L.A.'S GOLDEN AGE,
a Novel

For information about this title or to order other books
and/or electronic media, contact the publisher:

Marquez Press
Pittsburgh, Pennsylvania
United States
info@marquezpress.com
www.marquezpress.com

ISBN: 978-1-73318-412-0 (hardcover)
ISBN: 978-1-73318-413-7 (paperback)
Library of Congress Control Number: 2020934934
Publisher's Cataloging-in-Publication Data

Names:	Schuler, Ron, 1963- author.
Title:	Angeleños : L.A.'s golden age / Ron Schuler.
Description:	Pittsburgh : Marquez Press, 2020.	Also available in ebook format.
Identifiers:	LCCN 2020934934 (print)	ISBN 978-1-7331841-3-7 (paperback)	ISBN 978-1-7331841-2-0 (hardcover)
Subjects:	LCSH: Los Angeles (Calif.) — Fiction.	Hollywood (Los Angeles, Calif.) — Fiction.	Immigrants — Fiction.	Family secrets — Fiction.	Genealogy — Fiction.	Historical fiction.	BISAC: FICTION / Historical / General.	FICTION / Hispanic & Latino.	FICTION / Family Life / General.	FICTION / Literary.
Classification:	LCC PS3619.C47 A54 2020 (print)	LCC PS3619.C47 (ebook)	DDC 813/.6 — dc23.

Cover design by Nick Caruso, with artwork by Mark Bender.
Interior (book) design by Melissa Neely, Neelyhouse Design

L.A.'S GOLDEN AGE,
a Novel

RON SCHULER

MARQUEZ

To those who lived it.

CONTENTS

THE FAMILIES: THE MARTÍN FAMILY

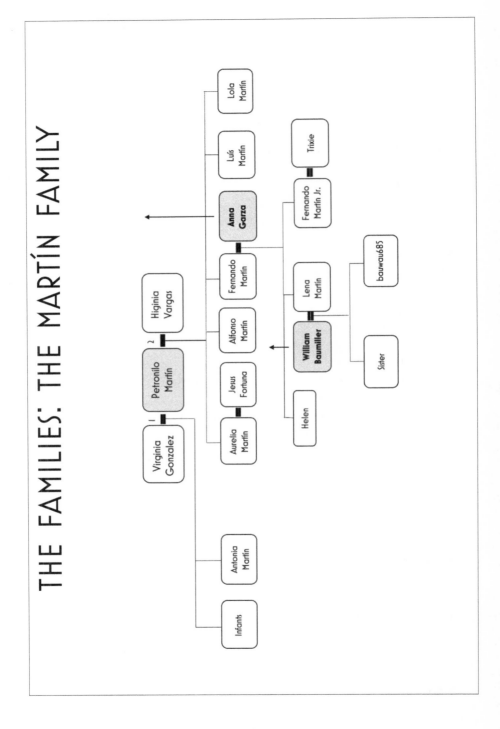

THE FAMILIES: THE GARZA FAMILY

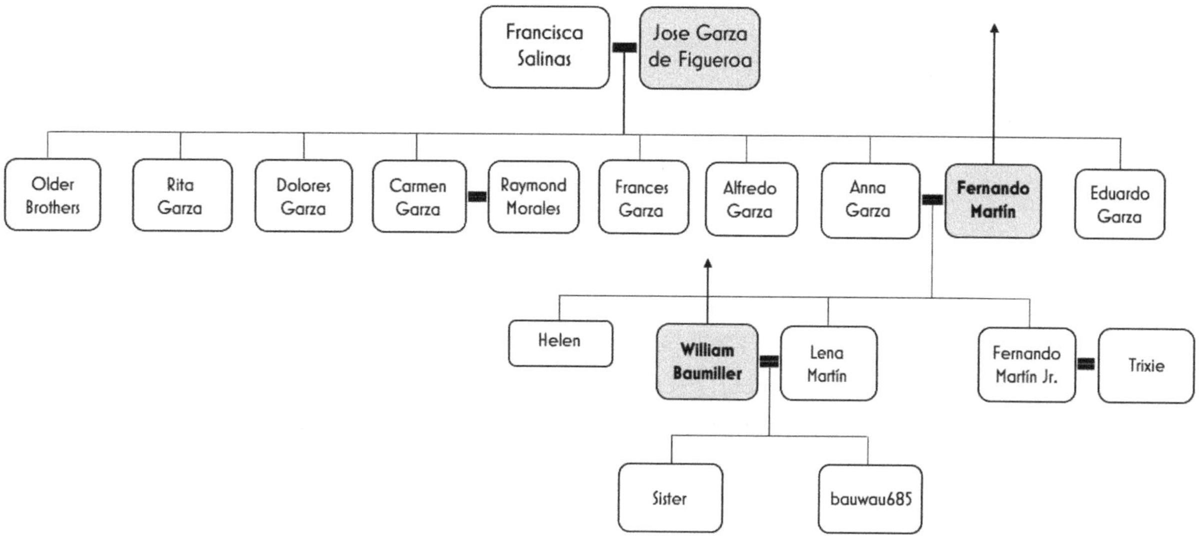

THE FAMILIES: THE BAUMILLER FAMILY

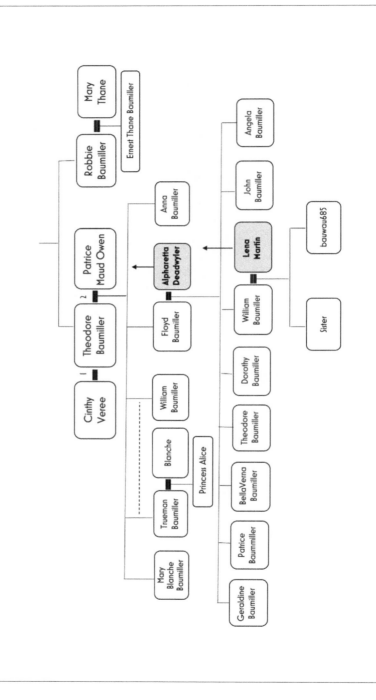

THE FAMILIES: THE DEADWYLER FAMILY

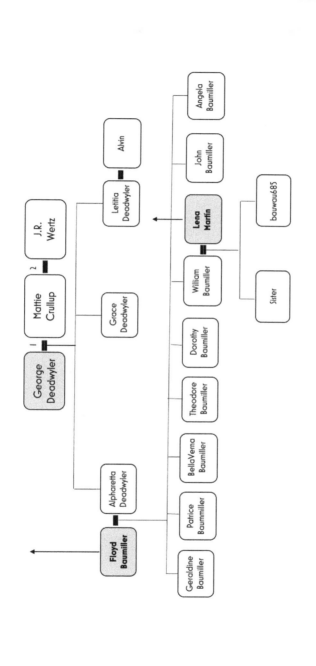

1
RAILWAYS

1.1
LOS CUERVOS, 1914

The wavy-haired boy, all of ten years old, strode out to the well, a bucket dangling from his right fist. His head erect, his chest sticking out, the child wore a tight frown as he stared into the distance. Like Juan sin Miedo, *la versión española* of the Grimm fairy tale about a dauntless boy who set off in search of fear, little Fernando Martín had none.

Since his father, Petronilo Martín, had left a few days earlier on horseback on one of his frequent overnight commercial expeditions, Fernando found himself, once again, the man of the house. He was used to it, for as the sounds and scents of random gunfire drifted more often through the hills toward Susticacán from the city of Zacatecas, where the Federal Army of Mexico had only recently fallen to Pancho Villa's forces, his father's rides to nearby Jerez de Garcia Salinas seemed to come with greater frequency and urgency. The house servants were missing that day — lit out, perhaps out of general alarm, or perhaps to take a side. Fernando's Mamá and big sister Aurelia were tending to the baby — María Dolores, whom they all called Lola — and they needed water from the well. Little Luís was only four years old, and Alfonso, the big chicken — Fernando's thirteen-year old brother — made excuses and wouldn't go. That left Fernando to venture out to the well.

At the well, Fernando spied them: rebels, camped under a nearby clif-frose tree, with big hats and big mustaches, big rifles and big bandoliers strapped across their chests. "Hey, boy," one of them shouted. "We need water for our horses." The words hung in the air, tentatively, more like a question than a rough demand. Fernando drew up his bucket full of water and easily hoisted its heavy load to sit on the ground. He turned his gaze at the man who had addressed him, and looked him right in the eyes, deadpan, like a wildcat looks at a coyote — without contempt, without dread, without any emotion at all. He turned back to the house. One hundred-fifty bowlegged steps out to the well, three hundred back with the bucket full. "Hey, boy ..."

Later that day, Fernando's father, Petronilo Martín, was coming home. In the distance Fernando saw the dust kicked up by his father's horse, but as the sun disappeared into the mountains, when the senior Martín reached the house, from inside the boy could only see dark blue outlines of his father as he dismounted and prepared to enter. Now inside, lit up by candlelight and covered from head to toe in a coat of yellow sand-dust, Petronilo nonchalantly tossed a heavy pouch of gold coins onto the table where the family took their meals.

It was another successful trip — but Petronilo was particularly quiet and subdued that evening. Slipping past the rebel positions and selling his wares in Jerez or Zacatecas had kept the family going, but with the fall of the big city, he could see all too clearly that the great wooden doors on the gateway of opportunity that had helped him build his legacy were closing. The life that the Martín family had enjoyed at Los Cuervos — the familial tranquility of farming on their own modest lands, selling their crops and wares nearby, haciendo el ponche,[1] the sense of being a proprietor and living a good life at Susticacán — was about to disappear. Perhaps forever.

Fernando Martín was my grandfather.

What does anyone remember about one's grandparents, decades after they're gone? Their visits around the holidays, of course — but because holidays are meant to be special days, my memories of them don't usually provide me with very meaningful insights about them. What I remember most about my grandparents during the holidays are episodes of them lining up for photos, and other episodes of them washing dishes at the kitchen sink.

What occurs to me when I close my eyes and attempt to reach more deeply into my store of memories about my grandparents are the times

---

1   Making the punch (i.e. distilling liquors).

I spent staying overnight at their Northside Drive home in Montebello, just east of Los Angeles. As I move about the house in the virtual reality of memory, I can hear the sounds of their voices — the pitch and timbre of them, their moderately thick cali-mexo-spanish accents, switching between English and Spanish words from the kitchen to the living room, back and forth, back and forth.

I remember mornings with KFWB-AM news, repeating in endless loops with the sound of a fake newswire always tapping in the background, and the *Herald Examiner*, which seemed like an old person's newspaper to me, with old person's comic strips like "Beetle Bailey," "Maggie and Jiggs" and "Blondie." I smell the deep, dark-roasted coffee — we almost never had it at home — and I hear the gurgling of the stainless-steel percolator. No one made soft-boiled eggs like my grandmother — to this day I don't know how she made them so special. I can walk outside into the lanai between the back of the house and my grandfather's detached playroom. I can poke around catching bees and orange skipper butterflies in their beautiful tiny backyard garden, with the lush, soft, perfectly-manicured dichondra lawn, the camellias, the lemon and avocado trees, and I can play in the concrete drive-in courtyard of my grandfather's modest Spanish Revival apartment buildings next door, just outside the cinder block wall and the dutch doors of the lanai.

My grandmother calls me and I go back and sit at the round, glass-topped wrought iron table in the lanai for lunch, a plateful of my grandmother's fried beef taquitos, smothered in my grandfather's handmade guacamole. Later I can find my grandmother sitting in her TV den, chain-smoking Salems, watching black-and-white Saturday matinee movies — Garbo, Hitchcock, Joan Crawford or Sonia Henie, with full-color commercial interspersions from Zachary All menswear ("big, tall and portlies") or Wilson's House of Suede or Adee Plumbing and Heating ("A-dee do!") — or the Loco Valdes show on KMEX-TV, canal treinta y quatro, en UHF. I can see my grandfather coming through the front door in his suit and tie after meetings Downtown, and retiring to his playroom and his pool table. Vikki Carr on the hi-fi, a fresh Highball on the bar, shooting pool by himself or teaching me how to shoot, whistling the first four notes of the "Tennessee Waltz" over and over again between songs and LP sides, my laughter when he shouts "El Sapo!" after sinking an unintended ball ...

My mother's father, the grey-haired man with the pool cue in white shirtsleeves and middle class repose, and the little boy at the well staring down the bandidos, are one and the same, yesiree. These memories of Northside Drive are satisfying, comforting as nostalgia, but unsatisfactory as biography. Their sensual persistence threatens to eclipse any recollection I may have of the stories of their lives before Northside Drive, often told by them only under protest, not to mention the stories they left untold altogether — the former, like a light drizzle of ephemeral raindrops, the latter, like the elusive spaces in between. *Dime, abuelos, por favor:* why so much shame over a little spring shower?

I have another vivid memory of riding in the front seat of my grandfather's "duchess gold" Cadillac Coup DeVille behemoth, before there were rules about kids and front seats, with my grandfather at the wheel. He was distracted, thinking about something else — perhaps an untold story — as we approached an uncontrolled railroad crossing. I remember an instant in which the speeding train came into my field of vision from my right, the screeching of the Cadillac's brakes, my grandfather jerking the wheel left, the spinning of the Cadillac's rear-end to the right, my body hurtling into the right corner of the passenger's side of the dash, the car coming to rest parallel to the tracks. I remember seeing the look of life-and-death anguish on my grandfather's face, if only for an instant, as the Southern Pacific train sped through and away, down the track.

Meanwhile, all I have had to hold onto from my father's invisible family are a set of abandoned rails, disappearing into an obscure horizon. I never really knew the Baumillers. They came to L.A. from the Midwest around the same time that Fernando and Anna Martín came from the Mexican border, looking for a fresh start in the West, but they moved away, and some of them died before I was born. For years my father's easy-going manner and unfailingly sunny outlook obscured what happened to them here, what they hoped to find here, the secrets the family tried to keep here, and what they lost.

These days, as questions occur to me, faster than I can answer them, about who I am, where I've come from, and about this country in which I dwell — I find myself walking down all of the empty tracks of both families, haunting them like a ghost from the future, looking for clues and traces, grasping at whatever I can. Through fragments of old conversations, recalled in spontaneous onrushes like familiar fragrances; through fifty year-old handwritten notes and fading printed photographs sliding around in an old shirt box; through almanacs and newspaper clippings, phone books and folded paper maps; through the opaque, bureaucratic finality of carelessly constructed public records and the prismatic results of mail order DNA tests, I am trying to piece together some version of the truth of the journeys of these families through a city that I left almost thirty years ago.

Several generations of the Martíns had lived somewhere in the vicinity of Rancho de Los Cuervos ("ranch of the ravens"), just outside of Susticacán, which itself was about ten miles west of the city of Jerez, at least since the early 1700s. The Indigenous people of Susticacán, the Chichimecas who had lived there for centuries before the Martíns arrived, had always claimed a certain independence from the various levels of Spanish government that asserted jurisdiction over the area for centuries. They put down their roots and began to farm in the area of Susticacán around 1562, in the midst of a hysterical Spanish "silver rush" to the Zacatecas region, and an ensuing brutal war between Indigenous tribes and conquistadors over the land and its precious metal treasures. Even as that war came to an end three decades later, with many Indigenous tribes capitulating and being coerced to sell their lands to the Spanish, the Chichimecas around Susticacán did not surrender their autonomy. They instead formed a Chichimecan agricultural commune and lived on subsistence farming and minor trade for two hundred fifty years. Their relative remoteness from the city of Zacatecas and its silver mines meant that the Chichimecas were able to cultivate their lush, green gardens without too much bother from the Spanish.

Petronilo's light-skinned forbearers were called *criollos* because although they were born in Mexico, they purported to be of Spanish blood. By the early 18th century, they had sidled into the area west of Susticacán — Los Cuervos — buying or staking their claims to the fertile land, and building small traditional ranchos upon which they farmed, with the assistance of Chichimecas and other Indigenous workers. Growing mostly corn and beans, but also squash and chile peppers and herbs, they also planted lush, green citrus groves, where beautiful, fragrant oranges and lemons flourished. Undisturbed by domineering large landholders — wealthy Spaniards and old-family criollos — life in and around Jerez was observed by many to be surpassingly good. According to a chronicler, Jerez was "picturesque and prosperous, with fine churches and houses, an active commerce, a college, theatre, jail, hospital and public gardens," and its surrounding fields were fertile. Its men, it was said, were fat, and its women were beautiful.

Petronilo — who was not fat, but rather lean and wiry, with the high cheekbones and hollow cheeks of a Hollywood Western movie star — thrived on the independence of Susticacán. One hundred twenty-five years after he walked the earth at the height of his powers, the fading imprint that remains of Petronilo is that he was stubborn, autocratic and skeptical, with the shrewdness of a baron and the larcenous grin of a pirate. Up until the fall of Zacatecas, Petronilo was left alone there at Los Cuervos, unmessed with and unfettered, to prosper on his own labor and cunning. Having learned how to grow strong and healthy crops from the green-thumbed Chichimecas of Susticacán, Petronilo was also known for the distillery on his little farm — probably engaged in producing mezcal, but also brewing *colonche*, a sweet, bright red, bubbly elixir fermented from the boiled juice of the bulbous red fruit of the nopal cactus that grew wild around the ranch. A steady supply of that *ponche* for the Chichimecas around Los Cuervos probably helped to make Petronilo a popular man.

Unlike his distillery, Petronilo's home life was anything but a bubbly frolic. At eighteen, he married Virginia Gonzalez, his contemporary in age, daughter of another local farmer. They started a family, but tragically, one child after another died in infancy. Their daughter Antonia, born in 1882, was the exception, although she too suffered from chronic illness. Then, unexpectedly, at 3 o'clock in the morning of February 16, 1893, Mrs. Virginia Martín succumbed to typhoid fever. At thirty-four, Petronilo, the ambitious farmer, suddenly found himself a widower with a sickly eleven-year-old daughter.

In late 1890s Mexico, success as a private farmer was inextricably related, both culturally and economically, to the composition of one's family. The assumption underlying Petronilo's ownership of land was that he was building a legacy for his descendants. It was one of the primary purposes of ownership, and of Petronilo's livelihood itself—to pass down what one had built to one's sons. The Chichimecas, engaged in communal farming nearby, did not worry about such lofty issues—land just existed, and people just worked on it. Meanwhile, while hired labor may have been relatively inexpensive, the economy of small farms relied heavily on blood-linked stakeholders—sons and brothers and nephews and male cousins—to go to work on the farm. The tragedy of Virginia's early death, and the deaths of his sons and daughters, undoubtedly left Petronilo grieving, but he could not be blamed if he also felt a dry bitterness over the fact that he could grow corn and beans so well, and yet had grown his blood-line so poorly.

Finding a new wife was not a matter of romance for Petronilo, but an existential imperative. And rather than woo, Petronilo annexed. A few years after Virginia's death, in the Summer of 1896, he fixed his eyes on a seventeen-year-old girl—twenty years his junior, with many years of child-bearing ahead of her. She was the orphaned daughter of nearby Los Cuervos farmers, with pock marks on her pale, round cheeks. Family legend holds that Petronilo kidnapped Higinia Vargas and brought her back to his ranch. However, Higinia's uncle Francisco Vargas was probably only too happy to give his consent for the little "child" to marry Petronilo, as the official documents indicate. One less mouth for the Vargases to feed, after all.

Higinia settled into Petronilo's home in 1896 almost as a big sister to Antonia, who was by then fourteen years old. Two years later, however, Antonia also succumbed to a fever. The following year, in 1899, Higinia gave birth to her first child, daughter Aurelia, followed by Alfonso two years later. Then Fernando, Luís and Lola. All of them were healthy babies on their way to being healthy boys and girls. At last Petronilo's blood-line had sprouted, growing soft and thick and fleshy, like his corn and his squash.

The defeat of the *federales* at Zacatecas on June 23, 1914, in what became known as *la Toma de Zacatecas*, put a stop to what had been almost two decades of gently improving prosperity for Petronilo Martín and his little ranch at Los Cuervos. The visions that Petronilo had that night came true. The cash market for his crops and his liquors came to a standstill almost overnight. No one in the city seemed to have any cash left, and the export market—via rail—was interrupted by the occupation of the railways by Francisco "Pancho" Villa, the mercurial revolutionary general who would become famous to Americans for his later exploits along the borderlands. First faced with mere declining fortunes, Petronilo soon saw that the Revolution had another objective. He heard stories that elsewhere in the state, at gunpoint, rebels forced large estateholders — the *hacendados* — to leave their land. He saw formerly wealthy citizens reduced to sweeping the streets of Zacatecas. Then, as the months wore on, Petronilo began to hear whispers around his ranch. "It's not your land," he would hear from local tenant farmers sympathetic to Villa's cause. "Your grandfathers stole it." Tempers flared quickly amid the food shortages and the general uncertainty. The church was sacked. A neighbor was shot and killed. The vultures were circling.

One evening in May 1916, Higinia gave Fernando a little sack with a change of clothes, and told him to hold it tightly as the family left the ranch, left Los Cuervos, and headed for Zacatecas. In the dead of the next evening, they entered the Zacatecas station of the Mexican Central Railway, on a hill overlooking the city. Fernando climbed aboard with his family, and sat down on a wooden bench inside the railcar. It was his first train trip. All through the evening, Mamá and Papá would tell him to keep his head down and his mouth closed, as they rode through the parts of the country where rebels were on the move. Occasionally, sneaking glances out the windows of the railcar, he could see lights in the distance.

They reached the quiet border crossing at El Paso at dawn, and a few sleepyheads stood in line ahead of them. The Martíns told the U.S. immigration clerks they were headed for Douglas, Arizona, where some of their neighbors from Los Cuervos had gone. One of the clerks dutifully noted in his paperwork that Petronilo had no teeth.

They caught their breaths in Douglas. Petronilo brought what gold coins he could collect and carry with him from Los Cuervos, but they didn't last long. He went to work on the Southern Pacific Railroad — at age fifty-six, after years as a prosperous farmer and distiller, finding himself loading and unloading boxcars to keep his family fed and clothed. Fernando passed his twelfth birthday there, and his older sister Aurelia got married to one of the boys from Los Cuervos, Jesus Fortuna. Jesus got a job in the copper mines nearby in Bisbee, Arizona.

Life in Douglas was hard, but at least for a time the Martíns felt some small comfort from working for wages without being terrorized by raiders. America, at least, seemed like a stable, relatively calm place to live; it seemed, for the moment, better than what they knew of the hostilities they last encountered in Los Cuervos.

That flickering sense of comfort disappeared abruptly, however, during the Summer of 1917. Copper prices were falling and so were wages at the mines. Reds, socialists from the IWW, came to town to try to organize the miners. They launched a strike against the largest mining company, Phelps Dodge, in May, after Phelps Dodge had rejected all eight hundred of the IWW's demands. The owners of Phelps Dodge said there was a war going on in Europe, and claimed that the strike was "pro-German and anti-American." With the county sheriff lending his support, Phelps Dodge recruited a posse of over two thousand white men — including about a thousand from Douglas — to arrest the "disturbers of the peace ... those strange men who have congregated here from other parts and sections for the purpose of harassing and intimidating all men who desire to pursue their daily toil."

The angry white men moved like an army through Bisbee on the afternoon of July 11, 1917 and arrested two thousand striking miners. They forced about 1,300 of the detainees, at gunpoint, onto boxcars and sent them out of town, 155 miles away to the godforsaken borderland railroad town of Hermanas, New Mexico, where they deposited them, penniless and without food or water. The company seized control of all communications and travel to and from Bisbee and Douglas, and for the next few months, hundreds of people trying to enter or leave Bisbee were "tried" in a secret sheriff's "court," and were deported on threat of being lynched if they ever came back.

"*Vienen a capturar a los rojos* ... they're coming to get the Reds, no?," Fernando asked his father. "*Si, hijo*," said Petronilo.

"What are these Reds?"

"*No lo sé, hijo*" answered Petronilo, "*Pero no somos Reds.*" We are not Reds, he told his son. But he wasn't sure.

Douglas went into lockdown. The white citizens' crusade was anti-union, to be sure, but it was also anti-foreigner. Even families who had lived there for a number of years wondered if they would be packed away on a train and sent south of the border. Although Petronilo and his family were not labor agitators, and they may not have looked like so many of the darker-skinned Mexicans who had also come to Douglas and who numbered among the strikers, they certainly didn't look or sound like entitled white locals, either, struggling as they were trying to speak enough English to make their way around town. When it was safe to get away, further away from the company muscle-men and the dangers of the border, they packed up and left for California, where they heard they could earn money working on farms.

Fernando's earliest memories of living in California were of picking lemons for day wages in Corona, about fifty miles southeast of Los Angeles in Riverside County. Petronilo, Jesus, Alfonso and Fernando all worked in the lemon groves, picking fruit and setting gopher traps. Fernando was fourteen now, wearing his first pair of long trousers. What he knew of picking lemons, just four years before, was the joy of grabbing yellow prizes from a tree on the family ranch, taking bold and juicy bites out of them, perversely relishing their sourness, and hurling them like bombs at his playmates at Los Cuervos. What he knew of life, just four years before, was playing pranks on the nuns who purported to be his teachers, climbing trees and hills, and running up and down and through the streambeds nearby. Now what he knew about lemons, and life, was all wrapped up in earning pennies for bread and beans.

But pennies were not enough to sustain them, and Petronilo knew there was work for higher wages in Los Angeles. He hesitated — the lemon groves at least seemed more familiar to him than what he had heard about the big city — but his antsy eldest son Alfonso knew their best opportunities were in the factories, foundries, oilfields and transport lines, in the noisiest, smokiest corridors of the metropolis. "*Lohz-AHNG-hell-ays*," Fernando heard his father pronounce, over and over again. "*Lohz-AHNG-hell-ays*."

Reluctantly, Petronilo led his family west to *Lohz-AHNG-hell-ays*, to the big city. In 1919, Petronilo and Higinia and his unmarried children — Alfonso, Fernando, Luís and Lola — moved into a little house on Bloom Street in Sonoratown, a few blocks away from the Central Plaza in Los Angeles. Petronilo got a job as a streetcar motorman with the Los Angeles Transit Company; Alfonso worked nearby on the Southern Pacific line.

It could not have been a more foreign world to Petronilo. The streets were clogged with people and smelly automobiles. He could hear folks speaking his language as he passed through the Plaza, and while the smell of carne asada cooking in streetside stalls was familiar enough, south of the Plaza, in the darkened commercial district, he encountered the noisy, exotic temptations that threatened to break apart his family — the dance halls, the billiard rooms, the *burdeles*. On Bloom Street, there was no room for planting in his little fenced-in front yard. There was no cactus, and nothing to brew, and anyway there was this thing called Prohibition that was coming into effect. And even though the sun was shining, everything looked grey to him.

More so now than at any time since he had brought his family to El Paso in 1916, thoughts of Los Cuervos haunted him. How many more gold coins could one more deal have gotten him? What if they had waited out the terror? Was anyone else brewing the *colonche* now? Would it have been better to die on their own land? The cruel irony occurred to him daily: now that he had grown his blood-line, he had no land on which to grow his corn and beans. He had nothing to pass down to his unruly children, other than having brought them to this squalid city life. He wondered aloud why God had bothered to give him these children.

Fernando, meanwhile, rarely gave Los Cuervos another thought. As he watched his toothless father, sitting on the front porch at Bloom Street in his Transit uniform and muttering to himself about what had been lost, all Fernando wanted to do was to get away.

1.2
ROSEDALE,
KANSAS, 1919

As Floyd Baumiller, my other grandfather, clutched his raggedy coat around his throat and set out for an almost-two-hours' walk in frigid air down Vine Street and then westward, from the Labor Temple at 14th and Woodland in Kansas City, Missouri to his family's rented home on Booth Street in Rosedale, on the other side of the state line in Kansas, he got the joke. It smacked him on the forehead like a northerly December squall. If the streetcars were running, he'd take the streetcars home. But he worked on the streetcars, and he was on strike. So the streetcars weren't running. So he was walking home. An almost two-hours' walk. To another blessed state of the Union. It hurt his teeth to laugh about it on the cold evening of December 12, 1919.

Stepping-lively through several darkened blocks of warehouses and vacant lots, past a pack of stray hounds collected around some edible found treasure, their noses poking up to sniff in his direction as he orbited them, Floyd encountered a row of dimly-lit boarding houses. He was tempted to knock on a door and ask for a bed for the night, knowing that he'd get one for nothing if he'd only ask for it. But he just wanted to get home and sleep in his own bed, next to his wife Alpha. It was then that he caught the eye of a friendly milkman on his wagon. Floyd lay down on a bed of milk bottles and listened to the clink-and-clop-and-clink-and-clop of the wagon as it made its way through the otherwise quiet evening. He shut his eyes for a bit, pretending he could sleep if he wanted to.

He guessed it was going to be like this for a while. The morning before, he joined the men of the Amalgamated in walking off the job, leaving the tracks of the Kansas City Railways silent.

The Kansas City Railways Company had only recognized the union — the Amalgamated Association of Street & Electric Railway Employees — a year and a half ago. Seven months after the contract with the Amalgamated was inked, however, Floyd and the rest of the men were told by the union heads to walk out again. The union heads told the men they needed to stand in solidarity with the laundry workers unions. Floyd wondered to himself what the consarned laundry workers had to do with putting bread and milk on his table at home, but he didn't ask any questions. He complied. The railway workers were off for five days before the union heads sent them back to work. The union heads assured Floyd and the other men that it was all for the cause of the working man.

As the year-long Amalgamated contract was coming to an end in August 1918, Colonel P.J. Kealy, the president of the Railway, offered a five cent an hour wage increase, based on the idea that the Railway was going to be able to raise its fares from five to six cents. The Amalgamated wanted more, though, so after some discussion, Colonel Kealy agreed with the Amalgamated to send their dispute all the way to Washington to be decided, on the promise that the Amalgamated men would not walk out as long as the Railway abided by the decision. Floyd had voted for President Woodrow Wilson, had always voted straight Democrat, and he was pleased to hear that Wilson would be hearing about their demands for higher wages.

But, as the war was still on, it was some group of gentlemen known as the National War Labor Board that actually took up the question. They came down with an even higher wage increase — hooray for Wilson! — but they said it was all conditioned on the Railways raising their fares. When the Railways announced they were going to do it, the mayor of this Kansas City and the other Kansas City got all up in arms, and the utilities commissioners put their feet down. Then the lawyers got involved. There was no raise.

Floyd was starting to think that the whole system was rigged against them, that the company never had any intention of raising the fares or giving the men a raise. So did a lot of the other men. Standing in the middle of the main hall at the Labor Temple on Tuesday night, Floyd added his voice to the "ayes" in favor of a strike. No one was keeping their word, and they needed to understand how much it hurts us, Floyd reasoned. Doesn't anybody's word mean anything?, he wondered.

Now, atop a bed of milk bottles, Floyd was in the second miserable day of this strike. Eight days on strike, back in August 1917, was pretty hard, but at least there were fresh greens in the garden at home. Five days for the launderers, back in March, was pretty bad. How long was Colonel P.J. Kealy, in his three-piece suit and his sideburns and stiff collar, going to keep us out this time?

Fresh greens were harder to come by this time of year, he thought, as he wandered through his darkened neighborhood. It was past midnight. He wrenched his boots off in the front parlor of the little shotgun house on Booth Street, trying not to wake Alpha (short for Alpharetta), or the three little ones, all girls — six-year old Geraldine Marie, three-year old Patrice, and the baby, BellaVerna Elizabeth, whom they all called "the little Fern." Lumbering down the narrow hallway toward the bedroom, he thought some more about Colonel P.J. Kealy, trying not to get angry. Maybe he'd show some Christian generosity at yuletide. Maybe there'd be enough pennies left over for sugar cane candies for the girls' Christmas stockings.

"Nothing worse than staring at the sky and waiting for it to rain," Floyd's Pa used to say.

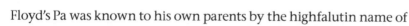

Floyd's Pa was known to his own parents by the highfalutin name of Theodore Aurelian Baumiller. Theodore, in fact, knew it was a highfalutin name, but over the years, he grew into it.

Theodore came to Kansas in 1880 from his father's homestead near Wabash, Indiana, bringing his new bride Cinthy, along with his older brother Robert and his family, Robert's wife Mary and their little boy, Ernest Thane Baumiller. Theodore and Robert came aiming to do what their father had done — work the land — and since so much of it was already spoken for back East, they hoped to spread out beneath the big Kansas sun in Woodson County, west of Fort Scott.

They set off from Indiana in their wagons early in the year, for the winter was mild that season. As they drove through Eastern Kansas on their way to the rented homestead that they had staked to begin their new lives upon, the ground looked hard and dull-brown. Sometimes the wind would whip up harshly, blowing their wagons to and fro, and there was an ever-present fog of dust hanging in the air, along with the scent of burnt ash. When they reached Woodson County, they heard from other townsfolk about the awful drought that occurred the year before, and they started to doubt themselves.

Near the end of March, a ferocious rainstorm raged through Woodson County. The two Baumiller boys, Theodore and Robert, ran out into the rain that afternoon like crazed fools, holding onto each other to stay upright against the wind. To their wives inside the house the skinny little men looked like earthworms wriggling skyward out of the mud. The women stood at the window and laughed at them, clapping their hands gaily. "Hey-ho, Robby!," called out Theodore. "What do you think of it!?" Theodore wasn't sure with all the rain, but it looked like Robert was close to tears. "We sure needed this," Robert managed to choke out. "I prayed and prayed for it. I was beginning to worry that we'd never have any rain."

The next day, their elation turned to fear. In place of an orange sunrise giving way to a clear blue day, a dense yellow fog muted the morning's brightening of the sky. At first, everything was quiet and still, but suddenly the unearthly peace gave way to a huge, growling gale, as strong as the rainstorm the day before. Instead of rain, though, the sky was now thick with dark sand. Theodore felt the hair on the back of his neck stand up as he looked out the window onto the horizon. He saw lightning in the distance but was unable to hear the thunder through the hissing of the flying sand.

Staring slackjawed at the storm that raged outside, his brother Robert watched as a big spool of rope left outside the barn blew over and started to roll away into the fog. Without thinking, before Mary could sputter, "Don't go out there, Robert," he was staggering against the wind, trying to retrieve the spool. All it took was a few seconds before little Robby was tossed up by the storm like a rag doll, thrown onto a gate post and knocked out cold. Theodore took one step out the door to fetch his brother before he felt the sting of sand particles, like tiny needles, against his face and in his eyes. He pulled back inside, coughing, grabbed an apron from the kitchen, tied it around his neck and face, and trudged out to where his brother was still lying. Mary, with a kerchief around her face, was right behind him, and with great difficulty battling the winds, the two of them brought Robert inside.

They managed to get Dr. Skinner to visit them from over near Yates Center when the storm died down, and the doctor said that Robert might have fractured his clavicle. He strapped Robert into a leather brace to keep his shoulder in place and a sling to keep his arm from moving, and told Robert to stay in bed for a while. For the pain, he said he might recommend whiskey if it weren't for the fact the Governor was trying to have it declared illegal. "Well, whiskey, for now," said Dr. Skinner, and maybe some weak tea and cold compresses, gently applied to the bruised area of Robert's shoulder. Mary quickly decided against the whiskey, but kept her own counsel.

Before he left, Dr. Skinner had other news — or rather, Cinthy did.

Sitting down at the kitchen table, Theodore breathed deeply and took full measure of his bride, barely out of her teen years, still wearing her wheat-blonde hair in ringlets. She peered back at him, her watery grey-blue eyes fluttering behind the blonde fringe that she wore straight over her forehead to the bottom of her brow, her cheeks blushing. He watched her as she looked away and fought to keep her lips straight and pursed. He took her hand in his. At last she was unable to contain herself. She looked back into his eyes and her mouth erupted into the sweetest, toothiest smile Theodore thought he'd ever seen. Then they laughed together. She was with child.

With Robert confined to his bed, Theodore worked alone on the planting the brothers had mapped out together. Row by row he planted corn, thrusting his axe down into the hard ground to make a slit in the dirt, then tossing in some kernels of corn, and kicking the dirt back over. On days when the wind and the sand whipped up, he wore rags as a mask and stayed out as long as he could before the sand in his eyes became too much. But he was happy. Mary sent her little toddler, Ernest Thane, out to the field one morning while Theodore worked. "I'm helping," he told his uncle, but of course he wasn't really. Theodore laughed and teased the boy while continuing to throw his axe into the dirt, row by row. The little boy was new life. Working the land and planting corn was new life. Cinthy's smile, and the infant they were waiting for, was new life. New life was worth shouldering an axe for.

Robert, however, was in a bad way. Some nights, he seemed unable to bear the pain. At the end of the day, after supper, before his eyelids dropped and closed by their own weight, Theodore would sit up in bed with his arms around Cinthy, and they'd rock back and forth and whisper to each other, just loud enough under the sound of the wind outside, about their future together. Then they'd hear Robert groaning on the other side of the wall. As they lay their heads down, Theodore and Cinthy drifted to a restless sleep, gliding unsettlingly from hope-filled whispering, to dreaming about sand, and the never-ending, moaning wind.

One relatively calm day in early June, while the wives and Ernest Thane were off visiting in Yates Center, Robert struggled to his feet, went out the door and found Theodore in the field. "Robby!", Theodore called out, startled. "What would Doc Skinner say if he saw you out here?" Outside, Robby looked even more pale than Theodore had noticed before, with dark circles under his eyes. "I should be out here with you," he sputtered, before his voice cracked into a dry cough, which in turn sent him whimpering from the pain brought on by the coughing. He coughed again and spat, into the dirt, and for a moment the two brothers stood silently as they studied Robert's sputum there on the ground. Theodore thought he saw blood, but said nothing. He looked at Robby's wet, squinting eyes and said, "We'd best get you back into bed, Robby, before Mary comes back and scolds us both." Neither of them mentioned the blood, then or later on when the women returned.

The sandstorms persisted, day in and day out, with some days being better than others, through much of the early summer. The Baumillers had almost become accustomed to them — trying to go about their daily business with kerchiefs around their faces, sweeping piles of sand out of the house, tying down anything that could be blown away — when Robert found a strange poem printed in the newspaper, said to be a prophecy written by a soothsayer from hundreds of years before named Mother Shipton:

Carriages without horses shall go,
And accidents fill the world with woe.
Around the world thoughts shall fly
In the twinkling of an eye.
Water shall yet more wonders do;
Now strange, yet shall be true.
The world upside down shall be,
And gold be found at root of tree.
Through hills man shall ride,
And no horse or ass be at his side.
Under water men shall walk;
Shall ride, shall sleep, shall talk.
In the air men shall be seen,
In white, in black, in green.
Iron in water shall float
As easy as a wooden boat.
Gold shall be found and found
In a land that's not now known.
Fire and water shall wonders do;
England shall admit a Jew.
The world to an end shall come
In eighteen hundred and eighty-one.

"The world to an end shall come / In 1881," Cinthy repeated aloud. The newspaper said that all the events predicted in it, except the last two lines, had already come to pass.

"Of course, it's hogwash," Theodore said. Little by little, though, from his tomb-like bedroom, Robert was seized with the idea of the impending end of all time. He saw it outside the window in the yellow-grey sky on mornings when the sand started to kick up fiercely. He tasted it in the drought and the dust. He had visions of locusts coming out of the sky in cloud-sized swarms and devouring all of Theodore's hard work in the field. And he felt it in the pain throughout his weakening body. His nights weren't getting any better, and out of the purest mercy, Mary had taken the unthinkable step of keeping whiskey in the house, feeding him spoonfuls when he could not suppress his night-time groaning. Robert found more evidence of the coming ruin of us all from the newspapers, in sermons and editorials, and in the speeches of Greenback politicians, who spoke of "a great black cloud" coming down upon the people, of "a death struggle" and "an ever-worse hell." Robert could see the cloud, and he was suffocating in its approach.

Theodore could see that his brother's delirious ravings were beginning to weigh down on Cinthy, and he couldn't help but resent them. He'd missed, though, how they were affecting Mary and Ernest Thane, though. After supper one night, Mary caught Theodore alone in the kitchen. "He ain't in his right mind," she said.

"It'll pass," Theodore said.

"Maybe ... but he ain't healing, neither. Everything's just getting worse. And ..." They were both looking out of the window. It was another gloomy dust cloud in the distance, strewn like a widow's black veil over the darkening horizon. "I don't know why he keeps saying those things," she said. "I understand why he's frightened. I'm frightened, too. If he should slip away, if he should leave me *here*," her voice cracked, "me and Ernest Thane —"

"I hired one of the Chrisman boys to ride us back to my folks in Warsaw," she said. "They'll pay him for his trouble when we get there." Theodore nodded. "I'm sorry to do this to you, to you and Cinthy. I'm sorry, I know it ain't going to be easy for her."

"Don't worry about us, Mary," Theodore said. "We'll be fine."

As he bade them goodbye two days later, he gave a pat on the head to Robby, whom Mary had liquored up for the beginning of the trip, and a pat on the head to Ernest Thane, and he gave Mary a kiss on the cheek. "Take care of my brother," he said. "We'll be here when you're ready to come back." But he doubted they'd ever come back. He put his arm around Cinthy, who was too far along to have joined them for the journey back to Indiana, even if she had wanted to. They watched Roy Chrisman's wagon roll away until it became a speck way out on the road.

Theodore brought on two farmhand boys, Stewart Williams and a little fellow they called "Bare," for room and board. They slept in the barn, helped keep care of the horses, and helped Theodore in the field. Still, Theodore had plenty of time alone in the field.

Nothing worse than staring at the sky and waiting for it to rain.

The corn was coming up, but it was coming up small, and some of it looked cankered. For days there would be nothing but hot sun and dust. Then, every so often, a quick summer rain would wash through, some of it so light and quick it was more of a vapor. But at least the air was calm for much of the late summer.

Theodore and Cinthy were still rocking and whispering in the evenings, Theodore reaching his tired arms around Cinthy's expanding form. In the half-darkness of their bedroom, they whispered back and forth about their unborn child. "If she's a girl, she'll be a little princess," Cinthy would say.

"You mean like a painted lady in Kansas City?," Theodore teased.

"No!," Cinthy would reply, giggling. "A proper little princess girl, in pretty dresses and yellow ringlets."

"And if he's a boy?"

"Then he'll be a miniature portrait of his father." And they would laugh. Their little bedroom, lit by the moonlight, was a little world unto itself, all that they could desire on a summer evening.

Early in September, however, the winds began to whip up again. It set them on edge. Robby and his delirium no longer inhabited the house, but still the idea of the end of time haunted them — especially Cinthy — as the sky grew dark again and the sand started to fly. During the days, Cinthy stayed alone in the house, crying, while Theodore, wrapped up in his mask, continued to work through the daily list of outside chores.

One afternoon Theodore came in and found his bride rolled up like a ball in her bed, seizing — almost shivering — from pain. It was a tad early for her lying-in to begin, she thought, but she was afraid it was beginning just the same. Out of caution, Theodore sent Stewart and Bare to fetch Dr. Skinner. After a quick cursory examination, Doc Skinner said that the baby was coming. The wind was picking up, and the sky was blackening, even faster than the sun was going down. Everything seemed to be moving faster than Theodore could think. From in the kitchen, he heard his bride wailing, and heard the low tones of Doc Skinner, trying to comfort her. An hour went by as quick as lightning, and then the terrible cries subsided. The house was silent. Doc Skinner came to Theodore in the kitchen. He said he was sorry but nothing more could be done, he said he was sorry, but they were both gone, Cinthy and the little girl were both gone. He said he was sorry. Theodore was on the floor. Doc Skinner said he was sorry.

And just like that, the world ended.

A year early.

Theodore gave himself until late the next day before he started making decisions.

The energy that flushed out of him the night before, leaving him like an old rag on the kitchen floor after Dr. Skinner left, returned with grim purposefulness as he approached the home of his neighbor down the road, Tobias. "Please do me the favor of telling Smalling," the fellow who let them on the property, "that my hired boys will work the place while I go back to Wabash for a season. They will harvest what's there and we's gonna pay Smalling what we can. And I'll be back. I'll pay him every penny I owe him."

"Good heavens, Baumiller," said Tobias, who had heard about Cinthy from people in town. "No one'd blame if you'd a-stripped down and run naked into the hills and never come back." Many men were capable of doing worse over less. Tobias wondered whether the young widower, all of twenty-five years old, wouldn't rather stay back in Indiana with his own people. Theodore had already given it some thought. It broke his heart just thinking about returning to Wabash to see Charles Veree, to give him back his precious blonde daughter in an oaken casket. How could he stay?

A few days later, with a simple oak box made by Stewart and Bare secured in the bed of his wagon, Theodore departed alone for the long ride back to Wabash.

Of course, he wasn't alone.

"When we get home, my dearest, your whole family will be there to greet us. I expect they'll all be in their Sunday best. Remember at our wedding how we laughed at old Uncle Anse, with his belly sticking out of that old black coat of his?" Just like on those howling windy evenings back in Woodson County, after miles and miles of driving, he went on whispering to his bride, until he was too tired to go on any further. And under a tree he'd lay his head and fall asleep, dreaming of his wife and their little girl. Hour after hour, he addressed himself to her, describing to her what he would see along his journey, and telling her how much he loved her and missed her.

He told her, as he finally reached his destination: "Look, Cinthy! My-oh-my, how green Indiana is today ... I know how much you loved it this way," he said as they approached their old home.

The funeral was mercifully short. They buried her in South Pleasant with her people. He went home and visited his Ma and Pa in Roann for a while, turned down their invitations to stay longer, and before he knew it, he was back out on the road again, telling Cinthy all about his plans for when he'd get back to Woodson County.

Floyd was born after the end of the world.

One of the conclusions that came to Theodore on the long road back to Woodson County, as he lay down his head under a tree, looking up at the stars, was that he knew he didn't have to be a farmer anymore. He was alone in the world, and he didn't have a calling for it now. Driving this wagon, though ... Theodore realized how much he appreciated the long, slow music of it, the syncopated horse hooves falling on the road, the squeaky wheel and its intervals.

Back in Kansas, he hired himself out as a teamster, hauling whatever needed to be hauled, rolling back and forth across the plain like a tumbleweed. Barely a year later, he received a letter from Mary Baumiller back in Warsaw, telling him his brother had passed. Robby's feverish visions of the end of time were over and done. His brother's world had ended in 1881. It gave Theodore pause to think about his departed wife and child, his departed brother, and his departed dream of working on the homestead. It gave him pause to think about the time before, the time that had ended.

But there was a new order to the world, now. Now, with Cinthy and Robby watching over him, drawing his team along in his suspenders and shirt-sleeves from atop his sturdy wagon, the skinny-little boy-farmer was acquiring a closed-mouthed dignity he had not possessed before. He'd wear a fashionable black hat, and wear it proudly, although some people would laugh at him with his cargo of random pieces of furniture, old pillows and bed clothes, calling him the rubbish man. He was unperturbed by it. They weren't his possessions. On the contrary, he began to prefer to think of himself as self-possessed.

Not long after receiving the news of Robby's death, Theodore met a serious Welsh girl named Patrice Maud Owen and began to court her. Her father, the county probate judge, had hoped for better for his daughter than a rubbish man. The judge eventually gave his blessing, though, and he officiated at their wedding. Then the children came — Mary Blanche; then the twin boys, Trueman and William. They'd lost William to a fever before Floyd was born in 1889; Floyd's little sister, Anna, came later. In time, Theodore aged into a white-haired gentleman with an impeccable brown mustache, sitting on his porch in Kansas City in his collar and necktie and vest, smoking a pipe. He was the very picture of a man with the highfalutin name of Theodore Aurelian Baumiller.

Floyd Baumiller had grown up with "transport" running through his veins, but horses were too slow for his hot young nervy-nerves. He had gone to work on the streetcars that careened around Kansas City, from which he made decent enough money to support his wife Alpha and their first two babies. And while neither Theodore nor Floyd would literally have to look at the sky and wait for it to rain, Floyd now found himself looking at the sky and waiting for a different phenomenon. Theodore never worked for a *company*, and Theodore never had a boss, and Theodore would never have occasion to observe that there's nothing worse than waiting for bosses and union heads to work out their deals.

Back when the streetcar men went out on strike for the laundry workers, Floyd stayed close by the Labor Temple awaiting the news of a breakthrough. When the call came, he'd be close by and ready to go back to work. So he endeavored to stay close by the Temple this time as well.

But something felt different about this strike, and soon he began to understand why. He started seeing the ads in the newspapers: "MEN WANTED ... STREET RAILWAY MOTORMEN AND CONDUCTORS ... Experienced men preferred. Those with no previous training also desired ... This is an unusual opportunity to obtain regular runs at once, and steady, permanent employment ... Details will be given at the employment office, second floor, Fifteenth and Grand Avenue, Kansas City, Mo. ... THE KANSAS CITY RAILWAYS COMPANY." The first time he saw one, he stood inside the main hall of the Labor Temple, thunderstruck.

One of the striking motormen, a fellow called Higgsy, came over and offered him a swig of contraband hooch from his flask. "Never touch the stuff," said Floyd. "Did you see they're hiring replacements for us?"

"Scabs? They ain't allowed to," said Higgsy.

"Maybe so," said Floyd, but his stomach turned sour thinking about it.

"If'n they do," added Higgsy, wiping his mouth on his sleeve, "we'll just have to burn 'em out."

On the next day, Saturday morning, Floyd was at home when the newspapers came. The night before, the headline was "Kansas City Will Break Rail Strike." This morning, they were reporting that the streetcars started rolling out of the car houses at 7 a.m., sixty-nine of them, with policemen on board.

The strike inched on, and every day, it seemed like more and more cars were leaving the barn. Floyd had heard they were getting hundreds of applications a day for jobs — fellows from St. Louis and Chicago, soldiers and sailors coming home from the war.

Not long afterward, the Railway managers were out spreading the word that all the workers who were on strike were welcome to come back to work and claim their old jobs, if their records were clean, but they had to do it by the end of the week, or else. At the Temple, the union heads implored the men to stay calm, to stay united. It was a bluff, they said. Floyd did as he was told.

Christmas Eve and then Christmas passed without a sign. While the Railway was giving the new transportation men a daily five-dollar bonus over and above their regular wages, Floyd's daughters' Christmas stockings were a little light this year. A few days after Christmas, Floyd was at the Labor Temple again, trying to find out what the union thought they could get done, but no one could say. They were all shrugging their shoulders, all on down the line.

On the night of December 29, Floyd was exhausted and went to sleep early. Barely five miles away, an explosion broke the peace of the pre-blizzard evening. Over at the 48th Street car barn, a dynamite bomb tore through the Railway's front office. A cashier named George Wilkinson lost an ear, and his brother J.T. was pretty badly banged up and burned. The next morning, as the blinding snow began to shut down the Railway lines — scabs were no match for Mother Nature — National Guard soldiers were marching through the streets, and the police were rounding up suspects in handfuls. This was what Higgsy was talking about, Floyd thought to himself. Drunken Higgsy said they'd burn 'em out.

Floyd stood under the grocer's awning with the newspaper that told the story of the bomb. If the union heads thought they could talk their way into getting our jobs back before, bombs weren't going to help their cause. An explosion like that, ringing out in the middle of the cold night, was more of an augur, a sign that all was lost. He knew then the union wasn't going to get him his job back. It wasn't in him to curse, not normally, but his frozen mouth let loose into the flying snow. "God-damn," he said. "God-*damn!*"

With the union in disarray and martial law in the streets, in early January Floyd started haunting the Railway employment office, seeing if he could get his old job back on his own. There were gangs of men waiting there. The first morning, a skinny fellow with a pencil-thin mustache, holding a rusty old clipboard stuffed with pages of names, came out and asked who was ready to work. One by one the men would approach and give him their names. "Okay," he would say, "report over to the side door ... okay, you can go, too ..." When Floyd stepped up, he gave the man his name. "No, not you. There's no work for you."

The next morning, same skinny fellow with the mustache and the clipboard. Same answer. "No work for you," he'd say. Same thing on the third day. On the fourth day, the skinny fellow paused. "Look, you're not getting it, bub. There's no work for you, period. Not now, not ever. Don't you realize you're on the black list?"

"What black list?"

"You walked out with the union. We's all done with you wildcat strikers. Colonel Kealy says no more union, no more strikes." Meanwhile, the union's lawyers were in Washington, appealing to the War Labor Board. A few weeks later, the Board put out its ruling: Kansas City Railways should rehire the men who walked out. Period. But it was the last thing the Board ever did, because the war was over. Hooray for Wilson. The Board disbanded, and after that, Colonel Kealy still never hired back a single striker.

On his way home, Floyd took the streetcar. There, in his conductor's monkey suit, was Higgsy, making change for the riders. Turns out he had taken the Railway's bait back in December and went back to work. "Hello, Baumiller," he said when he saw Floyd, grinning a wide grin as he reached into his vest pocket for his flask. "Drink?"

Drunken Higgsy.

Floyd was rounding the corner on 42nd Street toward home, passing the grocer, when a bright-colored label pasted on a fruit crate caught his eye. "Sunkist," it said. This wasn't serendipity, it had been on his mind. The green rows of orange trees, stretching out toward the bright blue horizon. Happy maidens with bushel baskets of sweet oranges. *"Lhas ANN-guhleez,"* he sighed. Los Angeles had been on Floyd's mind. He'd read the magazine articles. Fresh oranges. Fresh start. He remembered one article saying that anyone migrating to California had better assure himself that he had a saleable trade or a profession before making the trip — otherwise, he might be forced to take a job as a conductor on a trolley. He'd had a good chuckle over that one. Sounded like paradise.

"I got you a present, Mother," he said to Alpha as he walked through the front door. He handed her the Sunkist label, carefully peeled off of the grocer's fruit crate. They sat down at their little breakfast table, their knees touching. Floyd told her it was over, he was blacklisted. It was time to move on, as they'd often discussed. He proposed that he would go on ahead to Los Angeles, work a little, save some money, then he'd come back for her and the girls.

"Are you a wildcat, Daddy?," chimed in Geraldine Marie. "Kitty kat, kitty kat ..."

Alpha was silent. As far back as she could remember, when things got tough, men would leave, and they'd never come back. It's what her father did, leaving her mother alone with three little girls. "You know me," Floyd told her, his green-blue eyes fixed squarely on her black eyes. "You know I'm coming back for you."

The next morning they went to visit his folks, over on College Avenue, to tell them the news.

"You will come back for them," said Theodore, waving his hand over at Alpha and the girls.

"I will come back for them."

"I know you will, son," said Theodore, nodding. "I expect your brother Trueman and his wife will be joining you out there as well, soon enough. Your generation seems to be running to the end of your course here."

"What do you mean, Pa?," asked Floyd. "I guess I don't see Kansas City turning into a ghost town."

"I mean your generation of Baumillers. My father left Pennsylvania for Wabash. I left Wabash to come here to Kansas. You're leaving Kansas for ... for *paradise.*" He smiled. "It's what we do. We move on."

"And don't kid yourself, son," Theodore continued, "you're taking a risk when you move on. You leave behind what you know, for something you don't. The one thing I'll guarantee you, son, is it ain't a-gonna turn out the way you expected. Never does." Theodore could tell from his son's fidgeting, however, that he was more interested at the moment in calculations and preparations than in matters of fate.

Theodore sighed and put out his hand. "Take care of yourself, son," he said, and they shook on it.

After a few weeks of settling debts and making arrangements, one mid-February evening, Floyd packed a small bag of clothes, small enough to sling over his shoulder. Alpha made him four egg sandwiches, and down into his belt he stuffed the old Harrington & Richardson five-shot revolver, with a six-inch barrel and pearl-colored pistol grips, that Theodore had given him years before. "Maybe I won't get a shot off if I have to defend myself," he surmised, "but they are surely going to see me coming." At dawn the next morning, after skulking around the railyards in the dark, he threw his bag and then himself onto a boxcar on a westbound A.T. & S.F. train. He nodded politely to the other gentlemen who had already thusly boarded and found themselves places to recline comfortably in the dark.

"Hey, feller," piped up one of his traveling companions. "You got a egg sandrich on ya? I'll trade with ya for a pair-a socks."

By the full strength of morning, the A.T. & S.F. had pulled out and was humming down the rails, humming and drumming, rolling westward to *paradise*, and to the sea.

2
ARENAS

2.1
LA PLAZA, DOWNTOWN
LOS ANGELES, 1922

Red paper lanterns, strung from tree to tree around the Plaza for the occasion, a late autumnal fiesta, were gently swaying to the music. Mobs of young lovers, would-be lovers and punques from Sonoratown and Boyle Heights, from the Italian and Filipino districts and a few other nearby barrios were pushing in from the ring of fig trees at the edges of the Plaza. At the bandstand, Felix Luzero was leading his outdoor orchestra. Its pretty foxtrot tunes, wafting over the hats of the assembled revelers into the November night sky, hinted at the Spanish dance band roots of the orchestra's horn section, featuring the noisy Aranda brothers. The dancing couples on the makeshift dance floor in front of the stand — as a group, somewhat indistinctly bordered by the jostling spectators and stalkers — twirled and dipped in time. All through the night, the fiesta continued to draw the young people to the Plaza from the streetcars on Main Street.

Fernando Martín, now eighteen years old, now known to his *muchachos* as "Joe," was there, looking for trouble as usual. The motley *muchachos*, six or eight of them collected from the Foundry, the gymnasium, and a few other unmentionable places he'd been known to haunt, were there with him, forming a crescent-shaped gang of boy-men in ill-fitting coats and thrice-worn trousers. Joe, at the center of the crescent, with his pomaded wavy locks tucked under his hat, was not very tall, not very big, but clearly the leader of the bunch. The sardonic snarl on his face, and his puffed out chest, placed him at the top of the *muchacho* chain of command.

As their crescent pushed further into the Plaza flesh, they suddenly found themselves almost nose-to-nose with a sorority of Mexican dames, flapper girls in knee-length coats, dark stockings and cloche caps. The boys and the girls, from either side of the narrow chasm that separated them, eyed each other up and down. There was one girl who seemed to be Fernando's counterpart in command, a tallish, green-eyed girl with pale powdered skin, dark bee-stung lips, and a rose-colored feather in her cap. After a couple of beats, she turned her shoulders to face him squarely, placed her hands on her hips, cocked her head and grinned slightly at him, a peculiar upside-down grin.

Fernando's snarl quickly turned into a dumb, open-mouthed smile. He shot her two quick air kisses, rat-a-tat. Then he circumnavigated the inside of his lips with his tongue, ostentatiously bringing it to rest in his lower right cheek.

Now she turned her shoulder to him, gave him another quick once-over and returned fire with a piercing glance over the faux fur collar of her coat, like Gloria Swanson in *The Impossible Mrs. Bellew*, as she clucked her tongue at him. "*La caja esta cerrada,*" she spat at him.

With that, the comely young woman and her posse exited the encounter, and headed towards the bandstand.

"What?" asked Fernando. "She said 'the till is closed,' *caballero,*" said Freddie. "Yeah," said Stairways, "no smoochin' tonight, Joe."

He thought he detected a wink and a smile as she departed, but he wasn't sure. In fact, he wasn't at all sure what just happened.

Fernando was soon off to another minor conquest — a clown-nosed Mexican girl whom he spun around the dance floor, from whom he later stole a kiss and received a slap in the face, all in a night's work — but the green-eyed vamp stayed on his mind, leaving him with questions, like *where did she come from? And what gave her the right? ...*

Anita Garza had spent her childhood in Ambos Nogales, on either side of the Arizona, U.S./Sonora, Mexico border. She would always maintain that she was born on the American side — even cowed one of her older sisters into swearing on it, despite the fact that the contemporary records seem to point the other way — the ninth child and last daughter of the ten children born to José Garza de Figueroa, an itinerant day laborer, and his little wife, Francisca Salinas, in 1905.

The country of her birth was one of those facts, pitted against her unwavering powers of fantasy, that had met its match over time. If she believed strongly enough in something, over time, it became truth. In Nogales, when she was a child, the mayor, Adolphus Noon, was of Irish descent, as was the town marshal, W.V. Coughlin, the city attorney Frank Duffy, the tax assessor A.A. Doherty, and the customs duty collector, Con O'Keefe. While the town fathers and their busy wives all seemed to be Irish, at the convent where Anita went to school, Sacred Heart, the pastor, Father Louis Duval, was a French Jesuit, and her teachers, the sisters, were all French Dominican nuns. When asked about her own ethnic background, she would acknowledge being "Spanish," and then would assert with great confidence that she was also a little "Irish" and "French." Of course, there was no evidence that she was anything but Mexican, but with those green eyes, her pale white skin and jet black hair, the precise truth was ever shrouded in mystery, a mystery she curated diligently.

The Nogales of Anita's childhood was a boom-town, and so her father and older brothers, though uneducated and largely unskilled, could make decent money during those years. Up until Anita was old enough for school, the family bounced back and forth across the open border, between Southern Arizona and Santa Ana, the little town in Sonora where her parents grew up. But when Francisca brought Anita to the sisters for her schooling, Francisca — a woman with her own strong predilection for fantasy — seemed to stake her hopes on Anita. Anita was the special child, *nacida con un velo sobre la cara* — "born with a veil over her face," marked for destiny; the smart one; the green-eyed daughter among the family of brown-eyed girls. Francisca's doting influence helped to cocoon Anita within the little garden of the Sacred Heart Church, on the American side of the border, for a child-hood of chasing butterflies and hummingbirds amid the fragrant bee balm, the asters and the desert milkweed. As counterpoint to the tales of handsome young Mexican heroes rescuing beautiful bordertown maidens from the clutches of Apache marauders, told to her by her elder brothers, Anita learned the stories of the Bible from the nuns; and from the Jesuit, Father Duval, she learned to think of God as an all-powerful old padre, fondly regarded but often absent, a deity with whom one could nonetheless reason, if one were smart enough. As Colonel Savage once remarked, those convent-educated Arizona girls were "as smart and as wicked as they make 'em."

Sacred Heart was a center of cosmopolitan cultural expression in Nogales during those years, and Anita took it all in with wide-eyed curiosity. One autumn, a cabal of sincere *madres Mexicanas* and Irish-American busybodies among the wives of the chamber of commerce came together and created a "Bazaar of All Nations" for the benefit of the convent school under a huge tent on Grand Avenue. While Mrs. Con O'Keefe presided over the country store, there was an American booth, where fairgoers could buy "fancy" goods at "way back east prices"; a Spanish booth, managed by Mrs. O'Neill; an Alaskan booth, featuring ice cream and cake; a Japanese tea room; an "artistically decorated" French doll house booth; and of course, an Irish booth, "where the tired and thirsty will find 'soft' drinks, served in the good old Irish style." Meanwhile, the annual Sacred Heart commencement ceremonies were bona fide musical shows that drew the townspeople to the Lyric Theatre, featuring Spanish dancers, chamber music duets and quartets, and costumed musical cantatas, in which little Mexican girls obediently dressed up in the roles of such virtues as "Punctuality," "Perseverance" and "Generosity."

Anita first saw moving pictures at the Lyric, and at the Teatro Ramirez on the Mexican side of town. If pretend Japanese tea rooms and children's musicals were enough to stimulate fantastic thoughts in the brain of a smart young girl, one might imagine what movies became for her. As a five-year old, she and her seven-year old sister Frances and nine-year old brother Alfredo would crowd into front row seats to watch one reelers, ten-minute flickers about Pocahontas or Napoleon or the courtship of Miles Standish. The characters marched back and forth in front of painted indoor backdrops as full-length personages, distinguishable from each other only by costume first, then by their broad gestures. They told bold and simple stories that a five-year old could understand, perhaps even better than the grownups could. The movies and Anita were of similar age, and as Anita grew up, the movies were growing up right with her, her best childhood friend.

When Anita saw the story of Ramona, about an orphaned Spanish girl, played by Mary Pickford, who falls in love with an Indian, the story was depicted in the real outdoors, in a landscape that seemed familiar. Hollywood gradually became a real place in her mind, a place not too

44

far away from home, with fan palms and desert mountains that were not that different from the ones she knew. The only difference was that in Hollywood, romantic fantasies roamed the countryside, in the flesh.

As the movies started to grow beyond one reel, telling more complex stories, encompassing more detail, Anita was entering adolescence. On the outside, she displayed the armor of poise and confidence that the nuns had nurtured in her in the convent. But inside, the preteen girl was developing an interior life faster than she could even understand it, with a mix of complicated forces — yearnings, thrills, things that made her laugh and cry, and the inexorable pull of yet more and greater romantic fantasies. She saw *The Cheat*, a very popular, scandalous photoplay about a society woman selling her honor to a wealthy Japanese merchant. The sordid story seemed to be the thing that grownups talked most about, and Anita did file its narrative points away, to be relied upon later as a way of understanding the tales of betrayal, appetite, sacrifice and self-destruction that Hollywood so delighted in propagating — almost always, however, with a happy ending of sorts.

But the stories were less important to Anita than the world into which these romantic dramas invited her — a world of beautiful front parlors and lush gardens, alive with society parties, the neatly-coifed men wearing white tie and vest, the creamy-skinned women in glorious gowns, accented with jeweled brooches and feathers. Every woman of the world had a maid who dressed in black with lace trim, who fussed about her as she sat at her dressing table in a long silk robe, with hand-held beauty mirrors and brushes and exotic bottles of perfume.

All the men and women smoked cigarettes, and Anita learned the evocative subtexts beneath the practicalities of every move involving the cigarette. There were the intimate expressions on the faces of the man and the woman as the man gently taps a virgin cigarette on the side of his silver cigarette case; the devil-may-care offer and the daring acceptance; the expectant moment before the strike of the match, the white flame and the pivot of manly hands coming within a hair's breadth of the woman's face, caressing the air about her cheek, as the man lights the woman's cigarette; the way the cigarettes seem to float between their careless fingers as their lines of smoke rise and intertwine flirtatiously in the space between them, each draw on the cigarette approximating a kiss, a foreshadowing of a future intimacy. The movies were not only teaching Anita how to smoke, but how to hold a glass, how to walk across a room, how to dine, what to wear, what to live in, how to woo and be wooed, and how to love.

By the time Anita was becoming enthralled by this branch of learn-ing, Nogales itself was beginning to be threatened by disturbances from the South. Right around Anita's eighth birthday, a rebel army drove the Mexican federal commander, General Emilio Kosterlitzky, over the border into Nogales, Arizona. Not wanting to surrender to the rebels, General Kosterlitzky, who was well-known and liked by the Nogales chamber of commerce set, surrendered to U.S. troops. Bullets flew around Nogales that day. Ten of the fighting men died, and fourteen were wounded.

Kosterlitzky's skirmish was somewhat comical to the Nogalesos north of the border, who came out as spectators to watch the little conflict, while south of the border, the rebels took over Mexican Nogales. Two and a half years later, Pancho Villa brought an army of rebels to Nogales after losing a battle at Agua Prieta, one hundred miles to the east. From Mexican Nogales, Villa launched several raids on U.S. troops on the American side, spraying bullets around indiscriminately. Shortly there-after, a mass of U.S. soldiers descended upon the little town, and you could barely turn a corner without running into an Army man with his rifle. The border was closed up, controlled through a checkpoint at the Calle Internacional, manned by American soldiers on the American side, Mexican soldiers on the Mexican side. *"Ambos Nogales"* was now *"el uno o el otro Nogales."* At that point, Father Duval's successor, Father Deyrieux, closed the school. While Father Deyrieux favored a good breadth of education, he considered stray bullets outside the bounds of such breadth. Having concluded a sixth grade education with the nuns and learned some worldly ways from the Irish busybodies and Cecil B. DeMille, Anita came home from school at the beginning of the Summer of 1917 and asked her mother, Francisca — not so much literally but by the patterns of her pacing around the house — "Now what, mother?" *"Entonces,"* Francisca judged, "six grades ought to be enough for her"; but beyond that she had no immediate answers for the child of destiny.

A year later, another border incident gave Francisca further cause for concern. In August 1918, a confrontation between border guards erupted into a full-blown war between the two halves of the town, killing twelve, including the mayor of Mexican Nogales.

After that gun battle, Francisca had no intention of remaining in Nogales with her younger children. Her husband, José, and the older boys, in addition to one older daughter, Rita, who had gotten married, could take care of themselves, without her—especially Francisca's husband, who wasn't much interested in home life anyway. "José," she said to him after tracking him down in a Nogales saloon, "I'm taking the younger ones and moving to Los Angeles." He belched and laughed heartily. It was one of the last times she ever saw him.

Anita was staying in the house of a friend her own age from the convent, the daughter of a wealthy Irish family. They had offered to adopt Anita, but Francisca quickly derailed those plans. "*Lohz-AHNG-hell-ays*," Francisca told Anita. "*Hollywood?*" Anita's heart skipped a beat just thinking about it. Mary Pickford, Douglas Fairbanks, Geraldine Farrar, Wallace Reid, John Barrymore, Gloria Swanson. Hollywood! She knew that somehow she would get there, that all this moving picture education she had received was not for nothing. To live in that enchanted land was a dream come true for her, another fantasy becoming reality because she believed so strongly in it.

Not long afterward, Francisca and her little family—Dolores, Carmen, Frances, Alfredo, Anita and the baby, Eduardo—settled into a little house on Pleasant Avenue, east of the L.A. river in Boyle Heights. Anita was so excited about arriving in "Hollywood" that she resolved to take a milk bath, just like Mary Pickford in *Johanna Enlists* ("It's what keeps their skin so smooth and creamy," Anita asserted, taking a cue from *Picture-Play* magazine) and she even managed to convince Carmensa to help her. But Francisca caught them and put a stop to it after they had already poured two half-pint bottles into the bottom of the bathtub.

Francisca and Dolores took in sewing—Francisca would ultimately hold herself out as a dressmaker—while Carmensa and Frances sorted pages of sheet music at a music store on Broadway. Anita continued her photoplay habit at the Meralta, the Brooklyn and the Olympus Theatres, and her ukulele-playing brother Alfredo, who was always out for a good time, taught her the latest dances, one-steps and two-steps, the Grizzly Bear, the Chicken Scratch and the Turkey Trot, sashaying around the little front room. Each morning in Los Angeles gave Anita a reason to wake up smiling, and as she walked around Boyle Heights, she held out hope — no, she knew — that around any given corner, a movie star might suddenly appear.

A few years after they arrived, when Anita turned sixteen, she managed to get a job at the Paramount Dress Company on South Los Angeles Street as a sewing machine operator. In a room full of sewing girls, most of them Mexican, Anita stood out. She sprouted up during her early teen years, to a height of five feet and eight inches. Yet, despite towering over many of the girls amid the noisy chatter and the whirring of the late model Union Special industrial machines, her delicate frame — her narrow shoulders and her long arms, hands and fingers — and the deliberate way she moved — with the smooth, balletic flow and flair taught to her by the flickering, silvery likes of Norma Talmadge and Alma Rubens and Geraldine Farrar and, especially, Gloria Swanson — projected a serene, understated confidence. As she stood over the drafting table asking the designer questions about a new dress, her arms reaching out, *in the manner of a girlish lyric soprano at the Grand Opera House on Main Street*, leaning in with head cocked to the side, one knee bent and her foot on point, slowly tracing the outlines of the dress pattern with outstretched fingers, *she was like a marble statue of an angel, missing only her wings ...*

Or so thought Mr. Singer, the proprietor, as he sat behind glass in his executive office, surveying the scene. And of course, there were also those striking green eyes, her pale skin, and her black hair, done in Marcel waves, approximately, by sister Carmensa, in the kitchen on Pleasant Avenue. At the door to his office, Mr. Singer continued to watch Anita as he called out over the noise, "Yeah, yeah, Rexie — can you come here a minute?"

Mr. Singer's wiry little salesman, Rex Logan, jumped-to. "Yeah, boss?"

"Who's that one, the girl?"

"New girl, Anita Garza — you send some of your specialty work to her mother out in Boyle Heights."

"Right, right," said Mr. Singer, between chomps on his cigar. "Say, when's your brother going to stop by here with his camera get-up?" Mr. Singer had been planning a series of print advertisements for the Sunday paper, and Rexie volunteered his brother Hughie, a semi-pro lenser, to take the pictures.

"We need to schedule on a Saturday — and we need a model."

"There's your model," Mr. Singer said, waving his cigar in Anita's direction.

"Does Mrs. Singer approve?," asked Rexie.

"Mind your own potatoes, pipsqueak," said Mr. Singer. "I know what she likes. She likes 'subtle,' and that girl's got it. Set it up for next Saturday if you can, and in the meantime, keep your hands off the merchandise."

"Yes, boss."

On the next Saturday, Mr. and Mrs. Singer sat in Mr. Singer's office waiting while Rexie and Hughie Logan were adjusting their tripod floor lamps in a cleared-out corner of the work floor. "Yes, dear, yes, dear," Mr. Singer was saying as his wife explained for the third time that this operation might need to be shut down if she didn't like the looks of the model.

A few moments later, Anita walked in, with sister Carmensa by her side. "Look," said Hughie, "she brought her own fire extinguisher," referring to Carmensa. Rexie kicked his brother from behind. "Knock it off, Hughie," he whispered.

"Ah, Miss Garza," said Mr. Singer, bounding out of his office. "I'd like to present Mrs. Singer." Anita curtsied shyly, "Delighted to meet you, ma'am," she said. "I am so sorry we are late. The streetcars run on a different schedule on the weekend."

Mr. Singer caught his wife's eye, and they nodded to each other. "So nice to meet you, Miss Garza," said Mrs. Singer, smiling broadly. "I'm so glad your mother could spare you this morning. I'm sure we will make some very nice photos today." Across the room, Rexie and Hughie let out their sighs of relief in unison.

"Uh, thees-es my sister, Carmen," said Anita, somewhat nervously. She hadn't told her mother about the photographs; instead, she convinced Carmensa to keep quiet about them and come with her. "We thought maybe she could help me in the dressing room."

"Perfect," said Mr. Singer. He and Mrs. Singer proceeded to show her the dresses they wanted to feature and minutes later, Anita and Carmen were alone in the dressing room. "Okay, Princess Cuckoo," said Carmen, "let's get you changed." Anita giggled. *"Aqui estoy, otra vez,"* said Carmen, rolling her eyes. Standing before the full-length mirror in the first of the dresses, a high-waisted number with a crisp white sailor's collar, as Carmensa fussed with her hair, Anita blushed. When she walked out of the dressing room to where the lights were set up, she was Gloria Swanson again, just as she was on so many matinee afternoons walking home from the Meralta.

"A natural, eh, darling?," asked Mr. Singer, as Mrs. Singer marched toward Hughie to give directions.

A few hours later, Anita and Carmensa were back on a streetcar, heading back to Boyle Heights. "Well," said Carmensa, "what do you think Mamá ees going to say when she see these photos in the newspaper?" *"Ay Dios Mio!"* cried Anita. "I didn't think of eet!" Carmensa laughed.

Three Sunday mornings passed, and everyone in the house knew that the full-page advertisement for the Paramount Dress Company was going to come out on this Sunday morning, and that Anita would be the star of the page — everyone, except Francisca. The girls were all walking on eggshells that morning as Alfredo, not able to control himself, dropped big hints. "Mamá, would you like to see the paper this morning? ... Mamá, some of these new dresses are nice, you should take a look." Finally, Dolores opened the paper to the page and placed it right down in Francisca's lap, right between her nose and her sewing. *"Mira, Mamá,"* she said.

It took a moment for Francisca's eyes to focus on the page. Slowly, her hands came up from underneath and took hold of the edges of the newspaper. Out of her mouth came a little shriek, more like a chirp, unsupressable; and then, she just wept and wept and wept. Alfredo got up and quickly left the room, while Anita rushed over to her mother and dropped down on the floor next to her chair. *"Querida Mamá,"* said Anita, *"lo siento mucho!"*

When she could catch her breath, Francisca reached down and took Anita by the chin. *"Qué hermosa, m'hija.* They're beau-ti-ful." Then she swatted her on the head, hard, with the newspaper, and her tone shifted abruptly. "Who said you could have your photos taken?! When did you do thees? I don't know these people — "

"—Carmensa came with me!" said Anita, pointing.

From her chair, Francisca lunged at Carmen with the paper, but she was sitting too far away.

Once everything calmed down, Francisca was busy tacking the ad to the wall, putting it on display with obvious pride. "Listen, hija," she said. "*La próxima vez*, you tell me."

All was back to normal at the Paramount Dress Company two weeks later. Anita was busy winding the bobbin on her Union Special one afternoon when she caught a glimpse of a jaunty, vivid fellow, handsomely dressed in a light tweed travel suit and a flat cap strutting into Mr. Singer's office with a rolled up newspaper under his arm. The two engaged in animated discussion for some time, occasionally pointing at a page in the newspaper; after which, Mr. Singer went to his door and called out, "Miss Garza—could you come in here for a moment, please?"

Anita looked around nervously as she threw off her work apron, wondering what she might have done wrong. Mr. Singer, however, greeted her at the door of his office with a grin. "Miss Garza, I'd like to introduce you—"

"Howard Middleton," said the man in the flat cap, doffing it and bowing quickly. "I'm a scout with Bestwick Pictures."

"A *scout?*"

"Yes, that means I go around looking for the next big movie star and I bring them back to the studio for a screen test." This man was talking a bit too fast for Anita to comprehend what he was getting at. She looked at Singer, who just stood by with his cigar in his mouth, nodding. "It's like I told Mr. Singer here, we saw your pictures in the paper, and I think you've got something, we all said you've got something, around the studio, I mean."

"So, let me get right to the point, Miss Garza," he continued. "How old are you?, if you don't mind my asking—purely a professional question, you understand."

"Sixteen."

"*How* old are you?"

"Sixteen," Anita repeated.

"You're sure."

"Yes. Sixteen."

Mr. Middleton scratched his head underneath his cap and sighed. "Okay, well, you got me. Look, Miss Garza, I'd like to bring you around to the studio, show you around, introduce you to a few people, then put you in front of a movie camera. See how the camera likes you, you know. Then maybe they'll cast you in a picture — if the camera likes you. That's the idea behind the screen test."

Anita lost her breath. She asked Mr. Singer if she could sit down. "Put me een a movie?"

"I already know you look good in reg'lar pictures." He turned and spoke to Mr. Singer. "She really is a peach, isn't she? ... but look here, Miss Garza, since you're only sixteen, I'm going to have to get your parents' permission." He looked at Singer again. "You know, over at the studio, we live and we learn. Always get a permission slip for the younger ones."

"From my mother?"

"Sure, sure, your mother will do."

Later that day Anita found her little mother alone in the front room, sewing, and explained what had happened earlier at the Dress Company. Francisca listened without taking her attention away from her stitching, looking up only when Anita finished her breathless monologue.

Unlike her movie-mad daughter, Francisca was not one for going to the moving picture shows; she saw nothing charming in what passed before her eyes on the moving picture screen, and unlike Anita, she could not name a single picture star. Nor was Francisca much for reading the newspapers or absorbing the information therein. In Los Angeles, Francisca got her news in gossipy tidbits from the other Mexican seamstress "widows" and housemaids around the market, or at the Plaza, or in the pews at La Placita, Our Lady of the Queen of the Angels, just by the Plaza, or in the courtyard immediately alongside La Placita.

Not that Francisca was especially religious. She loved Father Duval in Nogales, his voice and his serene ways, and while she continued to attend Mass every Sunday once she arrived in Los Angeles, it was more of a social occasion than a moral retreat. She loved the bells of the church. She loved the christenings and the first communions and the weddings. There was even something beautiful about the funeral Masses. But she attended all of them as a society matron will attend the tea parties marked on her social calendar, and she stopped trying to force her daughters or Alfredo to go to Sunday Mass. Only little Eduardo went with her.

And so, as Francisca began to address Anita, she gave no concern about "mortal sin," and she held no hint of self-righteousness in her tone. Rather, she spoke deliberately and calmly, with the practicality of a dressmaker, as she told Anita what the La Placita gossips had told her.

"These movie girls and boys, they are no happy," she began. She said that Tomasa María told her that she read something about these two beautiful ones, a boy and a girl. They were married, and they went to France for a vacation. And the girl, she was beautiful but very sad, and she drank some of the boy's medicine because she was unhappy, and she burned her insides out and died. And there's a tall, good-looking boy who hurt himself in an accident, and María Concepción told her that she heard that after the studio started feeding him drugs with a needle, for the pain, he went crazy and now all he does is look for more drugs. And Mrs. Delgado showed her a photo of another girl from a magazine, with dark curly hair and a big smile, but Mrs. Delgado said that Mrs. Lopez heard from her niece, who cleans laundry in a movie mansion, the girl was "hooked on the happy dust." "Pobrecita," she sighed. And then there were all the liquor parties. "What will become of these boys and girls?"

The answer was no. No, no, no. "For your own good," said Francisca.

Anita was more perplexed than disappointed. Yes, of course, she had heard about some of these tragedies or rumors of tragedies — she even knew the names that her mother couldn't provide: poor Olive Thomas and Jack Pickford, poor Wallace Reid, poor Mabel Normand — but that didn't have much to do with what she knew about the movies. What was true to her was what she saw on screen at the Meralta. Beautiful women, handsome men, the way they dressed, the way they moved. The way they looked at each other. That was the truth. The rest was just things that happen to people sometimes.

Anita went back to the old Union Special sewing machine at the Paramount Dress Company, and never brought up the "screen test" again. A month or so later, movie gossip began to take hold of the newspaper headlines. In the *Evening Herald*, it said, "Girl in Tragedy." Accompanying the headline was a photo of a young woman, smiling, with dark, sunken eyes, in a garden hat and a low-cut gown, and a caption:

Miss Virginia Rappe, who succumbed after being stricken in Roscoe Arbuckle's suite in a San Francisco hotel. Police are investigating her demise.

"Comedian Speeds to S.F. for Inquiry," said a second article's headline, referring to Roscoe "Fatty" Arbuckle. Days later the *Herald* was saying that Fatty was to be indicted for murder, for having "feloniously attacked and caused the death of Virginia Rappe, the beautiful actress," at a wild weekend party. The salacious rumor was that he had raped and beaten her, viciously.

Anita hadn't heard of Miss Virginia Rappe and never thought much of Fatty Arbuckle's grotesque slapstick pictures.

"Girl in Tragedy." Anita studied the face of Miss Rappe closely. But in Miss Rappe, she could not see herself. In spite of what her mother might have thought, Anita was not and could not be "Girl in Tragedy." She was not the sad girl with the sunken eyes, she was not the victim. She was, rather, the sweet, flirty, independent-minded ingénue, like dozens she'd seen on the big screen at the Meralta. She was Gloria Swanson in-training. That was the part in which she had already been cast, whether anybody knew it or not. Whether there was a screen test or not. Whether there was even a movie, or not. No fat comedian would dare lay a finger on her.

That was the part she was playing on that November night, in the imaginary ballroom under the stars at the Plaza, when she faced down Fernando and his *muchachos.*

As she roamed around the Plaza that night with her girl posse, Anita caught glimpses of Fernando clowning around with his friends and attempting to boyhandle various random girls. On second and third thoughts, she began to admire his overall form. He sort of reminded her of the actor Richard Dix, with his broad shoulders and horizon-line stare, his grim mouth and resolute chin. She could imagine him fighting Apaches like Richard Dix, fighting outlaws like Richard Dix, fighting alligators like Richard Dix. She noticed his hands in particular. They were big, and they seemed to be on the verge of being fists at all times. It was slightly thrilling to consider them.

Several times over the weeks that followed, Anita continued to catch glimpses of Fernando around Downtown, which is unsurprising even in a city like Los Angeles, since Fernando rarely spent any time anywhere else but Downtown.

In fact, on the Saturday morning after the November fiesta where he first laid his eyes on Anita, those eyes of his opened, slowly and uneasily, on the dimly lit front room of an unnamed, rather Spartan speakeasy, a blind pig up an alley off Spring Street. No fancy chaises or marble bars for the late night patrons around the Plaza. Just an old dark room upstairs, wooden stools and tables, bowls of stale peanuts, and the cheapest bathtub gin you could find anywhere. Fernando's morning awakening that Saturday, on the hardwood floor in a corner of the front room, was another instance of an indulgence occasionally granted by the generous host of the joint, Nicky DeVity. It saved Fernando from having to go back to his father's house to sleep. "Well, hello and welcome back, Joe. You got a shift at the Foundry today?" Nicky was little more than a pourer of the mob's worst booze, but he was quick to develop a sense of loyalty to the strays who came to the joint for shelter and sustenance.

Fernando rubbed his eyes and struggled to his feet. "No, no work today," he croaked.

"Headed to the gym?"

"Huh? — yeah."

Nicky cracked a whole egg into a glass cocktail shaker filled with some chipped ice — he'd keep some in the icebox when he could, for special occasions, preferring to serve most of his dull-witted customers without using ice if he could get away with it — and poured a healthy dram of gin over the top, followed by a little syrup and the juice of a lemon. After a bit of shaking, he strained the mixture into a thick glass tumbler, gave it a shot of seltzer from a siphon bottle, and then, covering the top of the tumbler with his hand over a paper coaster, he slammed it down on the bar top. He served it up to Fernando, as it continued to fizz over wildly. "Normally I'd just put the egg white in here, but I know you ain't gonna have breakfast before some Palooka's gonna start punching you … they call this one a Royal Fizz." Fernando took the glass and tossed it back in a few impossible gulps, tasting a razor's hint of gin beneath the sweet creamy fizziness.

"Gracias, Nicky," he managed, before belching grandly. They laughed.

"I'll probably be along later to look at the floor show," said Nicky. "There was an oil driller in here, a wildcat engineer, coupla nights ago. He wanted to know about some prizefighting capers and I told him to go around and see the Newsies."

"I'm no newsy," said Fernando.

"I know that, son, but it's where you fight. And this wildcat, he's got some dough."

"What he doing in here, then?"

"Oh, a smart aleck, eh? Scram — time for you to go. You been in here long enough to pay rent now. Your great-grandparents should name me in their will."

"Gracias, señor."

The Newsboys' Club, managed by Carlo Curtiss, was down at the corner of Spring and West 1st Streets. Fernando's geography was mostly confined to Nicky's, a few other speakeasies, dance joints and whore-houses around Downtown, as well as the Newsboys' Club and the Hercules Foundry, at Boyle and Slauson, southeast of the foundry district near Huntington Park. If anyone was trying to send him a letter — and why would they? — they'd've sent it to Bloom Street, where his parents still resided, but in truth he did everything he could to stay away from there. What did they do for him? Nothing. What did he owe them? Nothing. For Fernando, who was busy trying to assume a different identity than the pathetic one his father had assumed, sitting on the front porch muttering to himself, it was a clean break.

Besides, he was busy. It was kind of inevitable that any strong, young Mexican lad working in or near the foundry district would end up prizefighting. The heavyweight champ, Jim Jeffries, worked in an L.A.

foundry — they used to call him the "Boilermaker." Fernando, if not large, was a strong kid, and when he went to work at Hercules Foundry, they sent him out into the scrap yard, where it seemed to be his job to move large heaps of scrap metal from one end of the yard to the other at the whim of his foremen. After a year at the Foundry, the back of his neck had turned a leathery red, and his wrists and hands bore the scars of many jagged little cuts.

Back in the Boilermaker's day, prizefighting in L.A. was a different game. Jeffries used to fight twenty-five-round fights, sometimes even longer ones. And Jeffries used to get a pretty nice pay day for them — thousands of dollars if he won, real money. Several years back, though, they outlawed professional boxing in L.A., which only really meant that you had to be an amateur if you were going to get paid for fighting within city limits. Then they had one of those pesky ballot questions and out popped a state law barring any fights over four rounds, and a maximum prize of twenty-five dollars. Down in Vernon, a nondescript unincorporated town abutting a Southern edge of L.A. proper where Jack Doyle set up his outdoor boxing pavilion, the Vernon Athletic Club, professional four-round fights became popular events, attracting the likes of Charlie Chaplin, the mayor's boss Kent Parrott, Will Rogers and Archbishop Cantwell as spectators. Meanwhile in L.A., the so-called amateur fighters kept plugging away, but prizefighting operated in the shadows — under the table, unheralded, small purses, pocket money for fighters if anything at all, based on small stakes wagers — with nickels and dimes trickling down to the fighters at the discretion of dispassionate gents like Carlo Curtiss, with no recourse or complaint after he'd take his carrying charges out of the prize. No celebrities came near.

To repeat: no celebrities came to the Newboys' Club at the corner of Spring and West 1st Street, where the fighters were all little men, ninety to one hundred thirty pounds soaking in sweat — sparring with each other in corners of the gym, hitting the bags, grappling with the outdated exercise contraptions, and loitering around waiting for a real fight. The spectators who did come to the Newsies were attracted by the anonymity, and by the smell of the easier small stakes. While stacks of green cash were flashed and passed around by Mr. Chaplin, Mr. Parrott and their ilk under klieglights in Vernon, watching popular match-ups who were presaged and advertised in the newspapers — these fellows sitting in the darkened back rows at the Newsies could open up their little purses and feel like big men, for a night, betting nickels, quarters and occasionally a dollar or two on faceless little fighters. Unassuming, most of these gamblers were gamblers-in-secret whose wives, neighbors and business associates never suspected. They were your basic bluenoses, but with a little wild streak — like that persnickety little Mr. V.M. Pruitt, the bank cashier, always with a carnation in the lapel of his tight-fitting suit; Mr. Mulk, the nervous, moist-browed fish broker, whose complexion ran from shades of abalone white to grunion grey; Eddie Chivers, the fidgety air compressor salesman and Lutheran deacon; Roeschenthaler, the junior mortician; and Mr. Joseph Iabone, the bread and cake man.

Mixed in among them, of course, were always a few sharps, without whom the ringside gambling economy could not have existed. They were the fast-talking fellows in straw hats and suspenders, the ones who held cash and wrote down bets in their little brown books, and who always seemed to know little bits of obscure information about a fighter — a hangnail, a weak left side, a blonde who broke someone's heart. The sharps kept the natural, uncalculated and unpublished odds balanced by their shrewdly muddled chatter. For the Mr. Pruitts of the world, betting on the little men in the ring was as much about reading the body language of sharps named Deuce and Obie as it was about picking fighters on their supposed merits.

Every once in a while an enigma would wander in and take a seat closer to the ring, within the reach of the overhead lights, confident enough to permit himself to be seen. On the Saturday morning after the November fiesta where Fernando first laid his eyes on Anita, the enigma known as Smitty first laid his eyes on Fernando.

Obie watched Smitty as he came through the door of the gym that first time. Not appearing ostentatiously wealthy, like some of the Vernon Arena gang, but rather well-tailored; in knickerbocker pants and high leather boots, he had the look of the sportsman about him. Obie was on him like a fruit fly on a November pumpkin. Wendell Groves "Smitty" Smithfield was an oilman — a Standard Oil engineer who cut his teeth in Southeast Texas and Southern California, and later prospected for the company in various far off locales, in Negev in the Sinai desert in 1915,

Baku in 1920, and lately, Ecuador. He was a little peeved to find himself with his wings cut, back in sleepy Los Angeles; and in his peevishness, he almost waved off Obie completely, when he noticed Fernando sparring with a redheaded fireplug of a kid, meaty but slightly shorter in stature. The fireplug was throwing body punch after body punch, but Fernando, wearing a manly close-mouthed smile and methodically shifting his weight to one or the other of his back feet at each turn, looked like he barely noticed.

"Tell me, who is that kid?," asked the enigma.

Obie was there to be helpful, of course. "You mean the taller one? They call him Joe—after that old wop fighter, Joe Grim." There was a lazy habit, in those days, of appropriating the names of champions or ranked fighters for undercard palookas. It was an easier way to promote a fight between two unknown kids, rather than using their real names. Take a champion, say, the middleweight champion like Harry Greb, the Human Windmill. Someone sees a younger kid boxing and thinks, "Boy-o-boy, that kid throws punches from every neighborhood—south, north, west and east, downtown and the heights—and he's fast, too." Like Greb. Rather than say, that's Jack Nobody, an unknown, they could say, "That's Young Greb," and, immediately, someone who knew anything about boxing would know something about this unknown fighter. There was Young Harry Greb, Young Jack Britton, Young Jack Dempsey, Young Jeffries, Young Wilson, Young Walker ... sometimes there were more than one of each.

That "wop fighter"—an Italian boxer, not someone who particularly fought "wops"—Joe Grim (sometimes listed as Grimm by an over-literate sportswriter) was an interesting choice of nickname for Fernando. The real Joe Grim's real name was Saverio Giannone, and he shined shoes outside the Broadway Athletic Club in Philadelphia until somebody let him in the ring. He was 5' 7", 150 pounds—not too far off from Fernando's own measurements, although Fernando was not as heavy. The real Joe Grim was known for two things—for standing up after every fight and giving a speech in Philly Itanglese about why the heavyweight champion Jim Jeffries should accept his challenge to fight, and for being able to take the worst punishment imaginable without going down. He didn't win much, and he could be a bloody mess by the end of a fight, but he never staggered, never passed out, and always left the ring with a jig and a smile, as if he had just come back from getting an ice cream.

Obie's sights were still on the enigma, trying to get him to spill some details about himself. Meanwhile, Smitty was focused on Fernando/ Joe, still getting pummeled by the fireplug's jabs to the body. All at once, however, Joe dropped his right heel, and pivoting on his left foot he unleashed a hook directly at the fireplug's maw, snapping his head back. The fireplug slumped to the ground, like an overcoat falling off a coat rack. His mouth was a muddle of blood.

"Quit horsing around over there," shouted Gig Rooney, the house trainer, looking up from his newspaper from across the gym. "C'mon, Joe, go get a rag and clean the boy up." Smitty, gasp-laughing over what he had just witnessed, asked Obie, "What's old sourpuss got against Young Joe Grim?" "Gig Rooney don't like Mexicans much," replied Obie matter-of-factly.

So Gig Rooney has a blindspot, surmised the enigma. Nothing inspired Smitty more than the prospect of humiliating smug old white men — in the oil business, in the prizefighting game, you name the turf — in spite of the fact that Smitty would undoubtedly become a smug old white man himself in not too many years. It set him to thinking; but before his engineering mind could come up with more than a simple framework of an idea for some mischief, Nicky DeVity sat down next to him and slapped him on his scapula.

"Old sport," said Nicky, noting Joe's attention to the fireplug's mouth, "I take it you just saw my young friend Joe's handiwork."

"Takes a punch pretty well," said Smitty. "I can see why they compare him to Joe Grim. The real Grim was a walking heavy-bag. I saw him fight Eddie Haney at the Standard in Philly once. Grim was awfully bloody at the end of it, but he always looked like he could stand up in there for another ten rounds. This kid has a little of that in him, without so much blood. Do they give him any time in the main ring here?"

"Very little," said Nicky, "despite I think he's one of the better fighters in this joint. They prefer Jews and Micks around here." Some of the fighters were actually newsboys who hawked newspapers on street corners, Nicky explained, and when Curtiss promoted a bigger event, like the annual Newsboys' Battle Royal, the white newsboys get all the glory, to the exclusion of some of the Mexican foundry boys like Joe. Smitty smiled. "You think he'll come out and tear it up with us tonight? I'd like to pick his brain a little."

"Sure, he'll come out. But he don't say much."

"That's alright, I'll be able to see his brain operate without him talking. Maybe better."

Joe showed up to present himself in wrinkled street clothes with a pair of seconds — his boy Freddie, who liked to say he was a fighter but mostly sat around the gym wearing a robe and watching his friends fight, and Stairways, the big-eared office boy over at the Foundry. "This your crew?" asked Smitty.

"You a trainer? You want to train me?"

"No, sir, I'm no trainer. C'mon, let's go have a drink."

The strange gang decided first to bumble upstairs to Nicky's joint for an aperitif. Nicky excused himself to see a man about a horse, leaving Joe and his *muchachos* alone with Smitty. "Anyone know how to make a decent Manhattan around here?," asked Smitty.

Joe strolled behind the bar and began to fix Smitty his drink. With some ice in Nicky's glass shaker, Joe carefully measured five parts whiskey to one part fancy Italian vermouth. "What the blazes? —" Nicky interjected as he came back into the front room. "Aw, he's almost done," said Smitty. "Let him finish." Joe looked up and exchanged a glance with Nicky, who stood there in front of him, a little miffed. Holding the shaker up to eye level, he then tossed a dash of bitters into the shaker and stirred it — evenly, carefully, almost delicately. He took a glass down from the cabinet and very slowly strained the contents of the shaker into it. Nicky, losing his patience at this point, nudged Joe out of the way. "Here, let me do this," he said, reaching into his secret stash for a canned cherry.

"Looked okay to me," said Smitty.

"Who taught you to make a Manhattan?," Nicky asked Joe.

"You did," he said.

"Shut up," said Nicky. "You spend too much time in here." Smitty laughed. Nicky turned to the *muchachos*. "You boys want a Manhattan? Let Uncle Nicky show you how it's done."

The celebratory Manhattans soon gave way to shots of cheap, acrid liquor, then a stumble down the staircase into the moonless alley below, criss-crossing through the back passageways of the darkest core of Downtown, amid echoes of drunken laughter and breaking glass. Next they went to a pool hall, then to another speakeasy, then to another speakeasy. Smitty made sure they were welcome wherever they lit by flashing his wad of spending cash. Smitty told stories that night that made Joe laugh, but Joe couldn't hold onto any of them any better than Smitty seemed to be able to hold onto his cash that night. The stories passed through him like bad hooch, and he pissed them away into the sewers. Somewhere along the way they lost Stairways, who went to sleep under a barstool.

By half past five o'clock in the morning, Smitty and Joe were strolling past the La Monica Ballroom on the Santa Monica Pier. "Well," said Smitty, "I guess that's proof positive that a fellow can still have a good time in the city of the angels. Been gone so long I wondered." Unaccustomed to receiving gifts, Joe haltingly thanked Smitty for the evening's entertainments.

"You're wondering what this is all about, aren't you?" asked Smitty, as he took a draw on his cigar. "I think you and I can make some good money. But first, you're going to have to get hurt."

Joe had heard about gamblers coming in and telling fighters to go to sleep during a fight so they could make big paydays. "I won't lay down," said Joe. "No, that isn't it," said Smitty. "I just think you're not getting to fight as much as you should because those saps over at the gym think you're too good. You have to let your face get bloodied a few times, let the odds on you settle a bit. Believe me, then you'll start getting some fights."

Joe didn't much care for the idea of showing other fighters that he could get hurt, but he understood where Smitty was headed. "What do I get out of it?"

"If I can get you onto the card in one of the newsboy nights out, in a bigger room somewhere, and you get in there and win, I can get you, say, three hundred smackers, maybe 350."

"Why not tell this to some kid down in Vernon, where they have big money?," Joe asked.

"Smart question, young man," said Smitty. "In the big money game, the show is rigged. I have no interest in playing with those swells in Vernon. Where you fight, everyone thinks everyone else is on the up and up — and they are, mostly. And when they aren't, I can usually see right through it."

"Besides," he said. "I've seen you drink, seen how you hold up on a bender. You're alright, son. You stand up pretty straight."

They sat on a bench, and Joe continued to listen. He looked out over the surf as the sun rose. He thought how strange it was that he could live in this town and never have seen this beautiful sight before. And he wondered how he would ever be able to spend three hundred and fifty bucks.

It was mid-December, in a dance hall on First Street, south of the Plaza, when Joe noticed Anita again. She saw him the moment he walked into the hall and she thought to herself, "There's Richard Dix, ready to fight an alligator." She was lying low, sitting at a table with her girls, and the evening's agenda was gossip, and maybe a dance or two. Joe was there with some of the boys — Freddie, Stairways, Tony, Osvaldo. They were sitting at a table across the hall, with no fixed agenda other than to be loud and have a bit of fun. The band, a small combo accompanied by a jazzy violinist, was chancing a Spanish take on some popular tunes — "Hot Lips," "Toot, Toot, Tootsie (Goodbye)," "Carolina in the Morning," and of course, "I'll Build a Stairway to Paradise." The moment Joe saw her, his neck snapped around again for a second look. The *muchachos*, even if they were paying attention, wouldn't have seen anything unusual in it, as he was always giving a second look to some girl. But Joe remembered this one from the Plaza that night. He remembered the quick little flirtation and her quick rejection. He couldn't take his eyes off of her.

Anita was doing her best to avoid looking across the room. She was keeping her head down, twiddling the back of her hat, while her girlfriends gossiped, occasionally breaking out into a chorus of giggles. Bowing her head, she snuck a glance over in his direction. He was looking at her! She looked away immediately, trying to appear casual, trying to appear engaged in her girlfriends' chit-chat. But she looked back again.

He was still looking at her.

The first couple of times she saw him looking at her, she could do little more than contain her surprise, lowering her eyes. After another tune from the band, she summoned some courage and looked over again. She smiled, politely. He smiled, and nodded to her. Now they were on speaking terms. What could possibly happen next?

Stairways was up and dancing around the floor with a little Filipina, to "Way Down Yonder in New Orleans." The boys were on their feet, whistling and taunting him as he tugged her around the floor. But Joe stood slightly apart from them, grinning in response to the spectacle, hands in his coat pockets, side-glancing over at Anita.

The band followed that with a straight-ahead version of "Wonderful One," and the floor was quickly flooded with couples getting up to dance to a slow tune. Two of Anita's girlfriends were swept onto the dance floor by nearby swains.

Joe fixed his eyes squarely on Anita's. As he began to walk over to her table, she got up and approached him. She reached out to give him her hand. He took it. In one almost balletic motion, or so it seemed to Anita, they were out the door of the dance hall — instead of onto the dance floor — crossing the street, and hopping up onto a streetcar heading west on First Street. They sat closely together in a seat in the back of the car. "My name is Anna," she said. "I'm Joe." He was still holding her hand in his. She turned his over to the top so she could get a better look at it.

"Where did Joe go?," asked Freddie, back at the dance hall.

"I saw him walk out with that dame," said Tony.

"What dame? He wasn't talking to no dame, was he?"

"I dunno."

Anita's girls were similarly perplexed. "She was here a moment ago — "

"Oh my, was she kidnapped?"

"No, I saw them — I thought they were going to dance, but out the door they went!"

"Who was he?"

"*Que loco, ¿no?*"

The streetcar trundled along First Street for what seemed like an eternity, past the lights of streetlamps and shops and signs that were reflected, shimmering, in Joe's and Anna's eyes as they studied each other's faces at close range for the first time. Neither of them was moved to speak much, and when they did, they spoke in whispers. As the streetcar turned south from starry First Street down darkened Bonnie Brae, any understandings they may have reached were conveyed and agreed upon only by their eyes, their fingertips, and their lips. It was the music without the words.

At West Sixth and Alvarado, they stepped off the streetcar and into Westlake Park. Down by the lake, Joe put down his coat for Anna, and they huddled together on the grass.

Something was different, for Joe. Usually he would have a few laughs with a girl, get drunk with her and steal a few empty thrills without giving any of it a second thought, without really feeling anything. Anna would not be stared down like the others. Her sly, green cat-eyes showed him no fear, ceded no ground to him. He saw the fangs in her upside down grin and shuddered. In Westlake Park he found himself thinking and saying things he'd never thought or said before, saying them out loud. Things like, *"Te prometo, te prometo."* He was drunk without drinking, he was bloodied in the ring and staggering on his feet. "I promise." He wanted her respect. Sitting there with her there by the lake, Joe strangely felt like there wasn't anything he wouldn't do to win it from her.

For Anna, the evening's adventure was all too familiar. The silent understandings, giving no care to the lights and scenery flying past them on the streetcar, their embrace in the dark by the lake ... she'd seen this picture before. Now she was in it.

Just past midnight, they climbed back on the "I" line and headed east back to Broadway. In her mind, she was humming a tune, the one from the dance hall. "Just you, only you / In the shadowy twilight / In silvery moonlight / There's none like you ... Oh, my wonderful, wonderful one."

From that evening onward, Joe and Anna were bound together by a mysterious invisible thread. It connected Anna from the Dress Company to Joe at Hercules Foundry, and from the house on Pleasant Avenue to the Newsboys' Gym, and to Nicky's blind pig. It drew them together in dance halls, or at improvised picnics, carnitas on a park bench at the Plaza or down in Pershing Square, or lingering in a storefront doorway in the dark somewhere on Ord Street, her head on his shoulder. Even when he was pummeling some poor boy in the ring. Even when he was on a bender with his *muchachos*. Even when she was watching Valentino at the Meralta. Maybe, especially then. Two beautiful youths, each of them planning their great escapes, running as fast as they could — dancing, laughing, and trying their level best not to trip over that damned thread.

Over at the Newsies, by late spring, Joe had come around to seeing the world as Smitty had mapped it out. Looking up from his newspaper, Smitty would catch Joe putting his face into the path of an errant jab from his opponent, mostly for show as Smitty had tutored, but catching a cut above the brow. Smitty was proud to see him bleed, just like Joe Grim used to bleed. And as Smitty had predicted, it was clear that Gig Rooney was beginning to notice Joe's cuts and bruises. He was paying closer attention to Joe's sparrings, making notes in his notebook. For what purpose, Smitty could only guess at this point, but he was pleased to see the arc bending toward his protégé.

These days, the fighter that Rooney was spending most of his obvious attentions on was a little Jewish kid whose father ran a delicatessen on Brooklyn Avenue in Boyle Heights. His real name was Friedberg, but in the tradition of the day, he'd been given another name around the gym: Young Benny Leonard. Leonard was a Jew, and this kid was a Jew, but that was about it in terms of any resemblance between the two — that's how lazy this nicknaming habit could be. Like the real Benny Leonard, however, Young Benny Leonard was a handsome, well-proportioned kid. Young Benny could've modeled for trophies. The real Benny Leonard was said to be a brainy boxer, a real tactician who would study his opponents for hours and figure out ways to play their weaknesses against them. There was no evidence that Young Benny was smart, although he did wear eyeglasses outside the ring, which made him look smart. So, if you were truly looking to figure out something about this fighter by his name, in this case the best you could hope for was that Young Benny Leonard was a Jew, and had a Benny Leonard kind of look to him.

Of course, Carlo Curtiss knew that none of that mattered too much. With the name and the look of the world lightweight champion, Young Benny Leonard could be depended upon to bring out a decent crowd to see him fight, at the right venue and on the right card. He could gain a following. If Carlo was going to put on a big show somewhere, after all, it was all about filling the room with duffs. Carlo had pulled some strings before for the kid and arranged to post him as undercard fodder at Vernon.

From Smitty's point of view, Young Benny Leonard was a decent enough fighter — not a power puncher, but he seemed to practice all the fundamentals well enough. Unlike the penny-ante gambling boys who haunted the dark corners of the gym — who had taken to betting heavily on the boy at Young Benny's occasional weeknight bouts, orchestrated by Gig Rooney himself — Smitty nonetheless felt there was something missing in the kid. His footwork, his punch sequences — they all seemed rote. While Joe never paid too much attention to Young Benny Leonard, Smitty was watching him closely and beginning to think there might be good reason for Joe to pay attention.

Meanwhile, as the Summer of 1923 began to bake the Downtown asphalt into asphalt pie for Downtown drunkards, Joe was busy with other things. He had joined a gang, for one thing. Not like a gang of larcenous hoods, though. Instead, Joe's was a gang of toothy, giggly post-teenage boys and girls who picked up in late night high jinks where Joe and his *muchachos* had left off the previous winter, trotting around the same old Downtown haunts, drinking and dancing and dancing and drinking, and eventually disappearing in private pairs into the dry hot darkness of the no-man's land between Downtown and Boyle Heights. With Joe's arms wrapped around his Anna, under a bridge or in another park somewhere, they'd sizzle and condense, and escape into the night, invisibly, as vapor.

Anna was sitting between her friends Elodia and Ylaria on a bench in the Plaza. Her usual upside-down grin was slightly subdued, if anyone was noticing. It was just after sundown on a Saturday evening in July. Stairways was there, as was Osvaldo and his girl Lores, and Tony and his new girl. Ylaria's dark-skinned *novio*, Jose, was lingering behind the bench, smoking a cigarette.

Joe was performing, front and center, doing an exaggerated old-timey cake walk, wearing a big open-mouthed smile and flashing his eyebrows. "This is how Stairways dances!," Joe said as he strutted around on wobbly legs, chicken-wing arms flapping. "Oh, come on, Joe!," Stairways protested, but the rest of the gang was belly-laughing. Even Anna couldn't hold back. "Like this!," said Joe, turning and wiggling his backside at them. "Come on!," said Stairways. "Let's go to this joint already!"

"So you can dance around like that some more?" asked Joe.

The gang was still laughing as they started for Nicky's for a drink. They'd only have one or two there, enough to screw up their puckers and redden their ears, before heading to their latest favorite wooden-floored piano joint, this one being down on East Second Street just off Main, where an upright bass player who played with tightly-closed eyes and a bald cornetist were cat-and-mousing with the piano player. And then it's off to the big wheel, the dance floor, "Swingin' Down the Lane" with mismatched duos from the gang — Ylaria with Tony, Joe with Lores, Osvaldo with Tony's new girl, Anna with Stairways, dark-skinned Jose with Elodia — hoofing, howling and hot-cha-cha-ing. Then it was a little "Oklahoma Indian Jazz" with Anna and Tony, Lores and dark-skinned Jose, Joe with Tony's new girl, Stairways with Ylaria, and Osvaldo and Elodia. As quickly as the tunes changed, so did the combinations, but as the hall began to thin out after midnight — after the unaffiliated, Stairways and Elodia, had already left and gone their separate ways — the lovey-dovey pairings settled down, magnetically, to their habitual end-of-Saturday combos, tune after late-night slow tune.

During a languorous "Tin Roof Blues," Anna rested her head in the crook of Joe's neck while his big arms nearly kept the rest of her aloft. Here is Richard Dix, she thought to herself as the buzz of the evening subsided, ready to wrestle his dance partner. Joe was a really good dancer. In the momentary quiet, the thought that had preoccupied her at the Plaza returned to her, full flush.

"Joe, I have something to tell you."

"You want to tell me you want another drink at Nicky's?"

"No, no es eso."

"You want the band to play the 'Charleston'?"

"No," she smiled, "... no."

As they walked outside together, the warm breeze smacked Joe's sweaty face like some of those punches Smitty told him to start taking. They stopped at the corner. He took her shoulders in each of his meaty hands and studied her face closely for a moment.

"*¿Estás embarazada?*" he asked.

"*Si.*" She seemed to be shrinking in front of him, shrinking right in his hands. "Yes, I'm going to have a baby." Now she pierced him through with her green eyes. Hey, no fair, he thought to himself. No fair to bring your weapons with you into the ring.

"Put those eyes away," he said, and he began to laugh. She smiled and buried her face in his chest. Then she looked up again. He wiped his forehead with his sleeve, and she reached up to fix his hair, and he remembered what he told her when they sat alone together at Westlake Park that first night. *Te prometo.* I promise. "I promise." The words tumbled again out of his mouth, as if he had no power over them. Now he was shivering, despite the heat.

"I know," she said.

She had taken this news to her mother only a few days before. Faithful Carmensa, nowadays Mrs. Raymond Morales, took her to see a doctor, who confirmed it. "Oh well, Princess Cuckoo," said Carmensa, "there's no turning back the clock now. You'd better not waste any time before you tell Mamá." In the front room on Pleasant Avenue, where the little mother had patiently taught her special child how to make beautiful dresses, Francisca sighed. "Well, m'hijita," she said without looking up from her sewing, "you are not the first in this family to tell me thees."

She had no bitter words for her daughter. "The way I have seen it," she said, "it all depends on how good the man ees. If the man ees a good one, then maybe years from now no one cares about a few months *antes o después de una boda, ni siquiera Dios*[2] — hmmm? You can still

---

2   ... before or after a wedding, not even God.

make a good home, *puedes mantener la cabeza alta.*[3]" She looked up at her daughter. "Thees muchacho, Joe — he ees a good one?" Anna smiled. It wasn't exactly how she would describe Joe. He was strong and tough and funny and handsome, and maybe he had a bit of a wild streak, but he also had a soft spot. You could see your own reflection melting in his eyes sometimes. "Bien," said Francisca, "you are a smart girl and if you love him enough then maybe you will figure out how to keep him straight. You will figure it out." She shrugged her little shoulders and returned to her sewing. "No one ever said everything ees going to be easy."

Anna wasn't worried about God. She thought she'd be able to convince Him it would all be alright. Meanwhile, in the movies, it always seemed pretty easy — all the problems, all the hardships were resolved in under ninety minutes. And marrying the man you loved — that *was* the happy ending, with the camera's iris closing in on the kiss of the happy bride and groom, and the theater organ music swelling blissfully. Real life, though, Anna thought to herself, it goes on and on, after the iris closes and the organ fades. Then what? Then, like her little mother said, you can make a good home, you can keep your head held high. She was a smart girl, and she'd figure it out.

"You'd be crazy to marry that boy," said her elder sister Dolores, as a last word on the matter.

After seeing Anna home to Pleasant Avenue, one kiss on her forehead and one on her mouth, Joe headed back toward the L.A. River, across the dingy streetcar bridge at Aliso, then aimlessly back down to the railroad tracks near the riverbed. It was a little after two in the morning. He had no fixed plan about where he was going to sleep that evening — perhaps after a stroll south through the edge of the foundry district he'd head back up to Nicky's joint, since Tony's mother would probably be a bit annoyed to receive a knock at the door at 3 a.m. For now, though, he was in no man's land, in no man's time.

Walking along the tracks, Joe started to cry. Not tears of joy, nor of sadness. More like the kind of deadpan tears a gravedigger cries after finishing all of his digging at the end of a tough week, knowing there's more digging waiting for him on Monday. Tears of reckoning, maybe, of

---

3   ... you can keep your head held high.

knowing more than you knew before and suspecting that you still have a lot more to learn. He didn't know, he was just crying because he had to.

Not far off from where he was walking, south of the tracks and east of Santa Fe Avenue, was the site of the Hercules Foundry, his day job. Among his crew there he knew bachelors who knocked around Downtown as he did, and jabbered gaily about their exploits every day. And he knew married men, who didn't jabber at all. Here, walking down the tracks, was a man whose only home was a woman named Anna, yet who was so scared that he looked down the railway tracks and, for a moment, contemplated an escape. Was there something in the darkness at the end of the railroad tracks in front of him that was more comforting than the unknown of being a husband and a father? Thinking about those words — "husband" and "father" — called to mind his toothless old father back on Bloom Street. Petronilo Martín wondered aloud too many times why he had children at all. Was Joe now just the unwanted, breeding more of the same? Mixing with the sweat on his brow, his tears assaulted the fresher cuts around his eyes and stung him.

What honor was there in leaving, though?, he asked himself. What purpose? Go north and pick crops? No, Downtown had staked its claim in him. Go back to Mexico? Mexico is dead. Los Angeles was for the living, Mexico was for the dead.

He hitched a ride back Downtown from a couple of South Gate punques who were looking for directions and he found a spot on Nicky's floor to rest his head for a few hours. Mid-morning, he was in the gym, hitting the speed bag when Gig Rooney grabbed his shoulder from behind. "Hey, Joe," he says, "Carlo says you're gonna fight Friedberg at the Armory, four weeks from this coming Thursday."

"Armory?"

"In Pasadena. Want me to tattoo it on your arm so you don't forget?" Rooney reached around the back of the bag and punched it back into Joe's face, then walked away laughing.

A few hours later, Joe was sitting in a corner of the gym with Smitty. "Young Benny Leonard!," Smitty snorted. Smitty's mind was racing. "Yeah, they keep putting Young Benny Leonard up against a kid they call Young Rocky Kansas, and they always fight to a draw." The real

Benny Leonard and the real Rocky Kansas were arch-rival lightweight boxers, and although Leonard was the better fighter, Kansas was known for holding his own against him. "Betting might be a push there anyway if you had the real guys ... They're looking for Young Benny to score his first real pay day. My guess is they're going to tell Young Benny to use you as a punching bag, just like the real Joe Grim, and he'll win on points. If you want to steal the fight from him, you're going to have to send him all the way to the far end of Queer Street."

"Kay-oh him? No problem."

"Yeah, maybe-maybe, you hot dog, you. Young Benny is fighting Young Rocky again in Vernon tomorrow night. You're coming as my guest. Wear a tie and a jacket, look smart. I'll pick you up here at 4 o'clock."

Joe showed up the next day in his frayed evening cruise-around jacket, wearing a string tie around the dingy collar of his shirt. Smitty laughed a little when he saw him. "Yeah, well I guess you could really use some clothes money. C'mon." They hopped into Smitty's cloth-topped yellow Bearcat, each took sips of coffin varnish out of Smitty's flask and headed down 1st Street toward Alameda, then south to Vernon.

As they entered Jack Doyle's Vernon Arena, Smitty's eyes darted around in every direction. "I'm remembering why I don't like this place," he said as he surveyed the crowd that was assembling for the evening's festivities. "Would you look at these swells?" Joe would never remember the names that Smitty was calling off as they made their way to their seats, in the lower level, but it went something like, "Darnit, if that isn't Rudy Valentino over there ... and there's Asa Keyes," the new district attorney, "that puffed-up lizard ... and over there's little Tod Sloan, the jockey ... and, see, that's Charlie Chaplin ..."

The names meant nothing to Joe. Besides, he was too busy feeling the rising sweaty moisture and the hot, smoky air and the percussive shouting and the mortal press of the thousands of people gathering for a newsboys' charity event at what would be the last-ever fights at the Vernon outdoor arena. Next week, Jack Doyle would be opening his brand new 7,500-seat indoor "Vernon Coliseum" nearby. Meanwhile, this was the biggest crowd Joe had ever been in. He stood in the aisle on the way down to their seats and did a half-turn, dizzily and almost involuntarily, looking up to into the rows and rows of wooden grandstands filling with more people. All this for a fight!, he thought to himself. He'd never seen or experienced anything like it before. Smitty tugged on his rough coat sleeve to keep him moving. "Don't worry," Smitty told him. "There won't be this many people at the Armory."

Most of the crowd was there to see the main event: the whistling middleweight, Blackie Rice, against the Whittier Flash, Bert Colima. Though Blackie had fought without much drama or fanfare for the past year, mostly in San Bernardino, his promoters touted him as a New Yorker, a Madison Square Garden phenom, a purveyor of fine fighting-you-wouldn't-know-about-because-you're-from-here-in-California. Colima, meanwhile, was wildly popular and a fast, straight puncher. Much of the wagering chatter that floated around them, down near ringside, was about Colima, although a few people mentioned another one of the night's scheduled bouts, between Sunny Jim and Steve Dalton.

Leonard and Kansas were deep in the undercard. Before them, though, was a fight between a couple of scrappy mugs — Mushy Callahan, making his debut, and Frankie Herman, who was probably standing on his last leg. Mushy knocked out Frankie in the second round, with a left-right combo that looked like it was delivered by a tin wind-up toy. Frankie collapsed like a rag doll and had to be dragged out of the ring by a couple of Filipino boys. Not many people in the crowd seemed to be paying much attention, though.

Next came Leonard and Kansas. They came out quickly at the bell, met each other in the center of the ring, and began to dance around each other like two fellows engaged in a comically intense polka. Within a few minutes they were both throwing punches at each other as fast as they could — right-left, right-left-right, right-left, and so on — as they continued polka-circling each other. The crowd was on their feet, laughing and cat-calling at the spectacle. Neither fighter landed much more than a glance on the other; punch-for-punch, it was one of the least effective displays of boxing Smitty could recall seeing in some time. Nevertheless, Smitty saw Joe leaning in and taking every punch, convulsing to the rhythm of the sad and sorry fight from his seat near ringside. Some fighters just can't help but feel the fight, any fight no matter how sorry, even if they're only watching it. I saw it, too, years later, as

I sat with Joe in his kitchen, his eighty-, ninety-year old body shifting violently back and forth in his chair in front of his little TV, feeling every punch that Julio Cesar Chavez landed on Meldrick Thompson ...

At the end of Round 2, the referee stepped in between Leonard and Kansas and called it a draw. The crowd continued to shout and carry on for several minutes afterward.

"Where I come from," Smitty said, "we wouldn't call that a fight."

Joe laughed. "That guy," he said, referring to Leonard, doing a vaude-ville boxing wind-up.

"Let's get out of here," Smitty said, "I don't like this place."

For the record, Bert Colima mopped the floor with Blackie that night under the klieg-lights, but Smitty and Joe were on to other things by the time that happened.

Four weeks later, Joe was hunched over with a towel around his neck, sitting in a makeshift, cinderblock dressing room inside the bowels of the Armory in Pasadena. His *muchacho*, Freddie the robe-wearer, was wrapping Joe's hands in bandages. The noise of the crowd outside the dressing room was loud, but Joe could hear that it was much smaller than the crowd that had dazzled him at Vernon.

Just an hour earlier, Joe was across the street at Library Park, sitting in the empty bandshell with Anna, who was crying. She didn't want to go in there, she didn't want to see him get hurt, and how could anyone think this was a good way to make their money?, and you're not going to do this anymore after tonight, no matter what happens, because you promised—no? Joe did his best to contain the firehose spray of her fears and emotions by bear-hugging her and kissing her hair. "*Te prometo,*" he said. "I promise you I won't get hurt. I'm the one who gets to do the hurting on the other guy," he said, laughing. "*Y, te prometo* ... there won't be any more fights after this one. This is it, this one's for us. Then, that's it, no more." She believed him, but she still needed to cry some more. And she needed to say, "*Porque me prometiste.*" She told him she'd wait there, at the bandshell, until it was over. Then they kissed again, and when he closed his eyes he thought he could see his future, or at least a bit of it.

Inside the Armory, Smitty was monitoring the bets that Obie was taking down in his little brown book. As expected for the Newsies' lowest undercard bout, they were running materially in favor of Young Benny Leonard—because, after all, who would bet on Joe Grim when Benny Leonard was fighting? Smitty, meanwhile, was taking as much action as he reasonably could without tipping the odds in favor of Joe, sending in some trusted oilpatch monkeys to drop cash anonymously with some of the other little-brown-bookies who were working the Armory crowd. He was pleased with how the room was moving, and pleased to see the bluenoses break open their purses. In these smaller fight venues, this is what Smitty lived for.

Freddie had the gloves on Joe's hands, and placed his own robe on Joe's shoulders. "That's for good luck," Freddie told him. "Give it to the other guy, then," Joe laughed. "He the one who needs good luck." "You are such a son of a bitch," said Freddie. "I hope he lays you out cold." Joe looked back at him with raised eyebrows. "No, not really. I gave Smitty a fiver and told him to bet it on you. Just hope your fists are half as fast as your mouth." A stagehand came in and said it was time to march.

As Joe and Freddie walked down the long aisle to the ring, the crowd got up on its feet and exploded with applause and cheers. He looked up and around, sort of the way he did at the Vernon Arena, but the room was much smaller than that arena. In the darkness he could see catwalks above him, where little boys sat dangling their legs down over the crowd. Unlike the open-air arena, there was a roof above that kept the force of the crowd's cheering down at ear level. It hurt his ears, and the curly hair on the back of his neck started to straighten out and stand up. "Nervous, Joe?" asked Freddie. "A leedle, maybe," said Joe. The nasally tenor voice of the announcer in the ring pierced through the random shouts and laughter as he welcomed the audience to the Newsboys' Battle Royal, and announced the fight with names Joe still had trouble getting used to: "Young Benny Leonard! ... Young Joe Grim!" Not Joe Martín, not Friedberg, but Leonard versus Grim. *OK*, he said to himself, as he puffed up his chest with a deep inhale.

The bell rang and Joe stood up as Freddie pulled away the stool. *I'm Grim, he's Leonard*, Joe thought to himself, putting "Friedberg" out of his mind.

Leonard bounded out of his corner and started into his usual rhythmic sidestep. Joe maintained his ground, though. *I'm not going to let you dance the polka with me.* Leonard moved to Joe's right, but instead of stepping back or to the left, Joe took a step in. Off balance, Leonard threw a couple of soft punches, which glanced off of Joe's raised gloves. Stopped in his tracks, recovering his footing, Leonard decided to go the other way to see if he could get the dance started. *I'm a stone wall and you're a little dog,* Joe thought as he took a big step forward to the left. *Not this way, either.* The ring was lit up brightly, and Joe could barely see anyone in the darkness outside of the ring, but amid an occasional shout he began to hear a few guffaws.

Joe could see that Leonard was getting frustrated. Now Leonard sashayed back to Joe's right, but instead of backing away from Joe's shift to the right, he barged past him awkwardly and began to circle around Joe's back. Joe resisted the temptation to turn around. Instead, he took a couple of steps back, keeping his back to Leonard during Leonard's half circle around him. Joe turned to the ringside crowd he couldn't see, at the right, and smiled a little with that mischievous open-mouth smile of his. The laughter rose as Leonard circumnavigated Joe, and Leonard threw a couple more soft punches on Joe's left as he completed his circuit.

"Come on! Ain't you gonna box with me, Joe?" Leonard asked him. Joe just kept smiling.

Leonard was now dancing in place in front of Joe, trying to figure out what to do next. Just then, the cries from the crowd sounded a little more indignant. Joe couldn't make out what they were saying, but he could tell they were growing restless. *The round must be ending soon. I guess if you want to box,* Joe thought ... Leonard was still bobbing up and down as if he were skipping rope as Joe stepped in toward him. Before Leonard could react, Joe planted his right foot firmly and let loose a cannonball left into Leonard's jaw.

In split seconds, Joe's mind raced along. Joe wasn't sure, but he thought he could feel Leonard's bones shivering, the backlash wriggling up his forearm as he pulled his punch away. Without skipping a beat, he stepped in further with his left foot and aimed a right cross at Leonard's mouth. He dropped his eyes as he stepped back and saw Leonard's feet landing flat and his legs stiffening. Looking up, he saw that Leonard's mouth was now full of blood, and he noticed Leonard's eyes going fixed and glassy. Leonard seemed unable to pull his arms up now. *Are you there, Leonard?* The referee seemed to be nowhere in sight. Joe pulled in close again and threw a hard one-two at Leonard's chest, followed by another big right to the temple; but Leonard was already crumbling from the chest hits. Joe saw his eyes roll back. Joe saw him down on the canvas, one knee up, his head back. He could hear him breathe-gurgling through his mouth. He stood over him, waiting forever it seemed for the referee to begin the count. The referee stepped in and hesitated for a moment to see if Leonard might be trying to raise onto his elbows or something, show a sign of game in him, but there was nothing — just the gurgles. As the referee waved Joe away and began his count, Joe repeated the number-words in his mind. Before he got to ten, though, Joe started to hear the crowd again, an indistinct roar that shook the ring. The referee suddenly grabbed Joe's wrist and thrust it upward. He had scored his kay-oh. One round and done. A couple of Gig Rooney's flunkies were in scraping Leonard off the canvas. Joe looked up, trying to make out the silhouettes of the boys on the catwalks waving and cheering. *Kay-oh, one round and done. Done forever.* The crowd continued to blast away as Joe exited the ring, suddenly feeling a bit lonely as he entered the darkness again. *Te prometo, done forever.*

Joe would always remember that night as the night he knocked out the champ, Benny Leonard. Even though it was only Friedberg.

Joe and Freddie could hear the other fights proceeding as Joe changed back into his wrinkled street clothes. Before too long, though, Smitty walked in with a big grin on his face. "18-1," he said, "and you beat it. You looked good out there, kid." "Gracias," said Joe. Moments later, Rooney's boys were carrying in Friedberg, who looked like he'd been thrown out of a building — grey complexion, red jaw, purple eye, bloody mouth. They put him on a cot on the other side of a partition in the dressing room. Joe could hear him trying to talk, but it still didn't sound like he was making much sense yet.

"Don't think he'll be fighting again," said Gig Rooney, indicating Friedberg as he strolled in and slapped Smitty on the back.

"What makes you so happy about it?," asked Smitty.

"You don't think I'm stupid, do you? I bet on your boy. Just 'cause he's a border cock-a-roach doesn't mean I can't make a few bucks off him." Rooney cackled as he made his way over to Friedberg's side of the partition.

"Forget that ass," said Smitty. "Here's what I promised you," he said in a low voice, digging a handbill-wrapped package of cash out of his pocket, like a cake from the baker's shop. "Here's your share of the winnings — $398." Joe's jaw dropped. "And," said Smitty, "here's a $20 tip from Rudy Valentino. He told me to tell you he liked your style." Joe was stunned by the sound of it all, although he still didn't know who Roody Whatsisname was. "Put it away, quickly, son. It's not exactly kosher for you to get all this cash."

"Gracias, señor. Muchas gracias!"

"I'd tell you don't spend it all in one place, but I heard about the dame you bull's-eyed," said Smitty. Joe's face turned red — he didn't know that Smitty knew anything about Anna. "Sorry, my friend, I should be more respectful," said Smitty, recovering. "Was that your girl I saw you with across the way, over at the Park?" Joe nodded. "Quite the panic, young man. Angel wings and everything. You done alright."

"I don't expect I'll see you around one of these joints again," said Smitty as he put on his duster. "I'm sure that angel has probably already told you you're not going to be fighting anymore. That's okay, though, you'll have some cash to get you started until you find some honest work."

"The Foundry," said Joe.

"Right, the Foundry," Smitty repeated, shaking his head. "I'd almost rather see you back in the ring," he laughed. "Well, my friend, good luck to you. I'll be leaving Los Angeles in two weeks." He explained he was going to check out a petroleum prospect in a "godforsaken place called Kirkuk," half-way around the world. Joe would probably never see him again. "Take care of that angel," he said as he spun out the door for good.

Exactly one week after Young Joe Grim sent Young Benny Leonard to a stretcher in the back room, on the morning of September 29, 1923, the bold boy from Susticacán met his beautiful Sonoran girl at the Pacific Electric Terminal and boarded a red car bound for Santa Ana. The boy was wearing a new suit coat and shoes, acquired with a small portion of his prizefighting receipts, and the bride-to-be, some four months with child and showing, was wearing a stylish new dress that she made (and let out a little) with her mother's indulgent assistance, underneath a form-obscuring long coat. The girl brought little blooms with her, one to pin on the boy's lapel, one to pin on her dress.

Santa Ana was then a quaint enclave of Orange County, forty miles southeast of Los Angeles. It wasn't too far away from where Joe used to pick lemons when he was a boy. Though it might not be readily apparent to us today why a young couple without means would choose to go eighty miles out of their way to be married, in September 1923 it was a dead giveaway. Joe and Anna were eloping, getting married without the fanfare of a family celebration. Anna was pregnant, of course, and neither of them could have afforded a big celebration even if they wanted one, and not getting any family involved was something that suited Joe just fine in any event. As far as he was concerned, he had no family. In September 1923, when young Los Angeles lovers eloped, they went to Santa Ana, specifically to the famous courtroom of the famous justice of the peace, John Belshazzar Cox.

Back in Los Angeles, one frequently read about swanky couples abandoning their families' fashionably overwrought wedding plans and sneaking into J.B. Cox's courtroom to receive their benedictions from the marrying judge. Hollywood stars did it, too. In 1919, a screen vamp known as Hedda Nova, star of *The Woman in the Web*, jilted a Russian grand duke and instead secretly married her director, Paul Hurst, in Justice Cox's little courtroom. Mr. Hurst signed the registry as Paul C. Hurst; Mrs. Hurst, by her given name, Hedwiga Leonie Kuzsewski, further obscuring the occasion from public ken. The newspapers eventually caught wind of it, nonetheless, and made "eloping to Santa Ana" sound like another romantic gesture of the movie colony. Santa Ana became Los Angeles' Gretna Green, and there were even a few bitter Los Angeles public officials who claimed that a large portion of the high divorce rate in Los Angeles followed from elopements in Santa Ana.

Judge Cox was also famous as the "Speeding Judge" of Santa Ana, having ensnared the likes of Douglas Fairbanks and Tom Mix and Bebe Daniels on traffic violations. Judge Cox sentenced Miss Daniels to ten days in the County Jail for driving 56.25 miles per hour in a 35-mile-per-hour zone in her Marmon Roadster, with the boxer Jack Dempsey at her side. But Bebe really didn't suffer much during her jail stay. Judge Cox visited her in jail and brought her a bouquet of flowers, while local restaurants and furniture stores fought over who would feed her and furnish her cell while she served her sentence. She also enjoyed a serenade of her favorite tango, the "Rose Room," from beneath her jail cell window, by Abe Lyman and his Orchestra, who drove down from the Cocoanut Grove nightclub to see her. The city of Santa Ana and the Hollywood film colony seemed to be enjoying an enormous in-joke together, with Judge J.B. Cox, the marrying judge, at the center of it.

Anna knew all about such things, of course. She knew about the way that Hollywood stars and starlets conducted themselves. This was the way to do it, and this was the way it was going to be done. And that's how Joe found himself taking the 40-mile red car ride to Santa Ana, with a boutonniere in his lapel, and Anna's slender fingers wrapped around his beefy hand.

Under the round lamps and skylights in the courtroom on the second floor of the courthouse, Anna's eyes sparkled. Joe couldn't take his own eyes off of her as she repeated the vows recited by Justice Cox, her voice echoing through the courtroom like a plaintive old love song, like the ones he used to hear the servants sing when he was a child. He was suddenly all too aware of his blundering awkwardness, his shabby trousers, his sweaty brows and pits, suddenly embarrassed by his new coat and shoes. Measuring himself against her in that moment, Anna had suddenly become to him that heavenly being who had bestowed her name upon her. She'd become Santa Ana — as the nuns of Jerez would say, the mother of Mary, the patroness and protector of all unmarried women bearing children. She was standing here in front of him, enveloping his humble, imperfect body with her eyes and her voice, indelibly assigning him his role in life, giving him his eternal purpose.

Moments later they were back in the mid-afternoon sunshine of Orange County, where everything looked plain again. They stopped at a grocery for sandwiches and bottles of milk, which they consumed without comment while sitting on a park bench. They window-shopped until it was time to go to the station. Then they watched the sun go down from their seats in the red car heading back to Los Angeles. Eventually, he fell to snoring.

Sitting next to her snuffling husband, Anna giggled. She reached in, grabbed his chin and kissed his ruddy cheek. In her mind she saw the camera iris closing in on the two of them in this little tableau, and she heard the theater organ music swelling. Having achieved a blissful ending, the picture was over.

But even she knew that wasn't true. The picture was just beginning. She squinted her green cat-eyes and studied him for a moment as he continued to snore away. Then she tilted her head, letting it rest gently upon his brown-bear shoulder.

"Keep your head held high, Mrs. Martín," she thought to herself.

Less than five months later, in February 1924, their little daughter Helen was born. She would've been my aunt, I guess, had she lived.

2.2
ANGELUS TEMPLE, ECHO PARK, 1925

As Floyd Baumiller rounded the bend along Park Avenue, strolling along the pretty Echo Park side of the street with his wife Alpha and their sleeping papoose Dorothy Theodora, he saw the crowds forming and heard the voices of would-be worshippers. They were a warm and familiar crowd to him, dressed in overalls and flannel shirts and rough coats, some wearing tattered cowboy hats, some wearing modest string-ties; their women, dressed in plain dresses, some still wearing their kitchen aprons. Some carried picnic baskets and some carried musical instruments — banjos, guitars, fiddles, mouth organs — and he could hear them playing and singing and whistling old-timey tunes up ahead, tunes he knew by heart. As he walked through them, he heard them exchanging their geographies. "Where do y'all hail from, friend?" He heard them answer Arkansas; he heard Illinois, he heard Kansas and Tennessee, Oklahoma and Missouri, Iowa and Texas ... stars on the flag, all of them, each representing miles and miles of good old American land. Land — all the faraway farms, the woods and streams and all the pretty homesteads that belonged to them in their memories, in their hearts and minds, if not under the law — that good old American land was their common currency.

Floyd's older brother Trueman and Trueman's wife Blanche walked ahead a few steps with their daughter Princess Alice, swinging on her papa's arm. Back home on East 4th, near Indiana Street, Geraldine Marie and Patrice were looking after the younger ones, little Fern and Teddy, Floyd and Alpha's five-year old blonde haired boy. It was a beautiful Sunday out, and Sundays were for coming together with a warm and familiar crowd of kindred souls, God-fearing ones — for worship, for learning, for thinking on and trying to understand what was happening around them in this landless city they'd come to, and in their country.

Blanche, in particular, was excited as usual about coming to see Sister Aimee preach at the brand new Angelus Temple, the beautiful, shining-white, 5,300-seat arena up ahead. Blanche received the Holy Ghost when she was ten years old, when her daddy took her to Topeka to hear Parham preach. When it happened to her, it was like the sky opened up. She stood up on her toes and reached both arms to the sky. Bathed in sunlight from a window above the pulpit, she said she'd smelled the scent of burning wood, and then she suddenly began to speak in the language of the angels, in a loud, clear, bell-like voice. Her daddy said he'd never seen or experienced anything more beautiful. Later, Blanche became a deaconess at the Church of the Nazarene on Orchard, back in Kansas City. Leaving her fellow communicants behind was the hardest thing about leaving Rosedale for Los Angeles. But she eventually saw the inconvenient journey as a truly spiritual one, one in which she, as a pilgrim, would continue to be a witness to God's power. She'd tell her neighbors, she'd tell the butcher and she'd tell the postman all about the sick people she'd known who were healed by the power of the Holy Ghost, and to all who questioned her she would maintain that God talked to her regularly. Coming to see Sister Aimee was for her like coming to an oasis, to be replenished and to receive the Holy Ghost all over again, so she could continue to impart God's message wherever she lived.

Floyd was never necessarily too convinced about all that, but he was respectful of it; and Blanche was mostly harmless, even if she did see fit on most days to pin Trueman's droopy shoulders down by her two Godly thumbs. Anyway, it felt good to extend the kinship of the day. And Sister Aimee was a good American, he was convinced about that, even if the preacher they'd heard that morning sometimes expressed his doubts about her.

That morning, they were at the Trinity Methodist Church. Fightin' Bob was the reverend pastor of the Church, a big beautiful stone-fortress of a place on the corner of Flower and 12th Street. Every Sunday, after the men's choir would sing out "The Old Rugged Cross" loud and strong, this little man with round spectacles and an easy smile would climb into the pulpit and begin to address the hundreds who came to hear him. Fightin' Bob had a Texas cyclone tenor voice that bumped along the plains of his sermons before taking flight. Then, as his voice rose up, that croaking tenor of his could fill the whole church with Bob's hellfire and fury. Floyd guessed that anyone with a decent head for stories could tell a good tale about Lot and his daughters or Joseph and his brothers, tales taken direct from the Bible, but Fightin' Bob took the time to relate God's word to what he'd seen around him, here in the city of Los Angeles, and Floyd liked all that. Because there was a whole lot to see and think on here.

Here, like at Angelus Temple, you'd see good, plain people — maybe acting a little less boisterous than the folks going to the Temple, even though some of them were the same folks. There were plenty of them who went to hear both Fightin' Bob and Sister Aimee on the same Sunday. They loved God, and most weren't too picky about what you call "Doctrine." They just wanted to fill the Sabbath with the Word. In the morning, it could be Fightin' Bob, railing against "modernists" and "weak Christians" and "Hollywood" and "corruption at City Hall," and in the evening, it could be Sister Aimee and her pageants and bands and healing miracles, preaching about how God wanted us all to be healthy and have good jobs and nice houses. They'd all get the feeling of the Holy Ghost at both Trinity and the Temple, but they also sure did hear some differing points of view.

Sitting in the pews at Trinity, to Floyd it seemed sometimes that Fightin' Bob was speaking directly to him, like he knew him. Floyd came here in 1919 convinced he was coming to the promised land, to "paradise," like his Pa said. He'd come to find that the promised land was broken, though. On the other days of the week, Floyd kept his head down and worked every day, and provided for his family as best as he could amid the brokenness, and he tried not to let it all beat him down. But on Sundays, it did wonders to hear Fightin' Bob shouting out with prophetic rage over it all.

Floyd was lucky enough to arrive in Los Angeles just as another nasty streetcar strike was cooling off there. Having already experienced the incompetence of the union, the Amalgamated, back in Kansas City — or maybe it was the government that let him down — he applied for a job as a free agent. Got a job three days after he arrived. No doubt he took it away from some poor union "committee" member. The Los Angeles Railway was an open shop by the time of the 1919 strike, and pretty much stayed that way afterwards. After working three and a half months, Floyd had saved enough to bring out Alpha and the children, and in a rented storefront with a parlor, bedroom and bath on the second floor, the Baumillers opened a sandwich and candy store on East 3rd Street, across the street from Second Street Elementary School and around the corner from Hollenbeck Park.

At first, it really did feel like "paradise." On beautiful spring days, folks would come out to Hollenbeck Park for a stroll or a picnic. The Park was a lush green oasis, with a long, narrow lake on which starry-eyed couples would escape the bonds of gritty Los Angeles earth in rowboats. They'd share the water with the swans, and with the dreamy reflections of rose bushes and willows, and an occasional palm tree or fern onshore. It was a garden of Eden, surrounded by grey streets, grey buildings and grey people in grey hats and coats.

The parkgoers, looking to put some color back into their lives, made for a good trade at the Baumillers' store for a time. In the summertime, groups of folks would get together and have "state" picnics — for example, a picnic for families who came to Los Angeles from Georgia, or another one for people from Indiana, and so on. They'd come for band concerts and Nazarene meetings, and a Fourth of July celebration — complete with a "confetti and serpentine battle" on the walk surrounding the boathouse; and being right around the corner, some of them might stop at the Baumillers for a chicken sandwich, hand-made by Alpha, who was with child at the time, or by nine-year old Geraldine Marie or six-year old Patrice, or for a bag of penny candy. The women in the family ran the store, while Floyd rotated as a motorman among various lines of the Los Angeles Railway.

As fall approached and the organized activities at the Park were fewer and farther between, the store attracted fewer customers, but the little shopkeepers on East 3rd Street remained steadily busy. One day in September, one of the greys, a fellow in a hat and overcoat, stopped in the store and wordlessly watched Alpha, six months pregnant with Teddy, as she sold candy to schoolchildren from the Second Street School. "May I help you, sir?", she asked the grey man. He told her "no, thanks," that he was just walking through the neighborhood and stopped by to see what was cooking. Over the next couple of weeks, they saw the same man sitting across the street on a bench, writing notes down in a book. Sometimes it was another grey man sitting there doing the same. Alpha caught one of them loitering around her garbage out back of the house. The kids were back in school, now, and the trade was getting very slow, as was Alpha as she reached her due date for the baby.

Then one day one of the grey men stopped by and tacked a notice on the front door, all smug like he was Martin Luther himself. "By order of the City Sanitation Department, Arthur Potts, Sanitation Inspector ... you have FOURTEEN DAYS to comply. Failure to comply will result in an order closing this establishment." Floyd and Alpha tried to make sense of all of the instructions—separate sink and cutting area for dressing the chickens; butter and sauces, such as the mayonnaise, to be kept in covered receptacles; new cleaning regimens for utensils and cloths; compost heap in back of premises will no longer be permitted; 14 different rules for handling eggs ... nigglingly close to what they were doing anyway, for cryin' out loud, but just different enough to cost them real dollars.

Floyd took a run at one of the lingering grey deputies, trying to talk some sense into him, but the deputy wouldn't have it. "Listen, mister, these aren't just arbitrary rules. We've got *chemists* with *college degrees* wearing *white lab coats* who can back all this up, based on *science!*" Floyd felt like he was getting taken out behind the woodshed and whooped with diplomas. Plus, Alpha was due to have this baby any day now, and they were already trying to figure out what it would cost to pay someone to mind the store while Alpha was down. It looked like the end of their little family store was nigh. It occurred to him that the deck was stacked for chain stores around here, anyway.

Meanwhile, Floyd had been recently assigned by the Railway to run the new "35" line, out at the end of the East Stephenson Line. It was a short line with a little trolley nicknamed "the Dinky," running a little less than a mile along Indiana Street from Stephenson Avenue to East 1st Street. Floyd would start at East 1st, with all the seats facing forward for the trip, and run the Dinky down to Stephenson. At Indiana and Stephenson, without turning the car around, Floyd would collect the cash box and the controls to take to the opposite end of the car. And then he would walk down the aisle and pull back each row of seats in the car, so that, presto, all the seats would be facing forward for the return the trip back to East 1ˢᵗ. Then, he would unhook the trolley pole from what was now the fore-end of the car, and hook the other trolley pole onto the new back-end of the car for the return trip. It was a nifty little system.

One day after work, just off Indiana, on the south side of East 4ᵗʰ, Floyd saw an old frame house for sale and talked to the owner, who told him it used to be the undertaker's. It had a nice big back yard. "They gonna send some fellers in white lab coats around here to tell me I can't have chickens or rabbits?"

"Nah," said the owner. "This here's Belvedere, not Los Angeles. It's what they call 'unincorporated' territory." The price was right and low, and the owner said he'd take a small mortgage; so shortly after Teddy was born, the family packed up and left their rented parlor, bedroom and bath and moved into a funeral home on East 4ᵗʰ. The new Baumiller homestead, on the frontier of Los Angeles.

From the pulpit, Fightin' Bob was railing. "I think we can get along very well for another hundred years without any other of these great scholars ... these great scholars that know so much that you can't ever find out what they know. *They* don't even know what they know! We've got enough brains to damn the world. I mean that. Like those fellers, those brainy fellers, that say we're all a-kin to monkeys or goats or cabbages, and not the creations of God Himself, in His image. Come now, really — what is all that education for, if it hain't to grow up men of character? Men who say 'yes' to God? We got plenty of brains around here, if we can only use 'em right."

Boy, I'll say, thought Floyd. All Floyd could think about were men in white lab coats, little clipboards in their hands, shaking their heads "no."

Even the frontier of Los Angeles was nothing like Floyd had once imagined it would be. That consarned Sunkist label showed lazy green hills of trees, as far as the eye could see, oranges you could pick right off the branch — like the Old West he deeply loved, but more verdant. Turned out, when he got here, Floyd figured out it wasn't so green here in Los Angeles. Turned out it was more grey, like those grey men from the Sanitation Department, except for a spot here and there, like Hollenbeck Park. Or the cemetery around the corner on Lorena Street.

But it wasn't just the lack of green beauty that disappointed him. For all those brave white Christian men who fought their way out here, who lived and died in the Old West, paving the way for our generation to make a life here on the Pacific coast of America ... *I guess I was expecting something different*, thought Floyd. He guessed he had a picture in his mind of place where a man could put his stake in the ground, breathe in the fresh ocean air, strike up a new covenant with God, and the United States of America, on behalf of himself and his family, conjoining with a reverent people in goodness and hard work ... but to find the downtown sidewalks, packed with the graceless, the worn-out and the unforgiving; the smoke and the noise; the cramped quarters; the unsightly displays of wealth among the dishonest and the profligate; the overpopulated, overlapping governments, hireable by the rich; the scent of contraband liquor hovering like a storm cloud over everything ... was this what all those brave men fought their way across the plains for?

For cryin' out loud, *Wyatt Earp*— THE *Wyatt Earp himself*— fought his way out here, too, and he was living out here somewhere. Was this any place for *Marshal Wyatt Earp* and his sacred Colt .45? Was this any place for his sacred horse, Dick Naylor? *Marshal Wyatt Earp* ... who took on the Clanton boys and lived to tell the tale ... who rode with some of the toughest lawmen and gunfighters there ever was ... who risked everything for law and order, and for pushing civilization out further West ...

Nobody around here seems to be aware of the real story about Wyatt Earp. *Funny*, thought Floyd, *in a town that loves to tell stories, in the moving pictures and in the Sunday newspapers and all, they don't have Wyatt Earp's story right at all.* To people around here, Wyatt Earp is a washed-up fight referee. Oh, Floyd remembered, as a child, reading about the Sharkey-Fitzsimmons fight up in San Francisco, about how Wyatt Earp was the referee, and how some people thought he threw the fight to Sharkey when he called a foul against Fitzsimmons. What a terrible shame to be remembered that way — as a two-bit cheater. Floyd almost wanted to go and visit the Marshal himself and tell him he knew all about his real story, tell him some folks knew better.

Pa knew folks who knew the Earp boys, and Pa was pretty sure he'd seen them himself on one of his trips West from Neodesha, back when the boys were out in Wichita. They were tough characters, they could get under your skin, Floyd supposed, with their quick tempers, but the only folks who really complained about them were those who either had mischief on their minds to begin with, or had no stomach for the frontier in the first place. Back when the newspapers were all full of the Sharkey fight, Floyd remembered people in Kansas talking about the Earp boys. In particular, he remembered his Pa telling him about how the Earp boys were out in this town called Tombstone, in the old Arizona Territory — back before Floyd was born — and Wyatt's brother Virgil was the town marshal, and Wyatt and his brother Morgan were deputies along with a fellow named Johnny Holiday. And how the Clanton boys and Billy Claiborne and the McLaurys, and bunch of other cow boys were coming into town all drunk and shooting and showing no respect for the law, and how they'd even threatened to go after the Earp boys; and how Virgil asked them to turn in their guns, but they said no. And how, in a gunfight between the lawmen and the cow boys, Virgil and Morgan and Holiday were all wounded, and Billy Clanton and the McLaurys were killed, and sharpshooting Wyatt Earp emerged unscathed, standing tall as a lawman, defending the good people of Tombstone.

Now that's a way to be remembered, thought Floyd. That man who aimed his gun at no-good cow boys could not have been the same man as the two-bit cheater that people out here in California accuse him of being. It upset Floyd to think about it, because, for starters, they were wrong about Earp. And because the law and order situation here in Los Angeles was none too good, and maybe we needed a few men like Earp to clean things up and keep 'em straight. There's Clanton boys behind every lamp post, and Prohibition or no, they're all raging drunk and looking for trouble.

Instead of a Wyatt Earp to stand up to 'em, though, as Fightin' Bob was just saying from the pulpit, "Our leaders these days seem to have nothing but excuses. If they ain't crooked themselves — and a lot of them are, as sure as I'm standing here, they are — they are weak men. They are men who lack courage. And a bucket full of their excuses ain't worth a mouthful of spit."

Amen to that, Floyd thought to himself.

But now we're all here: the heathens as well as the Christians; the whites, but also the blacks and the Mexicans. And, in our neighborhood — not really the frontier of Los Angeles, but he liked to think of it that way — there were also the Russians and the Armenians who cook their potatoes in fire pits in their front yards, and the little Japanese family, who come around asking if they can clip our dandelion weeds for soup. *Here we all are, in a big steaming bowl of Belvedere stew. We're all just poor tripe here. But at least I can have my chickens out here in the backyard,* thought Floyd. *I can carve and hew my funeral homestead the way I like it.* He built rabbit hutches back there, too, with little Teddy helping, sort of. Alpha sure knew how to fix up some good rabbit.

There in the pew at Trinity, Floyd snuck a little peek at Alpha and baby Dorothy. Both of them were dozing.

Alpha was a child when he met her, virtually a child when they were married. Sixteen-year old Floyd and his buddy Karl were out riding in a rickety gig one day. Up ahead, they saw a coach lying on its side in a ditch off to the side of the road. As they got closer, they heard and saw some girls in long mud-stained dresses climbing over the top of the coach. They sounded like they were squealing like little piglets. "Ho, Karl — I think they need help!" Floyd pulled back on the reins and they pulled over to the side of the road near the ditch.

"Are you girls alright?" Floyd shouted as he bounded down toward the coach.

Out from the coach window popped a little round head, a mop of black hair tied back, and bright black eyes staring back at him. "We were just playin'," said the little girl. The little heads of the two younger blonde girls popped out from other corners of the coach's architecture. "We're alright," the black-eyed girl said, "we're just playin'."

Floyd looked around to see where they could've come from. "It's getting late for you girls to be out here," he said. "Ain't your papa gonna worry 'bout you?"

"We don't have no papa," said the black-eyed girl as she rubbed her button nose on her muddy sleeve. "That is ..."

"Well, let us ride you home. Where d'you live?"

"Over that way," said the black-eyed girl, pointing yonder to a little frame house on the horizon.

"I'm Floyd, and this here's Karl." Karl tipped his cap and nodded.

"My name's Alpharetta Deadwyler," said the black-eyed girl, putting on a formal face, "and these here are my sisters. This one's Grace, and that little one is Lee-Lee. I mean, Letitia."

"Let us ride you home," said Floyd. Floyd reached out to take Alpharetta's hand as she climbed up from the coach out of the ditch. She seemed tiny down there, but now she seemed taller than he expected. "How old are you, Alpharetta Deadwyler?," Floyd asked. "Pretty old," she said. "I'm twelve years old. How old are you?"

Karl got out of the gig and propped himself up on the tailboard as the girls scrambled up into the seat, Alpharetta squeezing in next to Floyd. They chatted like chickadees until they pulled up the drive at Mother Deadwyler's house. Absorbed in their conversation, Floyd hadn't noticed Mother Deadwyler — Mrs. Mattie Crullup Deadwyler — until he heard her hard boot heels on the front porch floorboards. He looked up to see her standing there, larger than almighty life itself, with a shotgun half drawn.

Alpha and her sisters were flying out of the gig toward the house before Floyd could say a word. "Mama, this is Floyd and Karl, and they gave us a ride."

"Get over here, girls," she snarled at them. "What's your name, boy?"

"Floyd, ma'am. Floyd Baumiller. We didn't mean no — "

"Baumiller," she interrupted. "You the rubbish man's boy?"

"Yes, ma'am."

"What are you doing with my girls?"

"We just — " Alpha interrupted him. "We was out playin' by that old wrecked coach, Ma, and — "

"And we just offered to ride 'em home is all," piped Floyd.

As the story fairly set in with her, Mother Deadwyler loosened the flex of her shooting arms and wrapped one of them around her little Lee-Lee, crouching down to greet the babe as she tugged on her mother's long skirt. "You boys hungry? I dressed a chicken for supper. Here, boy, you take this bucket out to that well and get us some water for washing up."

Over time, during Mother Deadwyler's many blunt supper monologues, Floyd learned that her husband George had left the family a few years before and was now "cohabitatin'" with "a whore" in Kansas City; that she was "going it alone" and was planning to "*dee*-vorce" her "rotten husband" once she saved a little money for a lawyer; and that the little blonde girls looked like her own Crullup brothers and sisters, whilst Alpha favored "her no-good daddy" with her dark features. "I think he must'a been part Chickasaw," she asserted, without knowing one way or the other. "That'd explain a whole lot, though," she said. A few years later, that *dee*-vorce of hers hit the front page of all the papers: "Mrs. Mattie Deadwyler vs. George Deadwyler," went the headline, "Deserted Wife Supports Herself by Keeping Boarders."

He also learned that Mother Deadwyler had quite a head for stories. She said that they knew the James boys when she was a little girl back in Missouri — "and that Jesse himself sure was a handsome devil," she would laugh — and that she and George Deadwyler were living in Coffeyville, Kansas just before Alpha was born, and they were there on the day that the Dalton Gang rode into town.

She loved to tell the tale of the Coffeyville Raid. "Everyone around those parts knew the Dalton boys," she'd begin. "They were just one of the families you knew. The oldest boy, Frank, he was a strong and good-lookin' boy, and he became a deputy marshal, a federal lawman. The younger boys — Grat, Bill, Bob and Emmett — all looked up to Frank. They all wanted to be marshals, and they would all go out riding with Frank in his posses, going after the bad fellers. Then one day, when Frank was out hunting after a horse thief down in the Oklahoma Territory, he got shot up and died. After that, the younger boys, especially Bob Dalton, were pretty bitter about it, and they were even more angry that they never got comp'nsated for riding with the law. Frank would have seen to it, of course, had he lived, but since he wasn't around, the Dalton boys just wandered off the tracks. You'd hear stories about Bob being arrested for bringing hooch into Injun Territory, or about Grat stealing horses."

"After awhile it was inevitable, I guess, that they'd put together a gang, and they started robbing trains. Can you imagine? Robbing trains! They were brazen! They'd jump on and ambush the poor engineer and the brakeman in their cab, and while one of the gang would hold them at gunpoint, the other boys would march on down the center aisles of the train cars, snatching up all the cash and jewelry along the way. Down in the Injun Territory, they hauled in $10,000! Never a scratch on 'em, despite all the shooting. Once, though, the marshals arrested Grat, but he escaped by getting loose from his handcuffs and diving out of a moving train into the San Joaquin River. After they hit the trains, they'd ride off and head South to some godforsaken border town without any law in it. Then they'd live like kings for awhile, sometimes without even having to spend their cash."

"Now Bob Dalton was an ambitious fellow, tho, and even though they made a pretty good living robbing trains, Bob wanted something more than money. He wanted to be better than the James Gang. He kept telling folks he wanted to rob two banks at the same time, in broad daylight. That'd show 'em all how good he was. If I've seen it once, I've seen it a hundred times," Mother Deadwyler would say. "These young roosters, going to some outlandish length to prove themselves, as if anyone else even cared. Every time I see it I just hope and pray they'll learn their lesson before they end up dead. Unfortunately for Bob, though, he took a bullet before he could learn anything, poor bastard. Same with Grat."

"Anyways, Bob and his brothers were popping off about this scheme of theirs all over southern Kansas, and so the folks in Coffeyville knew about their plans for about month before the Dalton Gang came to call. And we were ready for them." She told how the Gang rode into town around 9 o'clock in the morning, and that while Bob and Emmett went into the First National Bank, the other boys went into the C.M. Congdon & Company private bank right across the street.

In one version of the story, it was Mother Deadwyler herself, eight months with child and almost ready to pop, who drew a bead on Grat Dalton as he left the front door of the Congdon bank and shot him "right square in the solar plexus." In another version, she and George met up with the Gang before they rode to town, and pleaded with them not to go when they heard about their plan. In yet another, George Deadwyler actually rode into town with the Dalton Gang and went into the First National Bank with Bob, and barely escaped with his life. "Should've thought to shoot'm then and there," Mother Deadwyler said.

In the end, the townspeople took down the Gang. They shot Bob and Grat dead, and they shot Bill Power and Dick Broadwell dead, and "they laid each of their pale carcasses out on the wooden plank sidewalk outside the hardware store, bullet holes and all. Emmett was the only brother who was there who survived — Bill Dalton wasn't there that day for some reason. Emmett got shot 23 times and still lived, but he got sent to prison for life." Later Floyd heard they pardoned Emmett Dalton and he moved to California, where, *it figures, he got a job making pictures.*

"Was Wyatt Earp there, in Coffeyville?" Floyd asked Mother Deadwyler. "Would've come in handy if he hadda been," she said. "But no, I expect he was shooting up outlaws somewhere's else that day." She paused to stare at Floyd across the dinner table, all squinty-eyed and ready to breathe fire. "If you're doing something wrong, you know, God's eternal wrath is around every corner, just waiting for you. Maybe he's a lawman, or maybe he's an honest citizen with a shotgun. But there ain't no getting away with anything in this life."

Floyd was scared of Mother Deadwyler, but fascinated by her all the same. Mother Deadwyler knew as much, and that was probably the reason that she did not protest when Floyd and Alpha went off to be married, when Alpha was just sixteen. Mother Deadwyler knew that under her watchful eye, Floyd would never be another no-good George Deadwyler.

After the service ended at Trinity, the Baumiller family walked down to catch the first trolley on their way to Echo Park. Someone left a newspaper behind, and Floyd managed to grab it before the onrush of passengers jumped on and took all of the open seats. While Alpha and the papoose sat below him, Floyd wrapped himself around a hand-hold pole in the aisle and scanned the pages of the paper. There were stories — some of them fresh, some of them ongoing reports on sordid drawn-out sagas — about the "fraud and conspiracy" conviction of Doheny the oil tycoon and Albert Fall, one of President Harding's men, over some oil leases; about some gangsters, some fellow named

"Farmer" Page murdering Al Joseph at the Sorrento Club; about some other fellow giving liquor to chorus girls; some picture actress with an obviously put-on name, *"Leatrice Joy,"* getting a divorce from her picture actor husband after he staged a "drunken debauch" — *whatever that is*; a man shooting his young fiancée then killing himself; twenty people losing $159,000 in a merger swindle ... it was hard for Floyd to think of all these things together, to hold them in the same thought as Bob Dalton trying to outdo the James Gang and getting shot dead in the street in Coffeyville in 1892. *Even if I was sitting here with a shotgun in my lap, I'm not sure I'd know who I was supposed to shoot,* he thought, laughing a little so as not to cry about it. *And while Marshal Wyatt Earp is remembered as a cheating fight referee, living somewhere around here on the edge of this town, Emmett Dalton of the Dalton Gang was making pictures in Hollywood, la-dee-da ...*

He knew it was best not to think about such things. Better to keep your head down and work hard and stay away from all of that as best as you could.

Settling in at the Angelus Temple, in seats up near the rafters, it wasn't hard to let all of that go amid a few thousand smiling faces, the impromptu finger-picking and hymn-singing while waiting for the service to begin. There was real Joy in that auditorium, not some put-on Hollywood Joy.

A little Mexican boy came around, passing out paper programmes. Way down on the stage below, four black women, dressed as angels in white robes, were playing guitars and singing a bouncy yet reverent version of the *Battle Hymn of the Republic* in four-part harmony. At the end of that, six tall gentlemen each dressed up like Uncle Sam came out, and each of them took a sentry post all around the edge of the stage. Soon they were joined by six women, each dressed up like the Statue of Liberty; and then each of the couples — the Sams and the Liberties — did a side-by-side jig as the orchestra played marching music. People stood up and clapped their hands and cheered to see them dance. Then, there was a long drum roll, and finally out came Sister Aimee herself — dressed up like George Washington, in boots and a long military coat, and a white wig and three-corner hat — strutting to the music, out to the center of the stage. The audience thundered its approval as she doffed her hat and wig and threw them into the crowd. Then the orchestra began to play "Enter His Court With Singing," and nearly the whole audience joined in as Sister Aimee sang it out, loud and clear and sweet.

After a couple more hymns, Sister Aimee — without her costume coat and boots — stood at the center of the stage in a long white dress. Standing in the spotlight, she seemed almost like a heavenly vision of a woman, not a woman in the flesh. With outstretched arms, she welcomed everyone, and the Temple rumbled with the congregation's reply to her. And then she began to preach, saying that today she was moved by the Holy Ghost to tell us "what we don't realize about what the Lord wants for you and me."

During her sermon, Sister Aimee told a story. "There was once a man who was having a tough time, he had to pinch every penny —," she said, causing the audience to laugh. "Well, now, maybe you know him!," she laughed. "Now, this man bought a ticket for an ocean voyage. And as he boarded the steamship, he said to himself, 'I must watch what I do with my few remaining dollars. I'll just buy some crackers and drink water with them for the duration of my voyage, so that will leave me with a small sum on my arrival.' Then the days wore on, one by one by one, and the poor man became more and more famished for a good square meal, and more and more disgusted with the crackers and water. And on the day that the steamer was scheduled to arrive in port, he could bear it no longer. If it took his last cent, he decided that he must have one more good meal."

"But when he made his way to the dining salon, and he saw first-hand all of its beauty and the fine food that was being served, course after course at the tables, the white linen and the shining silver — it all caused him to doubt. For such a fine dining room, perhaps he would not have money enough after all! Catching the eye of the steward, he inquired, 'Sir, would you please be kind enough to tell me the cost of a meal in that dining room?' The waiter looked at the man with amazement and said: 'Why, I don't understand what you mean.' 'I want to know how much one good, square meal at that table would cost me, please.'"

"'Why, you have a ticket for this steamship voyage, haven't you?'"

"'Ticket? Why, yes, of course,' said the man."

"'Then your meals don't cost you a penny. They are all included in the price of your ticket. Where have you been when we've been serving meals? Why did you not come to the table? Your place has been set and held vacant for you all the time.'"

"'Why, I've been sitting in my state-room eating crackers and drinking cold water, every day, because I thought I could not afford the dining room!'" The audience groaned its pity for the poor man.

"Oh dear ones," Sister Aimee concluded, "many of us have gone almost to the end of life 's voyage before realizing the good things included in our ticket. Salvation, healing, beauty, comfort, the power of the Holy Ghost and rich life in Christ are yours for the asking. Draw near today and cry out: 'Thou Son of David, have mercy upon me. I now appropriate Thy promises, and claim as mine the rich provision Thou hast made for me, even the double cure with its blessings for body and soul.'"

"My dear ones, too long have we wandered in weakness and poverty, when we might have had His strength and riches! Too long have we lain starving, when we might have been feasting in Our Father's banquet hall."

Sister Aimee said "you don't have to be a first class banker, or a lawyer, or a millionaire ... you've bought your ticket! The Lord loved to walk in the cool of the day in the tranquil beauty of the Garden of Eden, which he planted lovingly for man, whom he made after His own image. Your task is simply to come to His table, to obey Him, and to reap the rewards He made for you."

As she finished her sermon, the orchestra struck up a slow hymn, and Sister Aimee announced to the crowd, "Some of our dear friends are here with us, right here in the front row of this church, and they are down here tonight to claim freedom from pain and misery. Pray with me, my dears — pray that they might find comfort, pray that they might heal. Pray, my dears, pray! We all want a little of His healing power!" She went to each of the sick and lame sitting in the front row, with their crutches and their head bandages and wheelchairs, and as the orchestra continued to play, she rested her hands on each of their heads in turn. Up where the Baumillers sat, some people were crying as they watched Aimee bestow His divine power on the sick, as the conduit of His grace;

others started speaking in tongues — but they did so softly, since before the service the ushers did their best to spread the word that Sister Aimee wanted them to revel in the experience of the Holy Ghost "quietly, with the utmost respect to your neighbors here, and to those folks listening in on their radios at home." The effect was like a storm of unintelligible whispers, sha-sha-sha-ing across their section of the seats and around the Temple, as the orchestra played on. Blanche whispered her heavenly emissions right along with them.

On the way home, Blanche was in a state of bliss. She sat way back in her seat on the streetcar, with her head back and her jagged, crinkly chin pointed to the heavens, blinking slowly, her cheeks tear-daubed. "Such power and such glory ... did you feel it, Trueman?"

"Oh, yes, Blanche," answered Trueman meekly. It was call and response, like in the old Church of the Nazarene on Orchard. "Yes, I did." Their daughter Princess Alice snickered. "You stop that, young lady," said Blanche.

"What about you, Floyd?," Blanche continued. "Did you feel it?"

Sitting behind them in the car, with Alpha and the papoose, Floyd didn't answer.

He enjoyed it, and all — no question about it. All the pretty folderol, and all the music, and the high jinks down on that stage, and all that goodness and hope that Sister Aimee preached in her sermon, made him feel elated, he had to admit — a different feeling than he got at Trinity in the morning, to be sure. Tho' Fightin' Bob would say he was concerned that Sister Aimee's preaching was not based on Scripture. He would say he was concerned that there was no board of deacons watching over all that money that she raised to build that temple of hers, and that her "platform healings" and "tongues demonstrations" were hokum, at best — and at worst, they were "dangerously out of harmony with God's word, and with the experiences of all Christians of times past." And Fightin' Bob would suggest, without saying it too directly, that the temple and the orchestra and the whole big show was more about Aimee than it was about Our Lord. Still, it didn't seem to be hurting anyone.

Back at the house on East 4ᵗʰ, once all the children were put to bed, and the papoose was down in her little crib in her mama and papa's room, and once Alpha's head finally hit her pillow at the end of a long Sunday, Floyd found himself alone in the candlelit kitchen, the aroma of Sunday morning's breakfast still lingering. His Pa had sent him a recent edition of the *Kansas City Times* in the post, and he was anxious to catch up with the goings-on back home. As he studied the paper in the dim light of the kitchen, he absently reached up onto the metal shelf above the sink, pulled out a colorfully decorated tin and set it down on the middle of the wooden tabletop across from the old black stove. He pulled a mug down off the wall and ran a little tap water into it. Reading on, he sat down at the wooden table with his mug and his colorful tin; and before long, while looking at the department store ads, he was eating soda crackers from the tin and drinking water from the mug.

When he finally noticed what he was doing, he had to laugh out loud a little. Then he reached for another cracker. *I truly enjoy crackers and water.*

I never did think it was the Lord's job to provide me with any banquet feast, he thought to himself. *I guess I hope He don't mind that I don't want any champagne or any Oysters a la Rockefeller. I guess I hope I never have to be ashamed of it.*

He could complain about this or that, but he had his stake in the ground, and he had his arms and his legs and his wits. He had his funeral home on the frontier of Los Angeles, a big yard with rabbits and chickens, five healthy children and a good woman in his dear wife Alpha. He had the Dinky, not far from home. He had a good Sunday. And he had crackers and water. Contentment was Floyd's by-word.

<hr />

Barely a year later, Sister Aimee was in hot water after she claimed she had been kidnapped. People originally thought, when she went missing, that she drowned at the beach at Ocean Park, and two poor fellows died looking for her in the ocean. When she reappeared south of the border, a month after she went missing, she said she had been held for ransom in an old shack in Mexico. But as the grand jury tried to sort it all out, the newspapers gossiped that she was all-along cohabitating with a married man. Fightin' Bob had a field day with it all, and a lot of people like Floyd who used to be entertained by her and thought she was harmless, turned their backs on her. She still had her die-hard flock, but the Baumillers quit going to the Angelus Temple. Floyd was pretty sure Blanche still listened to her on the radio, though.

Floyd quit going to see Fightin' Bob, too. Although he liked it when Fightin' Bob lashed out against all the weak and corrupt politicians, he didn't like him getting too involved in elections — like when the Democrats ran Al Smith for the White House in 1928, and Fightin' Bob said the Catholics were fixing to take over the world and murder all the Protestants, or when Fightin' Bob ran for Senate against McAdoo in 1932. Fightin' Bob ran off his mouth one too many times and got his own radio station shut down. It was all a little unseemly to Floyd.

At length, there were no more Sunday visits to churches to hear preachers. At length, the Baumillers stayed home on Sundays, did their chores, and listened to the Zenith console radio in the front room — maybe sometimes to a modest Christian preacher, sometimes to rodeo shows ... at length, to Jimmy Wakely and His Saddle Pals, *Lone Ranger*, and *I Love a Mystery* ...

2.3
ARENA MOVEDIZA
SOUTH AVENUE 20,
LINCOLN HEIGHTS, 1927

Lieutenant Bill Lloyd, played with big fists by Richard Dix, has been tracking a brutal band of smugglers in and around Deadville, a little town on the Mexican border. If that weren't enough to keep up with, he's fallen in love with Carlotta, played by Helene Chadwick, a dancer who's turned out to be an undercover government agent. Disillusioned by the fight, Bill is about to resign his commission when he hears that Carlotta's father has been captured by the smugglers. He rushes into Deadville and attacks the dirty smugglers, mowing through a dozen of them with his two big fists like an aeroplane propeller. Carlotta's there, too, jumping out of empty pickle barrels and out from behind a fern or two, strategically crushing bottles and broken chair legs over the heads of some of the varmints just as they are about to attack Bill from behind.

Things seem to be going well for them until Bill and Carlotta end up cornered in an upstairs room at the saloon. Bill barricades the door, but the murderous army of smugglers is regrouping and is about to come and get them. They'll probably gun Bill down, but the hero and his girl are all too aware that she may be awaiting a fate worse than death ... the odds look bad for them as Bill reaches into his belt and pulls out his service revolver, which has only one shot left in the chamber.

They're making their last stand. The scene pulls in close. Bill leans in and gives Carlotta the tenderest of screen kisses, his buffalo-like chin creasing with ardor. Then he places the barrel of *his gun just underneath Carlotta's dainty jawline. Her butterfly lips quiver. She knows what's coming, what's about to burst through that door, and she wants him to pull the trigger. She reaches up and caresses his shooting wrist. Their moistened eyes are locked in an eternal moment of love and fate and despair. He rests his forehead upon hers. They close their eyes. He squeezes the trigger —*

— but wait.

They hear something we can't hear. The piano player knows — he's playing "Reveille" now. The Cavalry has come to save them! They rush to the window of their upstairs room and they cheer as the Cavalry gallops in and envelopes Deadville. Then, at the window, Bill and Carlotta smile and kiss again, this time crying tears of joy.

The End.

Mrs. Anna Martín awoke with a start. She was sitting in her little chair at her little table in the corner of her little kitchen on South Avenue 20. Her half-smoked cigarette was still smoldering in the ashtray next to her saucer and cup of coffee, also half-consumed. It was Sunday morning, and the vines in the little backyard smelled wet from last night's sprinkles.

She awoke with a start, thinking about the end of that Richard Dix picture. It was called *Quicksands*, and she had seen it the night before at the Lincoln, on Broadway, with her friend Gloria from the Dress Company. It had been awhile since she had been anywhere other than the factory, or the house of South Avenue 20.

She had seen the end of that Richard Dix picture before, before she and Joe were married. The picture was a few years old, in fact, and for some reason that's all they had to show last night.

In the little bedroom, Joe was still sleeping. He was awake last night, though, fading in and out anyway, and if it weren't for Mrs. Alvarez next door, Anna wouldn't have been able to get away to see the picture with Gloria. She needed Mrs. Alvarez to check on him, at least a couple of times, while she was out.

Now Anna was sitting in the little bedroom, next to the bed. Joe was breathing hard through his slumber, as if he were fighting his way out of it. The little bedroom smelled sick and sulfurous, like rotten fruit. She wanted to throw open the curtains, open the window, but Joe wouldn't have any of it. His eyes were red. He said the sunlight hurt them. He didn't say much else.

The doctor was coming today. They were fortunate to have him come. Anna sent a note down to Joe's manager at the Foundry, Mr. Hardy, that morning when Joe couldn't get out of bed, and she told him about it. Mr. Hardy liked Joe. He'd seen him fight a few times back in the old days. Whatever else he was, Joe was a good worker, and Mr. Hardy said he wanted to send the company doctor over. It had been a week or so since Joe went down, but the doctor called over and said he was coming today.

There was no doctor to the house when little Helen went down. And at first, anyway, it didn't occur to Anna that she needed a doctor. That hot morning in July, Baby was five months old and squawking in her little crib in the corner of the little bedroom Oh, it was so hot that day. Joe told Anna to keep Baby quiet, *estaba gruñón.*[4] Baby wouldn't stop, Joe left for work that morning without saying goodbye, the back of his head dripping with sweat.

After Joe left that day, Anna walked back and forth, back and forth, through the little hallway, to the little kitchen and back to the little bedroom, rocking and shooshing the little one. For a long time nothing worked, until Baby cried herself to sleep. Anna put Baby down that day and smoked a cigarette, curled up with a pillow and closed her eyes for a few minutes ...

On this Sunday morning, sitting next to the bed with Joe, Anna couldn't keep her eyes open, at least not until Joe was awake. "Where were you last night?", he asked, his head flat against the pillow, his eyes tilted at the ceiling. "Me and Gloria, we went to the Lincoln." Joe grunted. He was arching his back and stretching his arms. She closed in on him to feel his forehead. "A little warm," she said. He grunted again. "I got to piss," he said. She brought him the chamber pot. "Do you need help?" she asked. "No, just leave me."

She could hear him struggling in the little bedroom, could hear him mumble a bit from pain, but she obeyed him and didn't come in, not

---

4   He was grumpy.

until he called for her. "Take this. Gimme a towel." "You need to be cleaned?' "No, just a towel."

The doctor came mid-morning — Dr. Flynn. "Good, you speak English," the doctor said. She took him into the little bedroom, walked right in with him and went straight to the curtains. "Keep them closed," said Joe.

"Mrs. Martín, I'd like to examine your husband if I may," said Dr. Flynn. "It would be best if you waited outside the room." "Yes, doctor. Thank you for coming."

"How long have you been paralyzed?" the doctor asked Joe.

"Huh?"

"How long since you couldn't move your legs?" "A week, doctor," Anna said, leaving the little bedroom and closing the door behind her. She went back to her little corner of the little kitchen and opened up a motion picture magazine, lit up another cigarette. She heard the low murmurs of their voices, but couldn't make out any of the words.

On that hot July day, a Saturday almost three years ago, Anna just thought Baby was *enfadada*, a little cranky maybe. Baby started to cough and sputter, even hours after feeding, like she was trying to expel something from her mouth. By Saturday night, Anna thought she might have a fever, but it was hot out, and Anna's little mother and her sisters said not to worry too much about it, it was difficult to tell in the heat. But early the next morning, the fever was more apparent. Anna started to worry a little, but Joe didn't want to hear about it — just take care of the Baby, take care of the Baby, I don't know nothing. Monday morning Anna woke up and saw this coat, like mucus, a bleak, grey coat developing at the back of her throat; and Baby was struggling with it. "What have you gotten into, *pobrecita*?" she asked, as if Baby had gotten up in the middle of the night and eaten casein glue; and she tried to smudge at it, with her fingertip inside Baby's mouth, but somehow she couldn't get it, and in the early morning hours it felt almost like a dream, a nightmare about trying and trying and trying to wipe some spot clean of a black miasma, only to have it come back and grow larger and more virulent. But the dream-like quality of it faded quickly, even if the feeling of powerlessness did not, as it became apparent that Baby was having trouble breathing, her neck now swelling, her exhalations squealing softly like the earliest rise of a boiling coffee pot. Baby had stopped squirming around in the crib by Tuesday morning; whatever had Baby in its grip had shocked the kick out of her by then. She was turning so pale. The little Baby. She was turning so pale. And she wasn't eating. And Joe came home that night and it was a hot day, and he was beat down by the sun all day, out in the scrapyard, and he was tired. Anna was sobbing, her little mother and sisters were uninterested, no one was helping, no one had anything useful to say, there was no one to call. And Joe said take care of the Baby, I don't know.

And she said to him, "Joe — Baby is very sick, do you understand? Very sick."

So he sat down in the chair next to the crib, and he reached down in and felt Baby's forehead, he hadn't often done that, he hadn't often touched her even; and he sat and listened to her wheeze. Anna was down on the carpet, her head in his lap, her arms wrapped around his waist, crying softly. They spent the night that way, the lamp on the nightstand still burning.

Joe got dressed early and went next door to speak with Mr. Alvarez. He came back and told Anna, "We take her to the hospital." Mr. Alvarez drove them to White Memorial, the little family huddled together in his backseat. When the nurse took her, she knew immediately — she didn't say, but Anna was certain of it, the nurse knew what was wrong.

They were there for three hours before the doctor came and told them that Helen was dead.

Anna didn't remember much after that. Perhaps it was fortunate for her that she didn't. She'd have no recollection, as Joe did, of hearing the orderly in the hallway, asking about "the Mexicans who brought in that dead baby — we need to speak with them." She remembered that she wanted to bring home her Baby, just to have her for a little time longer; but she would not remember Joe trying to bargain with the Hospital, she would not remember hearing that they were going to perform an autopsy. "It's a public health matter, Mr. Mar-teen. We believe your daughter died of *diphtheria* and we need to make sure, for our records. We have to have an accurate count, you see? ...You want us to send the body to Zeferino Ramirez, the undertaker? He's down the street, he does most of the Mexicans. Such a nice man, you know him? ... No, I am sorry, Mr. Mar-teen, we could not possibly let you see the body. It was an infectious disease, and we cannot risk the chance of spreading it further ... Mr. Mar-tinn, we have papers for you to sign."

In fact, Anna never saw Baby again, never in the flesh. There was a little funeral at the Calvary Cemetery on Whittier Boulevard, which seemed like it was out in the country somewhere, closed little casket by order of the public health authorities; and then Helen was in the ground. Back home in Lincoln Heights, nowadays Anna would say to herself, when she would allow herself to think about it, that Helen was in the ground, far away from here, far away from her mother.

"Mrs. Martín?"

Dr. Flynn had found her in the kitchen.

"Mrs. Martín? I've finished with your husband," he said. "I've given him something for sleeping — I'm sure he's been a bit restless — you know, stir-crazy. Good for him to sleep a bit." He said that Joe was suffering from something they called Reiter's — "it's a kind of arthritis, a severe case, from an infection" — and they needed to treat the infection. He said the company would send their male nurse around here once a day for a week or so to administer a course of treatment — an eye wash for the pink-eye, a silver nitrate solution to flush "another infected area." Then, aspirin twice a day. "You can help, too," he told her, "by putting hot towels on his legs twice a day. Boil them in a pot, wring 'em out a little — hotter the better. They'll sting him, you know, but it's good for him."

"Will he walk again?," she asked.

"Oh, yes. He will. Might be a couple of months, but he will ... you're lucky Hardy likes the boy, or else they might not've given him the time of day here."

She thanked him, and he asked her if he could take a seat for a moment. Sitting across from her at the little table in the little kitchen, the doctor paused to clear his throat, took out his notepad and pen and began to ask her questions. He took her temperature, asked if she was experiencing pain, he said Joe was suffering from an infectious disease and he needed to know these things, and then, again clearing his throat and speaking slowly and awkwardly, began to ask her questions using words she did not know. Stammering something about *con-s-sortium*, or *c-congress*, or *c-conju-g-gation*, or *com-m-merce*, or *c-coition*, the words kept percussing on her eardrums — interrupting, no, assaulting the silence of the kitchen that morning, confusing her. He had told her before, "Oh, good, you speak English," but now she wasn't sure what language he was speaking.

"Mrs. Martín — do you and Mr. Martín sleep in the same bed?" He seemed to be apologizing for the question almost as quickly as he had asked it.

The truth was they rarely even occupied the same room since Helen was gone.

After Helen was gone, in the daytime, Anna would lie face down on the bed in their room and cry. In the evenings, she would lie down on the divan in the front room, smoking and staring at the ceiling. She would wait until Joe left for work in the mornings before closing her eyes, napping in short increments. Apart from making coffee, her attention to the rest of the little household was no better than intermittent. There were no meals waiting for Joe when he got home, and consequently, he started coming home later. Then he started coming home later still. She pretended not to notice, refused to acknowledge it in any way, secretly wanted to be alone, after all. But of course, she wanted to be anything but alone. She wanted Helen back. There were people telling Joe that she would snap out of it one day, and they told him to be patient. He wasn't a patient man at this stage of his life, though — really, he was just a boy — so instead he went through herky-jerky spasms of trying to comfort her, to staying out late, to staying out really late, to feeling guilty and trying to engage her in his awkward way.

But she was not to be engaged. Nor would she talk about Helen with her mother or her sisters. Instead she kept to her routine — almost machine-like, powered by an energy that wasn't her own — crying on the bed in the daytime, smoking on the divan in the evenings. Not that there was any comfort in the routine, but perhaps to have done otherwise would have been to surrender to something darker yet. Smoking cigarettes all night in the dark through the early morning light, crying face-down all day, were simply ways to transact her business. Which was emptiness. Which was a convulsive dry heave of blankness. Better than involuntary thoughts, though; better than involuntary questions about what she could have done differently, what she could have done to save her Baby. Better than the involuntary feeling that she would welcome this disease, this *diphtheria*, into her own body, *por favor Dios*, send the germs in and let it stifle her, then and now.

Helen was buried on July 24, 1924, and by April the following year, Anna was still avoiding contact with Joe. And Joe, still herky-jerky in his responses, was ever leaning more towards staying away rather than facing Anna, facing her grief, or facing their loss. They were like breadcrumbs bobbing around in the pond at Westlake Park, floating past each other without comment in the little house on Avenue 20 South.

One morning, Anna was in her crying phase of the day, face-down on the bed in their little bedroom. She rolled over on her side, and absently reached out to pat Baby's tummy. "My, my, but you are getting chubby, m'hijita," she said, a smile spreading across her lips. She tickled Baby's ribs, and Baby giggled. She grasped and held Baby's tiny wrist and studied her sweet, happy face.

Later that day, Anna had moved to a little corner of the kitchen, smoking a cigarette, looking out into the little garden, a little worse for wear, drinking coffee. She was going over that fleeting moment, that moment on the bed when Helen came to visit her. She was tracing over it again, checking herself. She was not asleep, she told herself. She was not dreaming. Her little mother stopped by and found her in the kitchen. Mamá told her it was probably a dream, but Anna got mad. Mrs. Alvarez said it didn't matter whether it was a dream or not. "Helen just wanted you to know she was alright," said Mrs. Alvarez. "This kind of thing happens," said Anna's little mother. "You know, *nació con un velo sobre la cara.*" "Ahh," said Mrs. Alvarez, "the *veil.*" "She was there," Anna said. "Okay," said her little mother, relenting, "she was there." "But it doesn't matter," said Mrs. Alvarez.

Helen had come to visit. That much Anna knew for sure. They had put her in the ground that summer day, out at the Cemetery. But then she came to visit. And she seemed to be doing fine. *I know she's alright now,* Anna thought to herself. *I know she isn't scared and alone in the dark and the cold ground.* That alternative had been haunting Anna's daily emptiness, no matter how hard she tried to banish those involuntary thoughts. Not that Helen's visit, that fleeting moment on the bed in the little bedroom, suddenly meant that Anna was *happy* ... that would be too much to ask of anyone, even if in hopeful moments Anna thought she was capable of happiness, some day. What she felt instead was that her daily emptiness had rolled over with her when she rolled over and found Helen on the bed; that it had capsized, ventral to dorsal. That instead of dead blankness, she now felt the beginnings of a living peace and quiet, a break, a fresh if still uneasy opening of her eyes to what was now around her.

The garden truly was a mess. There were dishes in the sink, days old, it appeared. An old food smell lingered. Coffee stains on the counter. Carpets needed sweeping, and there was dusting to do. The toilet and the bath and the bathroom sink were grimy. The sheets and pillowcases needed laundering. So did her housedress. She looked in the soap-streaked mirror. Her hair was matted and shaggy. Her eyes were puffy and her skin was blotched. It didn't seem like her reflection, it didn't seem like her home. It had all gone to ruin, but she could put it all back to right.

She started on herself. The next day she bathed and combed her hair, put on a different dress, a little makeup. The bathroom took little time at all, and then she was on to the kitchen. Mrs. Alvarez saw her later in the afternoon on the back porch, beating an area rug against the house, and smiled. At dusk Anna was at the little table in the kitchen, spooning up a meager portion of Campbell's Split Pea Soup from the stovetop, and slowly poring through the pages of a picture magazine that Mrs. Alvarez left for her. Joe did not come home that night.

Joe's license to be away had been unchecked for so long that he was growing back into the habits of his youth. His girl was *embarazada, le prometió* to give up the fights and to marry her, so they got married, and then came the baby, and then the baby died. And then the house was empty, the crib was empty, and his pledge to *Santa Ana* under the round courthouse lights was *por nada*. There was no baby.

He barely knew the baby. Her sounds and smells became familiar to him, though. He was sad she was gone, and sad mostly for Anna. But then Anna wasn't there, either. He would not, however, try to justify the uses of his time by somehow claiming that he was abandoned — the idea might've run through his head like a nursery rhyme, but there was still warm blood pumping through his heart. Out on the town with a new, more malevolent band of muchachos, he bragged and spit fire and posed with the best of them — better, really, as he was always out front of his compañeros, wherever he was, it was just his nature. He had an undeniable brutish charisma. On the outside, he would pursue his illicit nightlife with confidence; but if anyone really cared to look deeply into his eyes, they'd see all the way through to that sad and sorry, warm-blooded heart of his. If anyone really cared to peer deeply enough into those eyes, they'd find Anna. It should have been a dead giveaway. On the other hand, in these joints Downtown, no one really bothered to look anyone truly in the eye.

Meanwhile, Anna was pulling weeds and digging up the messy flowerbed in the sideyard of their home on Avenue 20 South. The neighbors, passing by, were happy just to see her outside the house, in the sunlight and the fresh air. Anna smiled and waved back to them; it was good to have nice neighbors.

Her home was healing. Soon, she would venture out to see Mr. Singer and see if she could get her old job back at the Dress Company. Keeping her hands busy was important, she knew that. Getting outside like this, and venturing out to take the streetcars down to South Los Angeles Street, that's what she needed to do. Once she did that, returned to the regular work day, she felt stronger with every step, and everything seemed to be falling into its proper place. Except that nothing would erase the sense of loss she felt, especially as she began to understand that in addition to losing Helen, she had been unable thus far to retrieve her lost husband. They were still just breadcrumbs bobbing around the house, their nearly wordless exchanges relating only to chores and practicalities. And over the course of a year and more of this, even though she was keeping her hands and her mind occupied with work and now, going out with a friend to see an occasional picture, she could feel her living peace-and-quiet wobbling inside her, threatening to capsize again.

"I didn't mean to imply — " the doctor continued, interrupting himself.

"No, doctor, I understand," said Anna. And well she did. "I'll be alright," she said softly. As Dr. Flynn said his goodbye — relieved that he had done his duty as a healer without having to discuss sexual intercourse openly, with a lady — and left her alone again in the kitchen, the anger that was erupting inside of her was a shock to her system, after months and months of going from blankness to an endurable solitude. She turned back and wretched violently before dashing to the sink and vomiting.

Joe was sleeping. She knew what he was; but she also knew what she saw in him. And she could also trace a straight line, God's straight line, from Helen's death, through her sadness, to his absence, to his paralysis. She paused as she entered the bedroom and stood in the doorway, head down, grimacing, pressing both arms out hard against the jambs, as if she were intent on breaking them and sending the header, and the rest of the house, down upon herself, upon Joe and everything else within its walls. She knew she had the power to destroy this house.

That house they lived in on Avenue 20 South is now long gone, torn down to make way for the footprint of the interstate freeway, the 5, ripping through their old neighborhood. The land on which it sat is now part of the pad of grass that supports a southbound on-ramp to the freeway. In the strip of land that is left there, some hairdressers from the salon in the building at the corner of Broadway park their cars; there's a little food carnival that will pop up there every once in a while. Across the street, there are a few houses that are probably of the same vintage as the one in which these things happened to Joe and Anna, in which they did these things, in which they felt these feelings, loss upon loss. It is all gone now. In the windows of those little houses across the street, one now sees only the bluish glow of TV screens. With the rush of the freeway behind, all else seems quiet and still.

Anna sat down in the bedroom. There were no apologies coming from Joe that day, or any day soon; the words *te prometo* would not fall out of his lips that morning as they had so easily before they were married. Indeed, even if they had, they wouldn't have meant the same thing to Anna now. She wouldn't ever listen to them or hear them the same way again, and he would not need cover that ground. That damned invisible thread that had connected them to each other ever since that night at Westlake Park, so long ago now, was now a heavy chain that neither could completely escape — in spite of the emptiness of their home after Helen died, in spite of their separateness of their lives of late. Lying in bed with a pair of useless legs, Joe was Anna's sick, feverish baby now. *"What have you gotten into, pobrecito?"* ... As angry-sad as she might have been when she concluded her interview with Dr. Flynn, she now had a mission. Nursing Joe back to health — presumably with the help of sisters and neighbors, she thought to herself, as she had to get back to the Dress Company and make a living for them both — was the one thing she now had to get done at all costs, to show him, *por Dios*, to show the world, to win the game, to claim the prize that had been lost when they put Helen in the ground. Bringing Joe to the point of standing on his own two legs, with the chance to stand in front of him, face-to-face, to look him in the eyes and to make her demand upon him, and perhaps to make her peace with him, was now her imperative.

For now, though, she wasn't thinking about the invisible chain that connected them. Instead, she was thinking about quicksand. *Arena movediza* is what her older brothers called it back in Arizona when she was a child, telling her macabre stories of caballeros getting stuck in the river mud of the Hassayampa, north of Phoenix. In her best moments she might fantasize herself as the lioness with the fallen, helpless man's legs in her stubborn chops; in her worst, she was still the poor housewife, the childless mother, unable to keep her head held high above the rising quicksand, unable to move, unable to escape. Soon, perhaps, unable to breathe.

Yes, alright, and *Quicksands* was also the name of the Richard Dix picture she saw last night. *Arena movediza*, on the screen. It made her feel strange, seeing it several years ago and seeing it again last night like that, like she had just awakened from a long, long sleep — one that began long before she met Joe, when she was dancing and playing dress-up in the front room at her mothers's, and ending just now, sitting in the little bedroom in the house on South Avenue 20, watching over Joe. It was as if one day Alfredo was playing his ukulele in the front room and Anita was clapping and dancing along, and in the next moment grown-up Anna was waking up in her little kitchen, with a half-smoked cigarette in the ashtray and a half cup of coffee resting in the saucer. One moment, she was sitting down in the Meralta on East 1st Street to see *Quicksands*, and the next moment she is waking up at the end of the same picture, at the Lincoln on Broadway, four years later.

Claro que si, that's not what happened. She hadn't gone to sleep for all that time. Maybe she was just wishing she had been, and maybe she was wishing she still were asleep.

She got up from her chair and crossed the room, and she dropped to her knees next to the bed, leaning over him as he snoozed, combing back his curly black hair with her fingers, her nose closing in on the waxy, bitter scent of his neck and shoulders. Here is Richard Dix, ready to wrestle his own legs, she thought to herself. Here we both are, both stuck in quicksand, sinking fast, with all the bad men — *and all the bad women, too*—just on the other side of that bedroom door. No cavalry is coming, no piano player playing "Reveille."

If you had a service revolver, and if it had only one bullet left in it, and if we were about to be overrun, Joe ... would you love me enough, Joe, to point that barrel at my chin, to rest your forehead on mine and close your eyes ... would you love me enough to squeeze that trigger?

She was not planning on losing, but she wanted to know.

3

CORRIDORS

3.1
DAGGETT GENERAL STORE AND SERVICE STATION, ROUTE 66, MOJAVE DESERT, 1934

That '26 Dodge Sedan has sure seen better days, and as it sits idling, a few yards away from the covered Shell pump station outside the General Store, it sure *sounds* like it has seen better days, too. The sunrise is still low in the sky, but the temperature has already reached eighty-two degrees. The father stands over the open flap of the hood, wafting the steam away with an old rag. The mother sits in the front seat on the passenger side, staring off into the distance, cradling her ten-month old little girl. The rest of the kids are up and prattling, opening and shutting the backseat doors and running back and forth and around the Store.

There is nothing and I mean nothing out here. Just a redtop road meeting the horizon, low red mountains in the distance, north and south, and sage-spotted flatlands.

The father nudges the hood flap down with his elbow to avoid getting burned and settles in behind the wheel. The passenger doors close, and the Sedan begins to pull away, back onto the redtop road.

Then from behind the store comes a little towheaded kid, six-years old, in dungarees, a drab tee and thick eyeglasses, speeding onto the road on his two bare feet. He runs without panic — straight-backed, eyes fixed on his target, his knees and his arms pumping up and down like pistons.

"Daddy, wait!" shouts Dorothy Theodora from the backseat. "Billy! We forgot Billy!"

Floyd Baumiller, behind the wheel of the Dodge, keeps his foot on the gas pedal just a beat longer than he should and then abruptly pulls over to the side of the road as if he's losing an argument with himself. He exchanges glances with Alpha before emitting a *"fercryinoutloud!"* as Billy motors up to the side of the Dodge, smiling a big apple slice of a smile as he piles into the backseat with his younger brother Johnny, 3, and his big sisters Dorothy Theodora, 10, and Fern, 17. Billy takes up residence belly-down on the floor of the backseat, happily propping himself up on his elbows as he resumes his study of the newspaper funnies.

"Boy — that is the last time you leave this automobile without my permission! *Is that clear?,"* says Floyd from behind the wheel.

Dorothy Theodora starts to cry. Then so does baby Angie, in Alpha's arms.

"Stop that! Quiet down back there!," says Floyd.

And as he begins to absorb himself again in the adventures of Flash Gordon on the planet Mongo, little Billy Baumiller thinks to himself ... "I know I could've caught that back bumper, I know I could've ... but what if I had roller skates? And what if I had rockets on roller skates? *Oboy!...*"

The occasion for this excursion through the Mojave Desert, because no one crosses it without an occasion, is an automobile trip from Los Angeles to Kansas City, most of the way along Route 66, precipitated by the delinquency of Floyd's eldest and most favorite son Teddy. About a month earlier, fourteen-year-old Teddy got upset with his father for some forgotten reason and ran away. Remembering the story of his father's route to L.A., Teddy rode the rails to Kansas City and ended up on the doorstep of Mother Deadwyler, now known as Mrs. Mattie Crullup Wertz. Alpha got the news from her mother by handwritten postcard, while Floyd heaved a paternal bear-sigh and made the news into an excuse for a family vacation. The big girls, Geraldine Marie and Patrice, were already married off and gone from the house on East Fourth Street — Geraldine to a road crew hunky, Patrice to a scrawny kid with buck teeth who wants to be a cop — so they didn't have to go. Meanwhile Mother Wertz admitted that she hesitated even writing to Alpha about it, since Teddy had done such a nice job with the firewood shed and the flowerbeds. Floyd couldn't decide whether to throttle the boy or tell him how proud he was. He would have a few days on the road to work it out, though.

If anything, Mother Wertz-*formerly*-Deadwyler was an even more imposing edifice of an old woman now, standing on the front porch of her frame house on Miami Avenue in the old Armourdale section of Kansas City, on the Kansas side of the state line, albeit without her shotgun. She was narrating their arrival, loudly, to no one in particular, as the Baumillers pulled up to the house in that Dodge. "Well, this must be Alpha. Look at that old car! How did they manage to get here in that old thing? Look at all those children!"

Once inside, the Baumillers got a chance to meet the not-nearly-so imposing Mr. J.R. Wertz, Mother Wertz's new husband of several years. A carpenter of slight build, he had a soft, somewhat high-pitched voice when he spoke, which was not often. Mother Wertz interrupted whatever he had started to say to inform them that Alpha's little sister Lee-Lee was coming over for dinner. Floyd walked in the front door just as Teddy was slinking into the foyer from the kitchen, hugging the side of Mother Wertz's staircase. "Son," Floyd nodded, grinning and rocking on his heels, his hands in his pockets. "Hiya, Pop," said Teddy, before heading to the parlor and into his mother's arms. And that was that.

Billy and Dorothy are outside, exploring the new territory, and some neighborhood children have gathered around to meet the new visitors from out of town. A husky boy in a striped T-shirt, a little older than Dorothy maybe, is their spokesman. "Where did you say you were from?"

"Hi, I'm Billy, and this is my sister Dorothy."

"Where did you come from?"

"Oh, we're from Los Angeles. We just got here in that automobile," Billy says, pointing to the old Dodge.

"You're crazy. You can't drive here from Los Angeles," says the bigger boy. "You have to take a train."

"We didn't. We drove here in that automobile."

"You can't drive! You're too little!," says a smaller boy in overalls.

"No, I didn't drive it," says Billy. "I was just a rider. Me and Dorothy and Johnny and Fern — "

"Los Angeles?" asks a freckly kid. "Is that near California?"

"It's *in* California, you dope," says the bigger boy.

"Tarzan lives in California!" says the freckly kid. "Do you know Tarzan?"

"We're playing 'pig slaughter'", says the bigger boy, "and now you're it!" He shoves a crusty, underinflated old football into Billy's gut, and it only takes Billy a second or so to figure out that "pig slaughter" is another name for "tackle the man with the ball." In an instant Billy squeezes out of the scrum of neighborhood boys and tomboys and breaks for open ground, the scrum uncoiling to give chase.

He proves to be faster on his bare feet than all of them, and as he speeds through the unfenced backyards near Mother Wertz's house, Billy suddenly realizes that there are fewer and fewer boys chasing after him, until he finds himself standing alone in front of an old red barn. He turns around to see them, the collected pig slaughterers standing like a fence a couple of backyards away, watching him with astonished looks on their faces, as if they are waiting for the sky to fall down upon him.

Then Billy hears a deep, slow animalian growl behind him, wheels around and finds himself staring into the wretched face of a mountainous, mangy one-eyed canine, laboriously propping itself up on its four muscular legs at its watchpost at the barn door. The boys start to scream. "Now you've done it!" says one. "Watch out! It's going to get you!" says another.

At that point, Billy is running again, the one-eyed canine coming after him fast, throwing off saliva and dog fuzz like automobile exhaust and barking like a hailstorm. The boys run off in all directions as Billy tries his best to outrun the dog. Still carrying that sorry football with him, he turns around briefly as he runs to see where the dog is, when he feels his feet sliding out from underneath him on something wet and slimy. A moment later he is face down in a mudpatch, rolling over to see the one-eyed canine's progress. And at the moment that Billy thinks the canine is about to jump on him, the dog suddenly stops sharply, its neck snapping back violently. It lets out a squeal. Billy realizes that the dog is attached to a long chain that runs all the way back to a spike in the ground at the barn door. The dog's gigantic jaws and tongue and tusks are only a few feet away from Billy's face, as the dog continues its furious roaring.

Covered from head to toe in mud, Billy appears at Mother Wertz's kitchen backdoor with his sister Dorothy. Floyd is talking with Aunt Letitia — little Lee-Lee — and her husband Alvin. "You've met my son Teddy," he says. "He's quite a boy, wouldn't you say?" Little Johnny, meanwhile, is wrapped around his father's leg, sobbing. "And this is my boy Johnny," Floyd says. "Papa," shrieks little blue-eyed Johnny, pointing to the door to Mother Wertz's basement. "I 'fraid of da door!"

"Oh," says Floyd, laughing, "come now, Johnny, it's just a basement door —," as Aunt Letitia and Alvin laugh along politely. Johnny is still shrieking when Letitia points past Floyd to the doorway where Billy and Dorothy are standing. "Hi, Daddy," says Dorothy.

"Billy!" shouts Floyd, "you can't come in here like that! You stay outside and wash off somewhere's, and don't come back until you're all cleaned up."

Dorothy takes Billy by the wrist and pulls him away from the doorway. "C'mon, Billy," she says. "I saw a spigot over here." Billy positions himself under the spigot as Dorothy turns the handle. "AAAAAAAAH!" screams Billy as he rolls away from the scalding hot water spewing out of the spigot. Later, at dinner around Mother Wertz's table, Billy sits next to Dorothy with a glob of lard thickly spread over the back of his red neck to prevent blistering, his ears and knuckles and upper arms still caked with dried mud, his hair sticking straight up. It is all Floyd can do to hide his disgust with the boy, turning to his son Teddy, asking him to tell everyone some more about how he rode the rails to Kansas City.

And little Billy Baumiller thinks to himself ... "*Oboy!* Fried potatoes!"

William Baumiller is my father.

He's eighty-nine years old now. To hear him tell the story of the family trip, eighty-some years later, with no living witnesses on hand to admit or deny the facts, he is somehow both the protagonist and an afterthought in the tale — which perhaps suggests a point to the story that my father has never seemed to fully acknowledge.

But it was always thus, apparently. Like that time little Billy volunteered to get up on the roof, tied in a primitive harness to Teddy's bicycle below and wearing a parachute-like contraption, while Teddy rode fast into the street. When Billy inevitably fell to the ground below like a sack of flour, he went out like a light for twenty minutes. Alpha and Teddy and Dorothy Theodora knelt around him, and when he came to, Floyd Baumiller called out to the boy from the front porch. "What's the matter?" he said, cackling. "Did the ground jump up and kiss you?" And then there was the time that poor little Johnny had gotten mad at Billy for some reason. Johnny positioned himself across the room from him, aimed the top of his head at Billy, and ran at Billy's gut from across the room like a human battering ram. Billy watched him in disbelief for a few steps and then stepped aside just in the nick of time. Johnny bashed his noggin against the wall and fell down crying. Floyd was sitting nearby. "What did you step aside for?" asked Floyd, irritated. "He was coming at me," Billy replied. "Well, you could've just let him!," said Floyd.

But more frequently, less subtly, it was Floyd introducing his sons to some visitor in the front parlor. "Here is my son Ted," he'd say, "and this is my son John, *and, get out of here — what do you want, Billy?*" The lore was that the blue-eyed and blonde sons of Floyd Baumiller got all the attention from him, while Billy — the middle son whose baby-blonde hair eventually darkened, the one with the darker skin and black eyes, the one who favored Alpha, who in turn favored that no-good George Deadwyler — was neglected. While his older and younger brother were deprived none of the fatherly attentions that young boys received back in those days, Billy was frequently left on his own, left to fill his own time.

Filling his own time became a knack for him, and ultimately a life-long habit. Our two-car garage could only fit one car in it when I was growing up. My father, who had built the garage — in fact, built the house in which I grew up, with his own two hands — had devised a way to use every unused piece of real estate not otherwise occupied by the car in that garage for the objects of his passion. He made things. And when he wasn't making things, he was making tools that could be used to make other things. So while my mother's preposterous two-tone Lincoln Continental Mark III, with the faux tire hub bump in the back, would be wedged into a tight corner of the garage, my father's eclectic machine shop encroached on it from all sides — even from an improvised, free-island attic suspended precariously above.

He has several lathes of different sizes — German-built lathes that emit the hum of a passenger locomotive engine when you flip their crisp switches, to dinky little Sears lathes that sound like the mechanized equivalent of a team of growling Chihuahuas. He has several milling machines, upright beasts with cutting tools that can be wielded upward and downward in vertical motion, including the one I liked to call Frankenstein's milling machine. He made it from spare parts. It is seven feet tall, with great brass spring coils, a lever that looks like it was copped from a slot machine, and bent sheet-metal platforms at various heights. On old wooden workbenches, he has pounds and pounds of machine dies, and nuts, and bolts, and screws, and drill bits, all arranged neatly within stand-up cabinets in little clear-plastic drawers. Mysterious artifacts — like micrometers, and hacksaw blades, brightly-colored plastic wire caps lined up like armies of marching soldiers, and little bellows attached to wire brushes — can be found everywhere you'd care to look. And the entire garage is covered with a thin, granular coat of black lube-soot and metal shavings.

When I was a child, my Dad didn't talk a lot. When he did, it was usually to make silly jokes. His attention might be zooming in through a magnifying glass on some small machine part he would be turning in his lathe, shading the shape of a piece of steel like a master sculptor, infinitesimal tolerance by infinitesimal tolerance — deploying almost manic powers of concentration to his task; while at the same time, he would be all too aware that his toddling son was walking to and fro under the canopy of machinery, getting into buckets and boxes of spiky and greasy things that he ought not get into. So, while continuing to work the lathe, sometimes he would put on a funny high voice that sounded like Mr. Moose's scratchy falsetto on *Captain Kangaroo,* saying silly things and making the toddling boy giggle. My Dad could do both at the same time — create an object out of steel, and keep a tiny tot's brain occupied and comfortable in his own skin and in his environment — both to great effect. This is where I wanted to be, until Mom called us in for dinner.

Now, at eighty-nine — Mom's been gone for seven years, leaving him again to his own devices after all this time — he's still in the workshop on most days, making steel parts and pieces on order for a small cult of side-hustling San Gabriel Valley mail-order entrepreneurs who have gathered around him, viewing him as a guru, a genius from the Iron Age. And now, at eighty-nine, with Mom gone, William Baumiller can't stop talking. He has become an irrepressible chatterbox, a braggart, one who roundly embarrasses his son and daughter as he accosts strangers and acquaintances alike with his rotating and repeating store of war stories and corny jokes and monkeyshines. We cringe and we smack our own foreheads, we mutter our protests under our breath, we can't look anymore.

I always said they were perfect for each other, my Mom and Dad — that Mom knew how to keep him in check. She was the one with taste, she was the one with the design idea, and he was the one who could execute, who could build, in three dimensions, the things she drew on paper. Without her, he was an inventor of fine, practical things that were unpleasant to behold; without him, she was capable of imagining a beautiful home on paper, and never getting to live in it. But Lena Martin Baumiller also had a bold, round and lively mezzo-soprano speaking voice that could fill the room, and she was adept at controlling the flow of a multi-party conversation. Ever the practical man, William Baumiller had great respect for his wife's talents, and seeing that she was effective, was content enough to retreat to the background, to be conversational wallpaper. Without her, now — at 89 — William Baumiller says what he thinks.

"So, why didn't your father like you?"

"I wouldn't say he didn't like me," my Dad says to me. "The other ones, my brothers and sisters, just needed him more than I did. That's what I think." Among the younger ones, the ones born in Los Angeles, Teddy was growing tall as a tree, and was strong and was not afraid of anything, but he was a little wild. He needed his father to try and tame him a bit. Dorothy Theodora was beautiful, artistic, sensitive — she played the cello — but when she came down with the epilepsy and started having seizures, she needed her father for comfort. Johnny was slow and emotionally stunted. While Billy attended Rowan Elementary and Robert Louis Stevenson Middle School like the rest of the middle Baumiller children, Johnny had to go the "Indiana Dumb School" — that's what they called it, the Indiana Street School for the Feeble-Minded — and Johnny needed his father's special attention sometimes just to keep him from hurting himself. And Baby Angie, she was the baby, and babies always need their father's attention. "There were a lot of kids, and my father did his best."

"And you didn't need anything?"

"No," he says, smiling that sunny smile that comes so easily to him. "I was fine."

Sure, Dad — *left for dead in the Mojave Desert, scalded by hot water and chased by a one-eyed dog, knocked out cold, on the receiving end of torpedo boy* — okay, whatever you say.

I used to love reading the *World Book Encyclopedia* when I was a kid. I'm sure Dad got me hooked on it. Any time a new topic gripped my fancy, I'd go to the appropriate lettered volume on the shelf and a new world would open for me. At age eight, I had the "E" volume open within twenty minutes after the Sylmar Earthquake occurred in February 1971, reading about historic earthquakes and chirping about the inaccurate improvised commentary of the morning TV newscasters. Yes, unfortunately, I was that kid. Oh, I liked riding bikes and building forts and playing street football and wiffle ball, too; but sometimes, I could lose myself for an afternoon, reading about the Renaissance, or the Presidents, or about English kings and queens, tracing their family lines through the *World Book's* easy-to-understand charts. Those lineage charts, in particular, fed my imagination, and it wasn't long before my feverish, impressionable brain was tugging at my Dad's toolbelt asking for information that would help me create my own improvised lineage chart. If it was good enough for Prince Charles, after all, why shouldn't I have one, too?

Naturally, my restless curiosity extended first to the family of our surname — especially since the details of it were so unknown to me. I grew up without having met any of my Baumiller grandparents or my father's Baumiller siblings, save for one car trip to Lake Tahoe when I was three years old, leaving me with a vague memory of meeting Uncle Ted, the red-faced, hard-drinking, Lucky-Strike-smoking, barrel-chested former forest firefighter, living with his third wife Jolene. Quizzing my Dad about the Baumillers yielded few vital facts for my chart, but I grew into a resourceful researcher. A letter to Uncle Ted resulted in a few photocopied pages from a family Bible entrusted to him by the late Floyd Baumiller himself, with many names and dates, entered somewhat haphazardly and sometimes cryptically. Through this and other research projects I had assigned to myself, I became an expert navigator of old newspaper microfilms and began to maintain a healthy correspondence with the California Department of Public Health Vital Statistics Bureau, and with genealogical and historical societies in Kansas and Indiana. By my mid-twenties, without the aid of the Internet, I had traced the Baumillers back through layers and down corridors, back eleven generations from me and my sister, back to a lapsed Mennonite, an eighteenth century Pennsylvania Dutch tavern owner named Gottfried Baumiller, who lived to be a hundred and seven years old — Gottfried Baumiller, the fire-breathing, beer-drinking Reformed Church deacon who, on his 100th birthday, cut down the tallest tree in the Skippack woods. My Dad loved that story when I told it to him. It confirmed that his genes were good enough to get him to age 100 himself — not for some lame Smuckers-sponsored *Today Show* birthday wish from Willard Scott, but for standing up straight at Frankenstein's milling machine in his garage, making things. He loved hearing the story, and I loved telling it to him.

The pre-Internet age was adept at perpetuating such legends as the one about Gottfried Baumiller, chopping down his big tree. Hundreds of legends such as these are etched out in quaint old fonts on scratchy, yellowing pages of American county "histories," written by itinerant scribbler-printers who roved from county to county, selling instant customized, made-to-order heritage in the form of big faux-leather-bound books for purchase by post, get yours today. And although the Internet and its tentacles perpetuate more than their share of bullshit — much of it improvised, some of it gleaned from that same pre-Internet hokum that gave us Gottfried and his tree — it can also shine a harsh light on what had previously been hidden from view. You know, like secrets.

I first met Dr. Joseph Eugene Courley while strolling through the 1930 United States Census on a genealogy website. Originally from somewhere in Illinois, he was living, at age sixty-one, on Stephenson Avenue with his wife of forty years, Lollie, only a few blocks away from the Baumiller homestead on East Fourth Street. He wisely informed the census-taker that he had no occupation, for as I later determined, he had once been a licensed physician, after a fashion — a so-called "drugless practitioner" under California law — but his license was revoked in 1923. Drugless practitioners were legally entitled to practice "any drugless art — the manipulative therapeutics, physiotherapy, hydrotherapy, dietetics — practically the entire gamut of natural therapy," as one practitioner put it. The requirement to receive a license was a high school diploma plus two thousand hours of practical experience through an internship, or three thousand two hundred hours of attendance at an approved medical college.

In a 1940 newspaper article about Dr. and Mrs. Courley's fiftieth wedding anniversary, it said that Dr. Courley had received his medical training in Illinois and served his internship at the Springfield Hospital and Training School, but that he had "also attended medical school in California." The couple moved to California in 1911, and it was Dr. Courley's misfortune to have chosen the Pacific Medical College for his California training. Or maybe the school chose him. At any rate, the school effectively closed in 1915, but during a 1923-24 expose it was revealed that the purveyors of the school continued to hand-out diplomas right through the 1920s. The whole thing was a diploma mill for quacks. Caught up in the heat of the investigation of Pacific Medical College, Dr. Courley lost his license, ostensibly for illegally prescribing medicines. While attempting to be reinstated in 1929, he had to admit to the state medical board that he had only attended Pacific Medical College for a few months after his arrival from Illinois, which called into question the credibility of his original credentials for the drugless practitioner license. The board took the matter under advisement, and Dr. Courley never got his license back. In the 1940 article, it was simply stated that Dr. Courley "retired from active practice about 10 years ago."

Floyd Baumiller would've first encountered him at Dr. Courley's office near the end of the cul-de-sac on Inez Street, a couple of blocks closer to East Fourth, where Dr. Courley apparently continued to practice without a license, on the q.t. The building is still there, now a converted shotgun stucco house surrounded by a wrought-iron fence, but the structure calls forth the building's original intention, with a waiting area in the front, and a long, narrow back section of the building, containing a hallway at the right side coming in from the waiting room and extending all the way to the back, with examination rooms on the left.

Floyd Baumiller was probably a lot like most of the patients Dr. Courley was seeing after his license was revoked during the 1920s — a soldier in the army of the hard-working poor, for whom professional medical care was mostly a luxury, unless the symptoms of an unnamed, unexplained malady became too great to handle with home remedies. Many of the poor folks in the neighborhood probably had no idea that Dr. Courley had lost his license. They only knew he was willing to see almost anyone, that he was willing to barter for his services and sometimes wouldn't charge for them at all, and that he would sometimes recommend pills and other medicines that could be obtained with a handwritten note from the doctor, through a fellow named Ralph at a back door of the Santa Fe Coast Lines Hospital, always wrapped in plain paper packages resembling bars of soap. For Floyd Baumiller, the fact that Dr. Courley may have lost his license was neither here nor there. In fact, sight unseen, it created a more favorable impression of the man when he first heard about it, having built up his own distrust of those government bureaucrats who spent their time tearing down good men at taxpayers' expense.

But Floyd wasn't the patient. Kids' colds and fevers came and went, scrapes could be bandaged. When Alpha went down, though — thirty-five years old, having borne five babies by the Fall of 1927, now suffering from pain and other "women's troubles" — Floyd asked around and came up with an answer, to go and see this Dr. Courley. Sometimes he could help without prescribing any pills, folks said. Sometimes he didn't charge you, folks said. So Floyd walked Alpha there, her arm in his, to Dr. Courley's office.

As he sat with Alpha in the waiting room, however, thinking about men in white lab coats holding clipboards and looking at all of the doctor's proclamations and certificates on the wall, the fine hair on the back of Floyd's neck stood on end, much in the same way that mine did when I first saw a photograph of Dr. Joseph Courley, the one that accompanied the article about the fiftieth wedding anniversary — when I first saw Dr. Courley's deep-set dark eyes, his wide jaw and wide, thin-lipped smile, jauntily cocked eyebrows and flat-topped dome. Floyd's hackles were up, from seeing the framed parchment on the wall. But maybe it was just sitting in any doctor's office, getting that queasy feeling.

"Why didn't your father like you?," I ask the eighty-nine-year old William Baumiller.

"I wouldn't say he didn't like me." William Baumiller has another theory. "I was a premature baby," he announces matter-of-factly. "You probably didn't know that."

"No, I didn't."

"Always ahead of my time," he jokes. "Anyway, I came out sickly and they wondered whether I would survive. And then, every time I got sick when I was really young, they were worried I might die. I think my father was scared to get attached to me. I think he hardened himself against it." Of course, I say to myself, that doesn't explain why he was still so cold to my father when he had grown past his early childhood years.

Kernels of fact, though — like little stones, dropping into the abyss — send back echoes of truth from the darkness of time past, from beyond the reaches of memory. The last few months of Alpha's carrying were tough ones, in part for the harsh low back pain, cramps and loose bowels during the unseasonably warm April of 1928, but also for the silence. As she wandered from kitchen to bedroom to parlor in the oppressive, thick air of the house on East Fourth Street, trying to find a comfortable place to rest and encountering none, a quietness prevailed. Some of it was her own. In between her muffled exhalations and emissions, she was saying nothing, answering nothing to the nothing put forth by Floyd. Floyd had also grown quieter as her condition evolved, as the reality of the child sank in with him. When Floyd and Alpha did speak to each other, they spoke in whispered factual assertions, yes-or-no questions and answers, no eye contact, devoid of emotional content, skimming the surface of each day and staying clear of the depths. Even the children were quiet — the older ones with some understanding of what was happening there, the younger ones, Teddy and Dorothy Theodora, merely responding to the atmosphere of intensity that enveloped the household, perhaps afraid of speaking up and getting the belt. For Alpha, living through her confinement in pain and silence, it felt like she was being punished at times, even if for Floyd, the silence signified only grief.

The doctor — not Dr. Courley — visited and said that the baby was coming sooner than expected, and out of a late May early morning Los Angeles fog came this wretched little creature, an inordinately small reddish-grey poppet with tiny hands and feet and a heaving chest, not crying as infants do so much as puffing, clicking, smacking. The doctor said this baby boy might not live until next week. Floyd's back straightened and his empty heart stiffened. He gave this baby boy the name William, after his own brother who died in infancy, Trueman's dead twin brother. Alpha laid nearby, weeping loudly, letting all the silence go at once.

It wasn't his boy, Floyd told himself. He thought back to sitting in Dr. Courley's waiting room, looking at all the doctor's proclamations and certificates on the wall. Alpha cried her eyes out saying, please don't take me back to see that doctor, please don't take me back. Fern, youngest of his Kansas brood at eleven years old, marched around the house as if she knew, throwing her father looks that said, how could you, Daddy, how could you? In the early hours of the morning, lying on his side in the dark and listening to this baby boy's labored breathing in the crib next to their bed, in the space between wakefulness and sleep, he knew better. It wasn't his boy. If he stopped breathing, it wouldn't matter. It wasn't his boy.

Greater access to previously sealed public records is certainly one way in which the Internet has blown the doors off of hidden or forgotten truths, but the mail-order Internet family history DNA kit is in the top tier of all bullshit erasers.

Not that these tests yield simple answers. They're not designed to be like the kind they use in court, the kind that can be used to convict murderers and rapists—those are a single crime-scene blood or semen sample versus a single, search-warrant extracted DNA sample from a suspect. Is it a match or not?—yes or no. Not like your family DNA sample—your spit, sent away in a plastic vial to the laboratory—versus an ever-growing population of DNA samples. Often, the results of these tests can be confusing, and they can easily be mistakenly interpreted. Mostly, they say things like, based on the other samples we've obtained, it looks like you're more like the French ones which means you might be French; or, it looks like you might be related to these people. Over time, there are shifts and adjustments. Over time, they get more samples. The more samples they have to work with, the more information is in the database; the more information is in the database, the easier it is to see different patterns emerging. It's like if the picture on your TV screen were made up of 100 dots, and you can only see 10 of them today; you get a clearer picture of what is going on when you see 25 of them, or 50 of them. If you're paying attention, you can learn to see the patterns, the direction of the changes over time, and you can begin to make some sense of them.

When my Dad, my sister and I all sent in our spit, the website told us we were all related, as father-son, father-daughter and siblings. So far so good, I thought to myself. For a few years I watched and noticed the number of Martíns and Garzas that began to show up in the lists of potential cousins for my sister and me. I also started to see the Crullups and Deadwylers show up, here and there. Did I think it was peculiar that I didn't see any *Baumillers?* No—these things take time, I thought to myself. There are shifts and adjustments to these results as the population of samples increases, I thought to myself. Maybe there just haven't been any Baumillers other than us who've taken the test.

I wasn't paying close enough attention to notice that there was a certain surname showing up in our cousin lists. Sometimes you just don't see what you're not looking for, even if it is right in front of your face.

> *Dear bauwau685:*
> *Based on our DNA results, I think we are related, but I can't figure out how.*

Because these websites are also social communities, they actually encourage people to reach out to other people on their cousin lists. It is an inexact science, however. The result is a bunch of half-informed searchers, blundering into other people's message boxes — blind genealogists trying to make sense of a proverbial elephant of DNA evidence by tugging at its inscrutable appendages.

Every once in a while, you get a message from someone who knows how to connect some of the dots.

> *Dear bauwau685:*
> *I noticed that your DNA test shows that you are also related to my cousins Dede and Philip, which means you and I must be related through the Courley line. Do you happen to know how you are related to the Courley family?*

Messages such as these are apt to get your attention, especially since, after over forty years of playing at this sport, you've never seen a Courley in your chart ... which is what first led me, playing hunches, to find Dr. Joseph Eugene Courley in the 1930 Census, living and working within a short walk of the Baumillers' place on East Fourth Avenue ... which is what led me to find that photo of Dr. Courley, the one that raised my hackles some seventy years after it was taken, the one in which the deep-set dark eyes, the lipless, close-mouthed smile, the jaunty cocked eyebrows and wide jaw were so eerily familiar to me ... which is what led me to investigate his checkered career as a so-called drugless practitioner ...

... which is what led me to remember a peculiar telephone conversation I had with my father's older sister Fern, a number of years before.

I never actually met Fern. I think she lived in Colorado with her husband for a while, and later settled down in the Imperial Valley. I remember seeing her when she stopped by once to borrow money from my father, but I never spoke with her. She was a large woman, perhaps taking after Mother Deadwyler, with blue eyes and a fleshy nose and cheeks, and unkempt hair. That's all I remembered about her.

Dad suggested I could call her and talk about family history with her — it would be the least she could do to take my call, considering she never repaid any of the loans he had given her — and that she would remember things about the time before my father was born.

Fern was cheerful when I called, and wanted to hear all about me and my life. Eventually though I eased her into a monologue about her childhood in Kansas and in L.A., a monologue by which she happily allowed herself to get swept away. She talked about how sweet her mother was with all the children, about how amusing Mother Deadwyler was, and about Coffeyville, and about how her father could be a stern disciplinarian, and how the brothers and sisters protected each other. How she and Geraldine Marie and Patrice, the older sisters, ran a little wild in the city. "We all married too young," she said. She talked about her father and the yellow cars, how much he loved them, and what a happy couple her parents were. Returning to her own life with her on-and-off husband, skinny Clem Paskell — they divorced and remarried twice — she highlighted a few of her life's regrets, including the fact that she never had her own children, and her spirits seemed to dip. "I've always been such a flibbertigibbet," she said, pausing from her chatty tour of her memories. "I could never keep my mouth shut."

And then she started to cry. "You sound so much like your father, do you know that?" she sputtered.

"I'm so sorry, Aunt Fern — but is anything the matter? Have I said something to upset you?" I hadn't said much of anything.

"Your father was such a good little brother — so smart, we could all see that," she said through sobs. "And I can never keep my mouth shut!"

"What's wrong?"

She continued to cry. "There was something I haven't told you, something that happened to my mother. And it involves your Dad. It was terrible, it was just terrible," she said.

"What happened?"

"No, I can't say it, I can't say it. Oh, I'm so terrible at keeping secrets — but I can't say it."

It was too surreal for me to be talking with someone I hardly knew and encountering such a well of pent-up anguish. She ultimately yielded nothing more to me than her raw emotions, barely a hint of anything I could pick up as fact, and she probably went to her grave thinking that while she was "such a flibbertigibbet," at least she never gave up the secret that she held about my Dad. Had she been talking with anyone else, any other stranger, perhaps she would have been right.

Years later, when initially I was just pursuing a silly theory by researching the shady life and career of Dr. Joseph Eugene Courley — like so many dead-ends I've pursued in the past — when I encountered that fiftieth anniversary photo of him, and I could look Dr. Courley in the eye for the first time, there was a moment. I had acceded to a moment in which the sum total of my Baumiller-less DNA results and Fern's tearful half-confession and my own father's deep-set dark eyes, thin-lipped smile, wide jaw and jauntily cocked eyebrows started to wrap themselves around my throat, leaving me breathless. Upon entering into that moment, I knew that I had figured this shit out. But I couldn't tell you the details of that story myself, because I wasn't there. And neither was Fern. Only one person could tell that story, that story only belonged to one person.

My name is Mrs. Alpharetta Baumiller and I live on East Fourth Street in Belvedere. I was raped by Dr. Joseph Courley. I was cramping up and bleeding and feeling quite poorly, so my husband, Floyd Baumiller, took me over to Inez Street to see Dr. Courley in his office. Dr. Courley led me down a long hallway to a little room in the back of his office, the one farthest from the waiting room where my husband was sitting. He asked me to put on an old cloth johnny-gown and to sit on this reclining seat before excusing himself. When he returned, he pressed a button and the seat went back, so that I was almost upside down, with my legs up in the air. He explained that he needed to buckle my ankles down, for my safety and comfort, while he performed his examination. He then proceeded to touch me in a way that made me feel very uncomfortable, but he explained it was necessary for him to do it, and that in fact, he might be able to help me and my problem by putting his hands on me. I couldn't breathe. He was touching me for some time, it was so awful, it felt like it must have been over an hour, and then he did it. He raped me. When he was finished with his business, he pulled up his trousers under his white coat and buckled up his belt and told me that

he was recommending more manipulation treatments for me and that I would start to feel better, and that I should come back and see him again next week. Then he left me there, with my legs in the air, buckled to the stirrups of the chair, until his nurse came in and found me crying and she freed me. I told my husband that I didn't want to go back to see this doctor, but he took me back to see him one more time. This time I wouldn't put on the johnny-gown and I just sat balled up in the corner of the back room and cried. The doctor tried to convince me to get into his reclining chair again, but I wouldn't do it, and then after a time he just let me go. After that, I never went to see him again, but I did see him around the neighborhood, and it was terrible.

It was her story, and hers alone. Even if she never told it that way while she lived, she's the only one who could tell it now. She could suggest some salient facts of it to her eldest two daughters, who might have let the substance of it slip to the third, Fern, in the imperious way that elder daughters wield secrets and data over a younger sister. But Alpha could not tell Floyd, much less report the event to the authorities. Even if Floyd had been privy to every detail — and he came to understand more about it than was ever expressed by anyone in actual words — he would have given her the same advice. What city police captain would take the word of a Belvedere housewife, a nobody, over that of a by-all-accounts-respectable *retired* physician — tall, well-dressed, well-spoken and distinguished-looking? Even if she had wanted to submit herself to such humiliation, what purpose would it serve? No, it was better to retreat, to get on with life and attend to her household — there was so much that needed to be done — and to forget it. Forgetting it actually seemed like it might be possible, until that baby boy was born.

I can only guess how much it must have irked poor Floyd Baumiller to watch this taciturn yet cheerful bespectacled child, this constant embarrassing reminder of bad decisions and limited choices, as he moved about by his wits and discovered his little world. There they were there at Mother Wertz's house, during that 1934 vacation trip, with Teddy squirming around like a bobcat looking to escape from his cage again, and with little Johnny messing his pants and screaming at his own shadow, when Mother Wertz asked Billy if he would help her in the backyard. "Little man, would you help your Grammy and take all these boxes on the back porch out to the furnace in the back?" Grampy J.R. wants to burn these things out there." Floyd watched from the kitchen as Billy sized up the stacks of boxes and then set to work linking together two of J.R.'s hand trucks with supplies he found lying around in the yard. He observed as Billy's thought processes unfolded, resulting in Billy carefully pulling the entire load of boxes out to the furnace in one trip, with great effort, through the use of his double-hand truck contraption. Of course, he wanted to shout at Billy, tell him just to carry the consarned boxes out to the furnace like his grandmother asked, but he kept his peace.

Pausing briefly to admire this little alien's improvised solution to the task in front of him, Floyd Baumiller turned away from the window and shook his head. *How could God have done this to me?*, he asked himself. *Why did He choose to give me this boy?*

Ultimately, Floyd's beef wasn't with Billy, and it wasn't even with Dr. Courley, this late in the plot. It was with God.

"You ready for some more coffee?" asks the 89-year old William Baumiller.

I am sitting at his breakfast table in his home, the one in which I grew up — east of East L.A. and north of Disneyland, in an older northern Orange County suburb. "Is there more?"

"Yeah, I just made some."

He pours me a mug, and I take a sip while studying my laptop screen. "Bleah," I say, nearly exploding in a spit-take. "Did you run this through the old coffee grounds?"

He smiles, and pops his eyebrows. "Yeah — can't even tell the difference, can you?"

I am weighed down by all this new information I am carrying this morning. I am carrying a hot, steaming platter of factual confirmations, explanations of coincidences and blind spots illuminated, and of almost a century of invisible shards and shrapnel, the probable causes of phantom pains endured yet unacknowledged, undiagnosed, untreated — and I am balancing all of it, all of it, all of it on my out-stretched left hand. I have figured this shit out, and it is very heavy. For now, though, there's this, and only this.

"You sit down and I'll fix us a real pot of coffee," I say as I get up from the breakfast table and head into the kitchen. "You ready for some cereal?"

"Sure. I think there's a new box on the top shelf — I just bought it at the 'Dollar Store' last week."

I reach up to the top shelf and bring down a box of General Mills Caramel Crunch with a gigantic Superman emblem on the front. Apparently eighty-nine-year-old men are the demographic General Mills was going for with this cereal box. I pour the cereal into two bowls, pour the milk, grab a couple of spoons and bring the cereal to the table. For now, there is only this.

And William Baumiller thinks to himself, "Superman Caramel Crunch ... *oboy!*"

3.2
AT THE CLUB, DOWNTOWN LOS ANGELES, 1938

**hen** they built the massive new Club building on the uncrowded edge of the downtown business district," writes one of the members, a man of leisure and an occasional ghost-writer for the ghost-writer for a well-known newspaper columnist, "it was like a completely unexpected mass had grown up overnight from the foot of the hillside, like a giant, ornate protuberance, to stand as sentry and watch over the little drudges of the city as they depart the cold certainty of downtown for the existential vagaries of Westlake and beyond. Made of steel and decorated with rose-colored brick and accents of weighty grey stone, the Club is a modern American Medici palace with a 600-car parking garage, especially commodious for the 1920s, to be frequented by those who would see ourselves as the nobility of Los Angeles: a thousand or so white male club members and our wives at the grand opening banquet, the dukes and duchesses of the independent city-state of Southern California. Gradually, downtown started to grow up and fill in around the Club, paying homage to it.

"Walking through the front entrance of the Club (a privilege enjoyed only by men, as lady visitors are only permitted to enter with an escort through a nondescript side street entrance) is walking into another time and place. Shiny floors of pink and grey marble, covered with enormous violet-and-gold print rugs; great gilt-edged and gilt-capped rectangular columns, festooned with living, perfectly groomed ferns and other greenery, supporting a one-and-a-half story ceiling, which itself is a stately grid of delicately hand-painted beams; under large clustering chandeliers, our overstuffed chairs and divans, populated by our overstuffed executives and professionals, smoking their pipes and cigarettes, drinking coffee with cream, reading newspapers, whispering in corners; the main desk, the command center, the familiar face of the concierge, his exquisitely manicured hands directing traffic while he smiles graciously, a snap from his fingers sending smartly uniformed lobby urchins into pre-choreographed patterns of hospitable productivity, his searching eyes meanwhile studying the face of each man who enters through the doors, to calculate his greetings, to keep the riff-raff out; off to the side, the newsstand, the cigar counter, the candy booth, the entrance to the florist and the eleven-chair barber shop and beyond. If one is fortunate enough to make it to the elevators, or the grand staircases, what wonders are awaiting above, twelve stories of an alternate universe of pleasure and repose: a full gymnasium with steamroom, a plunge or 'swimming pool,' game rooms for dominoes and cards and dice and chess and billiards, libraries holding some two-thousand volumes, *objets d'art* of incalculable value and impeccable taste down every hallway, ballrooms and private dining rooms, two-hundred and eighty overnight rooms; and at the very top of it all, the private 'top floor' of the complex, the site of the rooftop wintergarden, and the oh-so-private 'Bar in the Clouds.'

"At the time of the Club's opening, we might say there was no need for a 'bar,' per se, as that term might be understood today, with the Prohibition on. Of course, that would be a statement of fiction. Five years hence, it is even now somewhat difficult to remember how things worked during those dreary days, but they did work fine for the members of the Club, some of whom, regardless of our political stripe, enjoyed spirits in moderate quantities, having done so since returning from Europe and fighting our way through the saloons of the Great War; and we all know furthermore that Prohibition was initially designed to keep the hoi polloi from abusing liquor and turning its malevolent energies upon us, that it was never really meant to apply to gentlemen of means and higher rationality.

"And the other secret about the flow of spirits within the hidden rooms of the Club, both during and after Prohibition, is that it inevitably loosens everyone's jaws for the smooth and congenial conduct of Business. Yes, that's the other rule that is a statement of fiction, that members shall refrain from conducting Business inside the Club. What that really means is we don't want your valise at the table, we don't want your papers spread over the bar, keep your fountain pens in your pockets, boys. Instead, we are all expected to conduct our Business here in the civilized way: in between other Club entertainments, sitting at the small tables in the Bar in the Clouds or in a private dining room, Highball at the ready, voices only, in low, friendly tones: oilman to banker, contractor to congressman, magnate to magnate. The secrets of your hobnobbing are safe here, the outside world does not need to know that cats lie down with dogs, Republicans with Democrats, judges with litigants, stiff-collared deacons with well-dressed racketeers; the outside world need not understand that the world itself rotates on an engorged axis scoped from deep within the halls of the Club. Nor does it need to know that these collegial correspondences frequently carry on into the dense nocturnal air, when the Sandman roams the Southland, into hazy after-hours joints in other parts of town —

"But we digress. Five years hence, it is truly, even now, somewhat difficult to remember how we loosened our jaws during those dreary days. There was plenty of notice that the dreaded Volstead Act was coming before it came, and of course, those who could afford to do so stockpiled some favorite elixirs. The Club carried on for a while with that fiction, that it still possessed bottles acquired before the Act and that it was merely going through its dwindling stock while it continued to acquire new bottles through shadowy distribution chains. Then, after the lie about the dwindling stock was just too fatuous to maintain, the Club and some of its upstanding 'wet' members went through a brief period of intestinal panic about the future of spiriting within the Club's walls. It soon became clear, however, that some of the Club's most influential members, fine men from the federal prosecutor's office and the upper echelons of the local law enforcement establishment and the like, were all in on the gag, and that the Club would be free to acquire new supplies without fear of raids or prosecution, as long as it observed some basic rules: one, buy only from approved sources of the contraband; two, keep control over your stock, no backdoor sales, no tolerance of gray markets underneath the black market that serves the Club; three, no price gouging, unless it involves tourists; and four, keep it discreet within the Club itself, don't be ostentatious about your bounty, except with your better members.

"So, the Club was able to acquire a steady supply of bottles through-out Prohibition, typically delivered in broad daylight in unmarked panel delivery trucks coming up through the oil fields from ocean-side delivery points in and around Wilmington, near Los Angeles Harbor. Upon arrival, the Club's bus boys would come out and unload the freight, stowing it inside the Club in secret areas, such as within the footprint of the Bar in the Clouds on the top floor, which, incidentally, could only be reached by a separate, semi-secret elevator, and which, if the Dry Agents had been able to figure out how to get up there, could be closed off behind wood paneling in a jiff, hidden from would-be enforcers. No need for much more than that in terms of subterfuge. No need for underground tunnels or decoy trucks or back-alley password exchanges. Those were for the suckers, for the petty re-distributors and neighborhood pushers, and for those without any buying power. The Club had everything figured out. Occasionally the Club would even honor special requests, for special occasions or special members. A certain bottle of French wine, a certain case of champagne, a particular brand of English gin or Spanish brandy by request, procured, locked away and then handled only by the top craftsmen in the Club.

"Speaking of craftsmen, at the height of Prohibition, there was a Mexican fellow who they hired originally as a bus boy, who rose to become the favorite of the top floor regulars. During Prohibition, you would often hear the members say something along the lines of, 'I don't want anyone but Joe touching my precious bottle of Gordon's Gin.' Joe was a master when it came to the dry Martini. Also, he had a look; and this being Los Angeles, this being Hollywood, that was important, as important to the swells who came to sample his concoctions and who dressed in their downtown uniforms (their wide-shoulder, wide pointed lapel, high-waisted grey suits with bright-white, double-point folded pocket squares, art deco neckties, white shirts with French cuffs and wingtip shoes, or their standard black-tie ensembles for evening occasions), yes, as important to them as it was to the Club in setting the right image. Joe, like his fellow Mexicans, movie actors like Gilbert Roland or Leo Carrillo, was like a suave, manly continental-type sent over from 'central casting.' Gilbert and Leo would play Mexicans and Indians on screen, to be sure, but they would also frequently be cast as Greeks, Russians, Italians, Polacks, Slovaks, Spanish, Portuguese, Turks, Persians, even Arab sheiks. Well, that was Joe, with his dark eyes and thick, expressive brows, black hair Brilliantined back in wavy ridges, his face clean-shaven, dressed in the Club's tailored white notch lapel jacket with contrasting black lapel-top and cuff, double-breasted eight-button front, black bow-tie and slim black trousers with side stripes. The suit itself was of such construction that it made Joe stand up tall and straight, and from the looks and demeanor of him alone, he could easily've been a guard at the Tsar's Palace, or a Hungarian diplomat, or the doorman at the Waldorf-Astoria.

"Later on, when FDR signed the repeal and Prohibition was over, and liquors of all types were now readily available, Joe's mastery of cocktails, coupled with his presence behind the bar, became almost legendary. By that time, Joe's white dinner jacket already had the words 'Head Barman' embroidered near the lapel. Mixing a Martini, Manhattan or Gimlet, he is all business, his jaw clenched, mouth-closed tightly, swift, steady and duteous with his bottles and instruments. Then, on the pour, his mouth curls up on one side, his eyebrows raise and his nose points like that of a conductor on the last note of a concerto, and he waits for the first sip to be taken. With a note of approval from his holy communicant, he gives them back an open-mouthed smile, tip of the head in gratitude, tap of the top of the bar with the ball of his right hand. The men, the top floor regulars, love Joe's charm and his meticulousness, the gleam in his eyes, his gracious, unassuming banter, and above all, his great baritone laugh. Oh, and he can show off, too: pouring a cascade of champagne down a pyramid of champagne coupe glasses, or tackling a tray of Pousse-café nightcaps, a little pick-me-up that doubles as a magic show, in which he pours different liqueurs in layers into a stemmed glass, perhaps Grenadine, followed by a layer of Maraschino poured slowly over the back of a bar spoon, followed by a layer of Crème de Menthe poured the same way, leaving drinkers dazzled by the effect of a colorfully striped cocktail. Not that it tastes very good; but in this case, it is all about the picture, this being Los Angeles, this being Hollywood and all. When served in mixed company, the men and their wives adore it.

"But the men, the top floor regulars, love Joe most when it is just the men, without the wives, when they can coax him into talking about old downtown: the speakeasies, the wee-hour rambles, the boxing matches, the old hourly hotels and houses of ill-repute. He is not profound, nor even very articulate, but in his way he can convey a tenderness, a sense of nostalgia about those adventures. A small cadre of disciples, bachelors, older married men who have angled their home life in a certain way, might stay and listen raptly to his stories, right up until the last call. And at the evening's end, before Joe Martin has time to change back into his street clothes, his own regular suit-and-tie downtown uniform, he will get the questions. 'You know any of the new places, Joe? Where do we go now, Joe?'"

Mrs. Anna Martín got her wish. She was eventually able to stand toe to toe with her husband, face to face, and make her demands upon him, after nursing him back to health. And it worked. Joe Martín who came from nothing, as he would have said, was now very afraid of losing what he had. He went back to work at the Foundry, she went back to work on their home. The rhythm of work overtook them both, and during stretches in between the chores of living, they learned to laugh together again. More importantly, Mrs. Anna Martín was able to teach her husband-who-came-from-nothing how to dream a little with her.

As 1929 drew to a close, while the rest of the world seemed to be on the edge of worry over the stock market, Anna and Joe awoke each day smiling in anticipation of what was coming. For one thing, Joe was starting a new job, one which would require him to dress up and go to work in a Downtown building rather than hauling scrap metal around under the sun. Old Nicky, from that blind pig up an alley off Spring Street, remembered his one-time boarder and protégé when a friend of his in the "distribution business" mentioned an upcoming opening for a bus boy at the Club. At first, Joe hesitated, and the more that Anna needled him about the opportunity, the more irritated he became, until Anna came to understand the problem: Joe didn't know how to count change, and although he could read a little, he was shy about writing things down. But Anna knew what was good for Joe, and told him to grab the job. In the meantime, with little more than a few weeks before he would don the white jacket and tie, in the evenings after dinner, they sat at the little kitchen table and they counted change back and forth in drills; and in the mornings, on his way to the Foundry, she encouraged Joe to copy lines from the newspaper onto a scratch pad. On that first day, before he left for his new career, Anna put Johnson's baby powder on the back of his neck to keep him from sweating so much, fixed his hair with her fingers, adjusted his necktie, packed him up with a sandwich for supper, and with a good luck smooch she sent him on his way to the Club, onto a new life for both of them.

Also, Anna was carrying a child again, due to deliver in March. In February, the papers were still posting signs of hope that the nation's economy was going to ride out October's crash and that America was hitting on all six. Death Valley Scotty was spending $2,000,000 building a castle in Grape Vine Canyon; California oil chiefs were still cheerful; photos of bathing beauties frolicking in the moderate late February sun were captioned with taunts aimed at the wintry East; beautiful dress ads from Bullock's Wilshire were showing young women what "youth seasoned with sophistication" was supposed to look like; and there were still classified job ads for salesmen and bookkeepers. Late in her term, Anna went to see *Anna Christie,* in which "Garbo Talked" for the first time on screen. Anna had been watching the talkies as the picture palaces around her, one by one, converted to sound-only. Many of her friends were annoyed by how scratchy the sound was and how none of the talkies seemed to be as good as silent pictures — they weren't as romantic or as magical, even if there was a certain novelty to hearing each one of their favorite stars speak their first words; but Anna, remembering the flickers she saw in Nogales when she was a child, would say, "Never mind, they'll get better." Now, over two years after Al Jolson sang "Mammy" on theatre screens, the great, enigmatic Swede, Greta Garbo, was stepping out of her hermitage in Beverly Hills to speak, and the moment she opened her mouth — growling, in low, leonine tones, *"Giff me a visky, jinja ale on da side — and don't be stinjee, baby"* — now, for the first time, it seemed to Anna like these talking pictures were really something to look forward to. There was a whole new world, a beautiful one, opening up in Los Angeles for her — where Joe was wearing clean, nice clothes and earning good money working indoors, where pretty dance music wafted through her home from the radio, and where movie stars could really speak. Even the garden looked greener and brighter to her. And soon, there would be a baby. What more could anyone want?

Well, for one thing, you could want the baby to be here already. On the appointed day, Joe came home from work early, driving the Ford he bought shortly after starting at the Club, and took Anna to the Sisters of St. Joseph, to Santa Marta Maternity Hospital over on North Humphreys Street near Brooklyn Avenue. The baby came early the next morning. Remarking on Anna's light eyes, pale skin and stylish dark hair, her pointed chin and her upside down smile, the nuns were all saying, "Gloria Swanson just had a baby, Gloria Swanson just had a baby," and Anna was so embarrassed, but she was secretly quite proud. She named the little girl Elena Armida Martín — "Elena," after Helen, and "Armida," after a young movie starlet from Sonora about whom Anna had recently read — and Joe dutifully took care of the birth certificate with the nuns.

Lena Martín was my mother.

Later, Joe's parents, Petronilo and Higinia, visited him and Anna at their home. Joe had little contact with them since before marrying Anna six years before. Joe showed off his new car, and proudly described his new job to his father. *"Jesucristo, ¿cómo terminó mi hijo como sirvienta de la casa?"*[5] his father said. To Petronilo, it sounded like menial work, like what the servants used to do back in Los Cuervos. Meanwhile, Petronilo peered in to look at the little white bunny in Anna's arms, stone-faced. "I hope this one don't die like the other one," was all he could think of to say. They never saw much of each other after that.

There was no room in their house for such cynicism. Elena Armida Martín was born into a household that was almost overflowing with love and hope for her, where there had been an empty space waiting for her ever since Helen died. With the memory of wandering aimlessly up and down the railroad tracks in the middle of the night, not all that long ago, the memory of having nothing and being nothing, Joe stared in the mirror above the wash basin while getting ready for work, and he hardly recognized the huskier man in front of him, the man in the sleeveless undershirt with the shaving cream on his face; but as he studied that face, in his chest he could feel the transfiguration of his heart. Anna was with the baby — he could hear their indistinct but contented sounds from the bedroom, Anna singing quietly, the baby cooing back. Anna's little mother, Francisca, dropped by early and made the coffee, and now she was back in the kitchen stirring a pot of aromatic albondigas on the

---

5   Jesus Christ, how did my son end up as a maid of the house?

stove, the richly intermingled scents of mint and tomato and seasoned beef rising. The curtains were pulled back and the windows were open, and the fresh breeze kept those scents and sounds of the late morning circulating through each room, beckoning to him. Yes, there really was a "Depression" on outside, so the papers were now saying, without apology, but the Martín household was a home of order and beauty.

Until Francisca showed up one day, weeping miserably on their doorstep.

"¡Se llevaron a Eduardo!"

A Thursday afternoon in February, 1931. The Plaza was crowded with muchachos and muchachas, some four hundred of them. Some had just left afternoon Mass at La Placita, Our Lady of the Queen of the Angels; some of the women, with their handbags and grocery sacks, were looking to catch up on the latest gossip; and some of the men were just taking an opportunity for a nap in the sun after *el almuerzo*. Many of the muchachos, old and young alike, were between jobs, looking to find out who was hiring. Sometimes a truck would pull up to the edge of the Plaza and a white man would get out and shout out that he needed a few able-bodied men for a job. A few card games were in progress, and an old fellow had his guitar with him, stuttering over what to play next. And there were children, too.

There was just enough activity, just enough noise and laughter and music, to make it difficult to hear the assembly of men just outside the plaza, ready to surround it. Then came the sound of the hard heels of them, as they blocked all the ways out, as they came in and blocked out the sun. *"Stay where you are!"* came the announcement over a crude megaphone. *"¡De-tay-ner!"* While most of the woman circled around the younger ones, many of the men spun around, looking in all directions for an exit. There was none. That didn't stop a few of them to try to breach the line. A couple of younger men ran right into a line of officers and were turned around quickly and without drama by a brace of arms in blue jerseys and jackets; one decided to fight, and was clubbed by a couple of officers. He was clubbed, and he was down on the ground, and a couple of other officers came and took him away, straightaway, off to a waiting paddy van. It seemed like there was an inexhaustible supply of officers, they were coming out of nowhere.

"We've come to see your papers," shouted the officer in charge. *"¡Moo-énstros soos dock-you-mentos!"* Pairs of higher-ranking agents, wearing drab green ties, were approaching them in small groups, asking them for their papers. But who was carrying their *pasaportes* or any *papeles* with them to the Plaza that day? If they'd had any, they'd usually keep them at home, in a safe place — in the little cedar box on the nightstand, or with the baby's baptismal certificate from the priest. Some were offering to show driver's licenses; a few had identification cards from their employers; others were trying to show them envelopes with letters from relatives from Mexico, pointing to their addresses and apologizing for not being prepared. The officers spent a lot of time with each one of them, one peppering questions at them in English and broken Spanish, the other taking notes in a little book. Every once in a while, after listening to a muchacho try to explain what he was doing in Los Angeles, the lead officer would give a nod to an officer on the line, and two officers would emerge and take the muchacho away, putting him in one of the paddy vans with the one they beat up earlier.

It was hard to see a pattern, hard to understand which answers were the wrong ones and which ones were right — it just seemed like most of the ones they took away were able-bodied men, the kind those men in the trucks were also looking for.

Eduardo Garza, Anna's little brother, was there. He was just 21 years old, and like many of the others, he was looking for work. He would occasionally find some with the Southern Pacific, over in the rail yards, but being one of the younger ones and a *soltero*,[6] he was always the first to be sent home when there wasn't enough work for everyone. He spoke English pretty well, and his accent wasn't as thick as Anna's or his mother's, as he had virtually grown up in Los Angeles. His skin was lightish, but to the officers he was just another *bean-bandido*, with thick, oily-black hair, in a white T-shirt and raggedy trousers. He wore the uniform.

"Where did you take my friend?," he asked an officer.

---

6   A bachelor.

"What's that, young man?"

"What did you do with my friend, the one who tried to run outa here?" Eduardo repeated, nodding his head over to where that young muchacho got clubbed.

"You keep your mouth closed," said the other officer. "Are you saying you are with him?" asked the first.

"I'm not saying anything," said Eduardo. "I'm only asking what you did with him."

"Detail!" shouted the first, and out came a pair of deputies. "If you're so curious about it, we'll show you exactly where we took him," the first one said. They took Eduardo to a van and eventually drove him away. Mrs. Tafoya, who watched the whole thing from the courtyard at the church across the street, came by the house and told Francisca that the officers took away her son.

Walter Carr, the Bureau of Immigration's superintendent in Los Angeles — a fellow whose countenance vaguely reminded one of a cigar that had been put out in a dish of white cake frosting — had quietly put out the call for assistance a few weeks before. Agents came from the California border, from San Francisco, and even from as far as Eduardo's home town of Nogales, and Police Chief Stackel and Sheriff Traeger also pledged their support to assist in a planned raid that was intended to send a message to illegals in Los Angeles — and the message was "go home, or we will send you home by force." At exactly three o'clock on February 26, 1931, the retinue of immigration agents in olive-green uniforms, police officers and deputy sheriffs emerged from the side streets near the Plaza and engulfed it, leaving each exit from the Plaza impenetrable. After about an hour and a half of interrogations, they took away at least a dozen, maybe as many as about thirty Mexicans, as well as a few Chinese, and held them for further questioning.

Carr was operating under a policy set by President Hoover's Secretary of Labor, William N. Doak. With unemployment growing, the newly-appointed Doak announced he was going to improve the job situation in America by deporting illegal immigrants who were stealing our jobs, and Mexicans turned out to be at the top of his list. He directed immigration agents to deport every stray Mexican they could find — and he did not emphasize the need to figure out which ones were illegal and which were not. The Plaza raid was meant to scare them all, to create an atmosphere of psychological discomfort that would inspire many Mexican-Americans, regardless of their right to stay, to choose to go "home" on their own. (*Anyone ever remember hearing that word "self-deportation"? I used to laugh myself silly when I heard it.*) Now, though, after the raid at the Plaza, Carr's officers seemed to be regularly raiding the dance halls, the parties and picnics, and the *burdeles*, and pairs of uniformed immigration officers were rumored to be wandering around Boyle Heights and Lincoln Heights, knocking on doors. Meanwhile, you'd never know this even happened if all you did was read the newspapers — I mean, the English-speaking ones. It was news from that part of Downtown and surrounds that was overrun by the Mexicans — conducted in broad daylight but unseen by whites. It was a piece of history that was conveniently left out of the newspapers, except for some protest articles in *La Opinion*, the Spanish-language newspaper.

It was almost two weeks before Eduardo was released and showed up on Francisca's doorstep. She threw herself on him, crying inconsolably. He looked tired, his eyes looked a little bruised, and she saw that he had some cuts and bruises on his arms. "They hit you!," she said. "No, mamá — it was just a bunch of muchachos all jumbled up in holding tanks," said Eduardo. "It was *por nada*." Apparently they let him go because his English was a little better than some of the others who were in there. He'd heard that a few muchachos were put on trains and sent all the way down to Ciudad Juárez.

Eduardo slept for a day or so, and then joined his mother in the little living room, asking questions, agitatedly. "Mamá, where was I born?"

"En Nogales, m'hijo."

"No, I know that, Mamá — but on the American or the Mexican side?"

"No me acuerdo,[7] m'hijo." Francisca remembered it all as *Ambos Nogales*, without a fence down the middle of the Calle Internacional, without the checkpoints.

---

7   I don't remember.

"They kept telling me, when they'd take me out to ask me questions, that I should gather up *mi familia* and go back home. So, look at me, Mama, I am from Nogales, todos somos de Nogales. If I were to show up in Nogales next week, probablemente me tirarían por la frontera.[8] ¿Qué demonios quieren que haga?"[9]

Francisca thought long and hard about her youngest son, and about what was best. They had lived in Los Angeles for a dozen years now. The older daughters here in Los Angeles all had their own lives now, they didn't need her anymore. Alfredo was working steadily, even if he hadn't settled down with a nice girl yet. She loved going to Anna and Joe's, helping with the cooking and the cleaning and holding the little baby, Elenita, but they didn't need her there. Meanwhile, there were no jobs for Eduardo, and she could see he was falling into some bad habits — staying out a little too late, coming home a little drunk, getting into bust-ups, only God knew what else. He was a good boy, but things could change rapidly, especially with a lot of immigration agents roaming the streets, looking for an excuse to pick someone up and send them to Mexico. She couldn't bear the thought of him spending one more night in a holding tank, *con un paquete de perros*.[10] And she was so tired all the time. Her fingers hurt, and the sewing wasn't as good as it once was. She thought maybe it was time to go. They had family in Santa Ana, Sonora, south of Nogales. Eduardo's older brothers were there, maybe, and maybe they could help him find work.

Eduardo shrugged. "Mamá," he said, exhausted by the weight of all these questions, thinking about how he had taken to looking over his shoulder now at frequent intervals. "Mamá," he said. "Lo que crea que es mejor."[11] She said she thought maybe it was time to go.

They packed their things, just what they could carry. Among the ephemera in Francisca's suitcase, in amongst her clothing, her pin cushions and threads and sewing needles, was the yellowing newspaper with Anna's photographs in the old Paramount dress advertisements. Anna took the baby and went to the station to see them off. They said

---

8   They would probably throw me over the border.
9   What the hell do they want me to do?
10 With a pack of dogs.
11 Whatever you think is best,

their goodbyes. "Adios, m'hija querida," said the little mother to her child of destiny. "Don't you worry, m'hija," she said, shaking her little fist at Anna and winking. "You keep working on it and everything will be o-kay."

"Don't go to the train station no more," Joe said, after Anna told her about saying goodbye to her mother. "Don't take the baby near there." Joe had his own fears about what was going on around them. He was concerned that someone might mistake them for Mexicans going home, and they might throw them on the train.

Less than a year later, little brother Eduardo, whom Anna never saw again, sent Anna a note to tell her that their little mama had passed away in Mexico.

"You dirty spic! Pour me another goddamned rye!" Occasionally, some jobbie in the wrong suit would find his way onto the top floor, into the Bar in the Clouds, and proceed to dip his bill too deeply in the sauce. Once they get a little soused, they get harder to control.

"Pour me another goddamned rye, or I'll make sure you and your whole family get sent back to *Tia-wanna* where you belong!"

Just then, the bumble that was stirred up by the young jobbie's aggression was frozen, mid-bumble, and a hush came over the top floor, as the tall, imposing figure of the former Secretary of the United States Treasury entered the Bar in the Clouds. Even the drunken jobbie stopped in the middle of a malevolent lunge at Joe, looking sheepishly over at the Great Man as his presence filled the room.

"Is that young Mr. Crowley I see?," drawled the Secretary. "My, my — and a little worse for wear, too. Wouldn't it surprise your father to know that his son is a pathetic drunkard? No, I beg your pardon, Mr. Crowley — I shouldn't jump to any conclusions. Perhaps this encounter of yours with too-much liquor this evening was just an accident?"

"I — uh — I," sputtered Crowley.

"Well, I am sure you will think better of avoiding such accidents in the future, upon reflection, as you recuperate in the light of morning.

Meanwhile, my advice to you, young Mr. Crowley, would be to go home and attend to your father's desires for you and your prospects."

"Y-y-es, sir?"

"And do tell the elder Mr. Crowley that yours truly sends his best wishes, and hopes to inquire after the state of the electric motor-winding business. You may tell him I would be most gratified if he were to call my law office so that we might chat about such matters later in the week."

"Yes, sir."

At that moment, the Club's assistant manager and a couple of porters plowed into the top floor, stumbling onto the scene like the Keystone Kops. As the Secretary helped the assistant manager to his feet, he whispered to him, "I don't think Mr. Crowley here will give you any trouble on his way out." He handed the assistant manager a few bills. "You may put him in a cab — on me." Once the elevator doors had shut behind them, there was a smattering of applause as the Secretary approached the bar. "Joseph, my friend," he said, "how about a cup of your fine coffee?"

"Yes, Mr. Mack, comeen right up."

William Gibbs McAdoo, Jr. was already one of the most famous, most recognizable figures in American political life when he began to frequent the Club in the early 1920s. Over six feet tall, with deep-set grey eyes and high cheekbones and a long, aquiline nose that gave him the appearance of a Roman senator, McAdoo was indeed an imposing figure; a Southerner, a Tennessean, who had managed somehow to enter the highest circles of power, seemingly almost effortlessly, not only in New York and Washington, but also in Hollywood. Before the middle-aged lawyer joined the late President Wilson's cabinet, he was known as the "boy-wonder" who led the successful completion of the construction of the Hudson Tubes, the railways tunnels under the Hudson River that connected New Jersey to Manhattan. Later as Secretary of the Treasury, he was the architect of the late President Wilson's financial policy and was largely responsible for leaving the Federal Reserve System in place as America's central bank by the end of Wilson's term. A widower, McAdoo also managed to woo President Wilson's much younger daughter Eleanor and married her in a ceremony in the Blue Room of the White House. Not incidentally, he became one of the President's closest advisors on all fronts, including foreign policy. It was inevitable that he would run for President, but his own Democratic party twice thwarted his efforts to attain the nomination. In 1920, he lost after 44 ballots at the convention, during which his mortally ill father-in-law Wilson undermined his candidacy, hoping to be nominated for a third term; and he lost again in 1924 after a barn-burning 103 ballots.

Now, as a powerful Hollywood lawyer — the force behind the creation of United Artists, with a few little-known partners named Charlie Chaplin, Mary Pickford, Douglas Fairbanks and D.W. Griffith — in 1931 he seemed to be enjoying a hiatus from important work. Although he still had the look of a man who could be President someday, his loosened schedule was giving him an opportunity to settle into the enjoyment of some select vices.

Liquor, however, was not one of them. He was a fervent supporter of Prohibition, consistently stating both publicly and privately that excessive alcohol use was ruinous and that it encouraged poverty. Nonetheless, he liked a "warm and cheerful" bar as much as the next gentleman of leisure, and spent many evenings with Joe on the top floor, sipping coffee and philosophizing. No, his chosen vices were the *other ones*—namely, the companionship of women, and games of chance. As with liquor, such vices put the Secretary into the society of a great cross-section of men. He was quite accustomed to the company of both doormen and diplomats — as well as Mexicans. In fact, McAdoo loved Mexico and had been traveling there since 1921, in both official and unofficial capacities. More recently he had taken to flying down to the resort at Agua Caliente, celebrating alongside Hollywood stars and gambling at the Casino and the Racetrack. "I'll admit to you, privately, that I've taken an aeroplane down there with the pretty wife of a particular congressman a couple of times," he once boasted to Joe. "A little harmless fun, you know."

"Never mind young Mr. Crowley's bigoted eruptions," he said to Joe, once the mood had calmed that evening. "It's all just inebriated bluster, and likely to be misunderstood."

"They called me a bigot back in '24 when I ran for President," the Secretary went on, "and they tried to hang me alongside the Ku Klux

Klan, but I will say this to you, my friend: no matter what the newspapers say, I have had many great, beloved colored acquaintances in my life. Meanwhile, I can assure you that Herbert Clark Hoover is positively beside himself at the thought of having to receive a Negro in the White House parlor for tea. His valet would be well advised to keep a second set of undergarments for him at the ready for such an occasion." He smiled and sipped his coffee. "So much for the 'party of emancipation.'"

"Mr. Mack," said Joe, "I am worried a leedle." The Secretary always encouraged Joe to call him Mr. Mack, something I never realized when, as a child, my grandfather used to pretend-wrestle me, chortling *"Hey, Mack! What do you say, Mr. Mack!"*

Joe proceeded to tell him about what happened to his wife's little brother at the Plaza, and about the departure of Eduardo and his mother-in-law to Mexico. "Tsk, tsk," said the Secretary. "Our national economy is taking a plunge, and our President is flailing. Too bad his gigantic brain seems to be immune to notions of responsible monetary policy. This latest ploy, though, this immigration hustle-and-bustle, is all the invention of the President's Secretary of Labor, one Mr. Doak. And unfortunately, the air is thick with bigotry." He brightened for a moment and laughed to himself a little. "I knew Billy Doak back when he was a junior negotiator for the Trainmen's Brotherhood. Not the brightest bulb in the marquee, if you know what I mean."

"Listen to me, Joe," the Secretary continued. "Billy Doak has got to be informed that he cannot upset our social equilibrium. There are certain things you just musn't do. And furthermore, if you or your wife ever have any problem with any of these agents, you must call upon me and I will take it up with Mr. Doak directly. I would ring Hoover himself, but the President and I haven't been on good speaking terms ever since he stabbed me in the back over hog futures at the end of the Great War. Damnable *hog futures*! ... well, *he* is the President, and unfortunately *I* am not."

The evening wore on, and other members of the Club who were there that evening drifted in and out of the colloquium shared by Joe and the Secretary. As the lively energy of the bar subsided, and the last call was sounded, the Secretary leaned in again to listen to his friend behind the bar. "Stepping out this evening, Mr. Mack?" asked Joe.

"No, not tonight, Joe. Mrs. Mack is in the city, and I will have to take a rain check." The Secretary looked around as if concerned about who might be listening in. "One more thing, Joe," he said in a half-whisper. "The best advice I have for you in these trying times is ... you might appear to be a little less Mexican. I should say, you already *are* a little less Mexican — but you know what I mean."

"I understand, Mr. Mack. I understand."

It was easy advice for Joe to heed. Mexico was for the dead — he had long believed it. Even though he had recently seen his father's lips move, when they came to visit that time after Elena was born, he still consigned them in his mind — his family, all of them, except maybe Luís and Lola, the younger ones — to the realm of the dead and gone. Joe was not a Mexican at all now — even if he had been born in Mexico, even if he had an accent when speaking in English, even if he spoke Spanish at home — he was light-skinned Spanish, not dark-skinned Mexican. He was a manly, suave continental-type from central casting. He was no longer Fernando Martín (*mar-TEEN*), he was now Joe Martin (*MART-inn*). His family would not wear the peasant uniforms of the Mexicans in the Plaza. Joe would wear his Downtown suit and tie during the week, and at home on weekends he would dress like John Gilbert in his tennis clothes from the pages of a movie magazine, in light-colored pleated slacks and silky button-downs, maybe plus-fours and a snazzy Panama hat for working in the garden. Anna would be good at choosing for him. And for Anna, who was already in the habit of making herself nice dresses that set her apart from the crowd, he bought a fur wrap and a pearl brooch. Their little girl would be known as "Lena" — less Mexican than "Elena," dressed like a little Mitzi Green in baby-doll dresses, white socks and shiny black Mary Janes. This being Los Angeles, this being Hollywood, the image they would fashion for themselves would be as true as anything could be.

Of course, there were other, more practical concerns that needed to be dealt with. Joe had an entry visa that was almost twenty years old, and he assumed it probably wouldn't even be recognized by the officials now. Anna's right to be here was even murkier, and the more she explained the circumstances to him, the more he imagined her growing up right in the middle of the Calle Internacional, one foot on either side of the border. He procrastinated over pursuing naturalization, mostly for the very good reason that the country was in no mood to legalize a couple of Mexicans, even the "Spanish" kind. From here it would appear that my mother, little Lena, was their *"anchor baby,"* to use a phrase that some politicians now seem to love. They would get another at the end of 1932. Fernando, Jr. was his name on the birth certificate, but Anna did her best to make it sound more French by calling him "Fernand." When he was but a curly-locked toddler, though, they all began to call him "Junior" or "Joey," which stuck and suited him just fine.

Meanwhile, for Joe, there truly was a sense of being "anchored" within the jolly, pleasure-loving community of the Club, anchored within a loving home, anchored in the excitement of Los Angeles—and to stay anchored, it didn't seem like much of a compromise to jettison some dead weight. Like living in a Mexican-American neighborhood. Landlords had an unbridled right, it seemed, to say no to you if they thought you were Mexican (and did so with impunity), so Joe moved his way into whiter neighborhoods by increment. From 1931 to 1938, the family moved six times until they could finally buy their own house, each time moving further out of the barrios where the agents were knocking on doors. Joe saw no sacrifice at all in jettisoning the Roman Catholic Church, especially Our Lady of the Queen of the Angels next to the Plaza—but any of them, really. If the immigration agents in olive-drab uniforms were looking for Mexicans, they'd always find them in the churches, he surmised. The only time Anna would insist on going back was for the babies' christenings and confirmations, leaving the children with only a very limited idea of what church was all about. Joe told Anna to stay away from train stations, but also the Plaza and the outdoor produce markets, anywhere that crowds would gather. He had the Ford, and a driver's license—he would take her to get the groceries. She never did get a driver's license of her own.

And of course, Lena and Joey would not be permitted to speak Spanish at all—even if their parents spoke to each other in a mixture of that strange tongue and English. "Mamá, quiero leche," Lena would say. "M'hija, no Espanish—only eenglesh," Anna would reply. "You want meelk? Say it, m'hija—meelk?"

159

Anna was and is all too willing to comply with these rules, because it turns her favorite pastime into an essential mission. Just as Anna learned about dresses and cigarettes and love from the silent pictures, Hollywood is now doing its best to teach everyone who buys a ticket what Being an American is all about — even when the movies are set in exotic foreign locales, for it is understood by Anna and the other mothers with their children in tow that when Hollywood shows Paris on screen, or Budapest or Baghdad, or Istanbul or Havana, it is showing a studio-curated version of America to them, in English.

Taking her babies by their hands as soon as they were old enough to walk, Anna would lead them in little steps down the sidewalks, past the little front lawns and flowerbeds of the neighborhood, to the thoroughfares, to modest East Los Angeles picture palaces like The Jewel or The Boulevard, and together they would sit down for a whole day, watching newsreels and short subjects about the latest fashions or home appliances, or about traveling on ocean liners. Then, inevitably, up would come, say, a prestigious MGM picture, announced by the throaty roar of Leo the lion sitting under a banner that said, in Latin, *"ars gratia artis,"* or "art for art's sake." Sometimes it was a costume drama, sometimes a musical or a modern-day photoplay, with Nelson Eddy and Jeanette McDonald, or Norma Shearer, Joan Crawford or Clark Gable, or, of course, Garbo. Garbo wasn't exactly the best role model for a good American speaking accent — Shearer and Crawford and the others sufficed for that — but Garbo's worldly, poetic Swenglish did make it seem to her children that Anna's own dignified cali-mexo-spanish accent, daintily syllabilized in baby-bites through and around the clenched teeth of her demure upside-down smile, was not so far out of place in America as depicted by Hollywood; if Garbo could sound a little bit exotic and still be a denizen of American style and taste and breeding, why couldn't Anna be that as well? It was a message that Anna could impart without comment, merely by unleashing Garbo's example on her children, and it was a message that little Lena, in particular, absorbed in real-time, staring wide-eyed at the gigantic screen of the theater, which was all lit-up with romance and beauty just for her.

Now, since Joey has outgrown being shuttled around by his mother and prefers to stay home and climb trees and play football with the other boys in the neighborhood — his imagination being stirred up by comic books and by cowboy cliffhangers and kiddie comedies during less frequent visits to The Strand on Whittier Boulevard with his father or with his rambunctious little buddies — the trips to the other neighborhood movie theaters that showed the more sophisticated shows have become a mother-daughter habit; and those MGM and Warner and Fox features have become a mother-daughter cultural salon. They chatter endlessly about Adrian's costumes for Garbo — the form-fitting gowns, the high necklines, the trench coats and hats — or Orry-Kelly's, for Kay Francis — the low-cut fronts and backs of her sleek gowns and the sleeveless tank dresses, revealing many gorgeous square inches of Kay's powdery white skin, the fur accents both actresses wear. "Mama," Lena says, "you would look so beautiful in that one."

"Oh, sweetheart — where would your mama wear that?"

"Out to dinner, with Papa!" Anna did, however, adapt some of those fashions for her own use, cutting paper patterns for a copy of a dress from *The Painted Veil,* or another taking ideas from one of Garbo's costumes in *Conquest* — the buttoned top with the tight, high Bertha collar and the tailored long-sleeves with the puff at the shoulder. But it isn't always about the dresses: how they laugh together at Mickey Rooney in the *Andy Hardy* movies, how they cried together at the end of *Camille,* as Garbo dies of tuberculosis in the arms of her suitor, Robert Taylor.

Years later, when my mother was being consumed by dementia, I sat with her in my parents' house — east of East L.A. and north of Disneyland, in an older northern Orange County suburb — trying to figure out a way to relieve the anxiety that accompanied her other deficits, trying to give my Dad a moment's rest from the 24-hour job of caring for her. I tried sitting her down to work on a jigsaw puzzle, thinking it would encourage focus — but it only made her more fidgety, and it only made me aware of how little I understood about her disease. When all else seemed to fail, I sat her down in front of the TV and put on a DVD of *Camille.* She stared glassy-eyed at the TV screen as the opening credits passed, and after a few minutes, in one of the last coherent phrases I remember her speaking to me, Lena Martin Baumiller turned to me and said, with a little smile, "I don't think this one ends too good for her."

Now, near the end of 1938, eight year-old Lena is skipping up the aisle of the ornate Golden Gate Theater after watching Tyrone Power, Don Ameche and Alice Faye in *Alexander's Ragtime Band,* her right hand alighting on and bouncing up from the padded backs of the seats in each row as she moves closer to the exit. She is humming to herself and swooning, just a little, having developed a crush on Tyrone Power watching his earlier romance pictures with Loretta Young. "Mama, can I stop taking piano and take dance lessons instead?," asks Lena, thinking about the dance numbers in the movie.

"No, m'hija — piano ees good for you. You take piano."

"Please?"

"No, m'hija — eet ees piano for you," Anna says, catching herself think-ing about how much she loved to dance. It is a delicate balance, though, raising your daughter to be an American based on Hollywood movies. Sometimes it is too easy to enjoy all the trappings yet miss the real story, the part that's supposed to teach you that the dancing girls never get to marry Tyrone Power in the end. Fortunately, fashion continues to bond mother and daughter, and if the lessons on cultivating the tastes and habits of a little American lady are sometimes difficult to divine at the end of a certain picture, all's well when they hit the lobby, where they stop to look at the glamour photos and lobby cards of recent and future Fox attractions — Sonia Henie in her cute little skating outfits, a pretty blouse worn by Arleen Whelan, a beautiful high-lapel, two-tone suit worn by Barbara Stanwyck. Lena is overjoyed when her mother makes her an approximate little copy of that Barbara Stanwyck number — she definitely elevates the fashion game at Lorena Elementary that fall, and she never wants to take it off. Unfortunately, she grows a few inches over Christmas vacation and cries her eyes out when Anna decides it is time to pack it up and give the suit to the Salvation Army. But there will be other suits for her, other dresses, new shoes and pretty bows for her hair, because her mother loves her and is industrious, and because her papa loves her and is a good provider.

Meanwhile, the good provider is a night owl, typically still snoring away when the kiddies are up and ready to go to school, and he is off to work before they can return home. He has turned into a legend in his own household, a monarch who is only available for audiences with his progeny on weekends, wearing his Hollywood weekend clothes.

Back in 1932, six years ago when Lena was only two years old and Junior was just an infant, born that September, the good provider, Joe, was doing very well indeed on his way to the present day, providing more than just illicit booze concoctions to the jolly boys of the top floor. 1932 was a presidential contest year, and Hoover looked like he might be on the ropes, so inevitably there was speculation about whether Joe's late-night compadre, Mr. Mack, would throw his hat into the ring. But Mr. Mack surprised everyone and backed the hard-drinking Speaker of the House, old John Nance Garner, from the backwater hamlet of Uvalde, Texas. Presaging what would become Mr. Mack's campaign for the Senate from California, Mr. Mack began to stump around the state for Garner, but he nonetheless incidentally declared his support for a plan that would tax bootleggers on 100% of their income. After each of his trips around the state, he always returned to the Club, continuing to sip his coffee at the bar on the top floor, surrounded by his many imbibing pals — who understood that when it came to politics, there was a gentlemanly solid line between what one said in public, and what one tolerated in private. There were no hard feelings on the top floor about Mr. Mack's unworkable "bootlegger tax." Mr. Mack's social cross to bear, apparently, was that he hated liquor, but he also hated spending time with the humorless, joy-killing bluenoses who also hated liquor. So when he returned to the top floor, he was always looking for Joe with a late-night idea.

Putting Joe behind the wheel of his brand new Cadillac Sedan with a few cronies in the back, Mr. Mack would lead them to Santa Monica Boulevard in West Hollywood where, between two and three o'clock in the morning, there was an unmistakable vibration of human activity that was wholly absent from Downtown at the same hour. One evening Mr. Mack directed Joe's wheel to an old house with a big porch, just off Santa Monica, where the hidden murmur of humanity seemed to be particularly strong. Inside they found all number of somnambulist swells in finely-tailored duds, eyes bulging — several collected around a piano getting tickled and scratched by a smiling black piano player wearing glasses, another crew fixing drinks over a small but stylish art deco cart of contraband liquor over in the corner, several others collected on couches and attached to the drapes, playing footsie with garish young twisties who laughed too loud and fussed with the young men's lapels and collars. At the back of the front room, a frowning portly gentleman emerged from the door to another room. "All hail, the Future Senator," said the smartly-coifed matron with the beer-barrel voice, entering stage right and accosting Mr. Mack.

"Morning, Schotzie," said Mr. Mack. "This is Joe — he's from the Club. They tell me he knows how to pour your swill and make it taste like apple pie." He waved behind him. "And you know the boys."

"Hello, boys. Welcome, Joe. Don't worry, dearie, I won't put you to work, but Miss Schotzie would love to taste one of your Martinis — something crystal clear and lucid, like your man Mr. Mack here."

"Are they dealing in the back?," asked Mr. Mack, nodding over to where the portly man had just abashedly made his exit.

"I'm sure they've got a special seat saved just for you." Mr. Mack started for the room in the back, stopping for a moment to reach in and apply his fingertips to the wrist of a petite young redhead getting paragraphed by an earnest suitor still wearing his overcoat, hat in hand. "My, my, but don't you have just the *most beautiful ... pulse*, my dear?," said Mr. McAdoo, his soft grey eyes stealing her gaze away from the poor swain. *"Do you ever let it race?"* he asked, kissing her wrist chastely before leading her, blushing, her arm in his, to the back room. The poor swain, still standing there mid-soliloquy, never had a chance.

Mack's boys split up in all directions, leaving Joe to mix Miss Schotzie's drink over at the art deco cart. "Your dessert, Madam," he said as he served it to her, with a flourish, makeshift white towel hanging over his other arm. She looked into eyes as she sipped. "Very, very nice," she said. "You obviously know a few tricks." She patted and rubbed his shoulder as she went in for sip number two. "Stick around," she said. "Maybe you'll pick up a few more."

About quarter past five, Joe was sitting in a comfy chair with a giddy flaxen on his lap, tie loosened, nursing a melting Highball and watching as Mr. Mack was staring down some studio executive over the biggest pot of the night. Half the people in the room were lousy with booze and snooze, and the other half had eyes glued to the game. The studio executive showed his cards — a pair of tens, a pair of queens, and a six. "Pair of Jean Harlows, pair of Garbos, and a bit player," says the bank. "What about you, Mr. Mack?" Mack puts down two more tens. "Well, there's your other blondies," says the bank. Then Mack puts down three kings. "Full house — Gables and Harlows!" says the bank. "Too bad your last picture didn't do as well as that," the bank says to the exec, as McAdoo plucks out a couple of C-Notes from the mound of swag and inserts them into the strap of the redhead's gown. "Yeah, not a full house in the Southland," says the exec. "A round for the whole room, Schotzie," says the coffee-drinking McAdoo, "although I won't complain if anyone wants to join me in a java." The boys and the girls snicker. After an hour or so more of foolishness, upstairs and downstairs, Joe pulls up to the Club in Mack's Cadillac, depositing what is left of the boys and turning the wheel back over to Mr. Mack.

"You're a good man, Joseph." Every morning-after, it was always thus. "My closed-mouthed chum," he would say, with a pre-sunrise smile of satisfaction, as he would reach over and put a few bills in Joe's breast pocket. Often it was Schotzie's, or another place like it, but sometimes they might find themselves in a black club on Central Avenue, where the jazz music and the chatter and the flesh were all hotter than moviegoers would ever see or imagine; or the pure gambling salons, where grim-faced gat-men monitored the proceedings and sucked all the fun out of the wee hours, mainly for the highest rollers and the self-martyring obsessives; or sometimes it might be a nancy club in some house on the edge of Beverly Hills, where skinny boys dressed up like Ruby Keeler and Marlene Dietrich — the latter being quite a challenge, considering how often Miss Dietrich herself dressed in drag. McAdoo was quite the ladies' man, but he was fascinated by the drag mistresses and their little shows. What Joe was learning, however, was that for every taste of man, there is a place somewhere in greater Los Angeles where it can be indulged at four in the morning.

That Summer of '32, at the Democratic convention, McAdoo sank the chances of New York's Governor Smith getting a second bite at the presidential apple when he threw the California and Texas Garner slates behind FDR's candidacy. He returned home to L.A. to run for Senate, facing the Republican "wet" candidate, a north-state nonentity named Tallant Tubbs, and the Prohibition candidate, none other than Fightin' Bob himself, straight from the pulpit of the Trinity Methodist Church Downtown. Interestingly enough, in the Southland where the "thirst" for change seemed most palpable, as it were, Mack and Fightin' Bob finished one and two, leaving Tubbs to go back into his granddaddy's rope business. Fightin' Bob put out a statement, cynically inferring that Mr. Mack was a closet "Wet," saying "all we needed were a few more Prohibition votes." And a little more than a year later, as if to cash in on Fightin' Bob's worst nightmares, McAdoo's anointed candidate for the White House signed into law the death sentence for Prohibition.

Meanwhile, just after the election in November of 1932, Mr. Mack and Joe and the boys were returning to the Club after another after-hours odyssey, when Mack remembered that he left his topcoat up in the top floor bar. The boys dispersed and Joe and Mr. Mack walked through the quiet halls of the Club to the secret elevator. Once they ascended, Joe said, "I think they put eet behind the bar," and Mr. Mack said, "I'm going to try my luck with your slot machines, if you don't mind," as he strolled out into the wintergarden. The slot machines had been there as long as Joe had been working at the Club. It never occurred to him that someone put them there, or that anyone made any money from them. They were just there, another illicit source of fun and games for the top floor jolly boys.

When Joe came out to the wintergarden to fetch Mr. Mack, he stumbled upon a peculiar tableau. Mr. Castagno, the Club's graveyard shift catering manager, was helping some hood in a trench coat to unload one of the machines. Another fellow stood nearby, counting coins. And there was another figure just beyond them, in the darkness. Mr. Mack stood a few feet ahead of Joe, surveying the same scene. Castagno said to Joe, in an almost vaudevillian stage whisper, "Hey, Joe, you don't belong here right now."

"Fine morning, wouldn't you say, gentlemen?" said Mr. Mack, breaking the awkward silence, his voice electrifying the pre-dawn air with its bright Tennesseean, stentorian tones.

"You'd better get out of here, Joe," said Castagno again, slightly louder.

"Fine morning for a harvest," said Mr. Mack.

The mysterious figure in the dark started to move toward them. As he walked into the light of the Bar in the Clouds, Joe saw the full-faced man with round eyeglasses under a wide-brimmed fedora. "Mister Senator-Elect," said the man from the shadows.

"Mr. Gans — why, what a pleasure," said McAdoo. Bob Gans was well known to newspapermen and crooked cops alike as the slot machine king of L.A. If anyone were to stop and think, they would have realized that the slot machines in the wintergarden at the Club were only there through the vison and toil of a professional such as Mr. Gans. And the only way that they could remain there, discreetly, would be through the cooperation of a man on the inside. This was how Bob Gans operated. Wherever he went, spreading his brand of good cheer and lucrative machinery, he needed a Castagno to monitor and collect from the machines in the wee hours of the morning. That particular November morning he was only making the rounds because the weather was decent and he needed to get out anyway. But here he was.

"How may I report your bounty, if asked, Mr. Gans?" asked Mr. Mack.

"Well, I really wish you wouldn't, Senator. We have our trade secrets," said Gans. "But if you must know, we do all right here." They smiled at each other, their flashy grins catching the early morning light, a pair of gambling sharps waiting for the end of the play. If you were looking for them that night, you might have detected their teeth up here on the roof from all the way up in Pasadena.

McAdoo backed up slowly and put his arm around Joe, pulling him further into the tableau. "I know you can always use more friends, Mr. Gans," said McAdoo. "Gentlemen, I'd like to introduce you to your new partner, Joe Martin."

"We don't need any — "

"Shut up, Castagno. You were saying, Senator?"

"Joe is a very good man. He is my closed-mouthed chum. I'm sure he will earn his keep."

Gans came in close to Mack and Joe. "You're the head barman?"

"Yes, sir."

"Sure," said Gans. "Sure, we can spare a dime's worth, out of Castagno's share — you won't mind at all, will you Castagno?" Castagno, still standing in mostly darkness, blanched. "Will you, Castagno?"

"'Course not, Mr. Gans."

"Tell the Senator-elect about it."

"'Course not, Mr. Senator."

"You know, Mr. Martin, you could be useful in drumming up more business for us," Gans continued. "Okay," said Mr. Mack, "sure, he can be useful, but we don't need to get his hands too dirty. Just hand him his take on a regular basis and we will make sure the rest goes smoothly on our end."

The two men smiled at each other again. "Nice doing business with you, Senator."

"The pleasure is mine, Mr. Gans." They shook hands, and a half hour later Joe was going home with some $800 in his pocket. It all went to pieces, of course, in 1942, when the Club was raided and they confiscated all the slot machines, but until then, for ten solid years Joe was quietly on the gravy train, keeping his tax-free, illicit treasure above the ceiling light fixture in the hallway of his home until he ran out of room there. Years later, it amounted to thousands of dollars. It helped him buy the house on Woods Avenue — and also his first Cadillac.

The late-night and early-morning rambles continued as Joe's reputation rose, even as Senator McAdoo was forced to spend more time in Washington. Joe was the walkingest, talkingest, charmingest Funk & Wagnalls of L.A. after dark, and in that role, with slot machine proceeds rolling in on a regular basis, he was able to spend, as well as make, some regular money — out on the town. It also made him a minor celebrity among a certain set in the city, and he was frequently called upon to tend bar at Hollywood parties and private political fundraisers, soirees at the homes of real estate developers and oil executives, on the weekends. L.B. Mayer, the head of Metro-Goldwyn-Mayer Studios and also, incidentally, the head of the California Republican Party, and also, incidentally, a Jew, had him out to his home on Pallisades Beach Road in Santa Monica, to tend bar for a political event. On that occasion, L.B. told his Downtown friends, "Gentlemen, Joe here is a Mexican who tends bar at the Club. I'm having a Mexican from the Club to my home — which is of course very funny because the Club won't admit me and my brother Jerry — because it is restricted!" A few of the Protestant Republicans laughed the hardest at L.B.'s little joke. At the drop of the word "Mexican," Joe started sweating in his white jacket, but he kept his best head barman's smile pasted across his face for the entire event. He was tipped quite well that evening.

Now, six years after their first trip to West Hollywood together, at the end of a mostly undistinguished term in the Senate during which he divorced his wife, the daughter of the former President, and married a nurse who was almost fifty years his junior, William Gibbs McAdoo, Jr. has lost his bid for re-nomination and is returning to L.A. for one last hurrah.

"Look at you, Joseph—all grown up," says Senator McAdoo. "Thank you, Senator."

"Oh, come now, my friend. I barely own up to that title anymore. You know what to call me."

"Mr. Mack," says Joe. "Cup of coffee for you?"

"If I could trouble you for a Sanka?" he replies. "No, no—just a moment, Joe," he says. "If we are going to hit the spots tonight, perhaps I should indulge in the real item. Cup of coffee sounds fine."

"Comeen right up," says Joe.

McAdoo leans in and whispers, smiling and winking. "Joseph, maybe with just a little shot of bourbon in it."

"Your secret ees safe with me, Mr. Mack."

At the other end of the bar this evening is L.B. Mayer's successor as head of the California Republican Party, an ambitious, middle-aged district attorney from Alameda County, up north—a garrulous, chunky fellow with chunky hands and feet, eyeglasses, a high, squarish forehead, wavy whitening hair, drinking a Gimlet and chuckling and thigh-slapping with a few other lawyers. His eye is caught by the awkwardly mantidian, grey figure sipping from a coffee cup, and he broad-shoulders his way up to the edge of the bar and gets Joe's attention. "Is that who I think it is, Joe?"

"Yes, that ees the Senator. Has no been here too much lately."

"Gosh," says the district attorney. "I've never met him." Joe motions him to come over to the other end of the bar. "Mr. Mack, may I introduce you to my friend, Mr. Warren."

"Mr. *Earl* Warren? Why, this young man needs no introduction — it is a pleasure to meet you, sir." In many ways, Earl Warren could be considered the complete opposite of William McAdoo. In his day, McAdoo was thought of as a conservative Democrat; the much younger Warren, now, a progressive Republican. McAdoo is a man who, during a long career as a political survivor, loved to play the partisan angles and was adept at it; Warren, although the newly-appointed head of the state Republicans, has cross-registered as a candidate for state attorney general — as a Republican, a Democrat and even as a member of the "Progressive Party." He has openly declared that he will be a "non-partisan" attorney general, if elected, and he truly believes he will be, in his heart-of-hearts. Most significantly, however, Mack is an old school gentleman of grace and charm, with generous traces of Rascal in him, while Earl Warren is as square as a ham sandwich. Warren has also become a new great friend of Joe's at the bar on the top floor — *"Keep the Gimlets coming, Joe, they sure are tasting mighty good tonight"* — but he is a family man who likes to bring his wife and children to the Club. He is a top floor jolly-boy, to be sure, in an earnest, glad-handing sort of way, but not a West Hollywood after-hours jolly-boy. "Mr. Warren, let me offer my deepest condolences on the passing of your father," says Mack, referring to the matter that had been in the papers, the matter of the senior Mr. Warren's murder, in his own home, by an unknown assailant. "I lost my own father when I was but, well, younger than you are, I would guess — but my father had been ill for some time. I cannot imagine losing a loved one under such shocking and terrifying circumstances. I am deeply sorry for your loss."

"Thank you, Senator," says Warren. "Once he is gone, a father can't be replaced."

"How true." McAdoo had lost his youngest son, Ribs, to pneumonia only months before. As the two men size each other up, each of them taking in the nature of the man across from him, one of them knows very well that the other is a Bakersfield boy scout and will not be interested in the old form of late night shenanigans, and the other surmises that, whatever he may desire, the first is a nineteenth century egg crème dandy who lacks the youthful stamina actually to sustain a wild night out. "Your fellow legislator, Senator Johnson, was a mentor to me," says Warren. "Ah, yes, dear Hiram," says McAdoo. "A good man, and a Republican who was not beyond engaging in a little horse trading for the good of the country." The men who linger around them there at the Bar in the Clouds, watching this interesting picture as it develops, this display of generational baton-passing — they are determined to see that the conversation continues in a quiet open forum, after the Club has kicked them all out. So telephone calls are made, and one of Warren's G.O.P. cronies finds a lady script-doctor in Holmby Hills who suffers from insomnia and hosts an irregular "salon" of sorts — musicians, pulp scribblers, intellectuals, creative emigres of like metabolism who gather at her home, sardonically exchanging questions and answers with each other in the opaque language of nocturnal poetry — the kind of dialogue that always used to get rejected in Mrs. Delacroix's early scripts for Fox, before she understood what Papa Hollywood wants and learned how to play His game. "Do bring them over," says Mrs. Delacroix over the phone. "They sound *delectable*."

And so, once more, Joe Martin finds himself behind the wheel of Mr. Mack's Cadillac, driving out to the winding, tree-lined section of Sunset Boulevard beyond Beverly Hills at around 2:30 o'clock in the A-M, this time with Mr. Mack in the passenger seat next to him, and Earl Warren and his assistant, Olney, in the backseat. Car-sized gangs of the men who lingered to listen to them in the Bar in the Clouds chase them around the curves along the way.

They are greeted at the door by the tall, slender Mrs. Delacroix herself, dressed in a long back slip dress with a sheer bolero lace jacket, and a silvery sash at the waist, drink and cigarette in hand. "Come with me, gentlemen," she says. "So glad you called, the place needs a little livening up this evening." She sits the two star performers in comfy chairs on what becomes the evening's stage, as the strange collection of Hollywood *artistes*, Club jolly-boys and G.O.P. donors gather at the feet of the two masters. Warren slips right into the role of emcee, graciously interviewing Mack about the end of the Wilson administration, and about President Hoover. Meanwhile, Joe lingers at Mrs. Delacroix's plentiful bar. "This man knows his cocktails," Olney tells Mrs. Delacroix helpfully. "Does he? You know, you would think that this would be a required skill for most gentlemen of the smart set, but I find that most of the men I know seem to be quite careless with the way they throw around their booze." "Joe here is an artist," says Olney. "An artist! How precious!," she laughs. "Well, my boy," she says to Joe, the back of her cigarette hand coming to rest on his ruddy cheek, "*artists* are always welcome in my home."

The assembled crowd sits with rapt attention while McAdoo tells of the scene at President Wilson's deathbed, as related to him by his, (cough), younger ex-mother-in-law Edith Bolling Wilson — since he and Mrs. McAdoo were then in Los Angeles, while Mack himself was embroiled in the Teapot Dome case as lawyer to the late Mr. Doheny, and contemplating his second run for the presidency. Joe busies himself with the drinks, making sure that both McAdoo and Warren are modestly well-served with their spiked coffee and Gimlet "usuals," and putting glasses in the hands of the admirers, contributing to the effervescent 3-a.m. mood of the room. The crowd laughs as McAdoo tells a tall tale about a horse he once had in Tennessee, and Warren counters with a recollection of his beloved pet burro Jack, whom he used to ride in Bakersfield as a boy, provoking more laughter. A young actor, a regular in Mrs. Delacroix's salon named Brandon, interrupts with a question. "Senator, why did you support the Klan when you ran for president in '24?" he asks. A hush falls over the room.

"Well, now," says Warren, looking for a graceful segue.

"No, Mr. Warren, the young man has asked a question — a good one — and I am here merely as a guest of these fine people. It is my place to answer for myself here." McAdoo here pauses, his ashen face taking on the look of a man delivering his Last Will and Testament, with one chance to atone for his sins at the end of a long political career — a career inconsistent of its own principles and now becoming an anachronism. "Poor Hugo Black, our new Supreme Court justice, just went through some hot water of his own on this," he begins. "He admitted he joined the Klan, you know — said he had to do it, for political expediency. Then later he resigned."

"You know," he goes on, "the original Klan was born in the state of Tennessee, right at the end of the War Between the States. My uncle John, rest his soul, was a general in the Confederate Army. I don't know if he joined the Klan after the War — he was busy down in Texas — but that Klan, really a resistance army, was disbanded in 1869."

"Back in 1915, the second Klan was born — and I cannot deny that my friend David Griffith had something to do with it when he made a popular motion picture about the old Klan. The idea just took off again, you know. Meanwhile I had long since moved to New York, then to Washington, and I had no interest in the issues that kept it going. But I knew the people who joined, and I knew some of what they did. They were preachers and bankers, the fellow who owned the hardware store and the grammar school principal — they were all Klan members. By this time I most certainly did not share their ideals about the grandeur of the Old South, or about the place of the Negro in this world — but I had had more experience out in the world. Still, they raised money for the poor — even for the colored poor — and they had parades. That's what I knew about the second Klan."

"You, Mr. Warren — are you a Moose, by any chance?" The bohemians in the crowd snicker. "Yes, sir," answers Warren, "I am a proud member of the Loyal Order of the Moose. I'm also active in the Odd Fellows, the Elks and the Freemasons."

"Well, I'll wager you have a dandy collection of hats," says the Senator, the crowd breaking up in laughter. Warren chuckles as well. "Now, the Freemasons," the Senator continues, "take that august group. There have been times in our history when the Masons have been vilified as warlocks and devils — and worse. Isn't that correct?"

"That is true, Senator."

"And I would guess that, whether it was true or not, you would have us judge the Masons by the best of their members, and not their worst."

"True," says Warren, "but the Klan — "

"I didn't know them to be violent. I knew them as community leaders. Not at all like the *third* Klan ..."

"Well, as you say, I have had my run-ins with this so-called third Klan," says Warren. "There were a bunch of them who took over city hall up in Oakland. They burned crosses and spread lies to chase away the Irish

Catholics who were running things back then. There was a sheriff, in particular, a fellow by the name of Burton Becker, whom I prosecuted for corruption. He's in San Quentin now. This Klan that I saw — they were a bunch of thugs."

"That's what I understand, sir, says Mr. Mack. "But I was dealing with a different group. Here is what I hope someone will remember about this, when all is said and done, Mr. Warren. I was never a member of the Klan — I was not a Southern politician, like Hugo Black, and I did not have to join clubs. In fact, as far as clubs go, I like the one that employs our friend Joe here," there is a smattering of applause for Joe, "and that's about it. No," he continues, "I never supported the Klan. It was them that supported me, because I was born in the South."

"But you did, I recall, make some statement," says Mr. Warren.

"I remember exactly what I said. I said that I stood four square on the immutable guarantee of liberty contained in the first paragraph of the constitution of the United States that is for freedom of religious worship, freedom of speech, freedom of the press, and the right to peaceable assemblage."

"That is laudable, but — "

" — But what I do regret, Mr. Warren," says Mack, interrupting, his voice rising, "is that I wanted their support. I wanted their votes. And I wasn't willing to stand up and denounce hatred." The room is deathly quiet now. "When you get to Washington, when you get a taste of what you are capable of doing when you have the power in your hands," says the grey man, eyes closed tightly shut, "that's when you will feel that your courage and your principles will be most violently tested."

"Well, I'm not aiming to get to Washington, Senator. Law enforcement, right here in California — that's my mission," says Warren. There are a couple of "hear, hears" from the G.O.P'ers.

"You may not want it now, Mr. Warren, but one day there will be a throng at your door," says Mack, pointing his boney index finger at the crowd in the room. "And they will force their ambitions onto you. This is what happens to able men of achievement. And as the river of this throng's ambitions rises, you will begin to find it impractical to swim against the flow. The question is, will you conquer it, or will it conquer you? Will you emerge somewhere on the river's edge with your principles intact, or will you drown?"

It is hard not to pity the old man, this relic from a bygone age, as he struggles to his feet at the end of the soiree, wobbling on bad legs as he leans on his cane, licks his lips and checks his coat pockets absent-mindedly. Someone has sent for the old man's young nurse-wife Doris, who comes in smiling, fresh as a daisy, to take him home. It is the last time most of these people will ever see Senator McAdoo.

Joe drives Mack's Cadillac back alone to retrieve his own car Downtown. He has absorbed little of this political talk, understands even less of the nostalgia about Washington or Sacramento or old party conventions. What he knows is these two friends of his from the Club are important men, and by introducing them and pouring the drinks, he has helped to make a fine evening out of it for everyone. And now, everyone can go home and forget about this evening, because they have work to do, and they can come back to the Club later to see Joe, to enjoy a few fine cocktails, and perhaps have another night out somewhere, because for every taste of man, there is a place somewhere in greater Los Angeles where it can be indulged at four in the morning ...

Meanwhile, Anna is at her listening post, on the divan in the front room, lamp lit on the end table. Lena and Joey are tucked in and sleeping in their bedrooms. The neighborhood is as quiet as can be at this hour, so quiet she can hear the children breathing, so quiet she can almost hear the neighbors breathing inside their homes across the street with her front window cracked open. She closes the pages of a *Look* magazine with Claudette Colbert on the cover and trades it in for a *Photoplay* with Deanna Durbin on the cover. Drawing on her cigarette, she absently peruses an article about the Dionne Quints and their third motion picture. This is the part of every day when she waits. This is what it is like, during the dark hours of the morning, to wait. She smokes, she closes her eyes, she rubs and stretches her neck, she lifts and stretches her arms to the ceiling, she turns the pages of her magazines and the daily newspaper, she writes little notes to herself about what she needs from the grocery store, the five-and-dime. She listens to the breathing, and she will continue to hear the breathing until the grey light of the morning, when the sun is barely peeking, until the routine of the breathing is broken by the sound of tires coming to rest, the door of the

Ford shutting, the backdoor opening, his steps down the back hallway into the bedroom. By the rhythm of those steps, she knows. Not long afterwards, she finds him snoring in their bed. She picks his clothes up off the floor and pulls the blanket up to the back of his neck. Then she goes back to the divan, and lights another cigarette. This is the routine of breathing and waiting.

3.3
HOLLYWOOD BOWL, 1943

S inatra to Compete with Sonatas in Hollywood Bowl
  — The Manhattan (Kansas) Mercury

Frank Sinatra's Hollywood Bowl Appearance Brings Protest Mail
  — The Times (of Munster, Indiana)

Swooner Sinatra Outdraws Yehudi In Hollywood Bowl
  — The Great Falls (Montana) Tribune

Sinatra Fans Crowd Bowl; Slick Chickies Swoon to Frankie's
Croon 'Neath August Moon
  — Los Angeles Times

Frank Sinatra's Hollywood Bowl Debut Called Moaning Success
Hollywood — Aug. 15. — (/P) — Frank Sinatra's starlight serenade
in that harmonic holy of holies, Hollywood Bowl, was a
moaning — and — mooning success, by feminine reaction and by
his own admission.

The setting was ecstatic. The occasion, debated beforehand
by defenders and devotees of Sinatra's swoon-inspiring brand
of vocal expression, was auspicious. The sedate Los Angeles
Philharmonic orchestra provided accompaniment. A hovering
full moon, silhouetting the pine trees along with the bowl's rim,
and a phalanx of photographers popping flash globes at his every
gesture, supplied his stage properties.

Sinatra, a willowy figure against the amphitheater's pale blue shell, thus delivered himself Saturday evening of nine super-sentimental ballads before one of the largest throngs the bowl has embraced, and then spoke this piece:

"I understand there was quite a controversy over my appearance here. I only want to say that those who thought I shouldn't appear seem to have lost out in a big way."

His audience of sub-debs, bobby-soxed 'teen'agers, a heavy sprinkling of starry-eyed middle-aged women and a host of somewhat restive escorts virtually filled the bowl, despite the management's official announcement that they comprised the military limit: 10,000. The bowl's peacetime capacity is 20,000.

They giggled and chatted impatiently through 45 minutes of Moussorgsky, Rimsky-Korsakoff and Straus, rendered by the orchestra under the baton of Vladimir [sic] Bakaleinikoff, while waiting for Sinatra to complete a broadcast elsewhere.

Whisked to the bowl shortly after 10 p. m., Sinatra's appearance was greeted by a chorus of sighs and moans that eddied and surged almost unceasingly thereafter, reaching wailing wall proportions with "Night and Day."

This, ("My favorite song of all time," says Sinatra) was the real auricular tailspin of the evening. Plaintive sobs, gasps and gurlings [sic] reverberated from hills to shell and back again. Frankie was sending solid. He even had to admonish them: "Girls, girls! please!"
— The Daily Oklahoman

Lena snickered when her father told her about how some of the members at the Club, crowding around the Bar in the Clouds, groused about Frank Sinatra's upcoming appearance at the Hollywood Bowl. "The Hollywood Bowl is a beautiful garden oasis for beautiful music, not a greasy nightclub for goombahs," said one old-line banker who was definitely not affiliated with Bank of America, Martini in hand. "First, 'concert rationing'—now this!" The Bowl, required to keep its public crowds below ten thousand under the orders of the Harbor Defenses of Los Angeles and the 3rd Coast Artillery, had resorted to rotating its subscribers through its summer evening programs, and it was losing money. While our boys were busy subduing the Axis in North Africa and pushing in from Sicily to topple the Fascists in Rome, the inconvenience was too much for some folks in the champagne and symphony crowd, especially among some Hiram-Johnsonites who didn't think we should be in Europe to begin with, left especially peeved and rudderless now as Johnson himself lay in his hospital bed following a stroke that the papers called pneumonia. And now, on top of everything else, they were putting a crooner on our stage! An Italian crooner! Where the grousers saw calamity, though, Joe saw an opportunity to be a big hero to his daughter, and he began to whisper into the ears of his customer and friend, the attorney Mr. Sprague, to see if he could ask around about some tickets.

"I have four tickets in a box near the stage," Joe announced proudly one Sunday evening. "One for you, one for me, and one and one for two of your leedle girlfriends." "Oh, boy, oh, boy, oh, boy!" shrieked Lena as she hopped around the kitchen in her stocking feet. Little Joey was unimpressed. "That skinny guy? My friend Beano could prolly break his arm off in a wrestling match." "Jealous, jealous, jealous," Lena sang, "my kid brother's jealous, goody-goody-goody!" "Alright, sh-sh-shh, m'hija," chimed in Anna. "Time for you to jump into your bedroom and put on your pajamas. Vámanos, come on, Junior. Tonight ees a school night."

"But *Mo-oo-oo-m*," Lena whined, "I have to call Marie and Madeline to tell them the news!" "It can wait 'til tomorrow — bedtime, little girl!" "*Awwww*," Lena wailed as she and her kid brother boing and boinged down the hallway like unmanned pogo sticks. Anna kissed the top of Joe's head as he sat at the kitchen table with the newspaper. "She won't sleep all week," Anna said, her green eyes twinkling.

On Saturday night Joe drove them to the Bowl, the three 13 year-old girls — wearing red sweaters and white-collared blouses, wool skirts, patent leather shoes and, of course, bobby sox--lounging in the ample backseat of his Cadillac. Lena put her hair up stylishly, and the girls indulged each other applying makeup smuggled from Anna's dressing table, to which Anna had turned a blind eye. Marie brought a portable RCA Victor radio, and as the Philharmonic played "Pictures at an

Exhibition," they sipped sparkling apple cider from little coupe glasses under the electric summer sky and listened to Frankie on the radio, volume on low. Then there came the moment, like a thunderbolt from out of the heavens, and Frank had an other-worldly glow about him as he walked into the spotlight in his white dinner jacket, singing, *"Looking for the light of a new love ..."* Marie squealed, "Oh, Frankie!" at least twice, which made Joe squirm in his seat a little. But Lena opened her mouth and nothing came out; he had taken her breath away, and she sat there frozen, staring, with the fingers of both her little hands fumbling at the neck of her red sweater, her wide eyes shining.

As the last number, his current chart-climber "All or Nothing at All," was winding to its finish, Joe was bobbing around in his seat, trying to catch the eye of a PR man he knew from the Club whom he had spied in the wings; and having received the pre-arranged signal, he reached down and grabbed Lena's wrist. "Hold hands, girls — don't let go, follow me." With the shrieks and applause arising from the hillside behind them, Joe led them down around the orchestra pit, through an explanation shouted into the ear of a security officer and into a corridor behind the stage where, amid a dozen and a half or so bobby-sox-wearing "'teen'agers" accompanied by their necktie-wearing father-chauffeurs. Twenty minutes or so went by, and then Frankie came in for a brief appearance on the way to his awaiting car. "We love you, Frankie!" screamed one of the myriad. "Aw, and I love you, too, girls," he said, throwing them a smile and a wink. "Thank you so much for being here." And afterwards, once she got her voice back, Lena said that *he looked right at her.*

There weren't too many fathers of daughters at Kern Avenue Junior High School who knew how to get tickets for the one-night-only Frank Sinatra concert at the Hollywood Bowl in the summer of 1943. In fact, Lena's father might have been the only one. In any event, having been there to see him, getting a taste of the heady airspace of the foremost and the utmost, that August night seasoned Lena's worldliness as she entered James A. Garfield High School. She and her girlfriends, Madeline and Marie, looked at the world around them through a different lens. Naïve though they were about so many things — boys included — they knew a paradise of glamour and beauty, and they knew that it was somewhere not too far away from where they lived. It sparkled under the Hollywood moonlight, like sparkling apple cider in coupe glasses.

"I love my daddy," Lena wrote in her diary that night.

 **"W**hat Next, Corporal Hargrove?"* will be shone on October 3 in the Auditorium, just before the Football pep dance, admission only 19 cents. Come see the picture and support our student body fund!*
— The Garfield Log

The Red Cross Training Courses for girls kicked off last Friday. Alice Harpunian, Mary Francis Hohlmberg, Rita Teresa Gonzalez and Marie Garabedian, who received their first aid certificates last semester, were back to begin the home nursing training course, and over a dozen girls were there starting their course in nutrition. Many girls have taken these courses over the last couple of years as active preparation for Red Cross work.
— The Garfield Log

June Beaudine played the gracious hostess to forty Garfieldians at a party in the patio of her home Satruday. Her royal highness's older brother Albert went all out and decorated the patio with crimson and blue paper streamers, which attractively showed the Beaudine's high school spirit. The boys and girls were served buffet style, out of doors, a menu of sandwiches, potato chips, salad, and punch. A real party, though, is never complete without dancing, and in this field Henry (the new boy from Roosevelt) proved to be quite a jitterbug with his partner Lena Martin.
— The Garfield Log

Unlike in previous years, Garfield students will not be called upon this semester to build model airplanes for the navy. Last semester, the woodshop boys of periods four and six built forty models of fifteen different planes that were packed up in crates of six for shipping.
— *The Garfield Log*

Pat Nunes's brother Joaquin, a former Bullpup "B" letter-man, is now with the para-troops in South Carolina. Joaquin was on a radio broadcast recently telling about what it is like to jump from a plane. "A guy gets scared every time he jumps, he never gets over his nerves," he said. Now that General MacArthur is the boss of Japan, Pat says he's hoping to see his brother again soon. We all wish Joaquin the best of luck.
— *The Garfield Log*

Any girl can be attractive if she will pay attention to what makes people look twice: a neat, well-groomed girl, clean from the top of her shinny hair to her pollished shoes. A few of the girls from each grade who present attractive illustrations of neatness and grooming are Joy Bettles, Raelene Pavletich, Lena Martin, Glenda Dorado, Marie Simmons, Helen Mencken and Mary Jo Nostromo. ... Last week, Lena Martin presented a picture of fashion and neatness at the Viceroys's Mid-Autumn Mixer, looking charming in a yellow cap sleeve dress.
— *The Garfield Log*

Bench Machine Shop for Girls, I and II, is being offered once again, subject to adequate student enrollment. Course features filing and burring, bench drill operation, tapping and threading, and decimal equivalents. Vice Principal Skoner says that if not enough girls sign up, he might entertain the case of a girl possibly joining the boy's Bench Machine class, but no promises.
— *The Garfield Log*

Garfield's Dream Girl

Hair	*Raelene Pavletich*
Nose	*Jackie Rogoff*
Mouth	*Catherine Avedissian*
Smile	*Babs Spooner*
Teeth	*Beverly Bogdan*
Personality	*Alice Manookian*
Talent	*Yvette Plonk*
Athlete	*Betty Handel*
Intelligence	*Frances Mortshaw*
Sweetness	*Lena Martin*
Shyness	*Elsa Lopez*
Dimples	*Janet Hernandez*
Giggles	*Mary Ann Banicki*

— The Garfield Log

Sad news that death came to a Garfieldian on the island of Mindanao in the Philippines over the summer. Private FC Oscar Naranja of the 1st Battalion, 24th Division apparently got caught in a gunfight with the Japs in the jungle near Sarangani Bay. Hirohito's surrender came too late for him, though. He was considered "missing in action" until August, when his family received confirmation that he had died in the fight. Always smiling, Oscar was a member of the Squires and the Garfield Print Shop. We mourn the death of PFC Oscar Naranja and are proud to say he was a Garfield man.

— The Garfield Log

The just-so world of Lena Martin was defined on most days by the western sidewalk of South Woods Avenue, between 4th Street and 6th — her house at one end, and Garfield High at the other. Increasingly, it included the tidy, green-lawned, little stucco homes of her girlfriends, scattered within blocks of South Woods Avenue in and around Belvedere Gardens. On special occasions, such as at Christmastime, it encompassed the windows of the department stores on the Miracle Mile — Bullocks Wilshire, The Broadway, Desmond's, Coulter's, the May Company. And on Saturdays and during weekdays in the summer, it extended down to Whittier Boulevard, to the Golden Gate, the Boulevard, the Royale or the United Artists Theatre. Of course, that's where Lena's world really opened up, unfolding like a paper fortune teller to reveal plantation homes in the Antebellum South, sophisticated nightclubs and hotel lobbies in present-day Manhattan, elegant staterooms of transatlantic ocean liners and romantic dining cars on the Orient Express, Swiss chalets and Scottish castles, and mysterious little cafes in Istanbul and Budapest.

Her people, the characters who lived inside the territorial limits of her 'teen'age cloisters, were all beautiful, from her impeccably dressed and coiffed Mom and Dad, to Madeline and Marie and her other initiated girlfriends in their smart little dresses and hair-bows, to the fresh-faced stars who inhabited her carefully curated scrapbooks in bold, super-human, magazine-page color — Tyrone Power, Betty Grable, Judy Garland, Dana Andrews, Gene Tierney, Dorothy Lamour, Frank Sinatra and Gene Kelly ...

During an era of black and white movies, it was color, though, vibrant color, that ignited her childhood imaginings, whether it was in a movie magazine or one of her mother's dresses, and it lured her along to acquire colored pencils which she used to create her own colorful Hollywood at home. Inserting herself into her mother's daily habits, her sewing and her fashion eye, Lena began dreaming up and sketching out elegant fashions, fanciful and colorful costumes for her favorite pink-skinned stars. She styled herself as "Lena of Hollywood," after the Montana dressmaker "Irene of Hollywood" who dressed Ginger Rogers and Carole Lombard and now, as Lena was about to enter her sixteenth year, she was designing the pristine-white, silvery-satin-flesh-baring ensembles of platinum blonde Lana Turner for the upcoming movie *The Postman Always Rings Twice*—oh my, and you thought there wasn't any color in those black-and-white movies. Be that as it may, when Lena looked in the mirror, most mornings before school, "Lena of Hollywood" was who was staring back at her.

Her schoolmates knew less about "Lena of Hollywood," and more about Lena's earnest openness, her big smile, greeting everyone — objectively, the biggest smile in the room. In Lena's just-so world, everyone was part of the social universe — hey, *the gang's all here!*— even if some people came from another neighborhood, or didn't dress as well, was more or less smart in school, more or less charming. Everyone had a role to play, in Lena's universe, just as the MGM or Warner Brothers movie character actors and actresses could all be identified and classified by their quirks — their accents, their unusual laughter, their funny walks and their funny-shaped bodies — they were not to be shunned or ignored, but celebrated as part of the cavalcade of Hollywood, or Garfield High in Lena's case. "*Why do you talk to her?*" she would sometimes be asked by a snooty classmate about a Garfield High bit player; "oh, I think she's very nice," would be her answer, because everyone was nice, everyone was *part of the gang* — unless they proved themselves to be unreliable.

"*Why do you talk to him?*" might have been an appropriate question, in fact, after her first encounter with a quiet, muscly, dark-skinned boy with a great pelt of unkempt hair (a kind of frontiersman's pompadour, a coonskin cap without the coonskin) on top of his head, who always wore a white T-shirt and jeans with rolled-up cuffs. Billy Baumiller sat behind Lena in Mrs. Frigg's homeroom class, and the sight of this wild beast-boy piqued her curiosity. Summoning up the courage that most other girls could not, because a wild beast-boy could play no role in the conventional worlds of most other girls that wasn't malevolent or in any event scary, Lena turned around to ask him if he had a pencil she could borrow. "Oh, sure," Billy said in a gentle, uplifted voice, because he always had pencils, and he carefully handed her a sharp one with an unused eraser tip.

Lena's friend Marie, that day's putative asker of the "*why talk to him?*" question, sat by and watched as Lena accepted the wild beast-boy's gift with a giant smile, objectively, the biggest smile in the room. Marie looked at her friend with a knowing smirk, until the moment passed on sufficiently for Lena to lean over and safely whisper to Marie, "He's *cuuute.*"

Lena and Billy developed a kind of kinship, a kind of walking and talking camaraderie, as he frequently ended the day walking her from the School, from one end of South Woods Avenue, to her home, at the other end. She would never admit that these were *dates* — flashy, chatty boys like Oren Flunger and Lee Tartshoogian were always lining up to take her to a dance, or to a movie — but she was intrigued enough to let Billy walk her home like this, just the same. And he wasn't like a lot of the other boys, who talked about the automobile they wanted to buy, or how important their fathers were, or how Principal Stack was such a dope. Billy just asked questions. Lena did most of the talking.

"They finally changed the window display at Bullocks Wilshire last weekend," says Lena, as they walk. "They took out the swimsuits and the sand and palm trees and they put in a fox hunting display, you know, with beautiful autumn leaves and mannequins wearing white breeches and riding boots? It's very classy, very tasteful. I don't think I've ever heard of anyone in California going on a fox hunt, though, you know? I wonder if we have foxes here. I know we have mountain lions. Did you hear about the young couple picnicking in Griffith Park who were attacked by a mountain lion? Well, I mean, I don't think they were actually attacked, they were enjoying their picnic when all of a sudden this lion comes up to them. Can you imagine that? That's really scary to me. I think mountain lions are a lot scarier than foxes, in fact. I suppose if we didn't have fox hunts here, we could have lion hunts. I mean, why not, right?"

"You'd like to go on a lion hunt?"

"Me? No, no, no — ha-ha — I'm too scared of lions. But if they were wearing those costumes, with the boots and the white breeches, I certainly do like the way they look. You, you're big and strong, though, you'd probably be really good in a lion hunt. I mean, well, you wouldn't have to wrestle one, probably, but if one happened to attack you, you know ..."

As she walks and talks, she sizes up the quiet wild beast-boy, and she knows and understands his type. Not too long ago, but like a century ago, back when Lena was just nine years old, *Wuthering Heights* came out, and people told her she looked a little like the actress who played Cathy, Merle Oberon — which is interesting, if not only interesting but true enough, because Merle Oberon's press clippings were always filled with vague mish-mosh about her being from Tasmania, or perhaps from India. True enough, though, because Lena's face was a similar teardrop-shape, with a high forehead and deep, dark, slightly slanty eyes. Anyway, before she became "Lena of Hollywood," Lena could squint in the mirror and see herself as Merle Oberon, a floating spirit haunting the moors, calling after Heathcliff, who was played by Laurence Olivier, a British actor who was made up to look swarthy and wild. This Bill Baumiller was a perfect Heathcliff — rough-edged, alone, a little lost — thought Lena — and not nearly as disagreeable as the onscreen Heathcliff.

Her walking and talking friendship with Heathcliff — Billy, rather — had been going on for a couple of months when her little brother Joey spilled the beans at home. "Lena's got a boy-friend!," sang Joey one afternoon after getting in trouble for hiding some of his soiled clothes under his bed. Anna was in mid-scold, a clutch of wrinkled laundry in her hands, when Lena waltzed in from her walk home from school, did a dancey little turn in their entry hall and dropped her books on a living room chair. Seeing an opportunity to interrupt his mother's ire and to take some of the sunshine out of Little Miss Sunny-Days, thereby silencing two birds with one expertly-slung shot, Joey started singing. "Lena's got a boy-friend!"

"A boy-friend?," asked Anna, right on cue. "Who ees this boy?"

" — His name is Jungle Jim," said Joey, "and he's a *monkey!*"

"*Mooo-oooom!*," Lena whined. "He's a boy and he's my friend, but he's not my *boy-friend!*"

"No entiendo, m'hija — your boy-friend ees a *monkey?*"

" — His name is Jungle Jim," Joey continued, "and every day during fourth period he goes out to the high-bar and puts on a show, swinging this way and that way, with one arm and then with two arms, then doing handstands on top of the bar, and *everybody* comes out to watch him ..."

"*Stop it, Junior! Mooooo-ooooom!*"

"Increíble," said Anna, shuddering. "Why he isn't in class?"

Joey was always trying to drop the dime on his perfect little sisterette, seeing it as his duty, no less. A couple of years before, it was Joey's unveiling of Lena's fashion sketches that first brought the topic of the "drape suit" (also known as a "zoot suit") home to South Woods Avenue. Not that Lena identified with any of the young Mexican men and women who sported the duds around Belvedere Gardens (after all, she wasn't a *Mex*-ican, couldn't be, they'd always told her she wasn't one), nor was it a case of consciously acknowledging what was on the beam, because poor Chicanos wearing funny hats was definitely not beamy. Perhaps it was a combination of the constructed drape suits of Joan Crawford, the *Wizard of Oz*, and Cab Calloway that got to her, who knows? But when a few drawings of young women in wide-brimmed hats, high-waisted, snug-cuffed slacks and long, high-waisted coats with peak lapels — her models' hands confidently resting on their hips, elbows akimbo like in the Wonder Woman comic book — showed up in her stack of sketches, quite good ones actually, Anna and Joey both immediately read them as zoot suits. Junior, as usual, piped up first: "Hey, Ma — look at Lena's fashion pick-chers! She gonna make suits for the 38th Street boys now?" Anna saw the pattern immediately in her head. "*Ohhh, nooo, m'hija, nooo,*" she said. "The War, *m'hijita,*" she explained, "eet is too much, too much cloth. The rationing ..." There was a War on, and it was unpatriotic to use so much material on one silly suit of clothing, or so everyone said, and it was good cover for what they really meant. When it suddenly dawned on Lena that she had been drawing *Chicana* clothes, amid Joey's unrelenting teasing, she grew embarrassed and retreated to her room. She was going to have to re-think a little about the future movie fashion design career of the famous Lena of Hollywood.

Looking up from his newspaper, Joe caught only the slightest wind of the South Woods Avenue zoot suit controversy burbling around him. Rationing, though, was a familiar enough topic in the Martin household at the time, with Anna counting stamps and working out compromised menus based on her blue and red points; and Rationing was certainly something that even encroached upon the war-less calm of the Club during the War. One of the Club's earliest casualties after Pearl Harbor was the good old American Martini. As with all the best practitioners of his art, in that day, the Martini was, first of all, a gin concoction (vodka was a most uncommon and somewhat unwelcome item of the bartender's inventory) and it contained some palpable ratio of dry French vermouth in its mixture — not a misting, or a mere adjacency, as is today's fashion, but some parts vermouth to some parts gin, all-in. Some of the better known barmen up the coast would insist that 5-to-1, gin-to-vermouth, was the best formula; others declared that the best Martinis had an 8-to-1 ratio. Unless prompted otherwise by an over-drinking thinker (thinking-drinker, drunking-thunker) at the Bar in the Clouds, Joe tended to stick to the calculation of one of the best barmen of the East that a 7-to-1 ratio brought the perfect dulling of the razory edges, a perfect fog descending to blur the sharp points and angles of a moonlit dip in a shimmering gin lagoon. Thus, when the vermouth in the Club's cellar ran out, Joe was forced to improvise. Ultimately he turned to a domestic sautern, at the tip of the tongue a slightly sweet white wine whose underlying body could drive to bitterness, backing off to a 9-to-1 ratio; and, *voila*, Joe's not-so World Famous Wine Martini, a Club feature as patriotic as a victory garden, was born. "Call 'em Victory Martinis," said square-as-a-ham-sandwich Earl Warren, now Governor-elect Warren, because he could not help himself. Ah, to be a lazy olive, floating in a shimmering gin lagoon ...

But zoot suits were also dancing through Joe's discomforted mind in those days. Driving through the streets of East L.A. in his Cadillac, a world apart from the Mexican kids he'd pass on streetcorners, wearing their jive attire, fingertips barely visible at the ends of oversized sleeves; he wanted to stop and tell them, warn them — *Why you need to show off? Why you not hide somewhere, not stand around in plain sight like dummies? Better you only come out late at night. Don't you know they're coming for you? Why you try so hard to be Mexicans?*

Not long after the commotion surrounding Lena's zoot suit sketches subsided in his own household, Joe found himself at work one day being informed by the Club manager that they had arranged to have him stay for the night in one of the Club's suites, Joe and his staff. "You fellas all live in East L.A., on the other side of the 'enemy' lines," explained the manager. They were now on day three of the disturbances: huge bands of sailors from Terminal Island, marching into central Downtown and East L.A. with bludgeons, yanking zooters down onto the sidewalks by their collars and then kicking and beating them bloody. Joe's busboy, little Manny, said his sister's kid, Jaime, was with his *muchachos* near Ford and East Fifth Street, minding his own *beeswax*, when a bunch of sailors jumped on him, pantsed him and then pissed all over him. Did the same to two of his buddies and a third one got away, ran to a patrolman, who cuffed him and sent him to the station. Manny said they needed him at home so he wasn't going to stay; neither would Felipe, who lived north of Downtown. "Manny," said Joe, "maybe not to wear the dinner jacket when you go?" Or maybe he should; the Club had changed the uniform just before the war and made lapels narrower. "I dunno. You got a sailor hat, *muchacho*?" Ford Boulevard and Fifth, *jeesus*, that was close enough to home that it got Joe's attention. "Call your wives and tell them to stay in, keep the children in, and lock the doors," said the manager. "And if any of your older children are tempted to wear any unusual outergarments and go loitering on the corner, better tell them to wait until after the Navy ships out. Chief Horrall's got an army of patrolmen out rounding up all those *Chicano gang members*."

"*Gang members*?" asked Joe.

"Yeah, those kids with the *snoot* costumes, or whatever they call them. Them clown suits, you know ..."

Joe called Anna and told her to stay inside. "Don't go to the movies," he said. Up in the Bar in the Clouds, there was casual talk being thrown around by the corporate drinkers over Victory Martinis and Bourbon Highballs. "Damned shame," said one. "We've let these Mexicans settle in too comfortably, and now look at them." "Somebody ought to shoot 'em if they're not going to throw 'em back over the border, right?"

"Did you read Ainsworth in the *Times* today?" said someone's corporate veepee. "He says fashions for young men around Firestone Boulevard are changing "*very rapidly*." He says anybody caught with strange-looking pants '*would rather be found dead, as maybe he will be*'!"

The men yukked. Joe could feel the sweat starting to bead up on the back of his neck. "Say, uh, Joe," said one of them, inevitably turning his mischievous attention to the man behind the bar. "You're a Mexican, aren't you?"

"No," interrupted another. "He ain't like one of them. He's a good Mexican."

"Is there any such a thing?"

"He's a good one — aren't ya, Joe?"

Joe was wiping down a particular area of the bar for the second or third time, not knowing exactly where to look. Finally, he looked up and tried flashing a smile at them. "*Espanish*," he said at length, his prodigious baritone rising from his diaphram. "I am *Espanish*, not Mexican." It seemed to satisfy most of them — either they had already had too much to drink and weren't thinking clearly enough to question him, or they were afraid to pipe-up and sound unsophisticated, like maybe they were supposed to know it meant, to be *"Espanish."* It was just ambiguous enough to catch people in their tracks.

"You shouldn't worry about those fat-heads," said the attorney Mr. Sprague to Joe once the place thinned out a bit. "You've got more going for you in your pinkie finger, Joe, than any of those stiffs has got all-told. In fact, most of them wouldn't be recognized by their own children if it weren't for their tie tacks and money clips." The attorney Mr. Sprague had made that sentiment living and real by getting Joe those tickets to see the crooner at the Hollywood Bowl; despite his accent and his south-of-the-border brow-line, he was entitled to be there, entitled to treat his beautiful daughter and her little friends to a paradise under the stars.

Meanwhile there was a War on and the old shenanigans — that which was the stuff of Joe's legend, his after-hours reputation — they were also subject to Rationing. With active military personnel, intelligence officers, federal handlers roaming the L.A. streets in and out of street clothes, even the crooked police were falling into line, at least on certain grey nights when attentions could be wrenched away from imminent Japanese invasions of the Southland coast. Governor Warren, in the months following the zoot suit beatings back in '43, would as much as admit that white hatred of Mexicans was a root cause of all the violence, that it was not simply the aftermath to the infamous "Sleepy Lagoon Murder"; and as it was, Joe was driving around the City with white knuckles, hunched over the steering wheel of his Cadillac, searching the sky for Japanese bombers, and living in abject fear of being arrested for driving with an accent. That's right, living in fear that he would be pulled over in his Cadillac and rousted out of the driver's seat by a cranky copper too old to be enlisted as a soldier-hero, rousted out to stand along the side of a dark road in his smart silk suit and tie, rousted to be strung up like a roasted Chicano on a spit as soon as he would open his mouth, his zacatecan, cali-mexo-spanglish, tumbling from his lips. A flashlight, a billy club, a tire iron — he imagined at any moment that he could feel one or any of them landing across his brow, extinguishing what was left of light and sense.

Joe couldn't get it out of his mind, reading about the unexplained death of José Gallardo Díaz, his head bashed in, his mostly-dead body found near a reservoir off Slauson, just near the river. In between the lines of the "Sleepy Lagoon Murder" newspaper articles he could see himself as a teen-aged bull, *el corte de vacuno más preciado*, swimming with his *muchachos* in a similar reservoir near the river. Ah, to be a lazy olive ... he remembered the names of the defendants in the sham trial that followed—Melendez, Padilla, Delgado, Reyes, and so on—and thought of them as names from his own childhood, and he could not take his eyes away the horrifying accounts of how these poor young men were being forced to stand up in court, stand there on display as the expert in the witness chair insisted that Mexicans had a "blood-thirst," and that they were born killers. Joe Martin, the "Espanish" fellow who secretly clipped newspaper articles about local Mexican boys and their heroics in the War and kept them in a plain grey envelope in his sock and underwear drawer, remembered the sting of reading that.

Joe was in fact pulled over one night, accused by a patrolman of weaving to and fro along Whittier Boulevard on his way home from a slightly later night at the Club. When he got to the station, it was only a half hour or so before his friend, the attorney Mr. Sprague, showed up and soon all was well with the captain of the night watch. Once the name of the Club was uttered, it was clear that the Club carried much heft with the loyal men in blue. Picking up Joe was all a big misunderstanding, "no worries, Captain." "It's alright, Joe, don't give it another thought," said the attorney Mr. Sprague. "We all stumble now and then," and he told him how badly his law partner, the attorney Mr. Goode, had stumbled as a younger man, and how he had bounced back and recovered. No one was the wiser, not even Anna, that Joe had been picked up that evening.

On those rare evenings during the War, though, when a few giddy customers, jolly-boys from the Bar in the Clouds, would get the better of him and he would find himself unable to resist an after-hours escapade, it gave him some sense of security if the attorney Mr. Sprague or his law partner, the attorney Mr. Goode, would ride shotgun. Because if there was anything that could save an uppity Chicano from being arrested for driving a Cadillac with an accent, it would be to have his mouthpiece along to do the talking.

Unfortunately, now, with the War on, the quality of after-hours diversions to be had around town had fallen off greatly; they were a lot less grand than they were, back in the day, back when Mr. Mack jauntily led the way into West Hollywood, back when the pursuit of a little illicit nocturnal pleasure had a sort of champagne innocence about it, even if the activities were nonetheless thoroughly wicked and degenerate. Now, there was dope everywhere, which Joe avoided like the plague; there was plenty of cheap gin and cheap whiskey, and plenty of five-dollar party girls who pretended they were dancers, thick-waisted girls from back East who never got discovered by the studios, some who scored bit parts as hat check girls on screen, shouting, already drunk or stoned by the time they stumbled upon you, croaking in unfiltered cigarette voices about what they would do for a twenty, what they would do for a twenty and a ten ... it was all Joe could do on some evenings not to simply drink and drink until he couldn't hear it anymore, drink until the scene became a strobing flicker of patterns and indistinct noise. And the winged-attorney Mr. Sprague, hovering over Joe as his guardian angel, would somehow see that he'd get home safely, somehow whisking him right past Anna at her listening post on the divan, tucking him in, kissing him on the forehead, and reminding him again that he had more going for him in his pinky finger than all those fat-headed veepees at the Club. Now Joe and his famous pinky-finger, now they are swaddled in his king-sized bed, alone, now in repose after a longish California autumn evening, after yet another late night, after-hours jag, his sleep however seized with the idea that malevolent personalities are operating through him, battling each other — one making social arrangements, announcing the evening's upcoming events like a carnival barker, *step right up, muchachos!*, the other recounting what actually happens during the evening — the barker getting pulled out of Joe's sinus cavities in the form of loud, self-awakening snorts and bubbly exhalations, the truth-teller coming up as cocktails and late-night snacks, the pungent taste of them surging up into his throat or through his nose at half-past four in the morning, leaving a horrible, acrid smack in his goopy dry mouth. The truth-teller takes him by the wrist and forearm and pulls him, against his will, to that reservoir off Slauson, that Sleepy Lagoon, and Joe is there looking down; but instead of looking down and seeing José Gallardo Díaz lying dead on the shore, he sees young Fernando Martín, *el corte de vacuno más preciado, un corte de carne ahora gris y malcriado.*[12] Dead beef in the gutter, good to no one.

In the morning, with one eye half-opened, looking around, he confirms that his guardian angel has abandoned him. The barker and the truth-teller are long gone, too. His temples seething with pain, like someone has drilled holes in them, and with a sour taste in his nose and throat, he falls out of his bed and marches on his knees to the cold porcelain toilet bowl and whimpers as he unburdens himself of the contents of his sorry sour stomach, twice, three times before cough-wrenching from his gut, rocking back on his haunches on the linoleum in his boxer shorts and sleeveless undershirt; he then picks that moment, that moment, to drag his own dead carcass, dead beef from the gutter, to drag it down the hallway, calling after Anna in a vomit-ravaged voice, "Ho-*ney?*", fumbling into the entry way of the house just in time to find Lena and Madeline preparing to leave for school, just in time to black out from shame, to pass out on the floor before them.

"I hate my daddy," Lena wrote in her diary that night.

---

12   The most precious cut of beef, now a cut of beef that is grey and spoiled.

3.5
FOURTH STREET, EAST LOS ANGELES, SEPTEMBER 1946

Although Billy wasn't home much to see it, Floyd Baumiller was in the middle of some kind of a freefall.

Over a course of years, it had begun to seem that each morning as the roosters in the backyard crowed and the sun rose on the Baumiller homestead on Fourth Street, there was hillbilly music on the radio, and there was fresh eggs and barefooted contentment for all in Alpha's kitchen — in spite of their lack of where-withal, in spite of the malevolent dark murmur of Los Angeles, the chorus of crazed city-fiends that threatened to envelope their weedy little Podunk neighborhood, in spite of all that they had endured. In all, it seemed to shape up just fine, over a course of years. Of course, poor pretty Dorothy was sick in the head, and so was Johnny. Baby Angie was now old enough to walk by herself to school, wearing the older girls' hand-me-downs but on most days preferring an old pair of dungarees with the cuffs rolled up, as she doodled pictures of horses in her composition books. Ted was in the Army, the 504th Parachute Infantry Regiment, at 5'-11-1/2" "just short enough" to get in and get himself dropped right onto the beachhead at Anzio in the middle of the night, right onto a flaming "T" in the sand of the beach. They would later hear how he hid himself in a bomb crater after he landed, throwing grenades and shooting at every sound he heard, but in the government telegram they received from his hospital bed in Capua, they made him sound like he was the second coming of Stonewall Jackson in-the-flesh. The older girls were all headed toward their first divorces just about then — but, you know, again, it all seemed to shape up just fine.

Billy's world, the one of his own making, was also a sure-enough, good-enough world. He had spent the summer working as a mail carrier for the Post Office, and in his humble and unassuming way he managed to raise the bar for productivity, to the point that a few of the older mail carriers had to take him aside and let him know that he was making them look bad. He dutifully brought his meager wages back to the homestead and dumped them into the pot, to be used by the family for anything the family needed, save for a few nickels here and there that he would squirrel away for a day with the cliffhangers — Buster Crabbe and Gene Autry and Red Ryder and the Westerns he particularly liked that featured the daring cowboy stuntman, Yakima Canutt — or for a Superman or Captain America comic book. Floyd was certainly sorry to see the boy's summer income disappear, and to hear that he turned down full-time work as a mail carrier to return to high school. Billy had friends, too: from his grammar school years, a motley collection of a few little Mexican boys who were always getting pushed around by thick-necked white bully-punks when Billy wasn't there to moderate their aggression with a combination of body language and diplomatic skills; from down the street, Sidney, the Japanese kid, whose older sisters used to put on puppet shows in their garage, and Paulie, the Greek; a coupla high-spirited, skinny Okies, Wilmer and Jay, whose propensity for five-and-dime larceny and junior varsity vandalism was happily tempered by Billy's indifference to such high jinks ... Billy and all his buddies were going to Garfield, instead of Roosevelt High where Ted and Dorothy Theodora went; all except for Sidney, who got rounded up with the rest of the Japanese families after Pearl Harbor and got sent to the desert. Billy was there to say goodbye when Sidney cleaned out his locker ...

But Billy also enjoyed his solitude, the solitude that was his natural dwelling place, his silk cocoon, within the walls of the house of Fourth Street and in its backyard barnyard. Solitude was where his three-dimensional imagination took flight — literally, when it came to building models of airplanes. Not being able to afford the wooden model kits that were sold in shops on Broadway, he used what he had at hand — initially, homestead mud from the backyard, carefully hand-shaped by the boy into uncanny miniatures of Douglas A-20 "Havocs," B-17 "Flying Fortresses," German Heinkel fighters and the like, based on newspaper photos, Coca-Cola trading cards, salvaged editions of

The Aeroplane Spotter journal, the wet models then placed on the iron grate in the family fireplace for quickfire hardening. More than once Floyd carelessly scooped out one of Billy's mud models and threw it away with the fireplace ashes. Billy learned that he had better keep a close watch on his makeshift kiln. Later, though, he switched to carving his models out of soft wood, a much more stable material, and not as vulnerable to Floyd's no-nonsense home maintenance habits. When they were finished, Billy would hang them from the ceiling in his and Johnny's room, with tacks and wire and string and whatever else worked. Although Johnny would normally wreck anything fragile, just as a matter of blind and blissful instinct, Billy calmed his tendencies toward destruction by telling him stories, night after night, about all the planes shooting this way and that through their shared bedroom sky.

"Maybe he's a smart one," Floyd would say to Alpha, behind closed doors, "or maybe he's not. To be honest, I couldn't tell you either way."

But Floyd was freefalling, as we were saying, with a terminal velocity that most paratroopers, even Ted, would never experience. He felt he was headed fast for his own shallow grave, rather than a bomb crater. And his pounding heart was screaming at him as he descended.

Amid everything shaping up just fine in the Baumiller homestead, there were things that only he knew, or that only he and Alpha knew, that kept him grim-faced and hunched over as he roved from fixing porch floorboards to varnishing fence-posts to changing belts on motor engines, things that followed him to work. First, there was the thing that everyone in the household should have realized but that no one was really paying attention to: that Alpha was slowing down. After eight children, plus two stillborns, you could hardly blame her. But it wasn't just that Alpha was tired; he knew better than anyone else in the house that Alpha was in pain, suffering, and it was women's pain. She would prop herself up better than he knew how to, cooking and washing clothes and looking after the children, but he would see her at the beginning and the end of each day, he would see her doubled-over, wincing, getting worse. His confidence in doctors with degrees on their walls long since exhausted, he wasn't sure what else he could do for her. He was patient and gentle with her, on the outside, and frantic on the inside.

Next on Floyd's list was Dorothy Theodora and the epilepsy. Her bouts were becoming more frequent, taking a greater toll on her sentient hours; easier to control and comfort when she was a child, now that she was a young adult, she was testing the limits of Floyd's physical capacity, already far beyond the limits of Alpha's ability to care for her. With the seizures coming more regularly, Dorothy was now no longer the skinny little girl with the pixie-bowl haircut; she was a beautiful young woman, with legs powered by wide Crullup hips, legs that could kick like mules' legs, kick the teeth out of your mouth. What Floyd knew, what Floyd and Alpha both knew but the other children did not, was that Dorothy would soon be sent away to live somewhere else.

On the appointed Saturday for it, Floyd packed a few of Dorothy's things in a satchel and drove her, alone, to the state mental hospital at Camarillo. He told her they were going somewheres that could help her, and Dorothy didn't protest. Alpha said goodbye from the porch as they pulled away. A couple of hours later they arrived together at the big, beautiful bleached building with a red tiled-roof and a majestic bell tower. Dorothy smiled a little. To Dorothy, it looked like what she'd heard a college should look like; to Floyd, it looked like a Spanish mission, stark white against the pinkish-brown Santa Monica mountains, or maybe like one of those secluded convents in the Alps where the Catholics keep their nuns. It seemed very peaceful, maybe almost eerily quiet, in broad daylight. Their initial excitement melted, though, as they sat down with a nurse to go through the drudgery of the paperwork. Midway through, Floyd thought about Johnny and asked, "How about slow kids? — you take them, too?" "No, sir, I'm afraid that we don't." Floyd thought of Billy for a moment, too, but failed to come up with a question about him before the nurse began to serve up more questions about Dorothy. When they were finished, the nurse picked up Dorothy's satchel as if to weigh it in her hands. "She won't be needing all this," the nurse said, frowning. Floyd gave Dorothy a one-armed squeeze and a kiss on the forehead as they said their goodbyes. Then, while Floyd drove home alone along Highway 101 as the sun went down, back at Camarillo, Dorothy Theodora settled in for a decades-long slumber, inside the walls of her pretend-college. But Floyd wouldn't let himself think of that. He saw no way around what they were doing with Dorothy, unfortunately. *It's just what you have to do*; and while Alpha cried and cried on the idea of it, then more and more on the reality of it, Floyd's sorry ticker screamed louder at him.

Back on the Yellow Cars, another kind of dread confronted him. At the beginning of the previous year, there was a tiny item in the Los Angeles newspapers that the Los Angeles Railway was purchased by a company called National City Lines for fifty million dollars. Floyd greeted the announcement with a mixture of pride and trepidation — pride that his business, his Yellow Dinky, and all the other Yellow Cars, were really worth something, fifty million smackers! They were a credit to the community! On the other hand, thought Floyd and many of his fellow motorman, *what's next?* The rumors about shutdowns began within weeks after that little newspaper article, within weeks after hearing from the brass downtown that we had new bosses. *Why would you pay fifty million dollars for something only to break it apart, to shut it down and kill it?*, Floyd wondered aloud. *Fifty million dollars! Is it possible that a number can be so big that in the end it doesn't mean anything?* Still, folks were saying that the fleet was old and decrepit, and that it was time for a change.

Floyd had long noticed the number of riders on the Dinky was in decline — as the man with the change drawer, he couldn't help but see it with his own eyes — and that this seemed to be coupled with an increase in the number of automobiles on the road. Of course, he couldn't help noticing all that at once. But, now, then: he loved the freedom of automobile ownership as much if not more than the next fellow, but it was irresponsible to think that all the people who rode the Yellow Cars would be able to afford their own jalopies, would be able to take care of them as he did, changing the oil and the filters and gaskets, and making sure the moving parts were sufficiently greased and road-ready. And kids, kids especially, had no sense about anything, including automobiles. Billy and his buddy Wilmer saved up a few dollars and bought, for next to nothing, a really sharp used '32 Ford Club Coupe and drove it around for a few days, whooping it up like mad, until Billy brought it home and parked it in the driveway at Fourth Street. "Consarn-it!," shouted Floyd, "you boys don't know how to take care of a *machine* like this," which happened to be nicer than his '26 Dodge. "Give me the key, Billy!" "Yeah," says William Baumiller, seventy-some years later, "He took the car away from us. Never gave it back."

Floyd looked at automobiles as machines that the very wealthy were privileged to enjoy, unless you were fearless like him and had the time to tinker. Thinking of all those regular folks out there, so few of whom seemed to tolerate getting their hands dirty, not to mention the effect it would have on traffic—it didn't add up to him. How could a city full of automobiles be anyone's sensible choice over the electrified railways of Los Angeles? Then reports started to filter in through the motorman's ranks about an article from a newspaper back East, the article about a retired Naval commander named Quinby who was sending letters to cities across the country, warning them that their streetcar lines were set to be dismantled by new owners coming in to replace them with motorbus lines. This Commander Quinby mentioned National City Lines in particular, and the "oil-rubber-bus combine" whose interests were best served by demolishing the railways: old General Motors, Phillips Petroleum, Firestone Tire and Rubber, and General American Aerocoach. They were the backers behind National City Lines, *and now they owned us. Of course, we already knew that those oil companies were crooked—remember Teapot Dome, remember Julian Petroleum, and how about them Rockefellers?* And he'd heard too much over the years about Alfred P. Sloan sticking his pointy nose into too much of America's business. Corporations, like doctor's diplomas on the wall, *were just pieces of paper after all, and they ought not to get away with so much.* And yet ...

He went on strike with the streetcar operators at the beginning of May. Floyd found himself to be a member of a union again, the A.F. of L., reluctantly, just before the War began, but there were no strikes during the War. Now, they were striking for higher wages, and National City Lines came back all too quickly, *suspiciously quickly* thought Floyd, with an agreement to pay more, so the strike was over in a few weeks. Then, at the end of May, Floyd got the news: line after line of streetcars were going to be shut down, either to be abandoned or replaced with bus routes, effective Sunday, June 30: the West Adams A line, the E line, the G, part of the Jefferson line, and the 10. And shuttles, too: the Edgeware Road Shuttle, the Gage Street Shuttle, and the Indiana Street Shuttle—Floyd's old Dinky. The A.F. of L. and the motormen had been bamboozled. The corporate bosses said, "Sure, we'll pay you more," and then they turned around and got rid of dozens of motormen. Including Floyd. There wasn't any room for the old motormen on the bus routes, they weren't trained for it. Floyd's career was over. Now he was to receive a pension, invited to turn out to pasture.

On Sunday, Floyd bought the newspaper. "You'd think that a man's whole career, his whole life, would be worth a couple of inches in the newspaper," Floyd said to no one, and no one heard. Instead of an obituary for the streetcars, for the Dinky, the pages were crowded with the preparations for the first Atom Bomb test in a lagoon of hobbled warships off Bikini Atoll in the South Pacific. There were photos of the pilot's smiling wife and daughters, the bombardier bragging about how he was going to nail the U.S.S. Nevada, dropping the bomb from 33,000 feet in the air, the fact that they nicknamed the bomb "Gilda" after Rita Hayworth in the movie and decorated it with her picture. That afternoon, Floyd and Alpha tuned in on the radio to hear the test, and the next day they saw the horrific pictures of the mushroom cloud in the newspaper. "Well, right there's your obituary," Floyd said to no one, and no one heard. His world had moved on to bigger things, a way you could murder a hundred thousand people in the blink of an eye; you couldn't any longer hold the peaceful simplicity of an electrified streetcar ride along Indiana Street in the same ambitious thought as a hundred thousand crazy people driving around Los Angeles in their smoking, poorly-looked-after automobiles. Even though the bombardier missed his target, those Yellow Cars might as well have been lying down there with those old warships in that Bikini lagoon that day, too, because the bomb destroyed it all. It destroyed everything small and humble in its path. Los Angeles was through with Floyd Baumiller, and now the Baumillers were through with L.A.

Shortly after the Fall Term began, Billy was sitting in third-period English class, taught by Mrs. Tibbings, a stout little woman who waddled up and down the rows of desks looking, at least to Billy, like the Little King from the cartoons, except without the moustache (mostly). She had given the class a surprise quiz the Friday before, and no one was particularly confident about how they had fared. As she continued her waddling up and down the rows, she held up one of the corrected quizzes from the stack in her hand, high above her little head; and she asked in a big voice, "Guess who scored the highest marks on Friday's quiz?"

The class retorted murmuring, and several students ventured guesses. "Was it *Frances?*" asked one junior girl. "How about *Buzzy?*" asked another. "Was it *me?*" asked Eldon.

Mrs. Tibbings stopped her waddle right in front of Billy's desk in the back of the classroom, where he was quietly putting the finishing hashmarks on a pencil drawing of a P-40 Warhawk on the back of his composition book. "*It was Billy!,*" she exclaimed, hiding none of her own surprise, which was enough to give permission to others in the case to express their own amazement. Billy looked up from his airplane, straightened up a little, smiling and shrugging. "*Oh!,*" he said, not knowing how he should respond. "*Thank you!*" Billy, the kid who wore only white T-shirts and blue jeans, shoes that hardly had any shoe left in 'em, who never seemed to be paying attention to anything ... well, that he was one of the poor kids was undeniable, but the idea that he wasn't paying attention was a common misapprehension.

Mrs. Tibbings's new-found high opinion of Billy's prospects kept him from switching out of her English class so that he could train with Coach Hamnet and the gymnastics team during third period. "Absolutely not, young man," said Mrs. Tibbings. "You have unrealized potential that needs to be cultivated," she said, and she seemed to feel that it was her destiny to lift this poor boy up.

The boy, Billy — he wasn't sure what she was getting at; but that left him with an open fourth period, with nothing to do. With gymnastics on his mind, he headed out to the horizontal bar rising above the sand out near the Boys' Field. There, in his street clothes, he would reach up and jump for the bar, and begin his silent training routine in his natural setting — in solitude. After a few test swings, he would cast-off and do a back-uprise to a kip, firmly holding his arms straight as courthouse columns with his weight slightly forward, his face uplifted toward the midday sun. Then he would do a couple of forward rolls, and, harnessing the momentum of his frame, would roll out into a few giant swings. It was the giant swings that attracted attention from boys coming out of the shop classes into the corridor outside of the "500" building, girls lingering in the quad nearby. The giant swings were slightly mesmerizing, slightly thrilling because one wasn't sure how he would halt his momentum, his V-shaped torso accentuated as he paused, upside-down, at the top of each swing. Early on he was dismounting with a simple somersault, but then he figured out how to do a proper layout. And without too much delay, he would be back on the bar again, trying to push himself further. Anyway, it was a lot safer than jumping off the garage roof with a homemade parachute. Occasionally, he'd hear someone call out, "Atta boy, Billy," or "Oh, yeah, fella — nice going!"

One afternoon a small but respectful crowd had formed nearby to watch Billy on the bars. When the bell rang for lunch period, the doors of the "500" building flew open and the shop classes started to empty out into the quad. Joey Martin and his buddy, Peanut-Butter-and-Jam, nudged their way to the front of the devoted little crew who watched Billy as he did his giant swings. "*Hey! ... Jungle Jim!*" Joey shouted, unleashing giggles and guffaws from the assembled crowd.

And Billy Baumiller thought to himself, mid-giant swing:

> *I had a little monkey*
> *His name was Jungle Jim*
> *I put him in the bathtub*
> *To see if he could swim*
> *He drank up all the water*
> *And he swallowed all the soap*
> *And the next day he died*
> *With bubbles in his throat*

And he kept on swinging.

Swinging through the air, flying through it on the dismount, Billy imagined himself as the living human embodiment of a P-40 Warhawk, gliding and diving through the occasional clouds above Los Angeles. That slightly dizzy feeling, that feeling of inertial pull and push, was the feeling of being free of cares, free of constraints. It was the feeling of being a child in a young man's body, soaring above the mundane Earth. On feet lighter than air he'd finish his walk back to Fourth Street, still feeling that giddy sensation of flight, right up until that moment when along comes the terminally free-falling Floyd, who clothes-lines him, yanking him down hard onto the cracked concrete sidewalk outside the old homestead on Fourth Street.

"Come here, boy," Floyd said. "I need to have a word with you."

The old man got right to the point, right there on the sidewalk. Mother was ill, and so was he, and they needed to get out of L.A. for their health. They were going to sell the old homestead, and he and Mother and Johnny and Angie were all going to move to the desert, "for the good air."

"Now, you," Floyd continued as though he were going through an inventory, "you, boy, are my last problem I got to deal with." The choice that Floyd laid out was simple: either you come with them to the desert and get a job to help support the family — "there's farms and quarries out there, the borax mines and so forth, so you'll easily earn a paycheck" — or, "You're on your own. That's it, there ain't no third choice."

"Do they have high school in the desert?"

"That's none of your account. Child's play is over for you. Now it's time to shape up or ship out."

Floyd told him he'd have a week to think things over. Then, down the street, Paulie the Greek offered up another alternative. "Shape up or ship out is right!" said Paulie. The War was over, but President Truman still hadn't declared it to be over, which basically meant that you were joining the Army during war-time, without so much "War" in it. "C'mon, Billy, let's go get us some of that G.I. Bill." On the whole, it sounded like a good idea to Billy.

The day after he made his decision, Bill Baumiller walked Lena Martin home from school for the last time. "I'm enlisting," he told her.

"In the Army? But the War is over."

"Yeah, but they still need men. No more fighting — just patrols and keeping order, I guess."

"So, are you going to Germany?"

"Sure. Or Japan, maybe, with General MacArthur," he said as he jauntily mock-saluted the General.

The two were quiet for a bit, quieter than they had ever been on one of their walks home, as far as Lena could remember. As they pulled up along the sidewalk opposite her front porch, she pivoted and stood face to face with the boy. Most of their conversations on their walks were side-by-side, but now they were face-to-face.

"When do you leave?"

"Soon. My Dad wants me to quit school early and help them move their house before I go."

"Where are they moving?"

"Palmdale." She had heard of it, but she didn't know where it was. She turned around to face her house, which seemed small to her just then. "Japan — just imagine! You're going to see the world!"

"Join the Army and see the Navy is what I hear," he said with a little smile. Without a beat she reached up and kissed him on the cheek.

And Billy Baumiller looked in her eyes and said softly ... "You have a very pretty house."

"Stay safe, Bill Baumiller," Lena said at length.

"I don't know if I'll ever see you again," she said brightly as she started to bound down the concrete walk to the porch. "But I hope I do," she said, pausing, over her shoulder.

Lena closed the front door behind her and leaned back on it heavily, exhaling deeply. With her eyes closed, her thoughts were flooded with dance parties and pretty dresses, with comfortable Flungers and Tartshoogians and their handsome lettermen sweaters, with corsages, and mortarboard and tassle. Looking around her bedroom, nothing much had changed in her pretty pink bedroom since she was seven years old, when she first discovered Tyrone Power. But by the time her arms and legs could flop onto her little pink bed, she couldn't help thinking of the smudged, fraying edges of the neck on Billy's T-shirt and the thatch of thick dark hairs that stood straight up at the back of his head; and as she tried to focus her mind on an idea of what Japan must be like, all she could come up with were snippets of Hollywood's Japan, jokey Busby Berkeley musical numbers and Bugs Bunny cartoons, and picture-books of world costumes from the school library. None of it satisfied, and now her pretty house seemed very small indeed. Her pretty pink bedroom was small, and for the moment, even her pretty pink heart was too small to hold everything she wanted it to carry at that moment, too small for the feelings that were enveloping her, that she couldn't name.

Meanwhile, as Billy headed back to Fourth Street, he thought to himself ... *I wonder what it's like to live in one of those pretty houses ...*

So Billy Baumiller entered the Army before the family finished packing up the house on Fourth Street, after saying goodbye to his Mom, his Dad, Johnny and Angie. Then he was himself packed up and posted like a Christmas present to Fort Bragg, North Carolina for a few weeks of basic training before being shipped off to Tokyo via the Philippines. With his paychecks going back to Palmdale to help support the family, he busied himself with his military chores. Six months or so after he left, Alpha died. Cancer of the cervix. Ted made it back home, for a moment, just in time to see her before she passed. They buried her in Palmdale, and then Ted lit out again. They told Billy after the fact; there was no question of his returning after she had already been buried, so he just carried on, half a world away.

Then Floyd moved what was left of them — himself, Johnny and Angie — up to the most god-forsaken place he could've come up with, had he been straining to think on it — more deeply scarred than

Hermanas, New Mexico, more wretched than Daggett, out in the Mojave Desert, or Uvalde, Texas — more hopeless, because it was where Old Chief Mulholland stole the water that L.A. needed to douse its corrupt orgy of charlatans, shysters and chorines underneath its oil derricks, palm trees and marquee lights — Floyd moved them to the consarned Owens Valley, to a hidden settlement of cast-offs east of the Sierra Nevadas, northwest of Death Valley, and west of the White Mountains and the Nevada state line. His nose must have caught the existential bitterness of the place in the wind and led him there, for he was drawn to this part of the world as if he were looking for an outward representation of what he felt in his soul.

3.6
SOUTH WOODS AVENUE, EAST LOS ANGELES, CHRISTMAS 1948

Bill Baumiller's time in Japan with the Army — well, that would be enough for another book, perhaps. At the end of it, in February 1948, a Navy transport ship dropped him off unceremoniously in Seattle, Washington with an honorable discharge and a little cash. After a quick trip to Canada with a couple of buddies, consisting of walking around downtown Vancouver for an evening, he got on a southbound train, vaguely heading back in the direction of L.A., but without a definite plan. On a whim, he got off the train at Dunsmuir, somewhere in the Shasta forest of northern California, wondering to himself, *"Is this a good place to live?"* After a couple of hours, first sitting in a diner, then in a park, reading a town "welcome" brochure, he thought better of the whole idea, and climbed onto the next southbound train.

Arriving in L.A., it was good to find familiar sights and sounds and smells after being so far from home. But then again, he didn't have a home, at present. Over a bowl of soup at a joint on Olympic, he thought of his mother, and of Johnny and Dorothy and Angie; and then he started to wonder whatever happened to his airplane models, the ones he had hanging from the boys' bedroom ceiling. He wondered whether anyone had bothered to save them. Or the comic books. Long gone, he mused.

Just then, a fellow he knew from high school, a Russian kid he remembered as "Cherrynose" walked in. "Of all the gin joints in all the world!," said Cherrynose, "if it isn't the *original 'Nature Boy' himself.* Weren't you in Japan?"

And Billy Baumiller thought to himself:

There was a boy, a very strange enchanted boy
They say he wandered very far, very far, over land and sea
A little shy and sad of eye, but very wise was he
And then one day, one magic day he came my way
And while we spoke of many things, fools and kings
This he said to me: "The greatest thing you'll ever learn
Is just to love and be loved in return"

He laughed. "Hi, Cherrynose. How've you been?" They caught up over another bowl of soup, and Cherrynose told him all about the comings and goings of all the Garfield crowd, some of whom Billy remembered well, others he wasn't sure he knew. So-and-so got married, this fellow was in college playing football, one fellow died in a car crash on the Pacific Coast Highway in the middle of the night, another is in a wheelchair after jumping off the Huntington Beach pier. Billy told Cherrynose all about Tokyo: about the Imperial Palace and the Kachidoki Bridge and the Ginza, and the football games and the rifle range, and singing songs and doing handstands on the watchtower.

And Cherrynose said, "So you just got back?"

"Yeah, just now."

"Ain't you seen your people yet?"

"Nah. They all moved away."

"Well, listen, Nature Boy," Cherrynose said, "You're coming with me. You're going to stay with me and my brother until you get your sea-legs. Plenty of jobs around, and all the factories love to put the vets to work."

Staying with Cherrynose and Cherrynose's indifferent older brother (Billy never did get his name) meant staying in the screened-in porch of the first floor apartment in a house on 8th Street, near the dead L.A. river. Everything smelled a little stale, but the couch out there was comfortable enough, Bill liked to listen to the night sounds as he dozed off in the evenings — the crickets, the owls and the occasional train. He slept well out there.

Cherrynose was right — there was no shortage of good jobs. Bill caught on quickly on the factory line at a tire company, then traded up to a plumbing fixture manufacturer, then to a sheet steel manufacturer; and in the process, he soon became aware of special subset of employees who seemed to exist in an exalted space within each of these factories: the machinists in the machine shop. They were tinkerers and troubleshooters, they used their brains, drew meaningful pictures from visions they had in their heads, and they made things with their hands. He started hanging around with these fellows during breaks and after-hours, and eventually he caught on as an apprentice machinist on the graveyard shift at a steel tubing company.

Living as a vampire on the graveyard shift was a piece of cake for Bill Baumiller who, as a serial nap-taker, was able to preserve a good chunk of daylight for jovial wandering. With a few dollars in his pocket and no responsibilities, he was able to spruce up his wardrobe a little; so, on a spring afternoon he was exploring Whittier Boulevard in his weekend best when he suddenly saw, from across the street, Lena Martin herself. There she was, emerging fresh-faced with a couple of girlfriends from a matinee showing of *Secret Beyond the Door* at the Boulevard Theatre, wearing a salmon A-line skirt and a white short-sleeved top. She was quite the picture, and he had to go and say hello.

Lena — now a ripe old eighteen years of age, a Garfield High School graduate — was in the midst of living an awkward year. In olden times, like in an MGM costume picture, she might have been considered to be beyond a seemly marriageable age. A few of her classmates, Marie and Madeline among them, had already snapped up beaux from the senior class; Madeline eloped with hers in Santa Barbara (or was it Oxnard?), and Marie was planning an October wedding. Lena, despite her sunniness, never managed to connect with the Flungers and Tartshoogians of the world — they had all moved on — although she went on plenty of dates. In addition to sending Lena to "business college" (to learn to type and take shorthand), Joe Martin had Lena wrapping gifts at the Club over the holidays, which led to a few dates with self-satisfied college boys, the sons of self-satisfied veepees. Joey, meanwhile, had knocked up a little blonde girl, Trixie, and after a series of bitter lectures from his parents who, unbeknownst to him, had real-life experience with the circumstance, Joey and Trixie did a shotgun hitch; and then Joe, Sr. stopped his lecturing and bought Joey a sensible beige '47 Nash Ambassador as a wedding gift. With no wedding in sight for her, on the other hand, Joe bought Lena a pale yellow 1948 Ford Super Deluxe convertible, which was a most stylish machine and one which ended up thoroughly intimidating many would-be suitors. One of them, a fellow named Hector, asked Lena out with the thought that he might get to drive her Ford, but Lena stayed glued to the wheel throughout the night and dropped Hector off at his parents' house at the conclusion of the date. There would be no second date for Hector.

"Hi, Lena," said Bill, catching her outside the theater. When she turned to look at him, her salmon skirt twirling with her, it was like a cool breeze had suddenly blown through Whittier Boulevard. Big as life, she'd never seen him in anything other than a T-shirt and blue jeans. Now, here was a man in front of her, a broad-shouldered, worldly man in a button-down shirt and slacks, shaven and clean-cut, with an easy smile, his warm brown eyes beaming back at her through his military-issue specs. Heathcliff was all grown up now. *"Bill!,"* she shouted. *"You came back!"*

A few days later, on Lena and Bill's first-ever date, Lena offered Bill the wheel of her snazzy Ford, and they drove to the Santa Monica pier. They enjoyed fish and chips and a long talk, after which Bill drove Lena home to South Woods Avenue in her own car, and then walked most of the way home to Cherrynose's apartment from there before hitching a ride with a delivery truck. On their second date, they saw *Call Northside 777* at the Gordon on La Brea. Joe was amused at the fact that Lena would let "this boy Bill" drive her car. "None of your other leedle boyfriends get to drive it, huh?"

"Well, he's a good driver," she replied. Joe laughed.

Over the summer, Bill and Lena would pile into the Ford with Lena's spirited Italian friend, Rowena, and Rowena's shy, gingery boyfriend Donnie, and go to Huntington Beach, where naturally Bill, despite the warning about the Garfield boy who ended up in a wheelchair, jumped off the pier. They laughed and chased each other through the surf and roasted frankfurters and huddled under blankets as the sun went down, and when they would pile back into the Ford in the evening, they were tired and their bellies were full and they were all smiles and giggles, listening to Peggy Lee singing *"Mañana is soon enough for me"* on the radio. On other weekends, they'd drive into the Angeles Forest for a picnic, or they'd go Downtown for a movie and afterwards look at the department store windows.

Joe and Anna decided it was time to get to know the boy; so, much to Lena's embarrassment, they invited him to lunch at the house on South Woods Avenue. Bill took it in stride, dressed nicely for the day and brought flowers for Anna. As the Martins talked with Bill over lunch, however, they discovered that he liked to fix things around the house. Joe suggested they all get in the Cadillac and go to Montebello to see the new apartment building he'd bought on Northside Drive. They were standing in the foyer when Joe remarked that the light fixture high in the ceiling was blinking on and off. Without delay, Bill turned off the power at the breaker and then helped Joe bring in a tall ladder from the garages in the back of the courtyard of the apartments. Still in his Sunday best, Bill unscrewed the cover of the fixture with his pocketknife, and as Joe held the ladder steady, Bill cut and twisted a few fresh connections for the fixture, then put it all back together. "Try the light," Bill said, after flipping the breaker switch, and Lena obliged. Of course, it worked better than before. "How wonnn-derful, Bill," Anna said. "I think this ceiling could use a coat of paint," said Bill. "I can do it for you." The smile on Lena's face was, objectively, the biggest in the room.

On their way back to South Woods Avenue, Joe begins to share a private dream of his that he has not previously revealed to his own family — that he'd like to build a new house on a lot next to the apart-ment building. He and Bill begin to discuss the project, and as the future begins to fall into place between the two men in the front seat of the Cadillac, Lena's own private dream begins to take shape as well. Not long afterwards, Bill and Lena announce to her parents that they are going to be married.

As they begin to tick off the requirements for even the modest wed-ding that Lena is planning — small, in the living room at South Woods Avenue — they realize that in order to get a marriage license, Lena needs a copy of her birth certificate. Bill has a little envelope of papers he's kept from the Army, and in it he has an official copy of his (*Father: Floyd Baumiller; Mother: Alpharetta Deadwyler*); he's all set. Lena asks her father to go with her to City Hall to get a copy of her birth certificate, and it turns out to be harder than either of them imagine, after the clerk behind the glass window comes back and apologizes, saying that they do not have a record of an Elena Armida Martin born on her birthdate. After a bit of back and forth, the clerk finally uncovers a birth certificate with a different spelling.

When she gets her hands on it, Lena can scarcely believe her eyes. First, of course, is the misspelled name, *"Marteen,"* like a bum note from the piano. But then, under her father's name, there is a box that says "Color or Race"; and inside that box is the word "Mexican," sitting there like dog doo in the middle of Lena's official origins. And then, also as clear as day, under Anna's name, the same thing: "Color or Race: Mexican." She cries her eyes out as her father brings her home from City Hall in the Cadillac. "How could you let this happen?" she shouts at her parents; "how could it end up so wrong?!" Joe had to admit that he was nearly illiterate when the nuns at Santa Marta's helped him fill out the paperwork on his little daughter, which of course was only part of the story. For Lena, it is a horrible act of negligence, another reason to write in her diary that she hates her daddy. Worse, though, was Lena's slightly overinflated concern that if people actually thought she were a Mexican, she might be prevented from marrying Bill because of the race listed on her birth certificate; or that she might be arrested for her presumptuousness, hauled in under the state's "forced sterilization" program so she wouldn't be able to start a family with Bill — yes, she'd heard the stories, whispered among the little old Chicanas in the neighborhoods as if they were telling stories about *la Llorona*, the evil spirit coming to devour all the children. Meanwhile, it wasn't too long ago, as Joe recalled to himself, that when Mr. Mack's daughter became engaged to an actor from the Philippines, there was public pressure to determine whether the actor was "pure Spanish" instead of Filipino, an aboriginal race. It would've been a different thing altogether if Lena's birth certificate said they were all "Spanish." "Mexican" implied "Indian," didn't it?

But the procedure to turn Lena into the little white girl she's always thought herself to be ends up being fairly simple, as the attorney Mr. Sprague deploys his partner, the attorney Mr. Goode, to get a court order signed by a friendly judge, a drinking jolly boy of a Club-loving judge, that provides for a corrected birth certificate to be created, on affidavits by the parents, who go from being "Marteen" to "Martin," and from being "Mexican" on Lena's original certificate, to "white." Never mind that they're still "Mexican" on their marriage license, if anyone bothered to track it down, still "Mexican" in their immigration records. Never mind that Lena's dead older sister, who didn't live to be old enough to marry, was and will always be "Mexican" in her official records, "Mexican" in the ground, left behind. With court order in hand, Joe and his daughter are back in the vital records office in the City Hall building, to receive the official evidence of Lena's whiteness.

I am sitting on the grass in Grand Park, looking past the bandstand, looking up at that iconic L.A. City Hall building, where the deed was done. It is Noche de Ofrenda, at the beginning of a week of Day of the Dead festivities. I am surrounded by Angeleño families who are here to commemorate the souls of their departed loved ones, creating makeshift altars to their memory, and we are all picnicking and listening to the band play gritty East L.A. Chicano garage rock. Goes well with the Tecate I'm not supposed to be drinking here in the Park. Most of the families have brought photos of their deceased relatives with them; some also have flags and hand-bouquets, or random artifacts of old clothing, like peaked military caps, printed T-shirts, a pair of old motorcycle boots; and favorite bottles of illicit hooch, favorite cookies and candies. They place their mementos on little corners of their picnic blankets, or they carefully add them as decorations to the artists' installations that line the walkways and the park monuments. Everywhere I look I see skeletons. The calaveras, the little skeleton figures by Posada or in imitation of his work, are sweet and nostalgic and comforting. Meanwhile, in mainstream Anglo culture, skeletons are evil spirits, villains, thugs who chase the Karate Kid around the gym. In my mind those kinds of skeletons might easily come to represent the spirit of a quack doctor from the old neighborhood. But here, they are the *abuelitos*.

I am thinking of my mother, and of Joe and Anna, but I am empty-handed. I have no offering for them today. I am also aware that I am alone in this crowd. My surname, pasted onto my father's identity at birth, falls awkwardly from the lips of the people around me as I introduce myself; but of course, even if my name itself is a lie, it obscures a secret, foul patrilineage, so I guess I can shut up and be grateful for that. Looking up at City Hall, lit up for night-time appreciation, it looks like a rocket ship, ready to blast off at any moment. I am thinking of my mother and Joe inside that rocket ship, rewriting my mother's history, whitewashing it for future generations, out of shame, from pretense. The show ends and the families pack up their altars, their family mementos, and they make their way home.

For now, though, there's this, and only this:

It is Christmas 1948, and my parents are set to get married within a couple of weeks, shortly after the beginning of 1949. Billy Baumiller, wearing unfamiliar tan dress slacks and a scratchy brown sportcoat, sits near the brightly lit and decorated Christmas tree in the Martins' living room at South Woods Avenue. On the radio, Gene Autry is singing, "Here Comes Santa Claus (Right Down Santa Claus Lane)..." Despite the awkwardness of new clothes, Bill Baumiller is, as usual, comfortable in his own skin. He sits back with his arm around Lena, who is beaming, and he is ready for just about anything.

"Bill, thees is for you." Anna hands him a gift box to open.

He sits up and pulls the strap of striped ribbon off the top of the box, which is embossed with the Bullocks Wilshire brand, and he opens it. Inside, underneath the tissue paper, is a crewneck sweater, fuzzy to the touch, with an indistinct, recurring pattern of silvery-gray, black and white, with an occasional splash of red. "*Ohhh*," says Lena, "look at that sweater! Isn't that nice?"

And Billy Baumiller ... struggles. To say something. Anything. He holds the box in his hands, making out as if to present it a couple of times as the topic of what he is about to say, but again, his words fail him, and he swallows hard and closes his eyes. "Th-thankyoo," he somehow manages. "M-may I use your bathroom?"

It had been a lot of years, a lot of years of scrounging for scraps, of having things taken from him, of losing things he'd put his heart and soul into, of losing people he'd loved. For years he'd refrained from any comment about it. Because there was no one to tell. When was the last time anyone had given him a gift at Christmas? Had he ever been given a gift so nice? Not since his mother was alive had he ... not since his mother was alive ...

Lena, kneeling quietly in the hallway outside the bathroom, puts her hand up on the door, and she can hear him inside fighting back tears, choking, gulping them down. She goes back into the living room and sits down on the couch near the Christmas tree. "He okay?" asks her mother. "He's fine," she whispers, mouthing the words more than whispering them. She reaches down and runs her fingers over the fuzzy sweater in the box.

A little while later Bill Baumiller comes back into the living room with a big smile on his face. He gives Anna a hug and kisses her on the cheek, and then he shakes Joe's hand. "Thank you very much for the sweater, Mr. and Mrs. Martin," he says. "It is really, really wonderful. I like it very much." Then he sits down next to Lena, and Lena squeezes his upper arm as they resume listening to Christmas songs on the radio, laughing at stories and drinking Christmas punch. Lena has already known it, but she is more sure of it now than ever. She has picked a good one.

4
NOIR

4.1
A VACANT LOT IN
BUNKER HILL, SUMMER 1949

There's a certain way that the human hand may be held that will maximize the terrible impact of its striking. Obviously, as Joe could've told you, the fist is the hand at its most malevolent, with all of its natural heft tightly concentrated, all the torque of the rest of the body behind it, like a solid boulder at the end of a battering ram hitting its target. When the primitive, hormonal response bound up in "fight or flight" is not the primary motivation for using the hand in a violent way, but rather a more complex emotional spur is at the root of its wielding, the hand may be uncoiled and used to create a great sound at the moment of its impact — the sound of one hand clapping against the hide of one's opponent *du jour*, loud enough to create a moment of public shame. Sometimes it takes an unimaginable cataclysm for the unconscious mind to send the appropriate signals to the innocent nerve-endings of the hand, resulting in its shaping into an instrument that delivers both the highest quotient of sound as well as the highest quotient of pain, simultaneously.

Then again, it can be just as true that when a large inanimate object, such as an automobile, for example, might strike a human body, one might barely hear a noise associated with it. Perhaps, if one were paying attention, one might hear the revving of an engine and the screeching of brakes on pavement, the scrape of tires on loose gravel — but as for the impact of the car on the body itself, perhaps one might hear very little. A muffled bump, perhaps, if one were actually sitting in the car. No matter that the car has done significant damage. No matter that a skull is mortally cracked open and bloody, leaving a neck internally severed from its spine.

It is stillness and silence that Detective Sergeant Ed Jokisch of the Homicide Division of the L.A.P.D. is soberly contemplating, standing in a partially paved vacant lot in Bunker Hill on a hot summer morning in 1949. This brutal tableau has been left here for his consideration this morning, and no one yet seems to have heard what produced it. By the look of tire patterns in the gravel, and a little fresh burnt rubber on the broken asphalt in the lot, this middle-aged woman, the one with the open skull, attempted to do battle with a car, and lost. If a woman dies in a gravel lot and no one hears it, did it really happen? "R-dubs," Detective Jokisch calls out to his fellow officer, Detective Sergeant R.W. Anderson, who is taking some measurements at the edge of the lot and making notes. "Hey, R-dubs, we need to canvas these apartments nearby. Gotta be someone who heard something."

Later in the day, the boys in forensic get hold of the body and manage to establish through fingerprint analysis that the dead woman has been going by the name of Carolina Mooney, at least some of the time, and that she has a local "rap" sheet that goes back almost a decade — arrests and a few visits to the clink for public intoxication, intoxication in an automobile, solicitation and morals charges — under the names Carolina Mooney, Rusty Jones, Sherry Jones and Sherry Allgood, among others. They also confirm that she died of massive trauma to the head consistent with being struck by an automobile, and that she had a blood alcohol concentration above .20%.

What the L.A.P.D. never figured out was Carolina Mooney's true identity. They didn't know, as I came to discover, that Carolina Mooney was born Paulet Webb in 1910 in Brevard, in the mountains of western North Carolina, to Wayne and Delma Webb. Father Wayne was a local postmaster, but died relatively young; Paulet was number six out of eight children born to the Webbs, and though she sang like a little angel in the choir at the Brevard First Baptist Church, Paulet was plenty fast with the boys and got engaged at sixteen to Marvin Purcell, a 22-year old boy from nearby Cleveland County who had been in Brevard working construction. Delma Webb made her daughter wait a year before they could marry, and by the time they did, Marvin was finishing up a plumbing course and was talking about starting a home and family out west. In L.A., they'd had a child, Marvin, Jr., who unfortunately died from a bout of enteritis when he was three years old. That's when Paulet began to drink in earnest. During the slow years at the beginning of the War, Marvin got a job with a defense contractor down in Hawthorne, working the assembly line on aircraft fuel systems. War work on the homefront was steady but colorless, paid decently enough but meant working long days with overtime. It was almost as if Marvin Purcell had already begun to disappear by the time Mrs. Paulet Purcell ran off with a door-to-door salesman. When that fellow turned out to be married, Paulet began to haunt downtown bars and after-hours joints, late at night, heading into an all-too-familiar descending spiral of addiction, random attachments and run-ins with the law. After 1943 or so, Marvin Purcell never saw or heard from Paulet again.

In those War years, it was perhaps always going to be the case that the men like Marvin who were left behind, the ones who never put on the soldier's uniform, were going to seem invisible to some — fairly or unfairly. But there is War work and there is other War work, and some of it makes invisible, ordinary men into minor celebrities. This was certainly the case for Hans-Dieter Schmatloch — ordinary, mostly, if also very tall and very handsome, with a broad, manly jawline and large white teeth, piercing blue eyes and wavy, beery-blonde hair. At the beginning of the War — the *European* War — Herr Schmatloch was a young but well-regarded computational physicist working with the Kaiser Wilhelm Society in Munich, essentially a high-brow mathematician, which is about as invisible as you can get in this world. He would have stayed in Munich were it not for the coordinated push by the Nazi regime to create lethal rockets to be aimed and fired at London, beginning in the late 1930s and culminating with the design of the V-2 rocket. Schmatloch was initially an unwilling draftee to the project, which landed him at the Peenemünde Army Research Center in 1939. Very quickly, though, Herr Schmatloch saw the advantages of lending his expertise to the War effort — where food and women and drink and song were rationed elsewhere in Germany, at Peenemünde and sometimes in Thuringia (after the Allies bombed Peenmünde) he and the other rocket scientists and engineers, especially those with pedigree and social status, were treated like barons, lavished with their heart's depraved desires as the rockets for which he calculated complex trajectories began their murderous rain on London in 1944 — and even more so when he voluntarily became a member of the Nazi Party, then of the SS, and had a snappy hat and uniform he could wear to impress the ladies.

He believed in rockets, he believed in mathematics, but beyond that, he wasn't sure what he believed in. Keep the wine coming, that was his motto. But as the Reich began to collapse in March 1945, he managed to get himself assigned with the group of rocket scientists who were being sent to Mittelwerk, then to Oberammergau, with the specific goal of avoiding capture by the Soviets. He knew he didn't believe in Soviets, *jedenfalls.* When the Americans caught him at Witzenhausen, he was still in his SS uniform, albeit with a bullet wound to the thigh that U.S. intelligence officials suspected might have been "self-inflicted." The uniform, and his quirky demeanor, obscured his significance to the Americans until his fellow rocket scientists manage to convince the Americans of his value as a physicist.

Eventually, they sent Schmatloch to Fort Bliss in El Paso, to Ordnance R&D, where the accommodations were spartan, and where there seemed to be little money for the research he and his German colleagues had agreed to do. But Schmatloch's spirit was not so easily broken, and he managed to make friends with some random Texas oil men who frequented the neighborhood near Fort Bliss, and he began wearing cowboy hats and boots. When the newspapers finally learned about the secret defections of German rocket scientists, Schmatloch became one of the poster boys of the program — the big-pawed German man-child in the Stetson, throwing around Texas slang in broken German-English: *"Hoddy, yowl*— vhy, ditt you see my rocket tump-ovah *chust now?"* Beloved by newspapermen for his outrageous quotes and his thirst for whiskey and good times, he began to attract attention from private defense industrialists on the West Coast, who laughed at his public antics and then carefully studied his German pre-War papers and treatises, and imagined how he could be useful to their development programs ...

In the service of his ambitions (evidence of his hidden but nonetheless well-developed political I.Q.), he managed to get himself transferred to the Navy, to the Naval Air Missile Test Center at Point Mugu, which put him a stone's throw away from the big California defense firms like Northrop and Hughes, who, one by one, took their turn at recruiting him. Now America was treating Schmatloch the way he used to be treated at Peenemünde — only bigger, better and more debauched. In addition to sampling all sorts of L.A. trouble on his own, he started showing up at the Club, sans cowboy hat, although he couldn't resist wearing the boots and the two-tone sport coat with the drop chevron yokes. Introduced around by the aerospace veepees, soon enough he felt comfortable showing up on his own, using someone else's tab, barging in with his "*Hoddy, yowl*" greeting and slapping the backs of poor Southland businessmen with his prodigious mitts. Why wasn't he thrown out? For Club management, it was a case of the man being so charming, if unsettling in a way that they just couldn't put their finger on, that they kind've had to close their eyes, wince, and hope it would all be over soon.

It was Joe's job to keep everyone feeling comfortable and happy. Isn't that at the heart of what a bartender does? Without judgment, without ego? Joe always had a smile for the awkward German giant, even when everyone around him was paralyzed by Schmatloch's presence. In the Bar in the Clouds, Schmatloch was quick to learn about Joe's uncanny nose for after-hours entertainment, and he began begging for Joe to take him out on the town. "*Cummon, Cho!*" Schmatloch would shout in his too-loud-for-the-indoors tenor voice, "*take me ouss mitt you!*" Eventually, he wore Joe down, and the two of them set off a couple of nights each week to explore the burlesque theatres until they turned out the lights and locked the doors, before moving on to gloomy hostess clubs, unlicensed booze dens, and even trolling MacArthur Park at three o'clock in the morning, Schmatloch putting Joe in an affectionate headlock and dragging him, staggering along the park's pathways. "Cho, Cho — you must call me *Hansel!*" Schmatloch's appetite seemed insatiable, his preposterously large mandibles and teeth almost literally chomping their way through wee-hours L.A.

"Were you there," asks one of the jolly boys this afternoon, "the time that big old Gulliver opened up his big chops and almost swallowed half a highball glass?" The other jolly boys laugh and slap the bar. "How 'bout that time when Mayor Bowron had the *Secretary of Commerce* in here, and Schmatloch was yodeling and sliding around on the carpet with bus basins on his feet?" "I'll bet that man-mountain has fleas the size of chipmunks!"

And off in the corner, eavesdropping veepees assess the German giant in quiet discussion among themselves. "I just don't know what it is about him," says one, "but he gives me the creeps."

"Is that because he used to be a Nazi?" asks his cocktail-tablemate. "Or is it because he reminds you of a cross between Frankenstein's monster and Koko the Clown?"

"What do you mean '*used to be*'?" They laugh.

The routine cocktail chatter in the Bar in the Clouds comes to a halt when through the door most incongruously comes Detective Sergeant Ed Jokisch and Detective Sergeant R.W. Anderson, as though they are stepping onto an exotic island, snatching off their hats and looking around like Abbott and Costello in short neckties and off-the-rack suits.

They had been having the same playful debate for a while now. Anna had gone to the movies with her son Joey and his wife Trixie, and they were emerging into the half-light of the theater lobby, somewhere between the darkness of the picture show and the light of day. "But Ma," Joey said, "people don't wanna see those old-fashioned pictures with those sugar-candy happy endings." The picture they had just seen was a John Garfield movie, *Force of Evil*. "That poor guy," said Anna, rolling her eyes. "He's so good looking, but he don't have en-n-y good luck. Cada vez I see him, he is mixed up with some no-good woman, or the policemen are chasing him, or the gangsters. Wouldn't it be nice for him if they put him in a nice romantic movie with a beautiful girl, for once, just for once?"

"Ma, no — he's a star. I'm pretty sure he's doing the pictures he wants to do. They're more like real life, you know?"

"Real life? Who wants to see all that? No m'hijo, you can *have* it." Anna was aware of a pattern emerging with all of these dark, new-style pictures: average guy meets femme fatale, follows temptation, someone innocent dies, maybe he's done the deed himself, and then the average guy gets pursued, either by the law or by evil forces, as he stumbles about the darkened city in a nightmarish haze of regret and anguish. Walking down the sidewalk now in the afternoon sunlight, Anna caught herself with an uneasy feeling of having left something behind, like wounded spirits were tugging at her, trying to drag her back to the darkness of the theater, the darkness of a bad dream, full of rotten people preying on the innocent, dark staircases and dead bodies, "like the rubbish" — what John Garfield said at the end of the movie. "Eso es no my real life, Junior." She acknowledged that a great Greta Garbo picture was a complete fairy tale — beautiful costumes, beautiful sets, a grand, romantic death for Miss Garbo at the end, heroic and perfect somehow, and when her light goes out, all the lights go out, and all that's left is the glow of her beautiful soul ... Okay, she could say, so, that's not my life, either, she could admit it — but who said we need to go to the show and see my own life up there? "No quiero ver, who cares?," she told her boy. "Oh, like in *Camille*, right?," said Trixie. "She was so beautiful in that one, what gorgeous clothes!"

"Nelson Eddy and Jeanette MacDonald, Fred Astaire and Ginger Rogers, all that Greta Garbo stuff — who lives like that, really?" Joey said. Anna still liked to see the pretty costumes, even if the picture didn't have a happy ending. *The Postman Always Rings Twice* was one of those dark movies — and those Lana Turner costumes really were something to behold; so was *Double Indemnity*, and Barbara Stanwyck looked so beautiful in that one. Those were among the more glamorous ones, though. More often than not, these "real life" pictures that Joey liked, they take place in dirty little motel rooms and apartments, the women dressed in dowdy bathrobes and slippers, the men *in short neckties and off-the-rack suits* ... "Y, entonces, Junior, those pictures that you like so much, they are a fantasy, too." Fantasy was a powerful thing, as she intuitively understood it. So why should you pick a nightmare over a fairy tale?

On the precise afternoon when Jokisch and Anderson visited the Club, Anna was sitting in her kitchen, pouring another cup of coffee out of the afternoon pot and thumbing through the pages of the *Examiner*. Her attention drifted out the backyard window, out into the sunny day, and she thought about planting some chiles and perhaps some basil, even though it was late in the season.

In the waning afternoon, the phone rang. It was the attorney Mr. Sprague. Anna had never met him, but she understood who he was and some of what he did. "I'm afraid I have some bad news," he told her. He explained that Joe had been picked up by the police, something about a woman who had been killed by a hit-run in Bunker Hill. "This will take some time to sort out, but I assure I will do everything I can for him." He told her, "Sit tight," and he would be back in touch.

He didn't say he was going to get him out, he just said he was going to do everything he could.

"Can I see him?" No, the attorney Mr. Sprague explained; they were questioning him.

She had always expected to get a call like this in the middle of the night, but it never came. She always expected it would be the hospital, or the sheriff visiting her door, hat in hand. She had always expected that, inevitably, the call would be about Joe's body lying on a slab in the county morgue. Over the years of sitting on the divan, smoking cigarettes and waiting, she had expected one day to receive some message of finality. But this was not that. There was nothing final here, nothing certain, except that in thinking about the attorney Mr. Sprague's cautious description of the events culminating in Joe's arrest, Anna saw the final and certain demise of all the stories she told herself about his late-night absences. She had understood all along that those stories were there, in her head, in order to cover up for wicked secret truths, because it made everything easier somehow; but now, having these few details from the call — a woman, a hit-run, Bunker Hill — she knew she could erase those other stories from her memory. She was free now to be disgusted with Joe's lifetime of habits, his malignant addictions, free to blow out the vigil candles and be angry — angry about the disruption of her day, angry about lawyers and "Sit Tight," angry about the unholy dark movies that Joey liked to see. Angry about the prayers she now made, angry enough to tell God: *"You butt out of this!"*

But fantasy was still a powerful thing. *Why should I pick a nightmare over a fairy tale?* The happy ending will not simply be that Joe Martin avoids going to jail, she thought to herself. The happy ending will be that it was a big mistake and he didn't have anything to do with this woman's death.

Después de eso, veremos[13] ...

---

13 After that, we will see ...

Detective Jokisch and Detective Anderson were initially quite skeptical that they would find anything useful at the Club. When they first arrived, they were simply following up on a routine lead that nonetheless seemed a little unusual, given the known identity of the woman — a matchbook with the Club insignia in the dead woman's purse. Wordlessly strolling up and down the aisles in the parking garage they had stumbled upon a cavern green '47 Cadillac with damage on its front grill and broken passenger side headlights. They checked the registration and eventually found out it belonged to the Club's head barman, Joe Martin. When they came up to the Bar in the Clouds, a hallowed place that no Homicide Division detective had ever laid eyes on, it turned out Joe wasn't there. He was downstairs in the Grill Room, going over inventory with some of the staff. The detectives pulled him aside and whispered to him about why they wanted to see him, because it seemed like you had to whisper in this hallowed place. Joe changed out of his white jacket into his wool suit coat and they took him away, but not before Joe told one of his bartenders to let the manager know he wouldn't be in that day.

Joe spent the night in jail after a night of police questioning. The next morning they brought him to the coroner's inquest in a narrow, windowless courtroom in the basement of the Hall of Justice. Rumpled but well-dressed, Joe sat in the witness chair and stared at the floor, staring at the alternating square linoleum tiles of terra cotta and deep dark green. They asked him if he was driving the Cadillac. Still staring at the floor, he answered. "Yes, I was driving the car."

"What caused you to drive to this vacant lot?"

After another long pause, still staring at the tiles on the floor, Joe said. "She was in the car. I was giving her a ride ... I pulled over and let her out in the lot."

"Did you hit Miss Mooney with your car?"

"No ... at least I don't think so."

An attendant from a nearby service station then testified that at about 4:45 in the morning he heard tires screeching and a car leaving the scene at a high rate of speed, as did a Mrs. Berry who lived in an apartment overlooking the lot. She was the one who ultimately called the police, when the dawn revealed the scene. A county forensic lab technician and Detective R.W. Anderson also gave their statements.

The coroner's jury was swift with its results.

> "In the Matter of the Inquisition upon the body of Miss Carolina Mooney, aka Rusty Jones, aka Sherry Jones, aka Sherry Allgood, Deceased, before the Coroner of Los Angeles County, we, the Jurors summoned to appear before the Coroner of Los Angeles County at Room 150, Hall of Justice, Los Angeles, California to inquire into the cause of death of Carolina Mooney, having been duly sworn according to law, and having made such inquisition and hearing the testimony adduced, upon our oaths, each and all do say that we find that the deceased was known as Carolina Mooney, a female, marital status unknown, a native of the state of North Carolina, aged about 43 years, and that she came to her death at the corner of South Figueroa and West Second Streets, Los Angeles, Los Angeles County, California, and that this death was caused by brain trauma inflicted on the deceased by an automobile driven by one Fernando Martín; and from testimony introduced at this time, we find that the death of the deceased was homicidal, and that the said Fernando Martín was criminally responsible therefor ..."

Joe was formally arrested, held without bail, for the crime of involuntary manslaughter, by order of the D.A.'s office, and the attorney Mr. Goode went back and reported the outcome to his partner, the attorney Mr. Sprague.

The attorney Mr. Sprague was busy with other things, though, for the moment. He was wearing two hats in this caper — as guardian angel to his good friend Joe Martin, and as one of nine board members of the Club. He called his friends at the *Times*, the *Examiner* and the *Herald-Express* and straightened out with them what would be covered and what would not be covered. The name of the Club would be left out entirely; that was simple enough, everyone understood that had to be the case. Even the city desk editor at the *Times* knew what his job was, but he couldn't resist shoving a jab back into the ribs of the fickle attorney Mr. Sprague by approving the inflammatory headline,

"MEXICAN BARTENDER ARRESTED" — it was just descriptive enough to be irritating. And then, in the body of the piece, they gave up Joe Martin's name as "Fernando Martín," as well as his home address, for all to see, including the neighbors.

But the guardian angel knew the real score. Asking around at the Club, it was easy enough to determine that Joe left that night with the ravenous German giant, Herr Hans-Dieter Schmatloch. The attorney Mr. Sprague sent out one of his investigators, Ears Molloy, who easily enough constructed a timeline: first, a little before the Club bars closed, to The Colony Club in Gardena to see the Stripping Co-Ed from Chico — Schmatloch couldn't stay in his seat, "the big German was on his feet, howling and whistling with his big fingers in the mouth"; then, after Schmatloch apparently got impatient — *"all I vhant is a lit-tal peese und tail!"*, around 3 a.m. they drove to a little hostess house off Slauson. At the Club, the boys all heard Schmatloch plead with Joe once he found out that Joe had a '47 Caddy. *"Ach, Cho—* you haff a *Caddel-ack?* You must let me trive it — *cummon,* Cho!"* he would say. The bouncer at the hostess house confirmed that the "big guy" got out of the driver's side when they pulled up, and when they left with the girl, the "big guy" and the girl got in the front seat ...

The attorney Mr. Sprague was never known to be a great trial lawyer. It was simply not the way he operated. If there was a problem to be solved, he was most adept at moving behind the scenes, whispering into the ears of the right people, letting the momentum of human nature play out in predictable ways ... When it came to the L.A.P.D., he always had to assess whether he was dealing with a crooked cop or a straight one. While crooked cops could be bought, at least temporarily, they could not be trusted. The attorney Mr. Sprague preferred to deal with the honest ones, the ones with a moral compass to guide them. Good versus evil, villainy versus innocence — good honest cops loved a good story. They lived for them.

Ears Molloy found Detective Jokisch at a coffee shop downtown and scooted into the Detective's booth across from him. "How's tricks, Ed?" "What's it to you, Ears?" Jokisch knew the man, and who and what he was. "Just wanted to make sure you knew that the Mexican bartender wasn't alone."

"Didn't mention anybody else," said the Detective.

"No, he wouldn't, you know. The Club, the code — "

"His funeral."

"Mebbe. Hey, Ed — you ever read about these German rocket scientists who come here? You know those Nazis who they got working for the government?"

"Yeah, I read about it. What of it?"

"You know there's one of those fellas hangs around the Club a lot."

"Aw, now, c'mon. What are you saying to me, Ears?" Ears had him hooked. Not only might he have the wrong man, no matter the complexities of the Club and its infernal code, but the right man might be a Nazi, in the flesh. Perhaps this wasn't just a case of a drunken accident in the wee hours of the morning; perhaps it was about a plague of evil infiltrating our streets at night, spreading death and threatening our way of life. Perhaps it wasn't about a Mexican bartender at all.

After spending the afternoon with Joe's impounded car, looking for other clues, Detective Jokisch went down to see Joe in his cell at the Hall of Justice. "I'm going to level with you, Mr. Martin," said Jokisch. "I don't think you were driving that car when Miss Mooney was hit."

"Why do you say that?"

"Well, for one thing. You're right-handed, aren't you, Mr. Martin?"

"Yes."

"Well, in a situation where a driver faces an emergency in front of him, a right-handed driver is more likely to make a hard turn to the right, whereas a left-handed driver — like maybe, a German scientist who is a left-hander — is more likely to make a hard turn to the left in an emergency. Looks to me from the tire tracks that we should have had a left-hander at the wheel."

OK, well, maybe.

Joe said nothing.

Jokisch laughed. "I found this in the backseat of your car." In the palm of his hand he held a cufflink with a broken clasp bearing the insignia of the Club. He looked at Joe's right-hand sleeve. "Missing this?," the detective asked.

Joe said nothing.

Joe said nothing more at all as he sat alone in his cell, with more time for contemplation than he might usually give himself on any particular day. He well understood his predicament. He was accused of being a Mexican bartender in a story about a white woman who died. The rest of the facts were a little hazy, but try as he might to deny his Mexicanness, they had him dead to rights on it. And as we all knew from the newspapers, Mexicans have an uncommon blood-thirst, whether they are wielding a switch-blade knife, or a Cadillac.

The rest of the facts were a little hazy because — well, what had his job been all these years? How had he provided for his family? He loved hospitality, he loved the creativity and showmanship of being the head barman, especially at the Club, and he loved the special social status he had been able to attain, by his wits and his charm; but all those extra dollars, all the side cash for Cadillacs and curtains and beautiful dresses — that was about being discreet. He was a professional tour guide and secret keeper, an impresario of private shows, the ringmaster of an invisible, nocturnal circus for affluent white male Club members, jolly-boys and callow veepees, a couple of generations of them. And what if he turned state's evidence on just one of them, even on one Nazi scientist, the Club gadfly? Would the regulars at the Bar in the Clouds still have the same nostalgic regard for him, seeing him standing behind the bar in his lily-whites? Or would they decide they had gotten all they needed from him, and he could be discarded like the rest? Bendable, undependable, expendable ...

Now the years of overindulgence seemed to overtake him in his cell, like the heavy, steamy smoke from a jailhouse laundry fire. A collage of moments, choking him, making his eyes water, suffocating him with the stifling guilt of having been to these places and done these things, having kept his own secrets from his own family. His beloved family. Now he was exposed. Now he just wanted to go back to being the jaunty continental-type behind the bar, impeccably dressed, the cocktail magician. He just wanted to go back to living-Spanish. As opposed to dead-Mexican.

From across the street, the old man watched Billy Baumiller through the dusty windshield of his beat-up pickup truck, watched him as he carefully placed the extension ladder up against the two-story front facade of the apartment building and checked its footing on the lawn below. He looked skinny. His work clothes were pressed and clean, though, and he had a good haircut and a suntan. He had the passing look of a young man who was doing mighty fine for himself, someone who had someone to look after him. It was a little jarring for the old man to behold, as he realized that he had never seen him that way before.

After Billy ascended the ladder to one of the front windows of the apartment building, the old man watched as the young man used sandpaper and a putty knife to remove the peeling paint on the second-floor window frame. He leaned into his scraping, working diligently, elbow to wrist, stopping occasionally to wipe his brow. Finishing one horizontal, he moved on to the next. Then, after an indeterminate amount of time, a pretty young woman in capri pants leaned out from the front porch below and called up to him. "Careful up there!" "S'alright," said Billy. She asked him if he wanted some lemonade, and he said "Sure."

With that, the old man got out of the truck and walked slowly, somewhat laboredly, across the street, over to the bottom of the ladder. "Howdy-hello, Billy-boy," said the man.

Bill Baumiller looked down and saw a shortish, stocky fellow in a suit coat and old pants, wearing round eyeglasses and an old gray porkpie hat. The old man doffed the hat and waved up to Bill. "It's yer-old ... it's me, uh, Floyd Baumiller," he said.

Bill blinked and smiled. He hadn't seen his Dad since before he left for Japan. "Dad? Oboy! What are you doing here?," he said as started to descend from the second floor, two-to-three rungs at a time. "Hold on there, boy, slow down, don't hurt yourself," said the old man.

Bill wiped his hands on a rag from his back pocket, and the two men shook hands. "I was, uh, in the neighborhood," said Floyd. "That is, I was down running a few errands in the city, then visiting Patrice and her new husband, and they told me where to find you. Thought it was the least I could do, to come and see how you were doing."

Just then, Lena came out with a nice cold glass of lemonade. Bill introduced his father to her, and she lit up with a big smile before the old man snatched his hat off again and put out his hand to shake, saying, "Fine to meet you, ma'am." As her smile collapsed a little, forming into a smaller, less grand one, she shot Bill a quizzical look and grasped the old man's hand. "Yes, I'm delighted to meet you, Mr. Baumiller. Can I get you a glass of lemonade?" "Oh, no thank you, ma'am. You know, acid, the old stomach — but could I trouble you for a drink of water?"

Bill had noticed the old truck, and was a little irked about being spied upon, especially in light of the news about Joe — communicated to him by Anna, who told them, "It's all a mistake, they have the wrong man, it will be fine." He and Lena had been repeating those words — "it's a mistake, they have the wrong man" — to themselves, to each other, for the last forty-eight hours. Bill then wondered for a moment if his father knew about Joe's dilemma and had come to gloat, but then it became clear that he hadn't a clue. It sure had Bill swirled up, though, and until he came down the ladder to see his father, he hadn't realized how much working on the apartment building had kept him distracted from it. Joe and Anna's new house had broken ground next door, and Bill wanted to paint up the apartments on the outside so that they would look good next to the new house.

Bill and Floyd sat down on the steps of the front porch, glasses in hand, and commenced a quiet chat. Lena stayed inside, occasionally peering out through their first-floor living room window to see them.

Floyd told Billy about how things were doing up in Bishop — that Johnny was working in a junkyard, cutting up old cars, and that Angie and her beau were fixing to get hitched up and move to Utah to be cowboys, up there with the wild Appaloosas. "Er, cowboy and cowgirl, I guess," he said, smiling. They didn't talk about Alpha, although Billy wanted to; nor did they talk about Dorothy Theodora. There were a lot of things Bill wanted to tell him — about Japan, about the things he was learning, about what he was hoping to accomplish — and a lot of things he wanted to ask; but somehow, it didn't seem to fit into the size of their little conversation. It was as if his Dad was focused on rationing his words, rationing the ones he would hear as well as the ones he'd say.

At length, Floyd Baumiller stood up from the steps to say his goodbye. "I can see you're doing fine here," he said. "That's mainly what I wanted to know."

"Yeah, Dad, we're doing okay here."

"This family of yours — they Mexican?"

Bill stuttered. "Uh-h, S-Spanish."

"Oh. Well, good to see you've got some people, boy. Your wife is a very pretty girl."

Bill smiled and nodded. "Works hard, too," he volunteered. Floyd laughed. "Alright, Billy-boy — drop me a line some time," he said, shaking Billy's hand.

"Getting late," said Bill. "You want to stay? We have an extra apartment room with a bed and bath. You could get an early start tomorrow."

"Oh, no, thank you, Billy-boy, but I'm going to head out of town and hit one of those motor hotels along the highway... Take good care," he said. And with that, he drove away.

Later that evening, Bill and Lena were lying down on the couch together, her head down on his chest, listening to the radio. "You're awfully quiet, Mister," she said, poking his ribs. "Everything okay?"

"Yeah."

"Did your father say anything untoward?"

"No. Didn't say much of anything really," said Bill.

Bill Baumiller fell asleep on the couch with Lena in his arms, listening to the radio, thinking about "his people" — about shooting pool with Joe, his new surrogate father, this man in his immaculate suit, drink in hand, his baritone laughter. And about how it was all a mistake and they had the wrong man.

"It was all a mistake," my eighty-something-year-old father told me a couple of years ago, when I first uncovered this case, the whole story about Carolina Mooney, among the annals of some old Los Angeles police files. "They had the wrong guy." The words came out of him like the answer to a math problem, matter-of-factly, unemotionally, betraying nothing of how it must have felt to live through it. Betraying nothing more at all.

My mother was long gone by the time I exhumed Carolina Mooney's memory. It is quite possible, though, that I would have gotten something more from her — perhaps a hot scolding for digging around where I was not wanted to dig, perhaps a flash of pent-up anger and disgust. Coming from one's own mother, of course, that's a powerful thing. For all her sunniness, Lena had grown to middle-age knowing that her "just-so" world would occasionally need to be defended, and over the years she had developed the heart of a warrior to do it. That bold, round mezzo-soprano voice of hers, the one that could fill the room, could wind its way around some brutal verbal weaponry. To this day, my memory of her rare slashings of me will occasionally creep up and unleash itself fiercely during late-night self-loathing sessions.

Please do not misunderstand me — my mother was kind and loving, and she believed in me; to her, I was the antidote for where we had come from, because I was going somewhere else, and her pride in me and my sister was palpable. But her response to my curiosity about our past, my incessant need to ask these uncomfortable questions, would have been to smite me down for asking, with medieval intensity. She had turf to protect, turf that was acquired at great expense, inch by inch, over two generations of living in L.A. as anonymously white, as quietly and unobtrusively non-Mexican as possible. *How dare you give that all away, after we worked so hard to acquire it for you! How can you be so ungrateful?*

Dad tells me there is nothing to see here. He is curious about a million things under the sun, but not this, and not about his own family. His innocence of his own origins, his lack of interest in them, his general contentment about the current state of his knowledge of them, come from the same generational outlook as my mother's. As children of the Depression, what matters to my father, and what mattered to my mother, is where we are today, and where we're headed. They worked hard to be unburdened by the elements of the past that threatened to limit and define them. And as I sit here with my Dad, listening to him retell the same stories of his most recent achievements in his garage-machine shop over and over again, drinking bad coffee, I understand that in the course of nearly nine full decades it has been his reward to forget most of what he knew about the deep past, to be unconcerned with it.

Here I am in greater L.A., sitting across from this man, pondering this mid-sip, my blood still racing through my veins. Having matured in the Digital Age, I'll confess that my greater fear is that of being disconnected. *"The wi-fi's down, where is everybody?, hook me up, are we linked-up?, did you link-in? I know a guy"*— the connection, we're always looking for our connection. The connection is knowledge, and knowledge is currency. I am sitting here across from this man, pondering this mid-sip, respectful of the secrets, of the stories they all told themselves to survive and move on. I really do understand. But after the last breath of every one of my ancestors has been extinguished, is there still not some sense in which, if I am anything at all, I am the survivor, I am the walkingest, talkingest, breathingest connection to where they came from, what they struggled against, what they survived, how they lived and loved? I am convinced that what happened here had meaning. That the truth matters. You had your burdens, I have mine.

In search of anything, anything I could learn about this Bunker Hill episode, I laid out what I had before a some-time L.A. prosecutor, on a "no-identities" basis: this Mexican bartender is held to answer for the death of a prostitute, after a coroner's inquest. "I'd say he's cooked, he's done," says the ex-prosecutor. "What if I told you there was no plea, that it never went to trial?" I ask.

"Are you telling me that?"

"I don't know," I say.

"Then I'd say the fix was in," says the ex-prosecutor. "But," he asks, "why would anyone care enough about some Mexican bartender to go to the trouble of fixing this case?"

A good question, Bob.

In search of anything, anything I could learn about this episode, I turned to tracing the origins of Miss Carolina Mooney, back through the police reports, down to census records, state birth, death and marriage records, right down to Miss Paulet Webb, the pretty Baptist choirgirl from Brevard, marveling at how easy it is to tell someone's life story, when you get right down to it — how easy it is to stalk the dead and dare them to come alive again. I knew her better than Joe ever did, no matter that their lives were forever altered by their brief association with each other. And by public records and newspapers, I knew her man as well: old Marvin Purcell, the jilted husband, died in the 1960s up in Porterville, north of Bakersfield, where some romantically-inclined obituary writer thought it would be appropriate to mention in Marvin's death notice that he lost track of his ex-wife, Mrs. Paulet Purcell, "many years ago, and always regretted that he had not been able to find her again." It occurs to me that I want to go back and tell Marvin, just to let him know what became of her. But if I were able to go back and fix that, restore some meaning to the life of an old plumber, what might I give to go back and prevent that car from hitting Mrs. Paulet Purcell in the vacant lot on that night? What else would I try to go back and fix?

But there is no fixing anything now. All these souls are now lost. The worst that they will have endured has already happened to them, and there is nothing that can change any of that. This is your penalty for going back and digging where digging was not wanted. Now, all there is to do is to let it wash over you; let the blood of Mrs. Paulet Purcell, aka Carolina Mooney, wash over you; let all the blood and sweat and tears of your fathers and mothers just wash over you. Be baptized and reborn in it. Build your altar to them in the park, listen to the band play, and stare up at the rocket ship. Whether you were digging for it or not, this is who you are — every particle of it.

The only things that can actually be fixed, apparently, are the things one finds on the ground, in the present. In the present day of the summer of 1949 and on the ground of this episode, the attorney Mr. Sprague had made good-and-certain that information about Joe's case was filtering to the right people within the L.A.P.D. The right *honest* people.

Chief William Worton was as honest as they came, a true patriot. War work had given him his compass.

Mayor Fletcher Bowron had his tail between his legs after the Brenda Allen scandal exposed the fact that a member of Chief Horrall's own Vice Squad was a business partner of Madame Allen's in a prostitution ring. You remember Brenda Allen, don't you?—her image splashed across the front pages of the newspapers: that hat, that veil, those sunglasses. With Bowron's reelection campaign running right through May, right through the middle of the aftermath of the raid on Brenda's and a grand jury hungry for details about possible bribes solicited for his own campaign fund, Mayor Bowron asked for Chief Horrall's resignation. While the L.A. charter required that the new chief would be selected from within, Bowron vowed to replace Horrall "temporarily" with an outsider who could come in and clean things up. He first tried to convince R.B. Hood, Hoover's G-man in L.A., to take the job; failing to move him, he called upon military advisors, who directed him to Worton, a Marine major general then serving at Camp Pendleton down in San Diego.

Worton had served in military intelligence in China in the 1930s. When the War began, he bounced around between Iceland, England and the U.S. until he was given a command in the Pacific, where he fought with valor in the Battles of Guam, Iwo Jima and Okinawa. After Hiroshima and Nagasaki, General Worton went back to China to work with nationalist forces to stamp out what remained of the Japanese resistance and to fire some warning shots at the Communist guerillas. He wasn't in San Diego for more than a cup of coffee before he was taking off his highly decorated Marine uniform and replacing it with gray gabardine. He had been appointed chief of the L.A. Police only a few days before Carolina Mooney's untimely death.

When the word started to filter up to him about a homicide case potentially involving a Nazi expat rocket scientist, it sounded like military intelligence must be mixed up in something, and he started to make inquiries. You know, you tend to solve the problems that are most familiar to you, in an otherwise unfamiliar job. Upon hearing that Herr Schmatloch had not even been questioned in the matter, he made a call to Point Mugu and politely invited the Navy's senior intelligence man there to come along to the Hall of Justice for tea, insisting that he bring his friend, "the German," with him.

"Admiral Simmons," began the Chief during their meeting the following day, "I'd like to thank you for coming and bringing our guest of honor." As Admiral Simmons looked on uncomfortably, Herr Schmatloch stood up and launched into a tirade about how he was being treated, that he had nothing to do with anything, and insisting that this was America and he had rights. Chief Worton was a small man, and Herr Schmatloch was looming above him furiously, not unlike the statue of Beethoven in Pershing Square. But Chief Worton was a cool customer.

"Let me invite you again to take a seat, Mr. Schmatloch," he said, dunking his tea bag. "We are all friends here — unless you're telling me that you don't want to be my friend."

"Vell, a man can nevah haff too many friends," said the German giant, shrugging out of his Beethoven pose. Chief Worton then explained that they were going to have a friendly chat, "with my stenographer, Miss Catto, here, I hope you don't mind," and that he intended that they should all "get to the bottom of the unfortunate accident involving the Cadillac the other night." "We have witnesses placing you at various locations connected with the event, Mr. Schmatloch," said Chief Worton, "and whether you are aware of it or not, you, sir, are a difficult one to be misidentified."

"Vut aksident?" asked the giant pointedly.

After conferring with Admiral Simmons, however, Schmatloch's demeanor loosened and he said he was ready to talk. With the stenographer tick-ticking away, Schmatloch led them on a colorful tour of the night's activities, sparing no detail. He gave an enthusiastic description of the Stripping Coed, the drive to the hostess lounge on hot wheels; then how "the chickie" — Miss Mooney — agreed to give him a good time. That's when things went "ganz beschissen[14]": Miss Mooney was asking for more money than they had agreed upon back at the hostess lounge, and she was "drunk as a skunk, passing out on da front seat. I told Cho, hey, help me get dis vun out of da car, let's go get anotha," but Joe was getting bounced around in the big backseat of his Cadillac by Schmatloch's erratic driving. Schmatloch swerved and pulled over in the

---

14 All shitty.

vacant lot and literally kicked her out of the car, pressing his prodigious feet into her ribs until she tumbled out backwards. When he put the car in gear, he thought she was still on the ground, but by this time she was staggering toward him like Lon Chaney, Jr. in *The Mummy's Ghost*. "I stepped on da gazoleen pettle und turned da steering vheel, and I vood guess she sigg-et vhen I sagg-et, vhich is vhen I hit her mitt da car."

Chief Worton asked his chief of staff to take Schmatloch out of the room for a moment. "Well," said the Chief. "What does the Navy have to say for itself?"

"Herr Schmatloch is a valuable defense asset and his continued participation in our rocket programs is essential to their success and to our nation's military superiority. Besides, you seem to have an open-and-shut case on the bartender," said Admiral Simmons.

"That's what I thought you would say," said the Chief. "I suppose if I call the brass at the Pentagon they'd say the same thing?" The Admiral nodded. The Chief leaned in close to the Admiral as he told him, "I don't want this in my city, do you understand? Not on my watch. You take that overgrown adding machine and keep him away from my city, put him on curfew, chain him up like King Kong if you have to. I don't want to hear about him going to burlesque shows, I don't want to hear about him going to the Club, and I certainly don't want him in here again telling me another story like that one."

As Admiral Simmons and Schmatloch departed, Schmatloch paused to address Chief Worton, "I vant to tank you for being my friend, Chief ... but I muss say, such a lot of fuss! Vot is vun whore, more or less, in dis town?" What was one whore, more or less, in Los Angeles, of all places?

Meanwhile, the attorney Mr. Sprague was meeting with his fellow board members at the Club. "They're not going to let him go," said one, "they've got a confession and everything."

"Gentlemen, all I am saying is that if they let him go — by some miracle, if that's the way you want it — I believe we all owe it to him to take him back here."

"That's preposterous!," exclaimed another member of the board. "We can't have a murderer in our bar!"

"If they let him go, then he's not a murderer."

"But he was in the papers."

"He was in the papers under a name no one knows him by, and there was no mention of the Club. Gentlemen, we got off easy."

"How do you figure?"

"Did you ever stop to think what he knows? Do you know how valuable that information is — about you?," said the attorney Mr. Sprague pointing around the room, "and you, and you, and you? He has been the soul of discretion when you've been out painting the town red together. He's protected you from yourselves, and from more than you know. His conduct has been the same as it's always been — even now, he has remained loyal to you, when his entire life and livelihood is on the line."

"How do we trust him?"

"What more do you need? Same way you always have — by asking him for his trust. It is what he lives for, gentlemen."

At that moment, the door opened and the Club's concierge — the one with the hands, from the lobby — came in with a telegram. "I figured you would want this without delay, Mr. Sprague. Sorry for the interruption, sirs. The Governor says hello to all of you."

Even if it might have been tidier to accept Joe's confession and move on, Chief Worton had been in the War. While he was in no position to fight with the Pentagon about Schmatloch, if the War meant anything to anyone, if it meant anything to Chief Worton, it meant that there was a right way to do things, and that innocent lives were always at stake. He granted Joe a small kindness, the likes of which seemed to be from a bygone era of Los Angeles — perhaps the type of kindness that only an outsider could have granted at that moment, an outsider who had spent so many years in places like Boston and China, where the question of whether anyone was "Mexican" or "not-Mexican" had no significance. Meanwhile, no one could have predicted whether or not Joe would've gotten the same shake with Chief Parker, who succeeded Chief Worton after a little over a year. Chief Parker might just as soon have said, "What's one Mexican, more or less?" But we wouldn't need to speculate about that. Joe went back to his job at the Club for a few more quiet years; the Club members were happy to see him behind the bar, and happy to be rid of the German giant, who soon afterward publicly announced that Billy Graham himself had counseled him to take Jesus as his savior, just before he signed a nice juicy contract with Hughes; and most of the members were never the wiser about what had happened. Chief Worton even became a member of the Club, a loyal patron of the Bar in the Clouds, with never a knowing glance exchanged. He was a cool customer.

The attorney Mr. Sprague pulled his Plymouth up to the curb outside the Martins' home on South Woods Avenue. He reached out and gripped Joe's shoulder empathetically as he said his goodbye, and Joe emerged into the broadest of broad daylights in sunny Los Angeles, walking the longest walk of his life from the curb to the front door, impossible not to feel the eyes of his neighbors upon him. He opened the door and went in to find what was waiting for him.

As Anna's hand hit Joe's cheek, her blood had rumbled up and her hand had unconsciously formed itself to deliver both the highest quotient of pain as well as the highest quotient of noise. "THWAK," it went, as she good-and-slugged her husband with her uncoiling, partially opened hand. The echoing sound of one hand clapping was shocking enough to Joe, but the sharp pain the former prizefighter felt across the ridge of his cheekbone was even more surprising as he found himself stumbling backwards into the corner of the doorway and the wall of the entry hall. The force of the impact sent him into a crouch near the floor, sliding down against the wall. He put up his hands up to ward off the next hit, which did not come. And then he started to cry.

Anna stood above him, unwound, frozen in the moment of release, slightly stunned that she had delivered a perfect strike.

"*Te prometo*," he said, between sobs, from his crouch on the floor.

As effective as the hand is as a human tool for delivering a kinetic blow, so too is the unexpected power of words — perhaps especially when they are not planned and thought out, perhaps especially when it has been surmised that two particular words have lost their meaning long ago, only to return and suddenly mean something again in the heat of an urgent moment.

He had not said these words to her in many years. He had not said them because he was careless, and he had not thought to hold the meaning behind them. Now he said them. They overtook him, and he said them. "*Te prometo*," he said, between sobs, from his crouch.

As they slammed across her face, the impact of these two words sent her into a like crouching position just across from her husband. She was crying, too, trying to catch her own breath. After a moment, she reached out her trembling hand and pulled one of his away from his face. She locked her fingers with his.

It was not a moment of forgiveness, nor would there be any forgetting. Just two fighters at the end of a long, bruising bout, acknowledging the sound of the bell.

They would both remember this bout, memorialize it for the rest of their lives, by not talking about it.

5
LET'S GO
FOR A RIDE

5.1
NORTHSIDE DRIVE, MONTEBELLO, 1950

The four of them would pack into Joe's new Cadillac — Bill at the wheel, Joe by his side up front, Anna and Lena in the back — and set off east on Whittier Boulevard, out to exotic locales like Brea, Olinda, Coyote Hills, Placentia, Carbon Canyon, La Habra, La Vida Springs and Yorba Linda, looking for "Model Homes." A row of three to five homes, completed, hooked up to utilities, furnished and landscaped by a tract home developer to show young families what it would be like to live in one of their newly-constructed houses. Behind the row of completed Models would be a small street plan, already paved and lined with beautiful sidewalks, with construction sites for each of the spec houses being built in the tract. A tidy little modern village in the making.

Driving through the open fields and the plentiful orange, lemon and avocado groves of northern Orange County, the Model Homes announce themselves on the horizon with brightly colored pennants flapping in the wind. The garage of the first home is the real estate office, where a salesman in a bright-colored sports jacket offers you brochures and floor plans. Then, you are invited to walk in and out of each of the ranch-style, shake-shingled Model Homes, with their wide driveways and pretty lawns — a chance to luxuriate for a moment in a brand new house, with a brand new house smell of fresh paint and fresh carpeting. Alone and without inhibitions, you can let your hands glide across the cool Formica countertops in the kitchen, the dashboard of the dual oven stove range — comes in off-white, aquamarine or goldenrod. Go ahead and touch the chrome-plated faucet handles. Press against the sliding glass door to the covered patio in the back. Do you see yourself here?

Can you see your reflection in this sliding door? The kidney-shaped swimming pool is an upgrade option ...

One Saturday afternoon, after wandering in and out of these Model Homes, they drove past some "owner-builder" tracts for sale — undeveloped lots, you buy and you build. It looked like good land, with good-sized lots, and there were eucalyptus trees. Then they stopped along the road at a little hamburger stand at the edge of a strawberry field, and had hamburgers and Cokes on a wooden picnic table in the sun. Then Lena said it, said the thing that started it all, as she dabbed her mouth with a paper napkin and stared off toward the Los Coyotes foothills. "You know, Bill — if we were to somehow buy one of those lots, we could have whatever house we wanted. You could build it," she said to him, with a gleam in her eye.

"Oh, yes," chimed in Anna. "Bill can make en-n-ny-thing." Bill Baumiller shrugged and smiled and nodded affirmatively, his mouth full of hamburger. Joe was quiet as mother and daughter read each other's thoughts. Joe thought it was a crazy idea, but he knew a wave coming when he saw one. On the way home, Joe announced to Bill, "Probably I could take you to see the banker. One of the members, you know. Maybe ... maybe I can help you get a loan for one of these ... tracts." As he said the words, he didn't yet realize that helping would mean co-signing for the loan. But he held faith in his daughter and son-in-law. He held his faith in their steadfastness.

That evening, Lena spread a dozen or so issues of *Sunset* magazine out on the breakfast table and paged through them one by one, referring to them as she started drawing pictures and floorplans of her dream homes, with colored pencils. Anna and Joe, next door at the house, were in the den watching Jack Carter on the *Saturday Night Revue* on the television. Joe sat slumped back in his chair with his legs straight out, hands in pockets, jingling his change and his keys, whistling the first few notes of the "Tennessee Waltz" over and over again at intervals. Anna, taking a break from smoking her Kools, had her reading glasses down on her nose and was crocheting the zig zag stripes of a future afghan blanket in brown and tan, her mind wandering along from Jack Carter, mugging and mincing, back to the strawberry field that afternoon, to the satisfaction of seeing Bill Baumiller up on the ladder in the entry hall of the apartments fixing the lights and painting the ceiling, to thoughts of a baby grandchild, my older sister, who was on her way ...

And Bill Baumiller?

He was stretched out on the apartment living room couch in his stocking feet — glasses off, napping.

Dreaming of oranges — fresh, sweet oranges.

Oboy!

THE END

AUTHOR'S NOTE

Prominently quoted material herein is attributable as follows:

Samuel Leavitt, *Dictator Grant: or, The Overthrow of the Republic in 1880* (New York, 1879).

"Mother Shipton's Prophecy," *Weekly Interior Herald* (Hutchinson, Kansas), May 13, 1880.

Col. Richard Henry Savage, *An Exile from London, a Novel* (New York: The Home Publishing Co., 1896).

"A Great Success," *The Border Vidette* (Nogales, Arizona), November 13, 1915.

"Sheriff Calls Americans to Help Oust Disturbers," *Los Angeles Times*, July 13, 1917.

"A Double Cure for a Double Curse," in McPherson, Sister Aimee Semple, *Divine Healing Sermons* (Los Angeles: Biola Press, 1921).

"Probe Cause of Girl's Death in Arbuckle Party - Comedian Speeds to S.F. for Inquiry," *Los Angeles Evening Herald*, September 10, 1921.

William G. McAdoo, *Crowded Years: The Reminiscences of William G. McAdoo* (Boston and New York: Houghton Mifflin Company, 1931).

"Sinatra to Compete with Sonatas in Hollywood Bowl," *The Manhattan* (Kansas) *Mercury*, August 5, 1943.

"Frank Sinatra's Hollywood Bowl Appearance Brings Protest Mail," *The Times* (of Munster, Indiana), August 11, 1943.

"Frank Sinatra's Hollywood Bowl Debut Called Moaning Success," *The Daily Oklahoman*, August 15, 1943.

"Sinatra Fans Crowd Bowl; Slick Chickies Swoon to Frankie's Croon 'Neath August Moon," *Los Angeles Times*, August 15, 1943.

"Swooner Sinatra Outdraws Yehudi In Hollywood Bowl," *Great Falls* (Montanan) *Tribune*, August 30, 1943.

Alan Knight, *The Mexican Revolution: Counter-revolution and Reconstruction* (Lincoln, NE: University of Nebraska Press, 1990).

With inspiration from back issues of *The Garfield Log*, James A. Garfield High School, East Los Angeles, California.

"Nature Boy," written by Eden Ahbez, published by Geraldine E. Janowiak obo Golden World. Lyrics used by permission.

Thanks to Melissa Neely (layout), Nick Caruso and Mark Bender (cover), and Victoria Blanco (editing). Thanks also to a few good friends who are patient readers, including: Mary Weir, Sally Edison, Tom and Judy Thompson, Steven Soto, Suzanne Sule, Carl Rothenberger, Kymberly Patsilevas, Virginia Starr, Suzanne Turner, Hildie Block, Richard "the typo hunter" Soto, and Raj Basi; special thanks to Kerstin for cutting me down to size; and to the following writing locales: in Pittsburgh, Cinderlands (Strip District), Local, Tres Rios, the former Union Standard, Iron Born Pizza (Strip District), the former Winghart's (South Side), Round Corner Cantina, Or the Whale, the former Brugge on North, the Lobby Bar at the Ace Hotel, Genoa Pizza & Bar; in New York, Chumley's, Lexington Brass and the Marlton Hotel lobby; and in Los Angeles, 24/7 and Library Bar.

ABOUT THE AUTHOR

A grandson of Mexican immigrants, **RON SCHULER** was born and raised in greater Los Angeles. He graduated from Pomona College *(cum laude)* with a B.A. in English and from Cornell Law School. He has been practicing corporate, M&A, start-up, technology and securities law in Pittsburgh for over 30 years. Schuler was a lead member of the City of Pittsburgh's legal team for the planning and construction of PNC Park, home to Major League Baseball's Pittsburgh Pirates, and was the author of the *Forbes Field II Task Force Final Report* (1996), the urban planning justification for PNC Park's location. He served as the founding chairman of Pittsburgh's community-supported jazz radio station, WZUM-FM. He is also the author of *The Steel Bar: Pittsburgh Lawyers and the Making of Modern America* (Marquez Press, 2019), an American history book set amid the legal profession in Pittsburgh. He is currently working on an illustrated history/memoir of Pittsburgh's elite baseball venues and their urban spaces, from the Civil War to the present, tentatively entitled *Seven Ballparks,* as well as a novel set in the American Southwest at the turn of the 20th century.

Also by Ron Schuler

The Steel Bar: Pittsburgh Lawyers and the Making of America (Marquez Press, 2019)

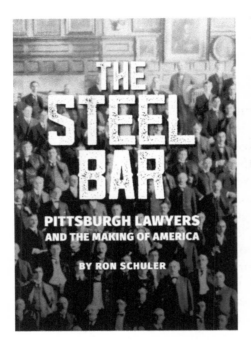

The definitive history of the legal profession in Pittsburgh, THE STEEL BAR examines Pittsburgh's role in the development of American democratic and commercial institutions and how its lawyers helped to shape American history in significant ways.

"Ron Schuler's THE STEEL BAR is a magnificent tour-de-force: It weaves together history, law and powerful story-telling to produce a dramatic, readable account of the people and unexpected forces that shaped our nation's legal system. This book belongs on the shelf of any serious student of law, history, and the role played by the bench and bar in forging America's remarkable destiny."

— Ken Gormley, *New York Times* bestselling author
and President, Duquesne University

"[T]he best and most engaging history of a city bar that I've read in many years. Far from being just another chronicle of a local profession, THE STEEL BAR shows how Pittsburgh lawyers played leading roles in the development of national politics, economic growth and social change. It's a great story written with verve, panache and wit that properly puts Pittsburgh at the center of the American narrative."

— Bernard J. Hibbitts, Publisher and editor of *JURIST*, professor at University of Pittsburgh Law School

During Pittsburgh's earliest days, Pittsburgh lawyers living as political outsiders on the frontier of America were actively defining the limits of political dissent in the young Republic. By 1902, however, Pittsburgh lawyers occupied top spots in all three branches of government at the same time: as U.S. attorney general and solicitor general, as a justice on the U.S. Supreme Court, and as a member of the powerful House Ways and Means Committee. This was not merely a coincidence. By the end of the 19th century, Pittsburgh lawyers were considered to be among the nation's most influential — for their role in the rise of Pittsburgh as the wealthiest and most important industrial city in America, as interpreters and curators of the earliest major American corporations, and as tacticians in the ongoing struggles between labor and management. During the Progressive Era and the rise of federal regulation, Pittsburgh lawyers fought epic battles against the government over the right to collective bargaining and the limits of monopoly power and local government self-determination. At the same time, the profession itself evolved in Pittsburgh, through wars and McCarthyism and the Civil Rights era, through the entry of women and minorities into the profession, and as stewards during the decline of Steel and the renaissance of a great American city.

SUPPORT THE
CHICANO RESEARCH CENTER

In the culmination of a long-held dream, a retired Central Valley high school educator and Vietnam *veterano* named Richard Soto opened the Chicano Research Center in Stockton, California in 2016-- starting it with his own lifetime collection of books, journals and ephemera relating to the history of La Raza and Chicano culture in the Southwestern United States. Ever since his college years, in the early 1970s, when he discovered that the libraries where he chose to attend college had little more than a dozen books on Chicano history and culture between them, Soto has made it his mission to build a collection that properly reflected the rich and beautiful history of Mexico and Mexican-Americans, and to make it available to all for understanding and appreciation.

Now housed in its own building, the CRC has over 15,000 volumes available for reading by the public, as well as a museum collection of Chicano artifacts, and it has become a hub for educational enrichment activities, cultural preservation, lectures and performances.

Please consider giving your support to this important repository of Chicano culture. The Chicano Research Center is a 501(c)(3) not-for-profit organization, and your donation is tax-deductible within the guidelines of the Internal Revenue Service, U.S. Department of the Treasury. If you would like to donate to this vital cultural resource, please send your support to:

Chicano Research Center
415 E. Main Street
Stockton, California 95202

¡A tu salud!